SILVER
CROSS

ALSO BY B. KENT ANDERSON

Cold Glory

SILVER CROSS

B. KENT ANDERSON

A Tom Doherty Associates Book
New York

SILVER CROSS

A Forge Book
Published by Tom Doherty Associates, LLC
175 Fifth Avenue
New York, NY 10010

www.tor-forge.com

Forge® is a registered trademark of Tom Doherty Associates, LLC.

Library of Congress Cataloging-in-Publication Data

Anderson, B. Kent, 1963–
    Silver cross / B. Kent Anderson.—1st ed.
        p. cm.
    "A Tom Doherty Associates book."
    ISBN 978-0-7653-2862-5 (hardcover)
    ISBN 978-1-4299-4811-1 (e-book)
    1. History teachers—Fiction.   2. Governmental investigations—
Fiction.   3. Conspiracies—United States—Fiction.   4. Treasure troves—
Fiction.   I. Title.
PS3601.N455S55 2012
813'.6—dc23

                                                                2012019973

First Edition: November 2012

Printed in the United States of America

0 9 8 7 6 5 4 3 2 1

In memory of Bill Anderson (1928–2011)

"Just keep working."

I miss you, Dad.

ACKNOWLEDGMENTS

I am fortunate in the extreme to be able to do what I do, and there are many people who make it possible for me to do it.

Ben, Will, and Sam Anderson have been the constants in my life. As my sons become young men, with all their individual challenges and difficult decisions ahead, I realize once again what truly remarkable people they are, and how fortunate I am to be their father. Their roads are beginning to diverge from mine, as they must, and none of us yet knows where those roads will lead. It is a journey, it is a process, and it never ends . . . but I am happy for them and eager to see what happens next.

While writing this book, I was delighted to reconnect with my critique group from years past. Michael Miller and Sami Birchall give me insight and thoughtful, honest perspectives on my writing. While the chairs once belonging to Dave Stanton and Judy Tillinghast are empty at the table now, I strongly feel that their spirits are very much with us.

My colleagues at *Slice* magazine and KCSC Radio continue to be supportive above and beyond the call, and my spiritual family at NWCC nurtures my life in more ways than I can even understand, much less name.

My agent, George Bick, is a gentleman and a professional—a rarer combination than one might think. He took a chance on me, and there is no finer advocate in the publishing business. He is always willing to lend an ear on nonpublishing matters as well, and I am grateful for this.

I am so pleased with my publishing home at Forge. From publisher Tom Doherty to publicist Alexis Saarela and copy editor Susannah Noel, the dedicated sales and marketing staff and phenomenal art department, there is nowhere I'd rather be. Of course, my editor, Kristin Sevick, is the one who drives this process. For starters, she is an editor who really edits, and her instincts are always on the mark, challenging me to be a better writer. She helped me to shape this story and the people who populate it, and I am most grateful for her fine editorial hand. Plus, she doesn't mind talking baseball, which is a plus in any relationship.

For research assistance, I would like to thank the following: Chad Bailey, information technology specialist with the Jeannine Rainbolt College of Education at the University of Oklahoma, for serving as computer security consultant; Michael DiRenzo of The Silver Institute; Ray Flowers of the Fort Fisher Historic Site, who gave me a private tour and pointed me toward additional resources; Darren Hellwege and Amy Leneski, for location details in Missouri and Michigan, respectively; Danny McClung, Oklahoma Highway Patrol trooper (retired) and aviation security officer with the Federal Transfer Center, for prisoner transfer procedures at the FTC; Charles Newcomb, friend for thirty years and licensed pilot, who keeps me accurate on aviation matters; Darrell Tracker, attorney, "freelance historian," and expert on the nooks and crannies of governmental operations; and Shellie Willoughby of the Office of Geographic Information, Oklahoma Conservation Commission, for answering questions on georeferencing technology. I am also grateful to officials of the Cripple Creek & Victor Gold Mining Company of Victor, Colorado, for a tour of their facility. As always, Rob Boss arms my characters in style, not only suggesting firearms, but tailoring his recommendations to the individual character.

Any errors of fact, or any changes I may have made, are certainly my own and not attributable to the above individuals or organizations.

I would like to extend notes of personal thanks to Terri Cullen, for her support and encouragement during the early stages of this book; and Martha Anderson, for her ongoing patience and flexibility.

Shortly after I began writing this book, my father, Bill Anderson, was diagnosed with stage four lung cancer. He was a gentleman and a gentle man, and he taught me everything I know about quiet dignity and courage, both in his life and how he faced his illness and death. He was a great reader, and no one was more proud than he of seeing my work in print. In the last few weeks of his life, the family framed a picture of the cover of my book *Cold Glory* and placed it beside his bed. I am told he would show it off when anyone came into his room. The last time I saw him, he held on to my hand for a long time before I left. Then he pointed at the book cover and said, "Just keep working." It seemed like a benediction, almost a blessing. They were the last words Dad said to me, and he died a few days later.

At the time we shared that moment, I was stuck in the writing of this book, bogged down, unable to focus. A week after Dad's death I began to work in earnest on this story, and I worked every day in the light of his memory and the good-natured nudge he gave me at the end of his life. It was one of the greatest gifts I have ever been given.

Read history, and you will find that the causes which bring about a revolution rarely predominate at its close, and no people have ever returned to the point from which they started.

—Rose O'Neale Greenhow

What will ye give me, and I will deliver him unto you? And they covenanted with him for thirty pieces of silver. And from that time he sought opportunity to betray him.

—Matthew 26:15–16

SILVER
CROSS

PROLOGUE

October 1, 1864—3:30 A.M.

The North Carolina coast, near the mouth of
the Cape Fear River

She woke to the sound of the guns, and as her senses adjusted, Rose Greenhow became aware of the ever-present wind and water. The sea had turned rough in the night. Then the ship was turning, turning hard. Waves broke and crashed, tossing the *Condor* side to side. Then more gunfire, and Rose knew with all certainty what she had to do.

She crawled out of the tiny berth and began to dress, moving quickly, silently, not even bothering to brush her hair. Rose found her heavy black wool dress and pulled it on, slightly askew. She grabbed the leather pouch from the post at the foot of the bunk and put the quarter-ounce gold coins into it, the checks drawn on the Bank of England, and then the papers, the dispatches for the Confederate secretary of state from the British commissioners—papers of no real consequence.

Then she took a thick envelope and caressed it as if it were the item made of gold, for indeed it was much more valuable than the coins. In the Tuileries Palace, alone with the most powerful man in Europe, she had watched Napoleon III write out the words himself—not trusting any secretary or clerk with the task—seal the envelope, and place it in her own hands. The emperor had held her hands and, in perfect English, said, "Go with God, madam. You carry the hopes of both our nations."

The ship lurched again, and Rose felt the sickening crunch of its bottom striking land. They had run hard aground. She tucked the envelope into a smaller leather pouch, then reached under her mattress, withdrew another package—a folded cloth, really—and slid it into a pocket of her dress.

More guns sounded, and they were closer still. The wind howled. She heard loud voices from the deck above. She quickened her movements. In the other berth, her maid was stirring. The younger woman sat up.

"What is it?" Elizabeth said.

"Lie down," Rose said. "I must go alone, Elizabeth."

"But—"

"You'll be fine. But the Yankees mustn't find me here."

Rose turned away and hurried from the compartment. She slipped the first leather pouch around her neck, keeping the other—the crucial one—clutched in her hands. Rose made her way to the deck of the *Condor,* the three-stack iron steamer that had been built in Scotland for the specific purpose of slipping past the Union navy's blockade of Southern ports. Drizzle hit her face; wind tugged at her. The guns were louder, now from two directions: a Union blockader, and the batteries from Fort Fisher, protecting the *Condor.*

It is not enough, Rose thought. She would not be captured . . . she would not be imprisoned. *Not again.*

She'd heard people call her the Confederacy's most "notorious" spy. Early in the war, she'd passed intelligence to General Beauregard that helped the South to win at Manassas. She had relayed messages to President Davis even during her imprisonment. But none were as vital as the letter she carried from Napoleon, the one she must put directly into Davis's hands. Publicly the emperor had said one thing—but alone with her at Tuileries, he had committed to a very different course of action.

The guns boomed.

Shadows moved along the deck. No lanterns burned—it was part of running the blockade, steaming without lights. The voices increased in number and tone. She saw a looming shadow in the waters of New Inlet, near the mouth of the Cape Fear River. Fort Fisher was perhaps three hundred yards away. She was almost home. Confederate soil was close. Perhaps . . .

No! She clutched the pouch. *I know what I must do.*

A sailor ran by her, swearing. Rose winced at his coarse language, making her way forward, holding the rail. She felt the wind on the back of her neck, the fine spray of water. To her right—*no, starboard,* she thought, *on board ship it's called starboard*—she saw the flash of light and heard the cannon roar. The *Condor* shuddered under her again.

She reached the wheelhouse and pulled open the door. The captain, younger than Rose by several years, stood in a cluster of men, one arm on the wheel, looking calm. "Mrs. Greenhow," he said, and bowed from the waist. "So sorry you were awakened. A spot of bad luck for a maiden voyage, but all is well. You will be more comfortable in your quarters. One of the men will take you—"

"What is happening, Captain?" Rose said.

"Pardon me, madam?"

"Will the Yankees board us?"

The captain put out both hands, as if patting the air in front of him. "You mustn't worry about such things. The guns from your Fort Fisher will protect us. We had the misfortune of having to steer around a wreck—a fairly recent one, I'd say. Now if you will kindly go . . ."

Rose shook her head, the fear rising within her. The ship was immobile, lying motionless, her keel against the bottom. The guns were relentless on both sides, dueling each other over who would claim the *Condor.* "I must get off this boat, Captain," Rose said, keeping her voice steady. She would not become hysterical, not in the face of these Englishmen, and certainly not to the Union sailors who would no doubt be swarming the ship in minutes. "Get me a lifeboat and some men. I must get to Fort Fisher."

The captain smiled, but he was straining to maintain his typically British nonchalant air. "We will wait out the night, Mrs. Greenhow. An unfortunate situation, to be sure, but not dire. The Union will not board us here, I assure you. The morning will see us safe."

A wind gust stirred the waves, and water broke over the bow. The *Condor* rocked against the current. Rose gazed out across the blackness of the sea toward the coast . . . toward home. She touched the pouch around her neck. "Now, Captain! A lifeboat!"

"The wench is daft," muttered an old seaman. "Serves us well, for taking a woman aboard."

"That will do," the captain said, and turned back to Rose. "Mrs. Greenhow, you must understand—"

"I am an emissary of the Confederate States of America, and you—and your ship—were engaged to conduct me safely to Confederate soil. This ship will sink, or it will be boarded, and I must be away from it when either of those things occurs. I will write to the queen and I will see that she is informed of your ill behavior, if you do not get me a lifeboat . . . now!"

The captain folded his hands together. "You are safer on board the ship. The current is strong here. We are not moving, but we are safe."

"Captain," Rose said, and lowered her voice. "Please. You must heed what I ask." She reached out and touched the ship's wheel. Her fingers were inches from the captain's. "Please," she said again.

The captain stared down at the wheel, and then slowly shook his head. "So be it." He turned to the sailors behind him. "Harlow, Roberts . . . you will lower the number one lifeboat and escort our passenger to shore. Find our other passengers, as they, too, are Confederate citizens, and see if they share Mrs. Greenhow's interest in leaving the ship now."

"I'll be damned if I will," growled Harlow, the old seaman who had spoken up earlier. "It's a fool's errand, Captain. Do you take orders from a woman, then?"

"Mr. Harlow," the captain said without raising his voice, "unless you mean to raise a mutiny here and now, you will take Mrs. Greenhow and anyone else who wishes to leave the ship."

Harlow was at least two decades older than the captain, with a gnarled white beard and stooped shoulders. He spat on the deck, between the captain and Rose. "Aye, Captain. I'm no mutineer, but I do this under protest."

"Your protest is noted, Mr. Harlow."

"Get your things," Harlow said to Rose.

Rose squeezed the pouch again. "All I need is here. And I require you to treat me with the proper respect."

Harlow stared at her. "Of course . . . my lady." He gestured at Roberts, a beardless boy who looked all of sixteen. "Go find the others."

* * *

The surf pounded the *Condor*'s hull. Even in the heavy dress, Rose shivered. She wished she had brought her coat to the deck, but now there was no time. Elizabeth pleaded to go with her, but Rose ordered her below. The young woman had been a faithful friend and dutiful servant, but this was not her battle, and Rose would not put her in danger. Rose stood on the deck in the hard, spitting rain and waited for the lifeboat to be ready.

The seas grew stronger, but the guns had fallen silent, though Rose could still see the outline of the Union gunship and the shadow of another ship, presumably also a blockade runner, that had run aground nearby. She waited, clutching her leather pouch.

"You carry the hopes of both our nations," Napoleon III had told her.

The men stomped onto the deck: Judge Holcombe, the Confederate commissioner to Canada, whom the *Condor* had picked up in Halifax; Lieutenant Wilson, a young Southern naval officer; the disagreeable Harlow; Roberts; and another young seaman named Jones. They climbed into the leeward lifeboat, and other crewmen began to lower it toward the sea. Wind gusts tore at the ropes. Rose grasped the side of the boat as the wind lashed the tiny craft and the rain stung her face. Her stomach clenched—she had never liked the water, never learned to swim, was always prone to seasickness, and this was worse than she had ever imagined. The boat swayed, hanging in the air above the water. Crewmen shouted. Harlow shouted back at them. Rose looked over at Judge Holcombe—his face was gray, and he was staring straight at her. She nodded to him, her mouth a tight line.

The boat touched the water, swells breaking across the bow. Rose, in the stern near young Roberts, drew in a hard breath, but she did not scream. She would not lose her dignity in front of these men.

The lifeboat cleared its davits. "Pull!" shouted Harlow from the bow. "Pull, damn you!"

Roberts and Jones had scarcely dipped oars into the water when Rose turned to her right, looking toward shore, toward the freedom of the Carolina coast. In the blackness of the night, she felt the wave as it caught the boat broadside. It was as though the hand of God had reached down and pushed the boat to the top of the breaker, where it hung suspended for an excruciating second.

Dear God, no! Rose thought. *Not after all this, not after all those who have died, not when I have the power to see their deaths were not in vain. . . .*

Then her thoughts turned to Little Rose, her daughter, in the convent school in Paris. *Thank God I did not insist on bringing her back with me. . . .*

The men were shouting, Harlow cursing the others, cursing her, cursing God and the waves. Rose dug into the pouch around her neck, and from it she withdrew the one containing the letter the emperor had placed in her hands. The letter that must not fall into Union hands.

She turned. The oars were torn from young Roberts's grasp. The boy—for he was, indeed, only a boy, Rose saw—was crying. Rose screamed his name. He looked toward her.

She extended the small pouch to him. "Take it!" she shouted.

"But, madam—"

She shook it in his face. "Protect it with your life!" For one instant she thought she could see into his eyes, even in the darkness.

"I will, my lady," he said, so quiet she could barely hear him.

She started to tell him how if they became separated, he was to see that the letter reached Richmond and President Davis. But the boat began to turn, capsizing as the wave receded and crashing back toward the sea.

The water rushed over her head, and Rose felt the waves pulling her. The shouts of the men began to fade. For a moment she had a grip on the boat, feeling wood splintering under her fingernails as she clawed for a handhold. But she was being pulled down, the heavy fabric of her dress and the pouch around her neck dragging her beneath the waves.

Her head broke the water one more time. Her hands raked the air. She could barely see Roberts, now three or four feet away. He was reaching toward her. But she could no longer fight the waves, and her dress pulled her under again.

CHAPTER

1

Present Day

T he sign on the office door still read WHERE CASES GO TO DIE. It was a white piece of paper with the letters in black marker, held in place by tape. A new nameplate was above the sign: MEG TOLMAN, DEPUTY DIRECTOR, RESEARCH AND INVESTIGATIONS OFFICE. The office was at the end of a short hallway on the fourth floor of an unassuming office suite in an equally unassuming office building in downtown Washington. The woman behind the office's desk wasn't thinking about research or investigations. She was wondering if she could get away with doing a lecture about piano music of the Romantic period and not mention Franz Liszt.

In the months since Meg Tolman had been named to run the day-to-day operations of RIO, she had learned that much of her job involved submitting reports to the offices of the attorney general and the secretaries of both Treasury and Homeland Security, the three departments that coadministered the agency. But she'd also learned why there had never been a person with the title of "director," why a "deputy director" was in charge. The titular director of RIO was the president of the United States. Twice a month Tolman had a personal meeting with the president's chief of staff. On two occasions she'd met with President Mendoza himself. In such an environment, it was easy to get distracted from her other world—that of part-time concert pianist.

Still, Tolman had farmed out as much of the administrative function of her job as possible to others in the office, so that she could still do actual work. RIO took cases that were referred from other law enforcement agencies—often strange and unsolvable crimes—and reviewed them to determine whether it was appropriate for federal resources to be committed. In most instances the cases were returned to the referring department. Occasionally they weren't. It was a strange and surreal existence, and Tolman needed her music to balance her life.

She doodled in a notebook, thinking about the lecture she was supposed to give in the afternoon at Northern Virginia Community College. She would talk about Schumann and Brahms and Chopin and even the "twentieth-century Romantics" like her beloved Rachmaninov, but Liszt . . .

"Liszt was a fucking show-off," she muttered.

She doodled a few music notes, a box, a cat, then put the notebook aside and turned to her computer to finish writing another report. She was plodding through an analysis of alleged federal civil rights abuses in a case from Ohio that had arisen from state police response to one of the recent waves of protests and general unrest sweeping the country. *Protests on the left, protests on the right,* she thought. *No one's satisfied and the cops are overmatched. What a mess—thinking about Liszt was easier.* She looked up from the computer when her cell phone rang.

"Hello, is this Meg Tolman?" said a male voice she didn't recognize.

"The one and only," she said, still looking at the Ohio case but thinking about what a prima donna Liszt had been.

"Ms. Tolman, this is Carl Troutman at New Hanover Regional Medical Center in Wilmington, North Carolina. You are listed as the emergency contact for Dana Cable. There's been an accident."

Tolman looked away from the computer. "What? Did you say Dana Cable?"

"Yes. Her insurance company lists you as her emergency contact."

"You mean Dana Cable the cellist?"

The man hesitated. "I don't know if she's a cellist, but her address is in Philadelphia, Pennsylvania, and her insurance company—"

"I haven't seen Dana in a long time, probably six or seven years. There must be someone else. . . ."

"You are Meg Tolman and you work in Washington, D.C.?"

"Yes, of course, but—"

"Then there's no mistake."

"Where did you say you are? North Carolina?"

"Yes. Wilmington."

"What's Dana doing there? What kind of accident?"

"I don't know the answer to the first question. As to the second, from what we can tell she was out walking on the seawall below Kure Beach that separates the Cape Fear River from the Atlantic. It seems she had been drinking, and it was high tide. A wave knocked her over. She hit her head."

"That's not right."

"Ms. Tolman—"

"No, no, you don't understand. That can't be right."

"Ms. Tolman, your friend has been in a serious accident. She's been in and out of consciousness and is in ICU. The nurses told me that she's said your name several times. Will you be able to come?"

"What?"

"She's asking for you, Ms. Tolman. You should come soon."

"What do you mean?"

"I don't mean to be indelicate, but if you want to see your friend while she's still alive, you should be on your way here as soon as possible."

Tolman gripped the phone. *Dana Cable.* She had a vision of the two of them playing Beethoven's Cello Sonata no. 2. It was Dana's senior recital at the Curtis Institute, and she'd asked Tolman to accompany her. She remembered the way Dana's long brown hair had fallen around her face as she bowed, lost in the music. Afterward they'd gone to a bar down the street, and while Tolman drank rum and Coke as Dana drank straight Coke, both of them confessed they never wanted to hear Beethoven's Cello Sonata no. 2 again. Tolman remembered Dana mumbling about wishing they could see her "back home" now. She'd come from some little town in the Ozark Mountains, and she was fairly certain she'd owned the only cello in the entire county. Tolman blinked away the memory.

"I'm on my way," she said.

CHAPTER

2

When she stepped off the plane in Wilmington, Tolman realized she'd come to the only possible place in America that was more humid than D.C. in August.

Although she hated driving almost as much as she hated Franz Liszt, she rented a car. It was her experience that there was no decent public transportation between Washington and Atlanta. Following the rental's GPS, she found herself on highways 74 and 76 within a few minutes of each other, made a wrong turn, crossed the Cape Fear River twice, and finally arrived at the sprawling New Hanover Regional Medical Center complex on Seventeenth Street.

She dragged her purse and laptop bag out of the car and found the main hospital entrance. Her blouse was dotted with perspiration from the coastal humidity by the time she reached the door. She was glad her hair was still short—anything longer than her very short shag would have wilted like dying flowers.

She asked for directions from a volunteer desk near the entrance, and in five minutes she found herself standing outside the ICU. "I'm here to see Dana Cable," she told the nurse.

The nurse picked up the phone, punched some buttons, spoke quietly. Tolman scanned the ICU waiting area: families congregating with fast-food wrappers in corners, an old woman crying while a middle-aged version of her held her hand and stared into space; a tired man with a salt-and-pepper beard sat with three teenage boys, periodically speaking in low tones about when they would be able to go in and see "granddad." Tolman turned away—there was tragedy everywhere. A former boss and mentor, a man who had betrayed Tolman and many others, had once said, "If you dig deep enough, you always come up with a fistful of tragedy." He'd been right on that one.

The nurse at the desk said, "Someone will be out to talk to you in a couple of minutes."

"What about this guy Troutman who called me? Who is he?"

"He's the unit clerk on the earlier shift," the nurse said. "But someone else will be out to talk to you."

"Who, the doctor?"

"If you'll take a seat, someone will—"

"I'll take it from here," said a voice in a deep Carolina drawl behind her.

Tolman turned and looked up at a tall man in polo shirt and khakis. "Who are you?" she said. "Are you the doctor?"

"Let's go in," the man said. He slapped a silver square button and the doors to the unit began to swing open. They were in a long hall. "She's at the far end, in the trauma section." He turned and looked down at Tolman as they walked. His legs were longer, and she had to trot to keep up. "I'm Larry Poe, New Hanover County Sheriff's Department."

"Are you the investigating officer?"

Poe didn't break stride. "Now that's interesting. Usually when I introduce myself in a situation like this, people say, 'Sheriff's department? Why is the sheriff's department here? Don't sheriff's deputies wear uniforms?' Things like that."

Tolman smiled. "I'm with the Research and Investigations Office in D.C. We're part of the departments of Justice, Treasury, and Homeland Security."

"I see," Poe said. "Three bosses. As much of a headache as it sounds?"

Tolman decided she liked Larry Poe. "More than I ever thought possible."

"Never heard of your department before."

"You and a couple of hundred million other Americans. We fly under the radar."

"Like NSA? No Such Agency, that sort of thing?"

"Hardly," Tolman said. "We're not that important. We look at cases that other departments think are worthless."

Poe stopped. "You're making that up."

She sighed. "No one would make up a job like that."

The sheriff's man started walking again. "Good point. The clerk tells me you're listed as emergency contact for Dana Cable."

"Apparently so. I didn't know it until the call came today."

"Haven't seen her in a while, then?"

"About seven years, since we graduated from the Curtis Institute."

"In Philadelphia."

"Right. She's a cellist. I'm a pianist."

"Thought you were with the three-boss office in D.C."

"That's my day job."

"Got it. Well, your friend went out for a late-night walk on the seawall, down at the tip of the Cape. Her blood alcohol level was nearly twice the legal limit."

"See, that's what doesn't make sense," Tolman said. They reached the end of the carpeted hallway. Poe touched another square button and another pair of doors swung open.

"She's in room three," he said, then stopped. Nurses in scrubs, and at least one doctor, were filing out of the room with the number three above it. One nurse drew the curtain across the opening. The doctor, a slim young African American man, pulled off his surgical cap and caught Poe's eye. He came toward them.

"Inspector," he said, nodding at Poe. "She went into coma about an hour ago. She coded ten minutes ago. The brain trauma was too severe for her body to handle. Is there someone else we should call?"

Poe nodded at Tolman.

"Are you a family member?" the doctor asked.

Tolman felt numb, her feelings on unsure footing. She hadn't seen Dana Cable in seven years, and they'd only kept in contact sporadically . . . a handful of phone calls and e-mails. Nothing at all in the last six months or so. "An old friend," she finally said.

"Oh," the doctor said.

"I know she had two brothers," Tolman said, "but I don't know anything about them. I don't even know where they live now. I think she said one is an accountant, and one was a college professor somewhere. I don't know where."

"We'll be ordering an autopsy," Poe said.

"Of course," the doctor said, and looked at Tolman. "I'm sorry." He moved away.

"Do you need a few minutes?" Poe asked.

"What?" Tolman said.

Poe gestured toward the door of room three.

It took Tolman a moment to get what he meant. "You mean go in there?"

"Yeah."

"No," Tolman said. "I don't want to see her dead."

Poe looked surprised. "You sure? There might not be a chance . . ."

Seeing death, even violent death, didn't scare Tolman. She'd even had a part in killing a man a few months ago, a man who was shooting at an unarmed civilian, and who had been part of a plot to overthrow the United States government. But seeing someone she *knew*—that was different. Her mother's car had gone over an embankment and into the Potomac River when Tolman was sixteen. In the backseat, she survived. Her mother didn't. At the hospital, her father—who had been called to the hospital from President Clinton's Secret Service detail—wouldn't let her see the body. *That's not your mom anymore,* Ray Tolman had told her. *That's just a container with a bunch of skin and bones and blood and muscle in it. That's all it is now.*

"No," Tolman said. "I'd rather picture her playing the cello."

"Okay," Poe said. "We'll need a couple of days for the autopsy. Do you want to claim the body? You mentioned brothers. Maybe they—"

"I don't know. I guess if she listed me as her emergency contact, though I don't know why she would, she must have wanted me to do something."

"We've searched her hotel room and released it. I have her belongings. There was a letter."

Tolman looked up at him. "What kind of letter?"

"It said 'In case of emergency' on the envelope. It tells what to do in the event of her death."

Tolman felt her heart slow down. "How many people carry something like that around with them?"

"Then you see why I'm here, and why this all looks a whole lot more complicated than someone getting drunk and going for a midnight stroll at high tide."

Tolman glanced at the closed curtain of room three. "She wasn't drunk."

Poe spread his hands. "Yes, she was."

"No. Maybe her blood alcohol level said she was, but Dana didn't drink."

"You hadn't seen her in seven years. Maybe she started."

"Both of her parents were alcoholics. Her father wandered drunk out of a bar one night when Dana was little and ran out in the middle of the highway, where a truck hit him and killed him. Her mother died of cirrhosis of the liver when Dana was in college. She and her brothers all swore they would never touch alcohol as long as they lived."

"People break childhood pledges all the time."

Tolman looked up at the tall man again. "Bullshit, Inspector. You don't believe that. You're playing devil's advocate with me. You know something's not right here."

Poe ran a hand through his short, graying brown hair. "Hungry? Ever had East Carolina–style barbeque?"

"No and no. I want to know why she was down here, and I want to know what happened to her."

"Did she know what you do for a living? Research and investigations, all that business?"

Tolman met the man's eyes. "Yes."

"Uh-huh. Let's get something to eat, Ms. Tolman. Then I want to take you for a little ride down the coast. We have a lot of daylight left."

As they turned toward the unit door, one of the nurses who had come out of Dana's room caught up to them, trotting from the nurses' station. "Excuse me," she said, and her voice carried the same soft drawling cadence as Poe's. "Is your name Meg? Were you a friend of hers?" She tilted her head toward the room.

"I'm Meg," Tolman said.

"She was in and out of consciousness ever since she came up from the ER," the nurse said. "She wasn't very coherent. And with the brain injury . . ." She shrugged. "But when she was lucid, before she went into coma, she said your name several times. She even grabbed my arm one time when she said it. She kept saying, 'Tell Meg, tell Meg.' I asked her who Meg was and what we were supposed to tell. 'Tell Meg,' she kept saying. Then after Troutman reached you and you said you were coming, I told her you were on your way. But right before she went into coma, she said it again. 'Tell Meg.' Then she said, 'The rose and the silver cross. Tell Meg, the rose and the silver cross.'" The nurse dipped her head. "Does that mean something to you?"

"*The rose and the silver cross.*"

"*Tell Meg.*"

And she thought of her mother, the way she'd been screaming at her over the seat of the car when she'd lost control. And she thought of Dana Cable and the good times in Philadelphia, a lifetime ago. The way they'd gone out after recitals, with Dana as the perpetual designated driver. She hadn't seen either of them dead, her mother or Dana, even though both of them had been talking to her—in very different ways—right before they died.

"No," Tolman said. "That doesn't mean a damn thing to me." She looked up at Poe. "Let's take that ride down the coast, Inspector."

CHAPTER
3

Ann Gray watched Inspector Poe and the short blond woman emerge from the ICU. Gray blended into the throng of patients' families and friends, sitting in a corner, a box of tissues on her lap, an old magazine open and unread beside her. Hospitals were easy places to conduct surveillance. Everyone looked out of place in a hospital.

Gray had watched Poe since he first arrived on the crime scene. Then she had been a tourist. In the Wilmington/Cape Fear area in the summer, that wasn't a hard role to play either. But she didn't know the short woman. She'd heard the name—Meg Tolman—when the woman first arrived at the ICU desk, but the name meant nothing. For now.

Still, Poe wasn't treating the Tolman woman like a typical friend or family member of a crime victim. He took her to his car, where she sat in the front seat next to him. Gray followed them, then watched as Poe took Tolman to a restaurant called Jackson's Big Oak Barbeque. She smiled—she'd eaten there yesterday, sampling the vinegar-based sauce for which eastern North Carolina was famous.

Gray waited. Forty-five minutes later the two emerged. She followed at a distance of three car lengths. When they crossed the Atlantic Intracoastal Waterway onto Pleasure Island and turned south on

U.S. 421, Gray sped up her rental and passed them. She knew where they were going. There was no need to follow—she would get there ahead of them and see what they did.

She drove through the tourist haven of Carolina Beach, with its seaside cottage and condo rentals and T-shirt shops and all things nautical. That gave way to Kure Beach, which was more family oriented. She was fast running out of land.

She passed the Fort Fisher Historic Site, with its remnants of the old fort, and the Aquarium at Fort Fisher, another tourist attraction. At the end of 421, the road widened into a parking lot. Only one car, a New Hanover County sheriff's unit, was in the lot. With the seawall barricaded by yellow crime scene tape, there was nothing for the tourists here today. They might stand for a few moments, watching the Atlantic Ocean on the left of the wall, the Cape Fear River on the right, the rock wall curving between the two, winding for more than six miles from the end of the highway to the spot where the river emptied into the sea.

Gray made sure she kept her camera around her neck as she got out of the car. A guidebook was another nice touch. She was a housewife whose husband had taken the kids to the public beach or the aquarium so she could have a few minutes of quiet contemplation. She wore navy blue walking shorts, a white polo shirt, and sneakers with white ankle socks. She was tanned, but not too tan. Just another middle-aged woman from Charlotte or Atlanta, admiring the water.

Poe and Tolman arrived five minutes later. But Gray still didn't know how Meg Tolman fit in to the equation, and why the sheriff's man was taking her to the crime scene. Gray took a few pictures of the seawall and the boat ramp, the camera straying to where Poe and Tolman were talking with the uniformed deputy who stood watch at the entrance of the seawall, the yellow tape running between a tree and a picnic table. In a few hours, she would know everything she needed to know about Meg Tolman, and how she might fit into Gray's new plans.

From inside the rental car, Gray's cell phone trilled. She reached in and looked at the caller ID, then smiled. "Hi, honey," she said into it.

"Hey, Mom," said the voice on the other end. Since getting a phone for his thirteenth birthday, her son called or texted her every few hours when she went out of town. "How's the conference?"

"On a break right now," Gray said. Poe and Tolman were stepping across the crime scene tape.

"You still coming home tomorrow? Dad's worried."

"Oh, Dad's worried? Nice to know that Dad's worried." She smiled.

"Um, and Ellis wants to know if I can sleep over this weekend. He got a new glass chess set from Germany."

Gray exhaled. How many thirteen-year-olds were more excited by chess than video games? "From Germany. Impressive. Tell Ellis's mother it's fine. See if they can pick you up, then Dad can get you from their house, if the house is still standing."

"The only way we'll tear the house down is if Ellis gets me in check with only a rook and a pawn like he did last time. See you tomorrow?"

Gray looked at the crime scene tape again. "I may be an extra day. One of our clients has a problem."

The boy sounded disappointed. "Okay. I'll tell Dad."

"Love you, honey," Gray said.

The boy hung up. He was thirteen, so telling his mother he loved her on the phone wasn't on the agenda. Still, he'd called her. There was something to be said for that.

She tossed her phone onto the car seat. Then she reached in the backseat of the car and straightened the overnight bag there. She zipped it up, making sure the CZ 75 semi-automatic pistol was covered.

Everything has changed, she thought. Then Ann Gray turned and took a few more pictures.

Tolman stood still, gazing past the crime scene tape. A yellow diamond-shaped sign read, DANGER – SLIPPERY ROCKS – SWIFT CURRENT. She stepped over the tape, Poe following. "How far does this go?" she asked.

"The seawall runs a good six miles to the point where the Cape Fear empties into the ocean," Poe said.

"How far out was Dana?"

"Not much more than a mile. There's a place where it makes a sharp curve to the left. That's where some tourists found her."

Tolman kept walking. The paved sidewalk gave way to the seawall itself. The visible portion of the wall was less than twenty feet across, with irregularly shaped and sized rocks sloping down on both sides.

Many of the rocks were broken, creating uncertain footing on the walkway. A little moss grew here and there. They stepped past a dirty white sock, an Aquafina bottle, a tangled ball of old twine. Tolman looked around. The parking lot behind them was deserted except for a woman with a camera.

"Lots of tourists come out here?" Tolman said.

"Oh, yeah," Poe said. "And we get fatalities from time to time, people who take walks when they shouldn't."

Tolman looked at him. "So what happened to Dana isn't all that uncommon down here."

"The fact that it happened isn't uncommon. Keep walking."

Tolman looked at him again, then returned to picking her way across the rocks. The wind came up. Water lapped at the base of the rocks on the ocean side. Ahead, she saw the wall begin its turn.

"A few more steps," Poe said, behind her. Then: "Stop. Look down."

Three steps into the curve, Tolman stopped. At her feet was a dark stain on the rocks. She raised her head, looking at the ocean on the left, the river on the right.

"And last night was high tide?" she said.

"Yep. You ever do much crime scene work up there with the Research and Investigations Office?"

Tolman was quiet. She knelt down, touched the bloodstain, raked her hands across the rocks. She looked at the ocean again.

"So she was walking this way," Tolman said, "and the tide came in from this direction." She pointed to her left. "Say the tide knocked her off her feet. It was coming from this way and this wall isn't all that wide. Why didn't she fall off into the river on the other side? How is it that this bloodstain is exactly in the center of the wall?" She touched the stain again.

"That's the question," Poe said. "And the guy who found her said she was laid out straight on top of the wall, right in the center, and her feet were pointing toward shore."

Tolman looked up at that. "Toward shore? Are you sure about that?"

"Paramedics confirmed it when they arrived on the scene."

"But if she was walking away from shore and a wave hit her, you would think her forward momentum would make her slip and fall with her feet in the direction she was going. Her body would have had to be turned completely around. Accidents don't happen that way. People don't wind up with their bodies neatly positioned like that."

"You see my problem, then."

"Someone else was out here with her."

"Maybe," Poe said. "Doesn't change the fact that she was legally drunk and in a bad place at a bad time."

Tolman stood up. "I don't know about the alcohol, but—"

"Yeah, yeah, I know, she didn't drink." Poe scratched his chin. "But dammit, this bothers me. A cello player from Philadelphia, with no connections to this area, on this wall alone in the middle of the night at high tide. And what? Someone knocks her in the head, positions her body very neatly, then leaves? Why? Not robbery. Her wallet was in the pocket of her jacket, and it had more than three hundred dollars in it. She was wearing an expensive necklace, a gold chain with a pendant in the shape of two music notes and two little diamonds inlaid into the notes."

"I remember that necklace. One of her brothers gave it to her as a graduation present, after her senior recital at Curtis."

Poe spread his hands apart. "Why was she in North Carolina? What was she doing here?"

Tolman turned toward shore. She watched a Coast Guard cutter pass on the Cape Fear River. Then she started walking, taking long strides, passing Poe. She thought of the Beethoven piece she and Dana had played all those years ago. Then the music in her mind stopped as abruptly as if the cello had been broken in half. "I'd like to see her room, if you can arrange it," she said. "I need that paper that says what to do in the event of her death. Did she have a laptop with her? I'll need that, too."

Poe folded his arms and looked down at Tolman, not speaking.

"Look, Inspector," Tolman said, "I'm in this, officially or not. For some reason neither of us knows, Dana asked me to be here. I can bring some resources into the investigation. I'm not going to go all federal on you and pull rank—it's your jurisdiction. But I need to do this, for Dana."

Without waiting for Poe to respond, Tolman began to trot along the wall. The woman with the camera was gone, the parking lot empty except for the deputy who stood guard. Her mind was racing. She needed her laptop. She needed RIO's databases. She needed time.

Poe's cell phone rang, and he spoke for a moment, then snapped the phone closed and caught up with Tolman. "I've had people canvassing the area," he said. "Someone at the Fort Fisher Museum remembers Cable. She was in there yesterday."

"Fort Fisher? What is that?"

"It's an old Civil War fort. It's a state historic site now, just up the road. You know any Civil War history?"

Tolman thought before she spoke. "More than I did a year ago."

"Excuse me?"

"Never mind. What about this place?"

"Fisher was one of the last strongholds the South had on the coast. There was a big battle here at the end of the war. Lots of blockade runners came through here, too. I'm no historian, but you can't grow up around here and not know at least some of the story. Lot of ships came through here."

"Was there ever one called the *Rose*? Or the *Silver Cross*?"

Poe's gaze sharpened. "I don't know. Look, we don't know why Cable was at the museum. Maybe she was doing the tourist thing herself. It happens."

"Maybe so. But I don't like 'maybe.' I want to know." She pulled out her phone as her feet left the seawall and she stepped onto the North Carolina shore. "If your Civil War fort has something to do with all this, we need an expert."

"Oh, and you know someone like that, do you?"

"Yes," Tolman said, and began punching buttons. "I do."

CHAPTER

4

Nick Journey only turned away for a few seconds, then Andrew was gone.

He and Andrew and Sandra Kelly had eaten dinner at a new Mexican café on the square in downtown Carpenter Center, Oklahoma, where Journey taught history at South Central College of Oklahoma. Sandra was a colleague and friend—their relationship still wasn't clear in his mind, and at forty-three he couldn't bring himself to use the word "girlfriend." But she'd been around a lot in the last few months, and Andrew had grown comfortable around her—a triumph no matter how he defined the relationship.

Andrew hadn't eaten much. He loaded up on warm flour tortillas but wouldn't touch the cheese quesadillas his father ordered for him. He was still a bit wound up from his day. In the summer Andrew attended a day camp for special needs children, hosted by a church in nearby Madill. Today had been water play day. Andrew loved the water.

They stepped out of the café and Andrew hooted loudly. Journey turned to say something to Sandra when his cell rang. "Hang on, Andrew," he said as the boy—tall for his age at thirteen—shuffled his feet on the concrete. He took a step toward the street.

Journey looked at the caller ID. He smiled and answered the call. "Well, hello, Meg," he said. "What's up in the world of RIO?"

Sandra Kelly screamed.

Journey jumped, losing his grip on the phone. Andrew was barreling straight into the middle of Texoma Plaza, the street that ran around all sides of the square. On the other side, a white pickup truck entered the square. The driver wouldn't be able to see Andrew, and was moving fast.

"Andrew!" Journey shouted.

Andrew was still running, arms flapping, fingers making their unusual motions. He looked vaguely toward his father, though he didn't make eye contact. The boy laughed, but it wasn't his genuine, happy laughter—instead the hysterical laughter that the autistic mind sometimes produced in response to his environment.

Journey began to run. "Stop!" he screamed. "Andrew, stop!"

Fifteen years and thirty pounds ago, Journey had been a professional baseball player, topping out at the highest level of the minor leagues before hanging it up and going to graduate school. He'd been fairly quick then, but he was a long time removed from that world now, just an overweight professor with high blood pressure. But his only child—a child with no understanding of danger—had broken away from him and was running free toward the traffic.

The white truck turned the corner of the square. It hadn't slowed down.

Journey pounded the pavement. Andrew had stopped, mesmerized by the light in the window of a store on the other side of the square. He flapped his arms. He hooted and laughed.

Journey ran. He heard Sandra behind him, a few steps away. She was running, too. He could see the truck's driver now, a man, big, with crew cut blond hair. Journey waved his arms. The man was thumping his hand on the steering wheel, listening to music, in a hurry to get where he was going.

Andrew was ten steps away, flapping and laughing.

"Andrew!"

His son looked at him. The truck's driver finally saw Andrew, laid on his horn. Tires screeched. Journey reached his son and grabbed a handful of his T-shirt. Andrew half-turned toward him and Journey wrapped his arms around him. The truck fishtailed. Journey enveloped Andrew in his grasp and angled their bodies toward the curb. Andrew stopped laughing as if an off button had been pressed.

Journey's leg went out from under him and he and Andrew tumbled to the pavement. The truck screeched to a stop, its grill three feet away from where they landed.

The burly driver erupted out of the truck. "Fucking retard," he screamed. "What's he think he's doing, running out in the street and standing there?"

Journey was breathing hard, cradling Andrew underneath him. The boy was squirming. Journey looked up at the driver. He was close enough to smell the man's sour breath. "My son is not a retard, and don't call him that. He has autism."

"I don't give a fiddler's fuck what he has. If you can't keep him out of the street, he ought to be somewhere he can't cause trouble."

Journey uncoiled himself from Andrew and got to his feet. He took a step toward the driver. "Look, he got away from me and that's my responsibility, but he has as much right to be here as you do. Probably more, with the way you were driving. You were going way too fast for the square, and not paying attention."

"Bull*shit*," the man said, and took a swing at Journey.

The driver had a good three inches and fifty pounds on him, but Journey was still quick enough to dodge the clumsy punch. In one motion, he stepped to the side and shoved the driver back until he was pinned against his truck.

"Fuck," the man spat.

Journey got an arm on each side of the man's chest and slammed him once against the hood of the truck. "Pay attention to your driving and watch your mouth, understand?" He never raised his voice. The driver's eyes widened.

A small crowd had gathered on both sides of the square, and a Carpenter Center police officer made his way through it. "Move along, Denny," he said to the driver. "You're lucky I don't cite you for both reckless driving and speeding. Speed limit on the square is twenty-five, and you were doing at least forty."

"The hell I was! There's no traffic here, and this stupid little—"

"Get in the truck and go home, Denny," the cop said. "And like Dr. Journey said, watch your mouth. I know Dr. Journey and I know Andrew, and we're all lucky that no one was hurt."

"This guy assaulted me! I want to file charges!"

"You swung at him first, Denny, and about forty people saw you. He was defending himself and his son. You're lucky Dr. Journey's a nicer guy than I am. If you'd said those things about my kid, you'd be spitting out some teeth right about now. So just go home."

The cop's name was Dale Gardner. He had a teenage daughter with cerebral palsy, and he volunteered at the therapeutic horseback-riding program Andrew attended twice a week. Journey knew him fairly well, almost to the point of thinking him a friend.

Journey let the driver off the hood and backed away several steps. "Go on, now," Gardner said. The driver shot a glare to all of them, climbed in the cab, and drove away.

"You okay, Nick?" Gardner asked.

"Fine," Journey said. He turned toward Andrew.

"You okay, Andrew?" Gardner said.

Andrew didn't hoot or whistle or laugh. His face had darkened. Journey said a few more words to Gardner, then when Journey turned back toward his son, Andrew shoved him backward into Gardner.

"Andrew!" Journey said.

Andrew made a throaty noise, stamped his feet, and spat in Journey's face.

Gardner raised his eyebrows in surprise. Journey heard Sandra draw in a sharp breath. A murmur went up from the bystanders. Journey wiped his face, struggling to hold his voice down. "Andrew, that's not appropriate. You don't spit. Come on, let's go back to the car." He reached out for his son's hand. Andrew raised both his hands and raked his fingernails down his father's arm. A red line of scratches appeared running from Journey's elbow almost to his wrist. He let out a sharp noise. "Andrew, no!"

Andrew responded to his father's raised voice by trying to scratch him again, but Journey caught his hands at the wrists and lowered them to the boy's sides, Andrew fighting him all the time.

He heard Sandra's voice: "Nick, what can I do?"

Sandra was a problem solver . . . always looking for solutions, and still trying to learn what Andrew was all about. Problem was, Journey didn't have the solutions either. He shook his head. "I need to get him up on the sidewalk. Come on, Andrew."

Andrew kicked at him, but Journey dodged, still holding his son's arms. They struggled toward the curb. People moved out of their way, gave them a wide berth, some staring, some talking in low tones. Journey heard one voice whisper, "If that were my kid . . ."

Gardner tried to help him, but Journey shrugged him off. "I can do it," he said. Andrew kicked his leg again, harder. Then the aggression stopped as quickly as it had begun. Andrew relaxed, looked at the ground, and started to whistle the three-note melody he always whistled.

Journey felt his heartbeat finally begin to slow. He closed his eyes and let out a breath. Andrew was a paradox—his functional age was about three years old, he was nonverbal, but he still had the body of a thirteen-year-old, which meant adolescence. And for Andrew, the physical changes in his body manifested themselves in aggression. So far, aside from one incident at school, the aggression had always been directed at his father. But this was the worst episode yet.

"You're bleeding," Sandra said, looking at the scratches on Journey's arm.

Journey looked down at the line of scratches. They were pretty deep. "Maybe it's time to trim his fingernails again," he said, trying for humor.

"I can help you clean up," Sandra said. She didn't look at Andrew. Journey wondered if she was thinking, *What have I gotten myself into?*

"No, it's okay," Journey said. "They're not too bad. We should take you home soon, though."

The crowd broke up, and Journey, Andrew, and Sandra walked to his old silver minivan. Andrew settled into the backseat and Journey buckled him in. Andrew continued to whistle. In the front, Sandra said, "I picked up your phone."

Journey had almost forgotten about the phone call that started all this. "What did Meg say?"

"She wanted you to call her as soon as possible. She sounded stressed." Sandra handed him the phone.

"Thanks." Journey pressed the redial button and in a moment Tolman's voice was on the line. Journey had worked with Meg Tolman eleven months ago, piecing together a harrowing conspiracy that almost toppled the entire U.S. government. Tolman had shot a man to save Journey's life, and he'd reluctantly agreed to become a consultant to RIO on any cases with a historical component. He wondered what Meg could be calling him about.

"What's up?" Tolman said. "Sandra said you had a problem with Andrew."

"Yeah," he said. "He ran out into traffic, then there was a little incident with the driver who almost hit him. After that Andrew got aggressive with me."

"Aggressive? What's that mean?"

"It means aggressive. It happens sometimes. Sandra said you wanted me to call back soon. Is something wrong?"

"Why do you always change the subject when I talk to you about anything personal?"

"You didn't call to chat about Andrew's development. What's going on?"

Tolman sighed. "You ever hear of Fort Fisher in North Carolina?"

"Of course," Journey said. "It was a major Confederate stronghold in the war. It was the last port to fall, a few months before Appomattox. Why?"

"You're on the clock, Nick. You're a consultant . . . time to consult."

"What does that mean?"

"It means, dammit, that I need your help. I'm in North Carolina now. I need to know everything about the fort, both historic and contemporary. I'll take care of the contemporary part."

"Okay." Journey glanced in the rearview mirror at Andrew. The boy was looking out the window at the square, very calm. The scratches on Journey's arm started to hurt a bit. "I'm not teaching this summer, so my time is flexible. I can do a workup on Fort Fisher for you."

"Does 'the rose and the silver cross' mean anything to you?"

"No. Should it?"

"Maybe. Connect it to Fort Fisher if you can."

"'The rose and the silver cross.' I've never heard of the silver cross, and the only rose I can think of offhand connected to Fort Fisher was Rose Greenhow. She was a famous Confederate spy who drowned just off the coast."

"A spy? They had female spies in the Civil War?"

"Lots of them," Journey said. "And Rose Greenhow was the most notorious. But what am I looking for, with regard to Fort Fisher? It would help if I knew which directions to look."

"Look everywhere," Tolman said. "I don't know yet."

"So this is a RIO case?"

There was a long pause.

"Meg?" Journey said.

"Yes and no," Tolman said. "I'm making it a RIO case. But this is also personal."

CHAPTER

5

Tolman spent three days in Wilmington's Hilton Garden Inn—the same hotel where Dana Cable had stayed. She and Larry Poe interviewed a staffer of the Fort Fisher Museum, who recalled seeing Dana Cable a few hours before her death. But Tolman didn't remember Dana ever having any interest in history, much less the Civil War.

Poe released Dana's room to Tolman. The letter marked "In case of emergency" answered no questions—it only instructed that Dana was to be buried in her family's plot in the cemetery in her hometown of Cassville, Missouri. Tolman contacted the funeral home in the small town and asked if Dana still had relatives in the area.

"No, she's the last of that family," the man at the funeral home told her. When Tolman asked what he meant, he told her she'd soon see, if she were accompanying the body to Missouri.

The autopsy showed that Dana Cable died of blunt trauma to the head.

So someone bashed her head against those rocks, Tolman thought.

The medical examiner also confirmed her blood alcohol level and said she had traces of bourbon on her clothes, arms, and torso.

As if someone forced her to drink, spilling the booze on her in the process.

Clumsy, Tolman thought. *Very clumsy.*

But she was still no closer to understanding what had happened and why.

Three days after arriving at the airport in Wilmington, she boarded another plane, this one bound for Springfield, Missouri. She called RIO and told the office she'd be away a few more days, but that she was now on an RIO case. Then she called her father and asked him to continue looking after Rocky, her cat. Tolman watched Dana's casket being loaded onto the plane, then took her seat for the flight to Missouri.

She'd arranged for a hearse from the funeral home in Cassville to meet the plane, and she rode in it for the sixty-mile trip to Cassville. The body was taken directly to the little cemetery on the edge of town. There was to be no funeral, per Dana's instructions, only a simple graveside service. Her letter had been adamant that she be buried in her family plot.

Cassville was deep in the winding hills and forests of the southwest Missouri Ozarks. Signs at the city limits billed it as home of Roaring River State Park. The funeral director had notified the pastor of the First Baptist Church of Cassville, the church in which Dana and her brothers had grown up. A handful of other people, perhaps twenty in all, hovered around the cemetery.

The minister approached Tolman as she climbed out of the hearse. "I'm Don Davison," he said, shaking her hand. "I was Dana's pastor when she was a girl here. You're her friend from music school?"

"Yes. Meg Tolman. I live in Washington, D.C., now."

The minister cocked his head a bit. "Oh. So did you know Barry, too?"

"Barry?" Tolman's memory played an annoying game of hide-and-seek with her. Then she had it—sitting in the bar after rehearsal one day, she and Dana talking about their respective screwed-up families. Dana had always been impressed that Meg's father was a Secret Service agent.

"But my oldest brother lives in Washington," Dana had said, sipping

her Coke. *"Barry's a minor bureaucrat, nothing glamorous. He's an accoun-tant, a bean counter. He doesn't understand me at all."*

"No," Tolman said. "I didn't remember that he lived in Washing-ton until you mentioned it. Did you or the funeral home notify him? And what about the other brother? I don't think I ever knew his name, but I remember Dana said he was a college professor. Engineering, I think."

Davison looked down at her. He was at least a foot taller than Tol-man, with a long face and large nose that made him look a bit like a hawk perched atop a fence post. "I gather you hadn't been in touch with Dana for a while."

"No, I hadn't. I was surprised she listed me on her insurance as an emergency contact."

The minister put a hand on her shoulder. "Nothing surprises me about that family."

"What?"

The casket was being offloaded. A few men from the community grabbed the silver handles. A few others looked Tolman's way.

"Let's walk over there," Davison said.

They walked to the family plot, and Tolman looked at the mound of freshly turned earth. Her eyes slid to the left, to the other two head-stones there. She assumed they were Dana's parents. Then she read the rose-colored stones.

EDWIN BARRY CABLE.

The birth date was August 24, 1976.

The death date was April 19 of this year.

Dana's oldest brother.

JAMES AARON CABLE.

Birth: November 2, 1978.

Death: June 27 of this year.

Her middle brother.

"My God," Tolman whispered. "What . . . what happened to them?"

"So you didn't know," Davison said.

"I . . . no." Tolman stared at the graves. Dana and her two broth-ers, all dead in less than four months. "What happened? Accidents or illness or . . ."

Davison lowered his voice. "You remember that shooting in Washington last spring? Bunch of guys calling themselves April 19 broke into this government office and shot up the place?"

Tolman tore her eyes from the grave markers and looked up at the minister. "April 19—I remember the date. That was the same date as the Oklahoma City federal building bombing all those years ago. They were a bunch of antigovernment nuts, said they wanted to continue McVeigh's 'work.' But it was a low-level office. It was"—*Barry's a minor bureaucrat. He's an accountant, a bean counter.*"—"an outlet of the Government Accountability Office. Barry worked there?" She had a flash of memory of the TV coverage of the attack, and she remembered the name of the dead man: Edwin Cable. "Edwin. I never made the connection from the news reports."

"He never liked the name Edwin," the minister said, nodding. "Always went by Barry. Edwin was his father's name and he didn't care for his father. But of course, the news media couldn't have known that. Those terrorists must have picked the office because it was an easy target. Who'd think a bunch of bookkeepers needed security?"

"But the shooters were captured right away, weren't they?"

"And they surrendered as pretty as you please. 'Martyrs for the cause,' they said."

Tolman swallowed, looking down at the grave markers. "What about the other brother?"

Davison's expression grew even more somber. "Jimmy took his own life. You're right, he was an engineering professor down in Oklahoma. He was upset about his brother's murder. He'd also lately been through a divorce. Bad one, so I hear. Hanged himself from a beam on his back porch."

Davison watched Dana Cable's casket lowered into the ground beside her two brothers. "I tell you, young lady, that I don't believe in curses. But if any family ever was, it was the Cables."

Ann Gray talked on her cell phone as she drove along Missouri Highway 413 outside of Springfield. "Her name is Margaret Isabell Tolman," she said. "She's the deputy director of the Research and Investigations Office."

"What the hell is that?" growled the man on the other end of the call. "I've never heard of it."

"Look it up," Gray said. "A simple Google search will tell you quite a bit. Tolman's father is a Secret Service agent, mother died in a strange car accident in D.C. when Margaret was sixteen. Margaret—she's known as Meg, by the way—went to the Curtis Institute in Philadelphia. She is quite a talented pianist."

"Why do I care about this?"

"Because *I* care about this," Gray said. "Please do not interrupt me. She met Dana Cable at Curtis, then later tried to make a living as a musician and it didn't work out. Her father's connections admitted her to the Federal Law Enforcement Academy, and she joined RIO after graduating. She's been there nearly six years. She was made deputy director late last year. Apparently her star is on the rise."

"Can this RIO possibly be a threat to us?"

Gray paused. "I can't answer that."

"Take her out," the man said.

"Just like that?" Gray said.

"Just like that. Not having another attack of conscience, are you?"

"Don't try to bait me. You've engaged me to do a very specific job, and I do it well, and I've protected and managed the investment well so far. If there's a threat to the investment, I deal with it, as you know. But I do not employ violence for fun."

"Take her out," the man said. "Deal with it now. I don't want to take any more chances, and I don't want to have to clean up after you."

The man clicked off. Gray drove on toward Cassville. She hoped she would be in time to catch Tolman at the cemetery. She was already days overdue, and she wanted to go home and spend time with her family.

The graveside service was brief, Davison quoting Psalms and Ecclesiastes and talking in short sentences about Dana's life as a musician, and the joy she derived from playing cello. He spoke of all the Cables being "at peace," and that one family should not have to experience so much tragedy in this life, but now they were in a place where such worries and tragedies were beyond touching them.

Davison asked Tolman what she planned to do, and it struck Tolman that she had no way to get to the airport in Springfield, and she didn't hold out much hope that there was a car rental agency in Cassville. "I need to get to the airport," she said.

The minister smiled. "I'd be pleased to drive you, young lady. Dana must have thought highly of you."

"I suppose so." The crowd broke up and began to move away. Tolman heard cars starting, low voices . . . an indistinct drone of white noise. Dana Cable—on a seawall in the middle of the night with her head bashed in, whiskey poured in her to make her appear intoxicated. Clearly, she'd been murdered, and the murderer had gone to some length to make it appear accidental; but yet, the killer was sloppy. The unnatural positioning of the body . . . the bourbon on her clothes . . .

One brother, dead in D.C. in an attack by a homegrown terrorist cell. One brother, dangling from a rope in Oklahoma. And Dana, on a slim wall between river and ocean . . . then, almost with her dying breaths, asking for Meg and talking about a rose and a silver cross.

This is crazy, Tolman thought, but she closed her eyes, trying to think of music again. In Dana's memory, she tried to remember the pieces they'd played together. The Beethoven sonata, of course, but they'd also partnered with a violinist and played trios by Haydn and Mendelssohn. They'd played the Chopin cello sonata, the only piece the composer ever wrote for cello. Now Tolman wished they had made more music together.

The music faded, and she was standing in the August heat of a rural Missouri cemetery. Reverend Davison had retreated to his air-conditioned car. The rest of the mourners were gone.

Except one.

A tall, well-dressed woman in her forties was walking toward her.

"Pardon me," she said, and her accent wasn't the laid-back drawl of the Ozarks. She sounded urban, northern.

"Yes?"

"You were a friend of hers?"

"I was. I brought her body back here. And you?"

"A casual acquaintance. This is all quite tragic." The woman swept a hand at the graves. "Her family . . . very tragic. Very difficult."

"Yes." Tolman wanted the woman to leave.

"I have something for you."

"For me? What?"

The woman handed her a manila envelope. "You may find some enlightenment there."

"What is it?"

The woman moved away, walking to a dark four-door parked at the gate of the little cemetery. Tolman undid the clasp on the envelope, pulled at the flap, and shook out a single piece of paper encased in a plastic sleeve. She looked up in the direction the woman had gone.

"Hey!" Tolman shouted. "Who are you?"

Tolman heard a group of cicadas singing, a car engine ticking, a little bit of a breeze. She began to trot after the woman, but she was already backing her car out of the cemetery. It turned right and was gone. With some effort, Reverend Davison climbed out of his car, an ancient Plymouth, and looked at her. She held up a hand—*wait.*

"Did you know that woman?" Tolman called to him.

"Can't say that I do," Davison said. He smiled. "Cassville may be a small town, but I don't know everyone."

"I don't think she was from Cassville," Tolman said. She turned away from the minister and looked again at the envelope.

Gray hadn't had much time to recon the area, but the fact that the cemetery was so small and the road beside it narrow meant it took less than three minutes to get into position. The hilly terrain worked to her advantage as well. A gravel path led upward less than fifty yards from the cemetery gate, across the street. A stone wall ran for some length as a property line, and it looked down toward the cemetery. She had the high ground.

She pulled the CZ 75 Tactical Sport from her overnight bag, then got out of the car, hidden by a copse of trees. She easily climbed over the low stone wall, then moved in a crouch from behind the cover of the trees. Still, the wall was perfect, and the Tactical Sport with its six-inch barrel made a pistol shot from this distance possible. An impossible shot, some would say. But they didn't know Ann Gray.

She crawled along the base of the wall, periodically poking her head up to calculate how far she was from the cemetery gate. When she was directly across from it, she stopped, raising the pistol and propping it on the wall. Meg Tolman and the minister were in her field of vision.

Tolman turned over the paper in its plastic sleeve and started to read.

28 July 1864

My dear President Davis,

Your emissary, Mrs. Greenhow, is most charming, felicitous, and persuasive. You must know that the French people have supported in spirit your noble battle in the matter at hand. It is, I believe, to the advantage of both commerce and culture that our peoples work in friendship. Do not be disheartened by our public acknowledgements in this matter. The business of nations must needs be conducted in the shadows at times.

The unlimited financial and military support of the French nation is at your disposal, sir. We wish an enduring friendship with the Confederacy, and Mrs. Greenhow is to deliver this missive to you along with a token of our friendship. We will endeavor to assist you by all feasible means, upon being granted legal possession of the Silver Cross. Mrs. Greenhow is to provide you with the details, and if you agree, I will send further documentation via duly appointed agents of my government.

I, and the French nation, await your reply. May God grant you wisdom in your decision.

Tolman looked at the signature at the bottom of the page.

Napoleon III

Napoleon III?
. . . *legal possession of the Silver Cross* . . .
Tolman remembered what Dana Cable had said to tell her: *"the rose and the silver cross . . ."*
Rose Greenhow.
The Silver Cross.
"I'll be damned," she said.

Davison frowned at her. Tolman slid the paper into its envelope and took two quick steps toward Davison's car.

A gunshot exploded into the ground where Tolman had been standing a second ago.

She dove to the ground, the knees of her pants scraping the grass. Another shot cracked, kicking up a spray of earth two feet to the other side of her.

Davison turned to Tolman, then looked across the road and said, "What—"

Tolman's mind raced. Her SIG Sauer 9mm was in her travel bag. She'd had it in the hearse ride from Springfield. Presumably the funeral director had taken it out before leaving the cemetery. She inched along the ground beside Davison's car. *There!*

She spotted the bag, in the open on the other side of the minister's car.

The shots were coming from across the narrow road that ran beside the cemetery. It was up a small slope, giving the shooter a perfect vantage point. As soon as she emerged from the protection of the car, she would be exposed.

Davison had ducked into the driver's seat. Tolman heard the engine start. *Shit!*

"Get in!" the minister shouted. "Get in the car!"

A few more inches . . .

Tolman reached the bumper. The bag was five feet away.

"Where are you?" Davison was yelling.

Shut up! Tolman thought.

She turned the corner of the car's rear bumper and flattened herself out on her stomach. Inching along, under cover of the bumper, feeling the exhaust vibrating inches from her head, she stayed out of sight.

She reached the other edge of the car. The bag was inches away. If she could only get to her SIG . . .

She snaked a hand from under the bumper, fingers reaching toward the bag.

Gray watched the movement, saw the woman under the car's bumper, and knew what she was doing. She probably had a weapon of her own packed away in the luggage. Gray wasn't concerned. Her work was almost finished.

She saw Meg Tolman's hand as it inched from below the Plymouth. She glanced to the left, saw the old minister cowering in the front seat, screaming incoherently for Tolman to get in the car with him.

Gray adjusted her aim by a few inches and sighted the CZ 75. She squeezed off two more rounds. One of them thudded into Meg Tolman's suitcase. The other sprayed gravel less than six inches from Tolman's hand.

Gray let out a slow breath. She'd taken three sets of shots. She carefully pulled the pistol from the top of the rock wall, lowered it, and crept along the wall to her car. She put the CZ 75 away, zipped up the overnight bag, and slid behind the wheel of the rental.

Five miles outside of Cassville, she made a phone call. "I couldn't finish it now," she said.

"I thought that sort of thing never happened with you," the man said.

"It can happen with anyone," Gray said. "Circumstances change. I took several shots, but the target moved. Also, there was a bystander, and I have no interest in bystanders here."

"But this Research and Investigations woman knows something is going on. She was a friend of Cable's, and she's alerted to our presence."

Yes, Gray thought. "Don't worry," she said, pointedly not responding to the man's statement. "I will tie this up."

"When?"

"When I can."

"We're watching, Ann."

"Don't be ridiculous," Gray said, and ended the call.

She pointed the car toward Springfield. She had a plane to catch. She missed her husband and her son.

Tolman heard the car, somewhere on the other side of the road. But from under the bumper, she couldn't see it. She waited two minutes, sweating, exhaust fumes breathing down her back. Then she reached out a hand. No shots.

She put her entire arm into the open, hooking the bag's handle. No shots.

She dragged the bag under the car, then inched back the way she had come, nearly burning herself on the exhaust pipe. On the other side, she opened the front passenger door of the Plymouth and fell into the seat beside Davison.

"My Lord," Davison said. "What was that? Are you all right?"

"I'm fine."

"Forgive me for my language, but what the hell is going on here?"

Tolman gripped the envelope with the 1864 letter from Napoleon III. She thought of Dana, Barry, and Jimmy Cable, all in their thirties, all dead within a few months of each other, all buried in this little country cemetery.

"I have no idea," she said.

CHAPTER

6

Tolman spent an interminable time giving a statement to the Cassville police, who took her contact information and looked at her as if she were from outer space when she presented her RIO credentials. The officer who took her statement had graduated high school with Barry Cable. It *was* a small town.

Reverend Davison drove her to Springfield and dropped her at Springfield-Branson Airport. In the small terminal, she pulled out her phone and called Nick Journey. "What do you know about Napoleon III?" she said when he answered.

Journey sighed. "Hello, Meg, I'm fine."

"No time to screw around," Tolman said. "I've been shot at today, and I'm a tad grumpy. Napoleon III. What would he have to do with the Civil War?"

Tolman heard Andrew Journey whistling in the background, then Journey said, "The Confederacy wanted the French to help them in the war, and Napoleon was with them in spirit, but he couldn't commit troops. He had problems of his own. Why all this talk about Napoleon?"

Tolman started moving down the row of airline counters, searching the arrival and departure monitors. "This is the same Napoleon? Short guy, hand in his coat?"

"No, no, Napoleon III was his nephew. He ruled France years later. Why do you—"

"This Rose woman you mentioned? The spy? It looks like she met with Napoleon and he was going to help the South."

There was a long silence. In the background, Andrew screeched, then laughed loudly. Soon he was whistling again. "Meg, where are you getting your information?"

"A letter. Napoleon wrote a letter and sent it with this Rose Greenhow. In it, he said the French were going to help the South if they gave him the Silver Cross. The 'silver cross' again."

"No, Meg," Journey said. "I mean, yes, Rose Greenhow went to both Britain and France to ask for their help with the Confederate cause. She was Jefferson Davis's personal emissary. But they wouldn't budge. They wanted Southern cotton, and they hated the Union naval blockade of the Southern ports, but they weren't about to commit troops. It's well documented. And besides, Napoleon—"

"I have the letter!" Tolman shouted. "A letter from Napoleon III to Jefferson Davis, promising French military assistance to the South. Apparently it went with Rose Greenhow. And it has something to do with Dana's death. And both her brothers have died in the last few months, too."

"If the French were going to help the Confederacy . . . I mean, there have been stories, legends, but nothing that could be—"

"Yeah, well, I have it. I think you need to tell me some of these stories and legends."

"The letter," Journey said. "Where did you get it?"

"I don't know."

"What?"

"A woman came up and gave it to me after Dana's funeral. Five minutes later, someone was shooting at me." She scanned the screens again. "How do I get to where you are?"

"What? Where are you?"

"Springfield, Missouri. That's not far from you, right? I should be able to get a flight. There are no flights to Oklahoma City."

"Try Dallas. Carpenter Center is closer to Dallas than to Oklahoma City."

Tolman read the screens. "There—American has a flight into

Dallas. It leaves in an hour, gets into Dallas at about seven-thirty P.M.
I'll get a car—more fucking driving—and come to you. How far are
you from Dallas?"

She slid into line at the American counter, cradling the phone
against her shoulder, digging in her bag for a credit card.

"About two hours from the airport to Carpenter Center. Get a
map when you rent the car."

"I'll get one with a GPS."

"Meg," Journey said. "This letter. We'll have to be sure. If it's
real—the historic ramifications would be staggering."

"I want to find out who killed Dana and why. Those are my ramifications."

"We'll have to be sure," Journey said again.

"That's why I keep you around," Tolman said. "See you in a few
hours."

After dinner and a short walk around their neighborhood, which was
equidistant from the SCCOK campus and Lake Texoma, Journey
turned on the TV for Andrew. Within a few minutes, Andrew lost
interest in Animal Planet and went off in search of a straw and a pencil, which he used to stimulate himself—or "stimming," as the teachers
and therapists called it. Andrew was working with a new therapist this
summer who was of the opinion that the stimming made him withdraw
further from the real world, and she asked Journey to gradually ease
Andrew away from the behavior. He was trying, with mixed results.
Andrew had been doing it for so long that it seemed part of him, and he
was always trying to find a way to locate the straw and the pencil. Some
of his bouts of aggression in the last two months had been in response
to their absence.

Journey sat down at his cluttered desk in one corner of the living
room and booted up his computer. Meg Tolman was on her way
here—he expected her around ten o'clock. And she was bringing a letter she believed to be from Napoleon III to Jefferson Davis.

Journey drummed his fingers on the desktop, tapping his left index
finger three times in rapid succession, then again. He was an American

Civil War historian. He only knew nineteenth-century France peripherally. But there were legends. There were always legends, mostly the domain of treasure hunters and conspiracy theorists. No one had ever seriously suggested that France was on the verge of militarily supporting the Confederacy. They were spread too thin already, with a bad economy and many other commitments.

Still, although Napoleon III was not as well known as his famous uncle and namesake, he usually got what he wanted. If he wanted something badly enough . . .

Journey started scanning history sites on the Web. Then he went to his bedroom and pulled down three volumes from his bookshelf. With a highlighter and a legal pad, he sat down to read.

Tolman arrived just before ten. When Journey opened the door, the first thing he noticed were the streaks of dirt on her face and grass stains on her black jeans and light blue blouse. "You don't look so good," Journey said, then smiled at her.

"Well, I started the day in North Carolina, was shot at in Missouri, then had to drive through at least twenty-seven construction zones between DFW Airport and this town. Is there any part of Texas or Oklahoma that isn't under construction?" She came through the door and tossed her bag onto Journey's couch.

The smile widened. "It's good to see you, Meg."

Tolman looked around at the clutter, the mismatched furniture, the books and magazines and papers. "First time I've been inside your house," she said.

"I didn't have much time to clean up," Journey said.

Tolman looked at him. Her gaze locked on his arm. "What the hell happened to your arm?"

"It's nothing."

Tolman looked from his arm to his eyes. "There you go again, holding yourself in. So where's the little guy?"

"In bed. And not so little anymore. He's gone through a serious growth spurt, gained four inches since you last saw him. He's only two inches shorter than I am now."

"How is he otherwise?"

Journey shrugged. "He had a pretty good school year. But you didn't come here to talk about parenting. What about this letter?"

Tolman eased herself onto the couch next to her travel bag and laptop. "Dr. Journey, you are an unusual man."

"Yes, I am. You want a drink?"

Tolman closed her eyes. "I never took you for a drinking man, Nick."

"What, your databases never told you that about me? I'm surprised you don't know what my favorite beer is."

"Let me guess. I'll say Guinness Stout."

"I'm more a lager guy. Keep trying. What do you want?"

"You really have booze in the house?"

"I keep it in a locked cabinet that Andrew can't get to."

"Bloody Mary, extra spicy," Tolman said.

He made the drink and brought it to her. She drank off almost half of it immediately. Journey watched her. "Tell me what happened," he said.

She told him all of it, from the phone call that sent her to Wilmington, to the deaths of the three Cable siblings and the shooting in Cassville.

"The letter," Journey said. "Let me see the letter."

"You're such a document guy," Tolman said. "I've never seen anyone get such a historical hard-on for old papers."

Journey smiled. "Let me see it."

Tolman dug in her bag, pulled out the plastic sleeve, and passed it to Journey. He adjusted the lamp and stared at it.

"And this was it?" he said after a time. "A woman just walked up and handed this to you?"

"She said I might find enlightenment there. That's the word she used, 'enlightenment.'"

"Let's not jump the gun. The paper seems right for the period. As for the handwriting, I have no idea. I'm not a Napoleon III expert. But I have a colleague who specializes in nineteenth-century Europe. I'll call him in the morning." Journey settled into the armchair beside the couch. "But two nonhistoric questions come to mind. Who was the woman who gave you this, and who shot at you after she gave it to you?"

Tolman ran her hand over the surface of her travel bag, felt the bullet hole there. "And how did she get the letter? And what the hell *is* the Silver Cross?" She rubbed her eyes and drank some more, this time slowly. "So what about this Rose, and old Napoleon? What does this mean?"

"I don't know how any of this is possibly connected to your friend, but I'll tell you some of what I do know from the historical side." He tapped the paper. "And keep in mind that even if this is authentic, it's incomplete. It mentions 'further documentation.'"

"I know you're not going to tell me we are going on another wild-document chase."

Journey smiled. "A good bit of history is about finding those documents. They're what tells us if things are real or fantasy."

"You said there were stories and legends."

"There are *always* stories and legends. Treasure hunters love them. People have spent decades searching for Civil War treasures. Books have been written about them, movies made about them. The Silver Cross? Never heard of it. But that doesn't mean anything either. Things are being unearthed about that era all the time."

Tolman rubbed her eyes and set down her glass. "So would the French really have helped the South?"

Journey shrugged. "There were rumors—see, more legends—from the beginning of the war that both the British and French would come in on the side of the Confederacy. The Union navy had blockaded all the Southern ports so they couldn't export goods. That meant the cotton trade with countries like Britain and France suffered. Plus, a lot of the aristocratic classes in Europe identified with the Southern culture and were on that side on principle."

"I'm guessing it would have made a huge difference if the French and the Brits were involved in the war."

"Of course. Especially after Gettysburg and Vicksburg in the summer of 1863, things began to look bad for the rebels. They were always outnumbered, but they began to have supply problems, and they were increasingly cut off from the things they needed to outfit the army. If France and Britain—or even one of them—had committed resources to the Confederacy, it could have tipped the whole thing on its side. It could have changed the outcome of the war."

Tolman sat up straight. "You're saying that if Napoleon III some-how acquired this Silver Cross from Davis, and he brought troops in, the South would have won?"

"I'm not saying they *would* have won. I'm saying it's possible. I'm saying everything would have been different. And think about it—a foreign power, committing troops on American soil, intervening in an internal conflict. It could have meant a world war, years before anyone thought of that term."

"Jesus, Nick. Let me see that again." Journey handed the paper to her. She read it again. "If all that had happened, the world map could look a lot different than it does now."

"Yes." Journey spread his hands apart. "And while it's an interesting exercise to contemplate that, it didn't happen." He pointed at the paper. "But no one has ever had any conclusive evidence that the French were seriously considering it. Moral support was one thing—committing money and an army quite another."

"Dammit," Tolman muttered, then said it again, louder. "What does this have to do with Dana? And why shoot at me?"

Journey nodded. "Let's look—"

He turned as he heard the sound of a door opening and a heavy step, followed by an ammonia smell. Andrew came into the room, eyes wide, body tensed. He stood by the chair and made a hooting sound. He stamped a foot. He glanced toward Tolman, then looked at the floor.

"What's the matter, Andrew?" Journey said, getting up. He saw the wet spot around the boy's groin area. "Wet already. I'll change you, then back to bed."

"Did I wake him up?" Tolman said. She looked at him. "Hey, Andrew." She glanced at his father. "You're right, he's grown a lot."

"He's not used to hearing another voice in the house after he goes to bed," Journey said, reaching for his son's arm. "Come on, Andrew, let's go to the bathroom."

Andrew jerked away from Journey's touch, then reached out as if to push his father away. "No, no, son, we don't do that," Journey said.

"Hey!" Tolman said, and her tone was sharp.

Andrew stamped both feet hard on the wood floor, then arched his fingers toward his father's arm.

"Keep your voice down," Journey said. "Loud, angry voices set him off and he responds with aggression." He turned to Andrew. "Andrew, put your hands down." The boy reached for his father. "No . . . no scratching."

Andrew made a noise deep in his throat and whipped his head from side to side, clawing for Journey's arm. Journey grabbed both his wrists. Andrew continued trying to scratch. He dug a thumb into his father's wrist, but Journey had trimmed his nails since the incident on the square and he wasn't able to break the skin.

"Andrew, no. . . ." The boy kept fighting him.

"What can I do?" Tolman said, behind him.

"I'll handle it. Andrew . . . Andrew, no!" His voice rose, and he seemed powerless to stop it. Andrew kept struggling. The boy tried to head-butt Journey. Journey dodged, still holding Andrew's arms, and lost his balance. Together they tumbled to the floor beside the chair, Journey breaking Andrew's fall with his body. The boy stopped struggling and was quiet.

Journey lay there with him, thinking of the beautiful child he had rocked and sung to and read to and walked with for the last thirteen years. Then he caught sight of the fresh scratches on his arm. He tried to be still, so that Andrew could see that it was safe, it was okay to be quiet.

After a long moment, Andrew rolled off him. Journey let out a breath. He caught the smell of urine again. Andrew whistled a few notes.

Journey helped him to his feet, then guided Andrew to the bathroom. Ten minutes later, he returned to the living room. The sounds of soft piano music drifted out behind him.

"Jesus, Nick," Tolman said. "Now I know what those scratches on your arm are."

"We're working through it," Journey said. "Nonverbal adolescents go through all the same physical changes that typical kids do, but they don't have words and they don't understand how they feel, so sometimes they lash out. It doesn't happen all the time."

"Will he go to sleep now?"

"Maybe. Or it might take him a while."

"Does he wake up wet like that every night?"

"Every night," Journey said.

Tolman stared at him.

"But we're working on it," Journey said. "Look, it's over for now. You came a long way to talk about this paper, and Napoleon, and Rose Greenhow and Fort Fisher and this Silver Cross." He leaned forward. "So let's talk."

CHAPTER
7

In the foothills of the Berkshires, along Route 23 at the east edge of the town of Hillsdale, New York, a few miles west of the Massachusetts line, a prim, colonial revival–style building sat to the side of the winding highway. It was an unassuming and unremarkable structure, red brick with white trim and forest green shutters, designed to blend in to the landscape. A small wooden sign near the front door read: THE ASSOCIATES. Beneath the words, in smaller print: *International Business Consultants.* The print below that was smaller still: *Established 1900.*

Inside, the building was comfortable but ordinary: a reception area and sitting room, and offices with computers, copiers, fax machines. Generic art dotted the walls. Unremarkable.

On the second floor, at the northeast corner, Victor Zale sat staring out the window at the shadow of the Berkshires and thinking that his country was coming apart at the seams. The sun was long down, the night full dark, and he watched moths bump against the screen of the open window. It was almost cool outside, even in early August. The radio had been giving heat advisories through the afternoon, since temperatures had topped ninety for three consecutive days. Zale had sneered at that. He was from north Georgia, where temperatures in the summer topped ninety for ninety consecutive days. They didn't know what heat was up here.

He'd finally had to turn off the television. The protests were getting out of hand—it was worse than the sixties, and that was saying something. On the left, the anti-big-business group, young and intellectual and fired up, was protesting everywhere. In the last few months, a group on the right—older and white and middle class—had sprouted to counter them, and they seemed to shadow them across the country. A few times the clashes had turned violent. A few times the cops had gotten out of hand. It was utter insanity, and to Zale, the upshot was that neither of them was accomplishing a damned thing. The Mendoza administration—*the "accidental presidency,"* Zale thought with disdain— was determined to remain above the fray, and so the protests went on and on.

The latest news was that the group on the left was organizing a huge rally in a few days, at Grant Park in downtown Chicago. The largest of the right-wing groups was assembling a counterprotest. Within a few days, a hundred thousand or more protesters were expected to descend on Grant Park. It would be laughable if it weren't so dangerous.

If only, Zale mused, *I could do something about these ridiculous protests and "His Accidency" President Mendoza could be blamed for it. . . .*

But Zale turned away from the thought. *First things first . . . other things to think about.*

The door to his office opened, but Zale didn't turn. Only one person came into this room without knocking. Zale swiveled around and looked at his partner, Terrence Landon.

"I want the bitch dead," Zale said. "We have to send the message that she can't fuck with us this way."

Landon winced. He fancied himself cosmopolitan and genteel and didn't approve of Zale's language. "Now, Victor—"

Zale leaned forward, rapping the stumps of his fingers against his mahogany desk. "No, goddammit! This is several times now that Gray's screwed us over. She gets on her moral high horse and starts to say what she will and won't do, and she forgets that she's an employee. She works for *us,* not the other way around."

Landon looked down, his eyes drawn, as always, to Zale's right hand with its three missing fingers. "It's true that some of her choices have been . . . troubling."

Zale snorted. "Troubling, my ass. She's making decisions she has no business making, and she's putting all of us at risk because of it. We've had to send cleaners in behind her because of her 'choices.'"

"But I don't know that killing her makes a difference," Landon said. "We have to tread very, very carefully, Victor. She's known all over the world, she's worked for everyone at one time or another. And yet—"

"And yet she's got this goddamned worldwide rep, but no one knows who she is or where she lives. She's either married with a bunch of kids or she's a lesbian. She lives in a little town in the Midwest or a villa in Spain. She was born in Canada or South Africa. Take your pick of the stories. Doesn't care about the 'why' of anything. Only when and where and how much."

"She's managed the project well," Landon said, hands fidgeting in his lap. "We've accomplished a lot of what we set out to do."

"Sure we have," Zale said. "We've made more money than ever before, and that means more leverage. But never forget what we're supposed to be doing, Terry—every dollar we put in to that account is about control. Every penny is about influence. It's why we're here." He shook his head. "But we could have done more. When Ann started deciding for herself that she didn't want to do some things for us, she became a problem, and now the problem's getting worse."

Landon was silent, then said, "What do you think happened in Missouri?"

Zale's face reddened. "I don't think for one goddamned second that she missed. Ann Gray doesn't miss. Not like that."

They fell silent for a long time, both men listening through the open window.

"Maybe it's time to shut the project down," Landon said, then looked at the floor, as if he were afraid Zale would hit him.

Zale said nothing, leaning back in his chair and running a hand through the frizz of his gray buzz cut. He stared across the desk at the small, neat, former banker.

"I mean," Landon said, "we're starting to have more risks involved. The business with the Cables hasn't gone away, and now with the Tolman woman from RIO interested in the Cables, the risks have increased. I don't have to tell you what it means if it comes out. Everything we've worked for . . . *all* of us."

"*All* of us?" Zale echoed. "You're not threatening me, are you, Terry? I know you're not threatening me." He lapsed into an exaggerated Georgia drawl. "That dog won't hunt, son. You best think long and hard before you go threatening old Victor Zale, you hear?"

Landon flinched. "Don't insult me, Victor."

"Don't fuck with me, Terry," Zale said, returning to his normal, softer accent. "But you might be right. Shut it all down and look for the next opportunity. This one has paid off more than any of us imagined, and there's enough money to keep our influence strong until the next project comes along."

"Yes."

"I think the time may be right to go with your idea on this one. Let's shut it down and tie up all the loose ends. Hide the money somewhere else for a while."

"Loose ends." It was a statement, not a question, from Landon.

"Loose ends. If you'd ever run anything operational before, Terry, you'd know what I mean."

"I handle money, Victor. You handle operations. But I still think going after Gray is a mistake."

"Well now, didn't you just say that you handle money and I handle operations? Yes, sir, you said that just now. So you count the money, tie off the accounts, and let me handle the operations."

Landon crossed his legs at the knee. "You won't find Gray if she doesn't want to be found."

"I've had someone on her for a long time."

"Really?"

"For nearly a year. I have a lot of people outside of this one project. I always cover my ass, Terry, and I don't trust anyone."

"I suspect you don't have anyone who is as good as Gray."

Zale turned his back to Landon, looking out the window toward the Berkshires. "Maybe not," he said. "But she shouldn't have fucked with us. I'll deal with her. And I'll deal with this RIO."

Landon left the room, closing the door very quietly behind him. After Zale heard Landon's footsteps going down the stairs, he turned around and faced his desk. "I'll deal with all of it," he said to himself.

He'd been dealing with the hard issues for over forty years, trying to make his country a better place, trying to protect it from those who had no idea of the things that must be done in the name of freedom. "The protected," as the army referred to civilians, could not comprehend what was done for them on a daily basis. Things that were done by men like Victor Zale, who knew what America was, and knew what it should be . . . unlike idiot protesters who naively thought they understood how the world worked. He'd known, even as he lay in a field hospital in Vietnam in 1969, staring at the bandages covering the stumps where his middle, ring, and little fingers used to be, that he would do whatever it took. Zale felt he'd actually gained something else when the shrapnel from the land mine sliced off his fingers. He'd gained understanding while he lay in the field hospital. Even then, watching the men on the ground being hamstrung by politicians in Washington and even worse, their uniformed lap dogs at the Pentagon, Zale had known that he would make a different choice, that he would leave the hospital a different man, that he would live the rest of his life in the shadows so that others could stand in the light.

From Vietnam to Baghdad, to this unobtrusive little office in the Berkshires, he had done what he had to do, to save America from itself. He'd had his revelation as a soldier, but he had spent most of the rest of his life as a civilian doing what civilians and soldiers alike were afraid to do.

And he would not be stopped.

Zale opened his desk drawer and took out one of several clean cell phones. *Time to clean up,* Zale thought, and he started making phone calls.

8

Journey made Tolman another Bloody Mary, took her bag, and tossed it into the spare bedroom. He jokingly called it the "clean room," since it was rarely used. The last time the futon had been slept on was three years ago, when an old friend from Journey's baseball days had passed through the area. He checked on Andrew. The boy was already asleep, and he looked at perfect peace. Journey was thankful he could sleep—many kids with autism had sleep problems, but it had never been an issue for Andrew.

Journey returned to the living room to find Tolman sprawling on the couch. "Long day," he said.

"Long day."

"You want to go on to bed? There's nothing in the other room but a futon, but at least it's clean. We can talk more in the morning."

"No, tell me what you have. Then we can find your friend the Napoleon guy in the morning."

Journey grabbed his legal pad from the desk. "He's not really my friend, but he is a colleague. Knows his stuff, though." He settled into the chair. "Every other year I teach a class called Spies and Espionage in the Civil War. Very popular, as you might imagine, even with nonhistory majors. So I'm more than a little familiar with Rose O'Neale Greenhow. But I brushed up a bit after your call."

Tolman sipped her drink. "You make a damn good Bloody Mary, Professor." She raised her glass to him. "Tell me about this Rose, and the connection to Wilmington and Fort Fisher."

"Her only real connection to Fort Fisher was that she drowned within sight of it. But we need to back up a bit and explain who she was and why she was on that ship at all."

"Can we have the abridged version? I'm sure it's a brilliant lecture, but let's skip the stuff like what color dress she wore and all that. I need facts that relate to why Dana mentioned her when she was dying, and how it relates to this letter."

Journey smiled a little. "You've been shot at today, so I'll give you a break. I'll stick to the highlights."

"Eternally grateful." Tolman crossed her legs at the ankles, leaned her head against the cushion of the sofa, and closed her eyes.

"Rose O'Neale Greenhow," Journey said. "I'll skip everything up to the beginning of the war, except to say that she was born in Maryland, and her father was a slave owner who was supposedly murdered by one of his own slaves. By the time of the war, Rose was a widow in her forties, one of Washington's leading hostesses, and strongly in favor of secession. She was what we would call today a Washington insider, having lived in the city for many years and knowing most of the powerful men."

"Knowing powerful men," Tolman said, eyes still closed. "What kind of 'knowing' are we talking about here?"

"Hard to tell. She may have had a few lovers, but she was discreet. Thought you didn't want irrelevant details."

"I don't. But if there's any sex in the story, that livens things up a bit."

"Uh-huh. Anyway, Rose knew everyone in D.C. and they all knew where she stood on secession. So after the hostilities started, she was in a position to know things. The first real battle of the war was at Manassas, or Bull Run, in July of 1861. In the days leading up to it, Rose used her contacts in Washington to find out the movements of the Union army. She passed that to General Beauregard, who was in command of the Confederate troops in the area. The battle turned into a rout, and it shocked the North. People had thought this thing would be over in a matter of days or weeks, but Manassas showed them the Confederates were serious, and weren't going away."

"I'm guessing the Union wasn't happy about this."

"You could say that. A little more than a month after Manassas, she was arrested by Lincoln's new Secret Service. She was held under house arrest, along with her youngest daughter, Little Rose. All the while she kept smuggling information south."

"Doesn't say much for the Secret Service that she was able to do all this right under their noses."

"Exactly," Journey said. "So after a few months they transferred her to the Old Capitol Prison, where she *still* continued running her little espionage operation. She was seen almost as a martyr in the South—a poor defenseless woman and her child locked up in prison. Rose was far from defenseless, but it still became a bit of a problem for Lincoln. A hearing was finally held on the charges of espionage, and the judge decided everyone would be better off if Rose was exiled to the South. When she arrived in Richmond, Jefferson Davis welcomed her as a hero."

Tolman sat up, wide awake now. "And at some point Davis sent her overseas as his emissary."

"He could think of no one better to plead the South's case in Europe. Davis knew he needed help, and he also knew that if he could get the assistance of either Britain or France—or better yet, both of them—that would go a long way toward legitimizing the Confederacy."

"So Rose went and made her case."

"She took her daughter with her, and she made a splash wherever she went. Rose Greenhow never did anything in a small way. She had a private audience with Queen Victoria, became engaged to a British nobleman, and wrote her memoir, which was a bestseller in Britain. But she never accomplished her goal: official recognition of the Confederacy."

"Then she went to France," Tolman said.

"Rose loved France," Journey said. "She thoroughly charmed Napoleon III. Saw him alone at Tuileries Palace. The emperor expressed all kinds of admiration for the South and especially for Robert E. Lee, but he was critical of some of the army's maneuverings in the West. Rose shot right back at him and said he couldn't possibly understand the enormity and scale of the conflict."

"So she wouldn't take bullshit, even from an emperor."

"That's right. She wrote in her diary that Napoleon was impressed with her and asked her to stay in France, but that he wouldn't commit to anything without England. Napoleon III may have had great ambitions, like his uncle, but he wasn't going to take a risk unless he saw a real benefit to France. Rose saw Napoleon one more time, for only a few minutes, the day before she left. She sailed to England, then boarded a boat for home."

Tolman pointed at the letter. "Could this letter have come from her last meeting with him, right before she left?"

"I suppose it's possible. But Rose's journal stops when she leaves England to return to America."

"And that's when she drowned."

"It's one of the great and strange mysteries of the war."

"What is?"

"Rose's death. She didn't have to die the way she did."

Tolman heard a little bit of piano still coming from Andrew's room, but otherwise the house was quiet. "Tell me."

"In England she boarded the *Condor*, which was specifically built as a blockade runner, to get past the Union navy's blockade of the Southern ports. It was a fast ship on her maiden voyage. She stopped over in Bermuda, which was often used as a way station at that time, then up to Halifax to pick up a few other passengers. The final destination was Wilmington. Early in the morning of October 1, 1864, the *Condor* was approaching the mouth of the Cape Fear River and got into a race with a Union blockader. Shots were fired, then the *Condor* ran aground. They weren't that far from Fort Fisher, and the guns from the fort protected the wreck. All they had to do was wait out the night and the weather, and they would have been fine."

"But Rose didn't wait."

"She demanded a lifeboat, went to the captain and begged him, threatened him, told him she had to get off the ship. Rose was almost hysterical, and this was a woman who never lost her cool. Finally the captain gave in. They lowered a lifeboat and as soon as it touched the water it capsized. Rose was wearing a heavy wool dress and had a leather bag around her neck with two thousand dollars in gold pieces and papers and such. It dragged her down, and she drowned within sight of Confederate soil. No one else died. All the other passengers and the crew who manned the lifeboat held on to the boat's keel and were rescued. Rose washed up on shore the next morning."

"Why did she get so hysterical? After all she'd been through, why then?"

"That's been the question for all these years. Was she carrying something that she believed to be so valuable she couldn't allow it to fall into Union hands, at any cost? Nothing she had with her was that explosive."

Tolman touched the plastic sheet. "But maybe it was," she said.

Journey waited a long time before replying. "Then why wasn't it with her things when her body washed up on shore? Or with the things she left behind in her cabin? How did this letter get to the woman who gave it to you today? There are too many holes in this little story. And we don't know that it's authentic."

"It doesn't explain anything about Dana, either." Tolman slapped the arm of the couch. "And it doesn't explain why I have a bullet hole in my luggage."

"There are always stories," Journey said, "but we're getting out of my expertise here. If this is real, the Silver Cross is something Napoleon III wanted very badly, to be willing to commit money and troops to the Southern cause."

"What did he want that much?" Tolman asked.

"I don't know. But we're going to talk to someone who knows more about it than I do."

"When she was dying, Dana said, 'Tell Meg . . . the rose and the silver cross.'" She looked at Journey, eyes never wavering. "We have to know."

"Yes," Journey said, meeting her gaze. "I think we do."

Half a block from Journey's house, on the other side of the street, a slim man in his late twenties sat in a rented Toyota Tercel that he'd picked up at DFW Airport, where he'd watched the American flight from

Springfield, Missouri, arrive. He'd rented the car under the name of Mark Barrientos, though that wasn't his real name. He hadn't done any kind of official transaction under his birth name in several years. The surveillance of Meg Tolman had been handed off to him, and he'd followed her through the endless Dallas suburbs, into the rolling plains of north Texas, across the Red River into Oklahoma, across Lake Texoma, and past the stone sign that read, CARPENTER CENTER, OKLA-HOMA, HOME OF LAKE TEXOMA, SOUTH CENTRAL COLLEGE OF OKLA-HOMA, AND A GREAT QUALITY OF LIFE!

Tolman had been inside the Tudor home with the sagging front porch for over an hour, and she'd taken her bag in with her. Barrientos didn't know who lived here, but that wasn't his job. His job, for the moment, was to follow and to gather information. He flipped open his laptop and sent an e-mail update that included the address where Tolman had gone—he would find out soon who lived here, and what the connection was to Tolman. Gray was in transit right now, but Barrientos knew she would find out soon. Ann Gray always found out.

CHAPTER

9

After dropping Andrew at his day camp at eight o'clock in the morning, Journey drove to the South Central campus, parked, and he and Tolman walked across the street to Uncle Charley's. As they walked, Journey said, "The guy we're going to meet is Graham Lashley. He's our resident specialist on nineteenth-century Europe. Interesting guy, if a bit pompous. He's originally from Barbados, then did his doctorate at the University of Kentucky. He doesn't like me very much, but he knows his stuff."

"Why doesn't he like you?"

"Thinks I'm an academic hack, the clichéd ex-jock history major. Also, I've missed a couple of meetings over the years because of things with Andrew, and he doesn't like that. I once overheard him mumbling about 'Journey always being off with that kid.'"

"Disharmony in the hallowed halls of academia?"

Journey shrugged. "It happens."

Uncle Charley's was a campus hangout, open from early morning until late at night, a favorite of both faculty and students. Graham Lashley was waiting for them in a corner booth, under a poster commemorating SCC's 1955 national champion basketball team.

"Hello, Graham," Journey said, sliding into the seat across from him. "Thanks for coming over to meet us."

"I must say that I'm intrigued," Lashley said in a melodic Caribbean-British accent. He turned to Tolman. "And you must be Nick's governmental acquaintance."

Tolman smiled. "'Governmental acquaintance.' I like that. I'm Meg Tolman."

They shook hands. "A pleasure," Lashley said. "Nick, you mentioned a paper you thought might be authored by Napoleon III."

Journey nodded at Tolman, who slid the plastic sheet out of her bag. She passed it to Lashley. He accepted it without speaking, adjusted his rimless glasses, and read.

Lashley looked slowly up at them.

"Not just another insignificant paper, if it's real," Journey said.

"I can see that," Lashley said.

Tolman looked back and forth between the two men. "Well, is it real?" she finally asked.

Lashley said nothing.

"Hello?" Tolman said.

Lashley looked at Journey. "What's your intention, Nick? Are you going to publish?"

"Graham, is it authentic?" Journey said.

"You didn't answer my question."

Tolman looked at Lashley, thinking how out of place he looked in a dark suit, starched white shirt, and tie in the corner booth of this casual college hangout. "Dr. Lashley, right now this document is part of a U.S. government investigation. When that investigation is complete, we'll make a determination about what to do with it."

Lashley ignored her, staring at Journey. "When you do publish, I want to be first author, not second."

"You're assuming a lot, Graham," Journey said.

"You're a Civil War historian. I presented a paper last year comparing and contrasting the two Napoleons. It's a natural collaboration for something like this, but I should be first author."

Tolman shook her head but held her tongue.

"So you think it's real or you wouldn't be talking about publishing," Journey said.

"I didn't say that," Lashley said.

"You didn't have to." Journey glanced at Tolman. "We're looking for insights on what it might mean."

"I think it's highly likely that it's real. When I was studying primary sources for my Napoleon paper, I read a lot of his original writings. Look at the 'N' in the signature. It's a very unusual shape. I've also read a fair number of documents that were forged, and some of them, while quite good, never get that 'N' right." He tapped the paper. "So this letter is to Jefferson Davis."

Journey briefly recounted the story of Rose Greenhow's trip to France.

"Greenhow," Lashley said when he'd finished. "I recall the name. Rather cagey of Davis to send an attractive widow to Napoleon's court. Napoleon III did have his vulnerabilities."

A waitress came over and took their orders: only coffee for Journey and Lashley. Tolman ordered an omelet. "I think getting shot at gives you an appetite," she said.

"Pardon me?" Lashley said.

"Nothing. Dr. Lashley, if you think this is real, what is the Silver Cross?"

"I don't know," Lashley said. "How much do you know about Napoleon during the time of the American Civil War?"

"I know nothing. Pretend I'm an incoming freshman majoring in, say, piano performance, who could care less about history."

Journey smiled. Lashley glared at Tolman.

"Nick, I guess I should expect this sort of thing from an associate of yours," Lashley said.

"You must be kidding," Journey said.

"You have very little respect for true scholarship," Lashley said. "It shows in your students, and in your . . . acquaintances."

"Dr. Lashley—," Tolman said, then took a deep breath. "Nick assured me you knew your stuff, that you were the right person to ask. If you're not, then we can go to any of the other God-only-knows-how-many historians who have written papers on Napoleon III. We need your help."

"Graham, the investigation is serious," Journey said in a quiet voice. "People may have been murdered because of this."

Lashley placed both his hands flat on the table and gave a rueful head shake. "Napoleon III was elected president of the Second French Republic in 1848. He staged a coup and declared himself emperor in 1852."

"Like his uncle, he was first a liberator, then a tyrant," Journey said.

Tolman's omelet came and she ignored it, tapping the table. "The Silver Cross."

"I have never heard of anything called the Silver Cross with regard to Napoleon, if that's what you want to know," Lashley said. He took a sip of coffee. "The fact that this letter says Napoleon is willing to commit troops to help the Confederacy in exchange for this Silver Cross is interesting, given what was going on in Mexico."

"Mexico?" Tolman said. "This doesn't say anything about Mexico."

"The word 'silver' says Mexico to me," Lashley said.

"My God, Graham," Journey said, sitting up straight. "I hadn't thought—"

Lashley adjusted his glasses again. "Napoleon invaded Mexico in 1862."

"Wait," Tolman said. "What? While the American Civil War was going on, the French were invading Mexico?"

"Oh, yes," Lashley said. "The timing was not accidental, either. The war here directly affected Napoleon's decision to go to Mexico."

"Why Mexico?"

Lashley and Journey looked at each other.

"Silver," Lashley said. "Napoleon was looking for silver."

CHAPTER
10

They all stared at each other.

"So I have your attention," Lashley said.

"Fill in the blanks for me," Tolman said.

"There are interesting parallels between that period and today in France," Lashley said. "Right now the French are in a financial crisis that threatens their entire economy. It was the same at that time. France had financial problems ever since Napoleon III became emperor. The country had a bimetallic monetary standard, which was based on a balance of gold and silver. But an influx of gold from America and Australia upset that balance, and then came the American Civil War."

"I still don't see what that has to do with Mexico and silver," Tolman said.

Lashley looked at Journey. "Cotton," Journey said.

"Cotton?"

"Countries like France and Britain imported their cotton from the southern U.S.," Journey said. "Remember the Union blockade of Southern ports? The Confederacy couldn't ship and sell cotton overseas to some of its biggest customers. The demand for cotton was high in France, so they had to look elsewhere for their supply."

"Yes," Lashley said, nodding. "India became the biggest cotton supplier to France." He spread his hands apart. "And India demanded payment in silver, which had become in short supply."

"And there was silver in Mexico," Tolman said.

"The world's biggest supply of silver was in the Sonoran mines," Lashley said. "Those mines were largely undeveloped. So in January of 1862, Napoleon landed troops in Mexico. His public statement at the time was that it was due to Mexico's refusal to pay its foreign debts."

"Was that true?" Tolman asked.

"Yes, but it was a fairly flimsy pretext for a full-blown invasion and occupation. Napoleon installed the Habsburg prince Maximilian on the throne of Mexico, and the mines were his."

"How long did this last?"

"About five years," Journey said. "After the war was over, the United States was able to pay attention to foreign affairs and started to notice what was happening south of the border. Maximilian was a weak ruler anyway and didn't last much longer."

"And the silver?"

"Oh, Napoleon acquired some silver," Lashley said. "But nothing near what he would have liked." He held up the letter. "And here is where we depart from history."

"What?" Tolman said.

"There is a legend," Lashley said, "that some of Napoleon's agents found a remarkable artifact, something so stunning, so beautiful that it was beyond comprehension."

"And made of pure silver," Journey said.

Lashley looked at him as if he'd spoken out of turn, then said, "Indeed. Whether it had been left behind by an ancient civilization, or recently fabricated . . . the legends vary. There are no descriptions of it, only that it defied human understanding. Its worth was beyond estimation—especially to Napoleon. You see, Napoleon was ambitious yet practical, spiritual yet pragmatic. If he could get his hands on this stunning piece of treasure—a treasure made of the very metal he so desperately needed—it would be a sign from God that He had approved of the incursion into Mexico. Maximilian's regime was always on shaky ground, right from the beginning, and Napoleon needed a public relations victory. So he supposedly sent agents everywhere from Brazil to Canada in search of this fabulous artifact."

Journey looked thoughtful, rubbing the scratches on his arm. "The letter would seem to indicate that this Silver Cross was found in Confederate territory. But they couldn't just take it back to Paris with them, considering French agents weren't supposed to be roaming around the Confederacy in the first place. If it was that valuable, the Confederates wouldn't just let it go."

"So Napoleon had to make them an offer they couldn't refuse," Tolman said.

Lashley nodded. "Perhaps. And consider this: Napoleon was a pious emperor, as most emperors are," Lashley said. "If the artifact was a cross, think what that would mean to him. The advantages were political, economic, spiritual . . . and highly personal to the emperor himself. The Silver Cross. You may have found the first piece in a puzzle that takes this from the realm of legend into history."

"And changes our understanding of the Civil War," Journey added.

Lashley looked at him, pursing his lips. "So it would seem. If the emissary had not died and had delivered this to Jefferson Davis, French troops may have come to the assistance of your General Lee. We could be sitting in the Confederate States of America at this very moment." He paused. "Well, perhaps the two of you would. No doubt those of my race would have fared quite differently."

Tolman was shaking her head. "This is . . . this is huge."

"Ah," Lashley said. "Our undergraduate piano major begins to see the light."

Journey smiled.

"I'd like to take this," Lashley said, putting his hands on the plastic sleeve.

Tolman grabbed it from him. "No, you're not taking this anywhere. Evidence in a federal investigation."

Lashley made the pursed-lips motion again, then slowly smiled. "One makes the attempt. What will you do with it? It is incomplete. It refers to further documentation. I presume that if you possessed such documentation, you would have it with you."

"This is all I was given," Tolman said.

"Who gave it to you?"

"I don't know."

Lashley raised his eyebrows.

Tolman ignored him and looked at Journey. "We should go," she said.

Journey stood up. "Thank you, Graham. You've been a big help."

"Wait," Lashley said. "Is that all? This is rather abrupt."

"It certainly is," Tolman said. "And you're not going to talk about this, Dr. Lashley. Not yet. You'll have full access to the document if and when it is released, and you and Nick can work out all the academic stuff. Until then, as far as you're concerned, this letter doesn't exist."

Lashley looked at Journey. "Nick, you can't allow this. This is a huge historic discovery. You cannot be a party to concealing it."

"I'm not concealing it. Be patient, Graham," Journey said. "It'll come around again."

Lashley stood up and took a step toward Journey. "I'll take it to the chair, then the dean, and the president if I have to. The president will want a find of this magnitude to be associated with South Central. You understand it's nothing personal. But I can't just pretend this doesn't exist."

"Now wait," Tolman said, stepping between the two men. Others in Uncle Charley's were looking at them. "There won't be any need to go through all that. Dr. Lashley, you've been very helpful, and your assistance will be noticed by the people who matter. You'll have your chance to publish this find, and I'm sure South Central College will be much better off for it. But not yet. You're just going to have to wait. Let's go, Nick."

As soon as they were on the sidewalk and headed toward the SCC campus, Tolman said, "You were right about one thing: he's an arrogant prick, all right."

"I didn't say that," Journey said, and smiled. "I just said he was pompous. I think he saw his ticket to a book deal and speaking tour, right in front of him, then snatched away."

"Yeah, well, that doesn't mean shit to me," Tolman said.

They crossed Taylor Drive onto campus, passing through the arching stone gates. "Meg," Journey said, "something's bothering me. You said this was personal. It's not really a RIO case."

"Now don't you start with me. How does Napoleon III lusting after silver and having a puppet government in Mexico get a cellist from Philadelphia murdered a century and a half later? And you know what? Both of her brothers died since April of this year, and I don't believe in coincidences." She stopped and leaned against a tree.

"Good God, Meg, you're shaking," Journey said. He touched her shoulder, then turned her toward him and put his arms around her. He felt the tension in her body, but otherwise she was perfectly still.

They stood that way, completely silent, for two long minutes before Tolman pulled away. "All right," she said. "All right, I'm just . . . I'm just wound up." She rolled her neck around, and they started toward Journey's office in Cullen Hall. "It's been a long few days."

Journey nodded, looking down at her.

"Don't look at me like that," Tolman said. "I'm okay."

"I'm worried about you."

"Don't worry about me. Yes, this case is personal. But something isn't right about it, whether it's my friend or not. You can see that. I know you can."

"Yes. I can." He touched her shoulder again, steering her across the nearly empty college common.

"What? I thought your office was that way."

"It is. New destination."

Five minutes later, they were in the piano studio of the fine arts building. It was small, only half a dozen instruments, but Tolman stopped dead in the doorway. "You're a saint," she said.

"I know one of the piano faculty, and students usually aren't in here until the afternoon," Journey said. "Enjoy yourself. If anyone bothers you, have them call me. I have a committee meeting in half an hour, then I'll be back."

Tolman squeezed his arm, watched him go, then sat down at the keys.

Two hours later, Journey came into the studio again. He waited silently at the door, listening to Tolman playing a softly flowing piece he didn't recognize. "Nice," he said when she finished.

She jumped.

"Sorry, didn't mean to startle you," he said.

She turned. "I get lost sometimes. I like the place where I am in the music. Beats the hell out of reality."

Journey smiled, leaning against the doorway. "What was that piece?"

"It's by Satie, the third Gymnopedie."

"Gym-what?"

"Satie made up the word himself. He was French, very mystic. He was sort of the new age musician of his time."

"It sounded mystical. I think Andrew might like it."

Tolman was flushed, sweating. She wiped her brow. "A hundred degrees outside and I'm sweating in an air-conditioned studio."

Her phone rang. She dug it out of her purse and spoke her name.

"Larry Poe calling from Wilmington, Meg."

"Hello, Inspector. How's it going on your end?"

"You don't have to call me inspector," Poe drawled. "Thought I'd let you know that another of the staff members at the Fort Fisher Museum recalled Dana Cable talking to a woman here."

"She came in with someone?"

"No. Cable came in not long before closing and was looking at some of the exhibits on blockade runners when this other woman came in behind her and started talking to her. Cable looked startled, but they talked for a few minutes."

"This woman? Tall, maybe midforties, brown hair about shoulder length?"

"That's right," Poe said. "Where did you—"

"She showed up at Dana's burial. She gave me something."

"What?"

"Later, Inspector. Get that description out."

"The witness didn't see her face. The description's very general."

"But she—" Tolman stopped, thinking about the little cemetery in Cassville, the blistering heat, the newly dug grave, the woman handing her the envelope. *"You may find some enlightenment there."*

But she'd never turned to fully face Tolman. She'd stood in profile the whole time and had quickly turned and walked away.

A professional, Tolman thought. The woman had had some kind of training. Although at least two people had seen and talked to her—the Fort Fisher staffer and Tolman herself—neither of them could give much of a description other than forties, tall, brown hair—a description that fit millions of women.

"I'll be damned," Tolman said. "I'll call you back soon, Inspector. Your people are doing good work there. Keep at it. Maybe someone else saw this woman." *But don't bet on them being able to describe her,* she thought. "In the meantime, can you send me Dana's things?"

"Her things?"

"Don't play dumb, Inspector, because you aren't. You're no hayseed country cop. You've now officially requested RIO's assistance—"

"Have I?"

"Yes, you have."

"That's good to know," Poe said. Tolman thought she detected a chuckle in his voice. "I like you, Meg. Quite a bit, actually."

"And that's likewise good to know," Tolman said. "I need to take a look at Dana's effects. You said she had a laptop?"

"She did."

"I especially want that. Send it to my office in D.C." She gave him the address.

"Do you ever wonder, Meg, why the feds are not well liked by local and state law enforcement?"

"No, Inspector, I don't wonder that at all. It's because we're such officious jerks."

"Just checking," Poe said.

Tolman laughed, closed the phone, and stood up from the piano bench. "I need my computer," she said. "It's at your house."

They crossed the common toward the parking lot, passing under towering elms. Tolman felt the thrill she always had when beginning a new case or learning a new piece of music. But it was tempered by something dark: the undercurrent of the death of a friend, a fellow musician, someone who had overcome the odds to earn her living performing and teaching music—something Tolman had not been able to do. And Dana Cable was a gentle soul, which was remarkable, in light of her family background.

Journey drove her to his house. "I hope you don't need your kitchen table for the rest of today, Nick," Tolman said, "because I need it for an office." She turned to her computer and went to work.

CHAPTER
11

Gray first picked up the tail in Los Angeles. She had flown from Springfield to Memphis, then on to LAX. She always traveled this way, adding layers of destinations so that she could pick up any watchers. It added extra days to her travel time, but it was how she had survived.

She saw the man as she deplaned at LAX. He never approached her, always five or six other passengers between them. Classic surveillance behavior. But she caught him looking at her twice.

So The Associates were on her again. She'd noticed other followers at various times in recent months. The giveaway was the watcher himself. Zale tended to use ex-military, and they all looked like Special Forces: muscular upper bodies, military haircut, dark clothes. Gray was sure all these men were excellent operationally, but they had a lot to learn about the finesse and nuance of the business. They didn't know how to make themselves forgettable.

Gray checked into a hotel at the airport in LA, prepared to spend the night. She would deal with her new friend tomorrow. She knew he would still be with her, and tomorrow she would see just how good he was.

In her room, she opened a bottle of water and took out her laptop. She read the e-mail from her man Barrientos, who was with Meg Tolman in Carpenter Center, Oklahoma. She did a search on the address he'd sent her and found that the house belonged to a man named Nick Allen Journey. In half an hour, she had the beginnings of a dossier on him.

Meg Tolman was good. In less than a day after Gray gave her the letter in Cassville, Tolman had made contact with a Civil War historian. *Very, very good,* she thought.

Gray wrote a quick e-mail to Barrientos and told him to stay with Meg Tolman. Then she wrote a note to one of her other people—a subcontractor who was not part of the project she managed for The Associates—and asked him to find out everything he could about Nick Allen Journey. She would have a more complete picture of him by morning.

Gray lay down on the hotel bed. It was too late to call home—her husband and son would already be in bed. She smiled at the thought of seeing them again, but the smile faded quickly. She would probably have to go out again soon. Tomorrow would be telling. Whether Zale's painfully obvious Special Forces man was still with her at the end of tomorrow would dictate whether she could relax with her family for a few days, or if she would have to leave them quickly. Gray would have to think about what to tell her husband and son. Perhaps a crisis with a troublesome client.

Not too far from the truth, is it? Gray thought, and drifted off to sleep.

The watcher was still with her in the morning. She spotted him in the American terminal at LAX, then she stepped out of line at the last minute and instead bought a ticket to Chicago on United. The move wouldn't divert him for long—but now, each was aware of the other, and Gray wanted him to be clear that she knew he was there.

She saw him get on the plane behind her—she was in first class, he in coach—then didn't see him at O'Hare. She waited, giving him time to catch up as she hailed a cab to take her to Union Station. Now Gray wasn't trying to lose him. She would deal with him on her own terms.

At Union Station, she watched some television, noting the media's

obsession with "Left vs. Right in Middle America," as they were calling the protest/counterprotest rallies that were planned for a few days
hence, not far from where Gray sat. Leaders of both movements were
interviewed. One railed about tax rates and the destruction of American values; the other prattled on about corporate welfare and government bailouts. After half an hour, Gray caught Amtrak's Hiawatha
train for Milwaukee. From there, a bus to Manitowoc. She didn't see
Zale's man, but he was there. He'd proven to be more than capable
of keeping up with her. Gray killed some time in the Wisconsin Maritime Museum in Manitowoc, on the banks of Lake Michigan, then
had dinner and went to a movie, some romantic comedy she had no real
interest in seeing. But she needed the time. She called home and told
her husband she'd be there in the morning.

In a coffee shop, she opened her laptop and read what her asset had
put together on the professor from Oklahoma, Nick Journey. There
were several payments to Journey from RIO. *So he's on Tolman's payroll,*
Gray thought. *Interesting. Most interesting.*

She read on, stopping when she came to the family section, which
detailed how his entire family had died in a car crash in California when
young Nick was seven. His father, Bruce Journey, was a laborer at the
naval base in San Diego, his mother, JoAnn, a homemaker and part-
time florist. Brothers: Mark, age nine, and Danny, age twelve. All were
pronounced dead at the crash site. Nick was thrown clear of the family's
station wagon and survived, only to be shuttled from one relative to
another, finally settling with an aunt in Florida. As Gray read about the
destruction of the Journey family, something seemed vaguely familiar
about it, as if she'd read it before, in another context, but she couldn't
recall where.

She kept reading: Journey's divorce from Amelia Boettcher, his
full custody of Andrew, and the boy's condition: profound, nonverbal
autism. Gray found that she actually became emotional when she read
about what a devoted father Nick Journey was. She thought of her own
son, the same age as Andrew Journey, of how intelligent and talented
Joseph was: chess champion, hockey player, and proficient violinist.

Gray's eyes blurred. She remembered another dossier she'd read
not long ago, about another young boy who played competitive chess.
That note—one throwaway line in the midst of twenty-plus pages of

data—had shaken her core, had changed her focus, had led her to make new decisions. Decisions that had put her in North Carolina, and then in Cassville, Missouri.

She looked at the screen of her laptop again. *Stay out of this, Professor Journey,* Gray thought. *Stay home and teach history and take care of that boy. Keep away from all this.*

But she knew he wouldn't. Reading the dossier, she knew that Nick Journey, Ph.D., wouldn't walk away. He would juggle being a father and a professor and a "consultant" to RIO. And if he'd read the letter from Napoleon—surely Tolman had shown it to him by now—he couldn't let it go. No historian would.

It made her admire the man, but it also made her a little sad. In her business, Gray never knew what situations would arise, and how they would have to be handled. She had to be ready for whatever came.

Shortly after midnight, Gray took a Manitowoc taxi to the waterfront and bought a ticket for the 12:55 crossing of the *S.S. Badger,* one of the best-known ferries on Lake Michigan. It made the sixty-mile, four-hour crossing to Ludington, Michigan, several times a day between May and October. At over four hundred feet, the *Badger* did double duty: it served as a car ferry, taking all manner of vehicles—even semi-trucks whose drivers didn't want to go all the way around the lake and fight through Chicago traffic to get to Michigan—and also something of a tourist attraction.

Gray had a car waiting in Ludington, and she would drive the final leg home. She frequently took the ship in season, and she'd never been followed onto it until now. At 12:55 the coal-fired ship—Gray could see the dark outlines of huge mounds of coal piled in the yard alongside its mooring—pulled away from shore. The late-night sailing typically had few riders, often a handful of truckers. No more than a dozen people boarded with Gray. They walked behind a chain to the left side of the cargo hold, where the vehicles would be secured for the crossing. Gray counted four tractor-trailer rigs and three cars.

As she put her foot on the first step up to the passenger decks, Gray turned casually. In the lights from the parking lot behind her, she saw Zale's man. Right where he should be. Gray had to give Zale credit—this one was better than most of the others he'd had tailing her over the last year. None of them had been able to stay with her this long. He had held on to the surveillance halfway across the country and back again.

Gray smiled. He was good, but she was willing to bet he'd never been aboard this ship before. The advantage was hers.

His name was Polk, and he had his orders.

Polk didn't know who Ann Gray was, and he didn't know how she was connected to The Associates. He only knew that she had seen him in Los Angeles, then seemed to have deliberately slowed down, as if she didn't care that he was there.

Doesn't matter, Polk thought. He liked the *S.S. Badger.* This overnight ferry ride across Lake Michigan was an opportunity. He had a Walther P22 with a suppressor in his backpack. He would catch the tall woman in a dark corner. Maybe she would decide to take a nap. The idea made him chuckle.

The *Badger* offered tiny staterooms for those who wanted to actually sleep during the cruise. Experience told Gray that about half the riders on the overnight crossing would take staterooms, while the others would stretch out in one of the TV lounges. On daylight cruises, activities abounded: bingo and games in the main lounge, a movie room, arcade, children's play area, and of course, lots of open space on the top deck. But after midnight, the *S.S. Badger* was quiet.

On the lower deck, she walked through the darkened main lounge, skirting the TV rooms and aft end lounge. A quiet, semi-enclosed deck area with scattered chairs opened toward the stern. Gray settled in to one of the plastic chairs, angling it so that her back was against a side bulkhead and she could see anyone who came into the area. She put her purse and travel bag at her feet, and she sat down to wait.

After half an hour, a sleepy truck driver wandered into the area and made small talk with her. She was polite but aloof, and eventually the man went away. Gray continued to watch the entrance. Once she thought she saw a shadow moving in the aft lounge area.

She bent to her travel bag, took out the CZ 75, and transferred it to her purse.

Polk watched from behind a wall, breathing quietly. The woman sat very still in her deck chair, looking out at the ship's wake. He gave her credit—she could be so still as to seem asleep, but he knew she was awake and alert. People drifted through the lounge at times, stopping to look out at the ship's stern. Some of them chatted with Gray. Some didn't.

At a few minutes past 3:00 A.M., Gray stood up, taking her bags with her. Polk took a step into the protection of a recessed section of the wall. She walked through the TV room. A dozen or so people sat in the chairs. Only one was awake.

Gray moved forward. Polk emerged from the shadows and followed her.

Gray angled past the closed Portside Bar and entered the main ladies' room, across from the cruise director's office—also closed on this crossing. She set her travel bag very carefully on the floor, counted to thirty, and emerged, turning quickly into the dark starboard hallway. She met no other crew or passengers. The row of staterooms was ahead, where some of the passengers slept.

She reached a breezeway that contained a set of steps to the top deck. On the other side of the open area was a strip of rooms: a maritime museum/quiet room, the ship's gift shop, movie lounge, arcade, and kids' playroom.

Gray closed her eyes, took a deep breath, and let it out slowly. She pictured the hallway beyond this point. There might be passengers sleeping in the quiet room. The gift shop—or Boatique, as the *Badger* called it—would be locked. She couldn't remember if the movie room ran DVDs on the overnight cruise. The arcade or the kids' area would be best. She'd only seen one child boarding the ship, an already-asleep toddler with her mother in the aft TV lounge.

She listened to the hallway forward of her position, hearing the low, constant hum of the ship itself, and the water outside. Above the ship sounds, she heard the footsteps somewhere behind her.

Gray turned toward the staircase and stepped heavily onto it, making a lot of noise. Then she put another foot on it, making noise there as well. She turned quickly, kicked off her flats, and ran for the starboard hallway in her bare feet.

Polk was passing stateroom #34 when he heard the slight clatter. He'd seen the central stairwell earlier when he did a quick recon of the ship after boarding. He entered the clearing from the corridor, feeling the warm breeze from the open deck at the top of the staircase. He ran to the stairwell, drawing the P22.

Polk's heart started to pound. He clambered up the staircase and stood at the top in the warm night air. The dark rolling water of Lake Michigan lay just beyond the rail.

He looked left and right. There was no movement, and the darkness was deeper here.

She'd only been a few seconds ahead of him, and there was no place to hide up here, only a long, narrow walkway before the railing of the ship.

She doubled back, Polk thought, then turned to the stairs. On the main deck again, he saw the shoes under the edge of the stairway.

Left or right? Port or starboard?

Polk dashed to the left, the side he'd come down a few seconds ago. He looked aft—he saw a crewman in dark shirt and khakis, carrying a garbage bag, crossing through the main lounge. Otherwise, nothing. He looked forward—nothing. No movement at all.

Polk turned and started down the port hallway, toward the quiet room and the front of the ship.

Gray inched her way down the starboard corridor, past the empty quiet room. The passageway was so still that it felt as if the entire four-hundred-foot ship was empty—except for Zale's man and her.

The quiet room and the other public rooms were in the center of

the deck. Corridors lined with staterooms ran along either side. Gray
stayed in the center of the corridor, hoping no sleepy passenger felt an
ill-timed urge to go to the restroom.

Gray moved sideways, her back to the staterooms. She passed the
gift shop, with its racks of *S.S. Badger* T-shirts and pens and postcards
and all kinds of nautical-themed kitsch. It was locked tight.

She listened for the steps. The man was coming faster. She passed
the movie lounge. The DVD player was off, the room dark. The only
light came from the hallway. Gray knew that each of these rooms had
entrances from either side. She wondered if her adversary knew that as
well.

Gray hurried past the movie room, then flattened herself against
the wall by the door to the arcade. She held the CZ 75 in firing stance
and inched into the doorway.

Nothing.

The steps had faded. She couldn't hear the man, which meant she
was either hearing more ship noise . . . or he had stopped moving.

Polk passed the movie room. The woman was still a few steps ahead of
him. He could hear her in the opposite corridor.

He raised the P22, took two more steps, and turned into the door
of the arcade.

Motion. Movement. *There!*

She was on the opposite side of the room, her head coming into
view in the doorway.

Video game machines lined both walls of the narrow room, their
lights flashing and glowing. In the daylight, they would be inviting to
kids and teenagers. At 3:00 A.M., the lights seemed grotesque.

Polk planted his feet and aimed his weapon across the expanse of
the room.

Gray only put half of her head through the doorway, the rest of it—
and most of her body—still concealed behind the wall. She had only
an instant to see the man and his weapon. She couldn't tell what it was,
but by the shape of the gun, it looked like he was using a suppressor, as

she was. A necessary precaution in a public place, even though the myth about sound suppressors was just that—they weren't "silencers." Even with the sound reduced considerably, no firearm was ever completely silent.

Down here, Gray thought, the ship noise would be a benefit. With a suppressed weapon and the natural sound from the engines, there was a good chance they still wouldn't be discovered.

The man took his shot as Gray pulled away from the doorway. The bullet slammed into the wall a foot from where she had been. She was right, though—between the ship noise and the suppressor, there was very little sound.

Gray spun into the hallway and the man fired again, trying to catch her in motion. Glass shattered—he must have hit one of the video games. She took two steps toward the children's playroom, then stopped.

The footsteps pounded away on the other side of the corridor. He was no longer trying to be quiet. Gray had no idea how many people were in these staterooms, but she willed them to stay asleep.

Gray shuffle-stepped toward the arcade, turning partway into it as she had before. The man was gone.

Polk raced into the children's room, the last one before the forward bulkhead and the two sides of the corridor came together. There were brightly colored "play huts" for small kids to crawl through, a table loaded with coloring books, a large plastic animal of some sort wearing a captain's hat. . . .

Polk stumbled over a bucket of crayons on the floor and went down with a crash, losing his grip on the P22.

He rolled over onto his side, quickly regaining his weapon. He swept the room—she wasn't here. Polk pushed himself to his feet and raced out the way he had come.

Gray leaned inside the arcade, leading with her bare feet, gingerly moving bits of safety glass from the shattered video game out of her way.

She picked her way around the glass to the opposite door of the arcade, wedging herself between the wall and the last game console. The man was in the hallway. He knew where she was, but she'd bought a few seconds by going toward the kids' area, then turning back.

Then a voice, male, very close, from the direction of the stairway: "What's going on? Hey, are you okay?"

No, Gray thought. *Go back,* she silently told the crewman. *Go back, go back . . .*

Zale's man scrabbled in the hallway. One step, two, three . . .

Gray kept her hand firmly around the butt of the CZ 75.

"Hey!" said the other voice. It was closer now, within a few steps of the entrance to the arcade.

Too late, Gray thought. She hoped the crewman had the good sense not to try anything heroic.

Zale's man ignored the voice. Gray could hear his breathing.

Keep coming, another step, then another . . .

Zale's assassin turned into the arcade, his pistol in front of him.

Keep coming. That's right . . .

Gray held her breath, invisible in the space beside the game console. The crew-cut assassin stepped into the center of the room. He kicked at a piece of broken glass.

Gray took one step from her spot behind the game console. An instant later, the crew member—young, blond, with a scraggly beard, probably a college kid—turned into the arcade.

"What's all this?" he said.

Zale's man jumped and shot him twice, catching him in the neck and chest, then stepped forward, bending toward the young man's body. Gray took another step from behind the console. The assassin was three feet away. He looked up from the crewman he had killed, and before he could raise his gun hand again, Gray placed a round in the center of his forehead. He toppled backward, tripping over the body of the young crewman, landing with his torso draped over the crewman's legs.

Gray stepped around the two bodies. She quickly went through the assassin's pockets and found his wallet. The driver's license was from Maryland, and the name was Craig Polk. It wouldn't be his real name, of course, if he was working for The Associates, but it gave Gray a point of reference. In the back pocket of his jeans was a cell phone.

Gray took it without looking at it, then moved away from the two bodies. She had no choice but to leave them where they were. If she'd been on an upper deck, she would have dragged them to the rail and lifted them over the side. But she wasn't confident she could take two bodies all the way down the corridor to the stairs, up the stairs, and over the side. They would have to stay where they fell, and she would have to be ready to cooperate, like any other passenger, when they were discovered and the questions began. She retrieved her shoes and her travel bag and reclaimed her seat at the stern. It was less than five minutes since she'd left.

It was still dark, and no one else was in the aft seating area. Gray took out the CZ 75, examined it a moment, then tossed it over the side and into Lake Michigan. It was a good piece of equipment, but she had no choice. After the bodies were discovered, whether in minutes or when the ship docked in Ludington just before 6:00 A.M., there would be questions. Passengers would no doubt be searched. There would be a delay in allowing the ship to be emptied.

Gray turned on Craig Polk's cell phone, then sat motionless. There was no cell service in the middle of the lake. A little after five-thirty, she acquired a cell signal. The *Badger* would be docking in less than half an hour. With luck, she would be at home with her husband and son by eight o'clock.

With the signal acquired, Gray checked the phone's call log and punched the last number called. After four rings, Victor Zale's drawling voice said, "Well? Is the bitch dead?"

"No, she isn't," Gray said. "Don't be so vulgar."

There was a breath-filled silence on the other end of the line.

"Have I caught you speechless, then?" Gray said.

"What did you do to him?"

"This changes everything. I hope you understand that. This was unnecessary and highly unprofessional."

"Shit," Zale spat. "You're calling *me* unprofessional? You are a hell of a piece of work, Ann."

"Perhaps. An innocent bystander died tonight, too, and there was no need for it."

"Oh, here we go. The assassin with a conscience. Well, it's over, Miss Ann. We're shutting it down and tying everything off."

Gray sat up straight. It was still dark behind the ship, off toward Wisconsin, but she could sense a faint glow of light in the other direction. "Excuse me?"

"The operation is over. Too many things have gone wrong, and we're shutting it down."

Gray looked around. No one was nearby. "I'll need to—"

"No, Ann, you don't need to do anything. I'm taking care of it."

"I've managed the project from the beginning. You can't be serious."

"Serious as I can be."

"That's a mistake. I'll take care of it."

"No, you won't," Zale said. "Tonight was a warning, Ann. Next time you won't see us coming."

Gray almost laughed. "A warning? No, tonight wasn't a warning, Victor. Your man wasn't up to the job. If he'd been a bit better, I would be dead now and we both know it. Next time, send a professional."

Gray never raised her voice—she thought it unseemly—but the rage was coursing through her, an unfamiliar emotion. Gray did not hate. She was a professional, and while she often worked with and for ideologues, she was not one. There was only the job, and the belief in one's own ability. But the uncouth and thoroughly unprofessional Zale had stirred anger in Gray. It had already been brewing, in the wake of Zale's recent decisions. The man killed with impunity, with no thought whatever to the consequences. For a moment Gray thought of that line in the dossier she'd read several weeks ago, a sentence about an eleven-year-old boy who liked to play chess—much like her own thirteen-year-old son.

Victor Zale, while wielding enormous power, was a little man who only possessed that power through others. He was a puppet and a puppeteer at the same time. A dangerous, foolish, immoral little man.

A man who must be taught a lesson.

"You think you're going to stay hidden from me?" Zale said. "You think I won't find you, Ann? You don't screw me over this way and get away with it. That's not the way it works."

"You'll soon find out the way things work." Gray's voice was calm, almost serene. She would not lose her dignity.

"Threatening me?" Zale roared. "It's over, Ann. All of it. Silver Cross is finished, and all thanks to you. I won't forget that."

"Goodbye, Victor," Gray said, and ended the call. She immediately turned off the phone and tossed it over the stern.

She heard urgent sounds behind her, people talking and moving. No doubt the bodies of "Craig Polk" and the unfortunate crewman had been found. Gray closed her eyes, trying to clear her mind. But it was difficult. She wanted to think of Rick and Joseph at home in Fremont, Michigan, waiting for her. She'd been gone nearly two weeks.

But she couldn't stop thinking about what she needed to do. Her mind raced, and she wondered what conclusions the reportedly brilliant Meg Tolman of RIO had reached. And she wondered about the addition of Professor Nick Journey. He could prove useful.

As the sun rose in stunning hues of orange and pink ahead of the *S.S. Badger,* Gray was thinking about Dana Cable on the seawall at the tip of Cape Fear, and she was still thinking about the Silver Cross.

CHAPTER
12

Tolman slept poorly, even though Journey's futon was comfortable and she was more than exhausted. She was also frustrated. After the morning meeting with Graham Lashley, she'd accomplished very little the rest of the day. She was able to connect to a few RIO databases and begin to build files on Barry and Jim Cable, and, reluctantly, on Dana. She woke up at four-thirty in the morning, the day after she and Journey met with Lashley, opened her laptop, and booked a midday flight to Washington. Sitting in Journey's dark living room, the computer open on her lap, she inadvertently tapped out the rhythm to one of Chopin's polonaises—not the *Heroic* or the *Military*, the ones everyone knew, but the fourth one, the *Funeral* polonaise. She'd played it for a recital years ago, but she hadn't thought of it in a long time. She didn't even realize what piece it was at first.

The cemetery in Cassville, she thought. *Dana and Barry and Jim Cable, all dead within the last few months.* Then she thought of the woman and the envelope: *"You may find some enlightenment there."*

Enlightenment.

A joke? A riddle? A code?

Gunshots from across the road.

The Silver Cross.

Tolman closed her laptop, then stood up as she heard a door open. Andrew Journey came around the corner, and Tolman flashed back to the first time she'd seen the boy, several months ago. A different place, a different situation. But he was the same kid, a little taller, a few acne breakouts starting to dot his face. But much was the same—the nut-colored hair, the big gray-green eyes, the loose-fitting clothes. *What do you say to someone who can't say anything back?* she wondered.

She found herself lost. Andrew and Nick Journey's lives, on paper, were an abstraction. Andrew was a statistic—part of the 1 in 110 kids with some form of autism. But here, he was a person—and she had absolutely no idea how to relate to him, if it was even possible to relate to him.

He didn't move, looking around the room as if something weren't right.

Me, Tolman thought. *I'm the thing that's not right. I'm in his world, and he doesn't know why I'm here.*

"I'm sure your dad will be up in a minute," she said.

Andrew whistled three notes.

Tolman looked at him.

He whistled the notes again. He still wasn't looking at her, but the whistling seemed intentional.

She whistled the notes back at him.

His eyes opened wider. He whistled three more, lowering the last note by half a step. Tolman listened with her musician's ear and repeated the pattern.

Andrew jabbed a flat hand in her direction, then whistled the original three notes.

"I like the second one better," Tolman said, then whistled it.

Andrew whistled the second, lower pattern, then broke into a huge smile.

Tolman returned the smile as Journey came around the corner, scratching his head. "I heard you whistling," he said, then looked at Tolman. "And I guess I heard *you* whistling, too, Meg."

"It was nothing," Tolman said. For some reason the moment had seemed private, and she didn't want to talk about it.

"He loves music, always has," Journey said. "Come on, Andrew, let's get you dressed. There's coffee in the kitchen, Meg. Thought you weren't an early riser."

"I'm not, but I can't sleep. I have to get back to D.C. Hopefully Poe sent Dana's belongings and they'll be at the office by the time I get there."

"You think there's something there?"

"I don't know, but I'm going to find out."

Tolman landed in D.C. shortly after three o'clock. She met her father outside and tossed her bags into the trunk of his black Crown Vic.

"Meg, there's a bullet hole in your suitcase," Ray Tolman said, as if it were a normal topic of father-daughter conversation. "Where did you say you've been the last few days?"

Meg Tolman settled in to the car, feeling the blast of air conditioning. "North Carolina, Missouri, and Oklahoma," she said.

"Oh, good," her father said, sliding behind the wheel. "Glad it wasn't anyplace dangerous, like Afghanistan or North Korea, where you might get shot."

"It is one hell of a long story, Dad," she said. "Do you remember my friend from Curtis, Dana Cable?"

"The cello player? Long brown hair?"

"The word is 'cellist,' Dad. Not 'cello player.' Cellist."

"She plays the cello, she's a cello player. What about her?"

"She's dead. Someone killed her, and she asked for me right before she died."

Ray Tolman's shoulders deflated. "Ah shit, Meg."

"Yeah. That's kind of how I feel."

"Ah shit," Ray Tolman said again, softer.

Meg glanced at him. She knew what he was thinking, and it was both unrealistic and understandable. Her father thought Meg should never have to deal with death again, after the way her mother had died. He, apparently, was planning to live forever.

"I can deal with it, Dad," she said. "That's what I'm doing right now, trying to figure it out. There's a lot going on that I don't understand."

"Yeah?"

So she told him. It was a more comfortable way for them to communicate. It was easy for them to talk about cases, one investigator to another—even though Meg knew that her father thought RIO wasn't "real" law enforcement. He was career Secret Service and had served on protective details for three presidents before moving inside six years ago. His daughter had inherited his ice blue eyes and cop's attitude, but little else.

When she was finished, Ray said, "Sounds crazy. Napoleon III? Civil War spies?" The Crown Vic crossed the Potomac into the District. "You said you went to Oklahoma. I guess you talked to that history guy, Journey."

"I was in the neighborhood," Meg said, "so I thought I'd go see him. I have him working the historic side of this."

"What are you going to do?"

"Take me to the office."

"Don't you want to go home first? That cat has really been pissing me off."

"Oh, come on. Rocky's a good cat. You're just pissed because you yell at him and he doesn't do anything."

"Yeah, it's a lot like having a teenage daughter again. What the hell possessed you to get a deaf cat?"

Meg Tolman waited a moment. Her tone softened. "I guess we sort of needed each other." She closed her eyes. "Speaking of people who need each other, how's Granddad? I need to call him."

"He's all right. They've decided that last round of chest pains was another mild heart attack after all. He's up to five heart attacks now."

Meg Tolman smiled. "And he probably gave the nurses all kinds of hell."

"You know it. Between cursing at them and telling stories about working for J. Edgar Hoover, he's everyone's favorite. But he's back at the assisted living place now. Go see him when you can. He'd rather talk to you than me, for some reason."

"I hope I'm that sharp when I'm eighty-nine. I'll call him soon. Right now, I have work to do."

He dropped her at the anonymous office building on Connecticut Avenue near Farragut Square, and she went to the fourth floor. Pulling her travel case behind her, she took a deep breath before opening the door of suite 427.

Tina, the raven-haired receptionist, said, "I thought you were going to be gone a few more days."

"Well, you never know," Tolman said. "Good to see the office is still standing."

Tina smiled. "I have a stack of papers for you."

Tolman grimaced. "Give them to Erin." After being appointed deputy director, Tolman had hired an assistant deputy director, someone who could navigate all the paperwork and let her still work individual cases.

"Some of them are 'eyes only' for you," Tina said.

"Later," Tolman said.

"What's that hole in your bag?"

"I was shot at in a cemetery in the Ozarks," Tolman said.

"I thought you went to North Carolina."

"I did."

"I'm a D.C. girl, but I don't think the Ozarks are in North Carolina."

"They aren't."

"Okay," Tina said, not pressing the matter. "And speaking of North Carolina, an overnight package came for you from Wilmington this morning. It's on your desk."

"Ah," Tolman said. "I need that. No calls. I'm officially unavailable the rest of the day."

At the end of the hall, Tolman went into her office, closed the door, and took off her shoes. The large FedEx package was centered neatly on her desk, in front of her keyboard. She sat down and rubbed her temples. That damned Chopin *Funeral* polonaise continued to run through her head. At some point, she would have to actually play it—that would be the only way to rid herself of it.

The package was from Poe. Good old Inspector Poe. His drawling, laid-back persona was deceptive. The man was sharp and easygoing at the same time, with a dry wit she liked. She hadn't seen a wedding ring on his hand, either. Under different circumstances . . .

"Oh, stop that crap," Tolman said aloud. There *were* no different circumstances. She hadn't been on a date in a year and a half, and Larry Poe was in North Carolina.

She tore into the package. There were clothes, all casual, neatly folded, a wallet, a purse, a yellow legal pad—and a little Netbook computer. Tolman paged quickly through the legal pad and found it completely blank. She poked around in the purse, but she found herself drawn to the computer.

If Dana held true to the way most people handled their personal laptops, it wouldn't be password protected. People seemed to think that since they were the only ones using the computer—it wasn't *public*, after all—they didn't need passwords. They stayed logged in to whatever programs they were using.

The desktop came up immediately, proving the point. Dana had used one of the popular web-based e-mail services, and sure enough, the computer was still logged in. "Thank you, Dana," Tolman said without thinking. She settled in.

There were nineteen unread messages in Dana's inbox. Tolman sighed heavily—she'd done this many times in the course of investigations over the six years she'd been with RIO. She had just never read the mail of a personal friend. Four of Dana's unread e-mails were listserv messages, all music related. Seven were work related, from colleagues at the George School, the Quaker prep school outside of Philadelphia where Dana taught. One was from Oberlin Conservatory, a follow-up on a student Dana had recommended. A confirmation for a book she'd ordered on Amazon, a dinner reservation . . . the normal things that made up a life.

Before she started to go down into the older e-mails that had already been read, Tolman caught sight of the drafts folder. There was one message in it, unsent. She clicked on the folder. The subject line was blank. The date was one week before Dana's walk on the seawall.

The addressee was mtolman@rio.gov.

"Oh God," Tolman said, and opened the message.

Hello Meg, read the salutation.

Tolman gripped the sides of the computer. She felt the tension in her hands, all the way up her arms to her shoulders, her neck. Her head throbbed.

Sorry I've been out of touch. Lots going on in my life. Well, not my life exactly, but you know what I mean.

Don't know exactly what it is you do down there with your research and investigations thing, but I may need your help. A woman called me and said she had information about my brothers and that if I would meet her at Fort Fisher near Wilmington, North Carolina (why there???), she would explain. I don't know who she is, but she knew things. . . .

Oh God, Meg, I better back up. I've been so out of touch, I guess you probably don't know. Both my brothers have died this year. Barry was killed in that terrorist shooting in Washington last April—remember he worked for the GAO? Jimmy committed suicide in June. I know you never met them and I never told you much about them, but now they're both gone. I am all that's left.

Something is happening.

I don't know what this woman

And that was all.

Tolman read it again: *I may need your help. . . . I am all that's left. . . .* And most ominous of all, *Something is happening.*

Tolman began scrolling through Dana's older e-mails, reading each one. Dana was pretty good about cleaning out her inbox, and she had no other folders. Apparently any e-mail she wanted to save stayed in the inbox and she deleted the rest. There were more concerning students of hers, a few additional work-related things. Then she opened a message with the subject line "Thanks," dated July 7 of this year. Not quite a month ago.

Hey, Dana,

It was good to see you, and Alex really liked seeing his aunt Dana. He still doesn't sleep very well and he gets so irritable, and I feel like I don't know what to do for him. Starting him on grief classes next Thursday. It's good that he's out of school. . . .

I'm glad Jim left you the house. I couldn't have stood to go in it. Glad you were able to come down and do some work on it, and your offer to put the money from the estate sale into a trust for Alex is really great. You know, Jim was a good man—I never said he wasn't a good man. I just said I couldn't live with him anymore. We gave it 12 years, and we were never right together. We put up a good front, and people were so shocked when I filed. But it was all a front. There was nothing underneath all the hand-holding and smarmy talk. We weren't really a husband and wife. But he was a good, good man. He never talked, so he never reached out, even when he was depressed. I guess that's what I've been telling myself.

Just a note to say thanks for settling the house. We can still be sisters-in-law, can't we? It's all about Alex now, and you'll always be his aunt.

Love, Melissa

Melissa Cable.

Tolman had learned from her preliminary research on the Cables that she'd filed for divorce from Jim on March 15, citing irreconcilable differences. She moved out of the couple's home in Norman, Oklahoma, where Jim Cable was a professor of mechanical engineering at the University of Oklahoma. Melissa Cable was an elementary school teacher. Their son, Alex, was eleven years old. Barry Cable was killed in April. Jim's divorce was final on June 15, ninety days after filing, according to Oklahoma law. He killed himself on June 27.

He had willed his house to his sister, but all life insurance policies and cash assets were split between his ex-wife and a trust fund for his son. So sometime before July 7, Dana had gone to Oklahoma to take care of the details of her brother's house. Tolman wrote "Melissa Cable visit" on an RIO notepad. She checked Google Maps: Norman was south of Oklahoma City and two hours or so north of Nick Journey's home in Carpenter Center. She remembered having driven past exits for Norman when she was in Oklahoma last year. She wrote "Norman, OK" on the pad.

I should have gone there yesterday, she thought. Then again, she hadn't known what she was looking for yesterday. The picture was starting to form, a blurry outline that she could begin to follow.

The Chopin was still bothering her, so Tolman dug out her iPod and shuffled until she found something that might drown it out. She finally settled on Carrie Newcomer, a songwriter she'd discovered a few months ago. The jangling acoustic guitars and Newcomer's earthy alto on a song called "Before and After" soothed her, and the Chopin eventually faded. She turned up the volume and started to dig further into Dana's e-mails.

She scrolled through more of the typical messages that made up a typical e-mail account, then stopped on one with the subject line "Barry." The sender was Jim Cable. The date was June 22, five days before Jim hanged himself on his back porch.

D,

Now that things have settled a bit from Melissa and Alex leaving and I'm starting to feel like myself again, I've been thinking . . . I believe there was more to Barry's death than just some random terrorist nutcases. He sent me something.

There's something happening here, and I don't know what. Going to check into it.

J

Tolman read it again.

"There's something happening here."

Tolman remembered the words *something is happening* in the unsent e-mail Dana had written her.

I do not believe in coincidence, Tolman thought.

She kept digging in the inbox. The last four messages were a series of exchanges between Dana and Jim in the days after Barry Cable had been murdered in the GAO shooting outside of Washington. Those messages were all about funeral arrangements, the family plot, contacting Reverend Davison, meeting in Cassville. . . .

Tolman clicked over from the inbox to Dana's "sent" file and she found Dana's reply to Jim, sent the same day as his message, about two hours later.

Into conspiracy theories these days?

Let it go. Those guys pled guilty to shooting up Barry's office. None of them will ever get out of jail. Don't look for things that aren't there. Let it go.

D

Tolman remembered the cemetery in Cassville, the three Cable siblings lying there together. She pictured the tall, nondescript woman pressing the envelope into her hand—*"You may find some enlightenment there."*

But she hadn't found enlightenment. She found only questions.

Tolman thumped her foot on the floor. Carrie Newcomer had given way to Miles Davis's "Straight, No Chaser." The Chopin was finally silent in her mind.

The three Cables: a spectacular, headline-grabbing shooting in a government office, the credit claimed by an obscure antigovernment group; a quiet suicide on a porch in Oklahoma; a bizarre "accident" on a midnight seawall in North Carolina.

Barry Cable, April. Jim Cable, June. Dana Cable, August, a few days ago.

She started to organize what she knew into chronological order. Not Rose Greenhow and Napoleon III and the Silver Cross—they were Nick Journey's department—but the here and now.

The point where the Cables entered the picture—culminating with Dana's death on the seawall—was in April, when Barry was killed.

Whatever Jim Cable had sent to his brother, it hadn't been sent to Dana. Or if it had, she didn't write about it in any electronic communications.

Tolman pulled herself close to the computer screen and logged into RACER—the custom search engine whose acronym meant Retrieval, Assessment, Correlation, Expression, Review. She was going to learn everything there was to know about Edwin Barry Cable and the people who had killed him, the shadowy extremist group April 19.

"Something is happening."

"It sure as hell is," Tolman said.

W hen the ship docked, Gray gave her statement to the police—other than a trip to the restroom and a stroll around the top deck at the very beginning of the cruise, she'd spent the entire crossing in her favorite spot at the ship's stern, alternately dozing and reading. Her bags were searched, her ID scrutinized. She gave the local police and ship's authorities her contact information and moved on. Apparently a couple of people in staterooms heard some indistinct noises, but no one saw anything. The police were visibly frustrated.

Other action had to be taken, and immediately. She rarely brought Ann Gray home to Fremont, Michigan, where she lived with her husband and son under another name. But this time she had no choice. It was a little over an hour's drive from Ludington to Fremont, and she came into town on Michigan 82, then turned north on Darling Street, passing the Fremont Library and police department. *My small middle-American town,* Gray thought fondly.

Within a few blocks she'd passed Daisy Brook Elementary School, where her son had attended, and curved onto Ramshorn Drive, the town's upper-middle-class enclave. After breakfast with Rick and Joseph, she e-mailed Mark Barrientos, the man she'd had on Meg Tolman and the professor, Nick Journey.

"Leave them for now," she typed. "We need to meet. Drastic measures are required."

Then Gray went to bed and slept for nearly twelve hours. She didn't know when she'd be able to sleep again.

Rick could tell she was distracted that evening. "That must have been one hell of a conference," he said at the dining room table.

"It was ridiculous," Gray said. "Three countries, six companies, six overblown CEOs, and the laws of all these countries. . . . I'm going to have to leave again, but I'm not sure when."

Rick looked at her.

"Don't say it," she said. "But you may have to take him to the chess tournament in Ann Arbor. This thing is about to blow up on me."

Rick shrugged, but she knew he was disappointed. The truth was, her husband liked the lifestyle her income provided. They had the best house in town, and he could be the hands-on father he'd always dreamed of being, without having to worry too much about earning a living. He would happily take Joseph to the chess tournament, and they'd get a hotel room and have fun. Joseph would call her from time to time and give her updates, but he would miss her. He was thirteen and he would miss her.

Maybe I'll make it to the first day of the tournament, she thought. *I owe them both that much. A little getaway with my family, participating in my only son's favorite activity in the world . . .*

"I'll arrange it so I can at least go down with you," she said. "I can catch a flight out of Detroit if I have to go again. But I want to be with you two for at least a day."

She went into the family room and played Xbox for a while with Joseph. He was a tall, gangly kid with her light brown hair, her husband's green eyes, and her own sense of pragmatism and logic. They had an easygoing relationship. He understood that he benefited from her business travel as well, and he also understood that when she was home, she was able to do things other parents couldn't, parents who were shackled to an eight-to-five Monday-through-Friday job. It was a trade-off, and they understood each other—as much as she could allow another person to understand her.

Joseph didn't complain when she told him to put away the Xbox. He never did. He didn't care all that much for video games anyway—he played them to keep up with what other kids his age were doing, but he would rather play chess. He'd placed in the top three in the state of Michigan the last two years, and this year he thought he would take the state title. Instead of a good-night hug or kiss—he was thirteen, after all—his mother high-fived him and he went upstairs.

Fifteen minutes later Gray's phone rang. She talked quietly in her study for a few minutes, then told Rick she was going out to run some errands. A shadow crossed his face, but he said nothing. He knew better than to ask. Gray made the forty-five-minute drive to the larger town of Big Rapids, and parked in a half-full student lot on the campus of Ferris State University. She wasn't likely to see any of her Fremont neighbors here.

She flashed her headlights once, and in less than a minute Mark Barrientos got into the car beside her. "Your husband won't be worried?"

"Not at all," Gray said.

"He knows nothing?"

"No," Gray said. "We've been married fifteen years. He still believes I am an attorney specializing in international mergers."

Barrientos was impressed. Most people in the business never married. Relationships were inconvenient and essentially impossible. Then again, Ann Gray was the best. She wasn't the ordinary, in this business or any other.

"I bet it's difficult," Barrientos said. "I dated a woman for a couple of months last year, and had trouble remembering what name I was supposed to use with her. Finally gave it up. Too confusing."

"It's a challenge," Gray said. "But it's a matter of priorities. My husband and son keep me going. When dealing with idiots like Victor Zale and some of the others I have dealt with over the years, they center me. I can come home to my pleasant upper-middle-class home in my small town in Michigan and go to PTA meetings and bake sales and hockey games. It's so uplifting to simply do some of the things normal people do."

"We're not normal people, Ann," Barrientos said.

"No. But we can experience bits and pieces of normalcy, if we are very, very careful."

Barrientos shrugged. "What do you want to do?"

"Zale sent a man to kill me," Gray said. She sat back against the car seat and rubbed her temples. "He's broken the rules now, the terms he agreed to when we entered into our relationship. That can't be allowed to happen."

"Agreed."

"He has already taken rash, foolish chances, unnecessary risks. I know men like Zale. They tend to use a nuclear warhead when a small-caliber revolver would do. Some of the things he's done . . . when I found out . . ." Her voice trailed off into the darkness.

"Ann?"

"He's dangerous. I never really understood how dangerous before."

"So you're going to hit him back."

Gray closed her eyes. Despite the sleep, she still felt fatigued. "It's not a matter of hitting him back. With Zale becoming unstable, he's going to be even more reckless. He's going to hurt even more people who shouldn't be hurt."

"You want to do something about the project?"

"Zale says he's closing it down, tying it off."

"Without you?"

Gray nodded.

"Son of a bitch," Barrientos said.

"Language, Mark," Gray said. "Take care in your language, please. But the terms state that I am in complete operational control of the project, including any shutdown. I've already taken some steps."

"You aren't going to go after Zale personally, are you?"

Gray waved her hand in a dismissive gesture. "The Associates cannot be allowed to continue. When Victor Zale falls, he will fall quite far."

"So, what . . . ?"

Gray turned and looked at her young associate. "Sometimes sacrifices have to be made."

"Ann, what the hell are you talking about?"

"We're going to reactivate April 19. They have much work to do."

* * *

She gave Barrientos detailed instructions. She knew he was surprised at her decision, but he was a professional—his face betrayed nothing.

Then Gray drove home, being careful to stop and purchase a few items at the grocery store. At home, Rick was already in bed. She sat down in her study to think. She needed time with her family, time to recharge. But Zale was shutting down the Silver Cross without her, and she didn't know if Meg Tolman and Nick Journey would be able to capitalize on what she had already given them in time to make a difference.

Then I will raise the stakes again, she thought.

She crossed to the wall safe she kept behind a print of Renoir's *At the Concert*. She punched numbers on the keypad, opened the safe, and withdrew a slim envelope. It contained one item: a very old paper encased in plastic bubble wrap. She had insisted on having the papers—both this one and the letter from Napoleon III to Jefferson Davis—in her possession when she agreed to take on the project. The Associates cared nothing for history. They cared only for how they could use history. They had been happy to hand over the papers. The papers themselves meant nothing to Victor Zale and Terrence Landon.

But Gray understood their value. She understood their meaning outside of what they accomplished, outside of Zale and Landon and those whom they both served and manipulated.

And now, the value had become even more substantial.

Gray found a box and carefully packed the bubble-wrap-encased papers in it. She handwrote a short note and slipped it in the package, then sealed it, opened her laptop, and pulled up the information she'd obtained since she left Meg Tolman in Cassville, Missouri.

Gray addressed the envelope to Nick Journey, Ph.D., 411 E. 7th St., Carpenter Center, Oklahoma.

She looked at the box. *Am I the hunter or the hunted now?* she wondered.

Both, she decided, thinking of Meg Tolman and Nick Journey, and of The Associates.

She would send the package by overnight mail in the morning, then Gray would spend some quality time with her husband and her son.

CHAPTER

14

Tolman ordered pizza at nine o'clock and met the delivery man at the office building's street entrance. Most of the other suites were dark. She nibbled the pizza and drank stale coffee, then settled in at her computer again. She considered what she already knew about Barry Cable: he'd left Cassville and attended the University of Missouri, where he received bachelor's and master's degrees in accounting. He worked for a large accounting firm's St. Louis office, then transferred to Chicago, and had moved to Washington to work for the Government Accountability Office eight years ago. The GAO was divided into thirteen "teams," and Cable was part of the Financial Management and Assurance team. He was single. He dated occasionally, had a few relationships of a few months, but was dedicated to the job. He swam at the Y every morning and was into classic muscle cars. He had a '68 GTO that he tinkered with on weekends.

He had started with the GAO's main headquarters on G Street, but the agency was growing, and a few "contract offices" were spread throughout the D.C. area. Two years ago he'd been transferred to such an office in Rockville. It was a small contingent, seven employees, all part of the same team.

Tolman scrolled through the notes she'd already made. The details were well known. On April 19, four men with automatic weapons burst into the contract office and opened fire. They destroyed government computers, shot out every piece of glass in the place, and worked their way toward the rear of the building. Barry was the only employee scheduled to be in the office during the day, with the other six at a training workshop in D.C. One of them, a forty-eight-year-old CPA named Corinne Barrett, was running late and stopped by the office to pick up some papers for the workshop. She was wounded in the arm, but she hid under her desk and escaped further injury as the killers quickly made their way through the office. The gunmen claimed to be part of an antigovernment group called April 19, naming itself after the day Timothy McVeigh blew up the Alfred P. Murrah Federal Building in Oklahoma City in 1995.

"We will finish Brother McVeigh's work," one of the shooters was quoted as saying. "If the GAO won't hold the government accountable . . . we will."

The four men were arrested as they left the building. They didn't resist.

"We are martyrs for the cause," said Jeremy Rayburn, an unemployed sheet metal worker from Spokane, Washington, who acted as leader. "You haven't heard the last of April 19."

Inside, Corinne Barrett had crawled from beneath her desk and called 9-1-1. Barry Cable was slumped over his desk, a cup of coffee and a cinnamon bagel at his side. One of the crime scene investigators had made a point of including in the report that the bagel was covered in the victim's blood. Cable had been shot five times. His office was at the rear of the building, but all the shooting took place in less than two minutes. It was a small building.

The members of April 19 pleaded guilty in federal court to one count of murder of a federal employee, one count of assault, and one count of conspiracy to commit an act of terror. All four men were sentenced to life in prison without parole. By the time Jim Cable was found hanging on his back porch in late June, the men who killed his brother were in the U.S. penitentiary in Hazelton, West Virginia, awaiting transfer to another facility to serve their sentence.

It was all very clinical. Police reports, official documents, trial transcripts. Statistics.

But somewhere in all that data was an answer that would set into motion the chain of events that led to Dana's death a few days ago.

Tolman reread Jim Cable's e-mail to his sister, five days before his death.

... I believe there was more to Barry's death than just some random terrorist nutcases. He sent me something.

There's something happening here, and I don't know what. Going to check into it. . . .

Did that sound like a depressed man on the verge of taking his own life?

"He sent me something."

Tolman sat very still.

"You haven't heard the last of April 19," Jeremy Rayburn had said.

But the silence since the shooting had been deafening. No one else stepped forward from the group. There were no threats of further violence. No pro-April 19 rallies at the trial. No messages from the group on Internet bulletin boards or websites. April 19 had faded away with the arrest, guilty pleas, and sentencing of the four members who carried out the GAO shooting.

Tolman closed her eyes. Everything was silent.

With almost every extremist group, noise was made when some of its members were arrested. The remaining members rattled their sabers and made pronouncements about what was coming next. None of that happened with this group. To be sure, they were loosely organized, but there should have been *something.*

She logged in to the Justice Department database and navigated to the files on domestic extremist groups. Each entry had a tag as to when the department became aware of the group, what their agenda was, what steps—if any—had been taken, and so on.

She found the entry for April 19 and said, "What the fuck is this?"

The date the Justice Department became aware of the group was April 19.

Extreme political groups did not exist in a vacuum. Even the groups on the furthest reaches of society, with only a few adherents, had some form of infrastructure: websites, bank accounts, real estate records. It had to be in place before the group took action. Weapons, personnel, transportation . . .

But the FBI had no record of April 19 prior to its appearance in Rockville.

She read the further notation in the file:

This group appears to have no organization that can be tracked.

There had been all kinds of news coverage about the group in the wake of Rockville, profiling their objectives . . . all information from the defendants themselves. There were no interviews with other members. Rayburn had told an interviewer from CNN, "You won't find us, so you may as well stop looking." The clip had been repeated over and over, with news analysts talking about its "ominous tone" and "dangerous portents," and wondering if the U.S. was on the cusp of entering into a new wave of domestic terrorism.

Journalists hadn't talked much about Barry Cable and Corinne Barrett, other than the obligatory feature story profiles in the days after the shooting. There was a footnote in a couple of stories that Barrett's medical bills had been paid by a mysterious "concerned individual" who remained anonymous. The focus of the media was the agenda of the killers. Barry Cable and Corinne Barrett became footnotes to April 19, and then April 19 itself became a footnote.

Like it never really existed at all, Tolman thought.

Or it only existed to carry out this particular shooting.

Jim Cable had written: *"I believe there was more to Barry's death than just some random terrorist nutcases."*

"I'll be goddamned," Tolman said. "You were right, Jim."

CHAPTER
15

In a quiet carrel on the fourth floor of SCC's Epperson Library, Journey sat with his laptop open and half a dozen books spread around him, wondering if there was a way to translate wispy legends and whispered comments into something verifiable about Napoleon III's Silver Cross—something for which he had apparently been willing to throw his government's support to the Confederate States of America.

And what could this Silver Cross possibly mean to Meg Tolman's friend and her brothers?

There were holes in the story big enough to drive a truck through, and Journey wasn't convinced of the connection. But as a historian, he was fascinated by the possibilities. It was almost like imagining an alternate history. What if the letter had reached Jefferson Davis? What if Davis had indeed turned over the Silver Cross—assuming he actually had it in the first place? What if French warships appeared on the American coast, landing troops in Virginia and Georgia and North Carolina?

Journey tapped his finger three times on the legal pad he'd filled with notes. *But Rose Greenhow drowned,* he thought.

And how did the letter get to the woman who gave it to Tolman? For that matter, who was the woman?

That part was Tolman's job. If the woman could be found, Tolman would find her. His task was to find the Silver Cross.

He threw down his pen in disgust, because he just wasn't finding it.

He'd been through a volume of Napoleon III's personal letters, the best primary source he could find. While there were many references to the French occupation of Mexico and the silver mines of Sonora, there was nothing about a valuable artifact, or any expedition into Confederate territory.

It wasn't until he started getting into secondary and tertiary sources that he even found any whispers—unsubstantiated rumors, things someone said to someone else. Lots of speculation, not much fact.

One of the books, written in 1954, mentioned that one of Napoleon's courtiers told his mistress twenty years after the fact that Napoleon had spoken of "a giant crucifix, almost as large as that upon which Our Lord suffered and died," and that "the emperor was determined to possess."

A 1971 article in an obscure British history journal included a one-paragraph notation of a conversation between a pair of British and French diplomats in 1864, with the Frenchman saying, "His Majesty is drunk on the idea of New World silver. He speaks of a single piece of treasure, for which he would gladly pay any bounty."

A French book from 1947 contained a lengthy section on Napoleon's adventures in Mexico. Many other books did the same, but this one held a full chapter on "The Emperor's Lost Treasure." Journey's French was not good, and he had to find a librarian who could translate for him.

It took nearly an hour, and the librarian commented, "It would help if the author knew how to write. A third-grader could write better than this."

Indeed, the book was poorly written. Editing was nonexistent. Journey downgraded the reliability of the source, but he was still intrigued by the content. The author's wild speculations conjured images of an ancient temple, built completely of silver and hidden in the deserts of northern Mexico. Other paragraphs went on at length about jewel-encrusted silver pieces that should rightfully be housed in France.

It was all hyperbole, but one short section caught Journey's eye.

L'empereur agents traversé la grande rivière et qu'il y a découvert un plus grand trésor que peut être cru.

Journey read the librarian's translation: "The emperor's agents crossed the great river and there discovered a greater treasure than may be believed."

"La Grande Riviere." The Great River.

The Rio Grande.

The text was suspect and of dubious reliability, but this author—who cited as his sources the letters of French soldiers garrisoned in Mexico at the time—believed that Napoleon's agents had crossed the Rio Grande.

Into the Confederate States of America.

"A greater treasure than may be believed."

No details about what this unbelievable treasure might be or where the French had gone after crossing the river.

But at least one account believed the French had left Mexican territory.

Searching for . . . what? A life-sized crucifix? A temple?

It was sketchy at best, laughable at worst. The legends were unsubstantiated by any primary sources. Journey threw his pen down again, and it bounced off his laptop and rolled to the floor.

Journey turned in his chair and saw Graham Lashley, dressed in a dark suit as always, bend over and pick up the pen.

"It is maddening, is it not?" Lashley said. "The Leveque text tantalizes, but proves nothing."

Journey took the pen from Lashley's outstretched hand. "You've read it?"

"I've read all of them, Nick, including a few you don't have here. This is my field."

The two professors stared at each other.

"You won't get away with it," Lashley said, lowering his voice.

"I'm not trying to get away with anything, Graham. This is a consulting project for the U.S. government. The college is aware that I do this. The dean encouraged it. It's no secret."

Lashley folded his arms. "Since that business at Fort Washita last year, you've been quite the celebrity, haven't you?"

Journey ignored the jab. "These consultations benefit the college, too. Faculty working on external projects is a good thing."

Lashley smiled, but there was no humor in it. "'External projects'? I hardly think concealing a find of major historical importance is what the college had in mind. But I guess I should expect no less from you."

Journey stood up and stepped toward the other man. Lashley's eyes widened and he took a step backward.

"So the famously cool Dr. Journey begins to show some emotion," Lashley said. "And while we are on the topic, don't waste your time with Sandra Kelly. She is as much a hack as you are. I voted against her receiving tenure."

"She'll be here long after you're back on Barbados and having trouble getting a job as an after-school tutor," Journey said, his voice rising. "And that's where you'll be if you don't leave me alone about it."

"That letter falls in my research area."

"I've already told you," Journey said. "After this project is finished. There's a bit more at stake here than academic politics, Graham."

Lashley's voice rose as well. "Oh yes, people may have been killed because of it. Yes, I remember that bit of melodrama. I believe you may have spent a little too much time with your secret-agent friend."

"This conversation is over, Graham. And if you don't let this go, and keep your comments about Sandra to yourself, then I'm going to come and kick your ass. Now get the hell out of my way."

Shaking with rage, Journey slammed his laptop closed, gathered up his legal pad, and walked away. People were staring—most of SCC had never seen him raise his voice or curse, and half of the fourth floor had seen him get into a shouting match with a fellow faculty member.

He tried to think of what he had learned about the Silver Cross. He had the same things he had when he started: innuendo, supposition, speculation . . . only more of it. He didn't know if he had anything that would help Meg Tolman. He was no closer to finding the Silver Cross.

* * *

Journey called home to check in with the sitter he'd hired to stay with Andrew for the evening, then headed for Sandra's house. She lived in a small house on the far west end of town, in a new subdivision populated mainly by younger faculty and grad students. She'd bought the house after she'd gained tenure last fall—it was her way of putting down roots in Carpenter Center, now that she knew her job at SCC was secure.

She was waiting for him on her front porch. Wearing flats, she was as tall as Journey. He stepped out of the car, kissed her cheek, and opened the passenger door for her.

"You're so funny," she said as she settled in.

"Am I?"

"No one opens car doors for women anymore, yet you do it every time. You don't have to impress me."

Journey smiled and walked around to his own side of the van. "I know, I'm quaint and old-fashioned. I also know you're an accomplished professional woman and very capable of opening a door for yourself."

"Maybe it's a generational thing," Sandra said with a smile. She liked to tease him about their age difference.

Journey shrugged, backing out of the driveway. "My aunt who raised me sort of pounded it into my head, that you always open the door for a lady. But she'd say, 'You don't do it because she's a lady, you do it because you're a gentleman.' I thought it was so silly at the time."

"Actually I think it's kind of endearing. Don't tell anyone. I'll lose feminist points for that. So Sarah is with Andrew?"

"I have her until nine o'clock."

"A little late for someone your age, isn't it?"

Journey smiled. The banter with Sandra was becoming more natural, bit by bit. She was interesting and sexy, and he was frumpy and outdated, but it felt good. It was still hot an hour and a half later when they left the restaurant and went for a drive around Lake Texoma. It was Friday, and the roads in and out of town were filled with boats and RVs, as they were every summer weekend. Journey cranked the air conditioner and they listened to "All Things Considered" on SCC's NPR affiliate.

"You know, you're getting better at it," Sandra said after a while.

"What?"

"Leaving Andrew with someone else. Actually getting a sitter so we can go out."

Journey shifted on his seat.

"I know you're still getting comfortable with it," Sandra said. "It's okay, and I appreciate it." She paused. "That doesn't sound condescending, does it?"

"No," he said. "I'm trying. But it's hard—"

Sandra raised her hand. "You don't have to explain. I don't know what it's like, but I'm learning. You're starting to let me see a little bit every now and then, the good and the bad. I'm a smart girl, Nick. I can see if you let me see."

Sandra reached across and put a hand on his arm. A gentle, soft, cool touch. It felt good. Amelia had been gone nearly four years now, and it had been at least five years before she left since she had touched him with any real affection. Journey had almost forgotten what the touch of a woman felt like.

"And you know what else?" Sandra said. "You only texted Sarah once during dinner. You're improving all the time."

Journey laughed, and it was an easy, natural response. For a while he wasn't thinking about Graham Lashley and Napoleon III and Meg Tolman's friend, murdered on a North Carolina seawall.

Sandra invited him in, and they sat on her red leather couch—"the only piece of furniture I've ever bought new," she said with a laugh—and talked for another hour. When the conversation slowed a bit, he took her hand, turned slightly, and kissed her. Her lips, like her hand on his arm in the car, were cool and firm. He broke the kiss much too soon, but still held her hand.

"Well, finally," she said, the little hint of a laugh always in her voice.

He smiled. "I'm a little out of practice."

"I like practicing."

She put her hand on the back of his neck and pulled his head toward her. They kissed again, more deeply. Journey felt light-headed. Sandra opened her mouth, and he felt her tongue, ever so lightly. They held the kiss a few more seconds, then broke off. Journey touched her shoulder, tracing a finger lightly across her neck. She shivered. They kissed again, quickly, and Journey lowered his hand to her breast. He left it there, unmoving, feeling himself growing hard. His motionless hand was a question.

"Please," Sandra said. "I want you to touch me, Nick."

He caressed her breast, very slowly, very gently, rubbing in an ever-widening circle, then finding the hardening nipple beneath the fabric of her blouse and rolling it between his thumb and forefinger. She drew in a sharp breath. With his other hand he traced from her neck to her shoulder. She shivered again.

He drew her to him and kissed her again, his hand still moving in circles on her breast. Sandra moaned and arched her back, then he slowly withdrew his hand, sliding it down to join hers, interlocking their fingers.

He kissed her mouth, her neck, her shoulder. She responded to him naturally, letting go. Her body had no tension—when he'd been intimate with Amelia, she'd always felt tense, as if she could never really surrender to the moment.

But neither could I, he thought.

He caressed Sandra's breast again, then held her hand.

"Not bad for a middle-aged, out-of-practice professor," Sandra said. She was a little out of breath.

"You think?"

"Mmm-hmm. You feel *good*." She moved around on the couch. "But, Nick. I don't want to go anywhere we're not both ready to go. You know what I'm saying to you?"

"Just this far," he said, then he smiled. "For now."

He kissed her again. He couldn't think of anything else to say. He didn't need to—the silence was easy, an exquisite moment of understanding and promise.

Journey traced his finger along the beautiful curve of her neck and he brushed against the silver chain she always wore. At the end of it, hanging perfectly between her breasts, was a tiny silver cross. He touched it, running his index finger across it.

"I don't think I've ever seen you without this necklace," he said.

Sandra smiled. "I never take it off."

"It's nice. Where did you get it?"

"My grandmother gave it to me when I made my confession of faith and joined the church at fourteen."

"Catholic?"

"Oh no," Sandra said. "Disciples of Christ denomination. Main-line, even liberal by some definitions. I'm from the rebellious Irish Protestant branch of the Kelly family. You?"

Journey shrugged, still looking at the pendant. "I think I'm sort of agnostic. Hung out with a lot of Unitarians in grad school, but I don't know. I'm pretty secular in general."

"You're suddenly very interested in the cross."

"This project I'm working on for Meg Tolman," he said. "It involves an artifact that Napoleon III wanted, something called the Silver Cross."

"You were feeling me up and thinking about Napoleon III?"

"Multitasking?"

"That's okay. I was mentally reviewing the presidential campaigns of Eugene Debs for a paper I'm working on. We are the sexy couple, aren't we?"

Journey smiled at her. It was going to be all right.

"So what's up with this project?" Sandra asked.

Journey looked at the cross again. "I've been going about this all wrong. It was a pious time. Rulers tried to out-Christian each other. Lashley said something about Napoleon wanting this item that would show that God approved of his invasion of Mexico. It makes sense."

"The symbolism would have been very important to him."

"Yes. And you know who some of the most reliable writers were among explorers? Priests. If the French crossed the Rio Grande, I'm willing to bet they had a chaplain—maybe more than one—with them."

"And chaplains with military units kept detailed journals," Sandra said, "so they could notify the families of soldiers who died in battle."

Journey sat up straight. "Yes! I need to start working it from the religious standpoint. I'll go to the library tomorrow after I drop Andrew off—"

"Tomorrow's Saturday, Nick. He doesn't have day camp on Saturday, does he?"

"No. No, he doesn't. Well, I guess I won't—"

"I could come over for a bit and stay with him."

"Sandra, you don't have to—"

"I don't have anything else going on tomorrow. I was planning to go to the gym and that can wait until later in the day."

Journey remembered the look on Sandra's face, in the square when Andrew had become aggressive. "But you don't—"

"Don't give me time to overthink it, or I might lose my nerve," she said.

There was hesitation in her voice, uncertainty—it was new territory for both of them.

"Okay," Journey said.

"Okay," Sandra said, then she leaned over and she kissed him again.

CHAPTER
16

After leaving Gray, Mark Barrientos made the three-hour drive to Detroit and checked in to a hotel. He spent the better part of two hours making phone calls and relaying Gray's instructions. The men had been on standby for months. They had already warehoused the materials. Gray hadn't known exactly when they would be needed, or even the precise nature of the assignment, but as always, she planned ahead, and as always, she was ready when action needed to be taken.

After he hung up the phone, Barrientos opened his laptop. The anonymous e-mail account had been created some time ago, but had been dormant ever since. Thinking of Gray's instructions, Barrientos began typing, working on the message. But he did not send it—that would come later.

He finally slept sometime after sunrise, then spent the day keeping tabs on the men in the field. At various times in the overnight hours, three yellow Ryder trucks loaded with fuel oil and ammonium nitrate left a Chicago warehouse. The first reached its destination in under seven hours. The second took nine hours. The third had a twenty-one-hour drive, arriving in its target city at a few minutes after midnight, as Friday turned to Saturday.

By then Barrientos was wide awake again. He remembered what

Gray had told him. The three distant locations had to be coordinated. They must operate simultaneously, even across three time zones. At 2:45 A.M. eastern time, he gave them the go-ahead to move into position.

Within ten minutes, the trucks pulled into parking areas adjacent to federal office buildings in Albuquerque, Kansas City, and Cleveland. Their drivers made quick exits to getaway vehicles that their partners drove, usually parked within two blocks. At the top of the hour—3:00 A.M. in Cleveland, two o'clock in Kansas City, one o'clock in Albuquerque—the three trucks exploded. The explosions were simultaneous in Albuquerque and Cleveland. The Kansas City driver's watch was a little off, and the explosion there came fifteen seconds after the others.

After Timothy McVeigh bombed the Murrah Building in Oklahoma City in 1995, many federal buildings installed new parking facilities, designed so that no vehicle could park directly in front of the buildings. Even with this architectural precaution, the blast had its intended effect. Glass and steel and brick and wood and granite flew. Nearby structures were damaged. The entire face was sheared off the Richard Bolling Federal Building in Kansas City, eerily similar to the Murrah Building years before. The fire spread rapidly across several blocks.

The A. J. Celebrezze Federal Building, at the northeast edge of tightly packed downtown Cleveland, absorbed less damage due to its "second skin" construction added after 1995, but most of the windows in the lower half of the thirty-two-story structure blew outward. The building's glass and granite panels on the lower floors became lethal weapons, careening through the air. Glass rained down onto silent East Ninth Street below. The tops of trees in the plaza across the street were sheared off and caught fire.

At Gold Avenue S.W. and Sixth Street in downtown Albuquerque, the Dennis Chavez Federal Building, at fourteen stories, was the smallest of the three targets. Although the truck was parked on the other side of a brick wall on the street, the blast still reached the building. Winds were strong and fire and debris spread rapidly through the downtown area. Rubble coated both sides of the downtown intersection.

Barrientos spoke to each of the teams as they made their getaway, and he told them to go to ground. They would receive further instructions later.

Barrientos logged in to the e-mail account, retrieved the message from the drafts folder, and pressed send. He sent many copies of the e-mail, all with the same wording. They read:

> April 19 is responsible for the bombings in Albuquerque, Kansas City, and Cleveland. There will be more to come. We will hold the government accountable. We are April 19. Maybe now the U.S. government and those who conduct business on its behalf will get the message.

After sending the messages, Barrientos sent a text to Ann Gray's cell phone.

The text read: "Message delivered."

For Victor Zale, there was never a state of being half-asleep or half-awake. He was either fully awake or deeply asleep. When the phone rang at just past four o'clock in the morning, he rolled over, instantly alert. He'd had more than his share of early morning phone calls in his life.

Before he could speak, a man's voice said, "Turn on your television."

Zale grabbed the remote from the nightstand. "What channel?"

"Pick one," said the voice.

Zale turned on CNN. The footage was graphic: ravaged buildings in Albuquerque, Kansas City, and Cleveland—truck bombs detonated simultaneously at 3:00 A.M. eastern time. Casualty reports were coming in, and the commentators breathlessly reported the fact that the late hour of the detonations meant there were few people in the vicinity. The death toll: three in Kansas City—two security officers and a homeless woman who had been sleeping in the shadow of the building; five in Cleveland—three security officers, an overnight data entry worker at the building's Social Security office, and a worker from a nearby bakery who had stepped outside to take a walk and smoke a cigarette. There were no fatalities at all in Albuquerque, and only minor injuries.

Zale sat up straight in bed as the CNN anchors introduced a

graphic of the text of the e-mail they and other media outlets had received a few minutes after the bombings.

"Goddammit," Zale muttered.

"To say the least," said the man on the phone. "Get your ass down
here. We have to talk in person. The usual place. I'll have a car waiting
for you."

The line went dead.

Still watching the TV, Zale called Landon. "Come on, Terry, wake
up. We have to go to D.C."

"What?" Landon said, his voice thick with sleep. "What time is it?"

"Doesn't matter what fucking time it is," Zale said. "Get dressed.
We'll take the Cirrus. I'll pick you up in fifteen minutes."

Zale had been a licensed pilot for more than thirty years, and he
kept his current plane, a four-seat Cirrus SR22, at the nearest general
aviation airport, across the state line from Hillsdale in Great Barrington, Massachusetts. Shortly after sunrise, the plane rose into the
sky, leaving behind the shadows of the Berkshires. A little over an hour
and a half later, with very little said between Zale and Landon, the plane
skirted the edge of Washington, D.C.'s restricted airspace and landed
at Manassas Regional Airport in Virginia.

A black Lincoln was waiting beside the tarmac, a driver in a business suit waiting for them. The sun was fully up, and the day would be
hot and humid. Zale and Landon ducked into the Lincoln. "You know
where we're going?" Zale said to the driver.

"Yes, sir," the driver said.

No more was said. Landon tried several times to engage Zale, but
Zale simply held up a hand and silenced him. Nearly an hour later, the
Lincoln crossed into the District on Constitution Avenue, navigated
through the Saturday morning traffic along the north edge of the National Mall, and turned onto Fifteenth Street. Without speaking, the
driver stopped by the Washington Monument and let Zale and Landon
out. With the shorter Landon trailing him by a few steps, Zale made
his way to a bench in the shadow of the monument and sat down.

Within two minutes, another man joined them. Wade Roader was
about Zale's age, midsixties, and like Zale, he wielded incredible power,
while most people did not know his name.

"What the hell is happening?" Roader said before he was even seated.

Zale looked around. A couple of men in suits—Roader's body-guards—hovered nearby. A young Asian couple with a toddler walked slowly by, angling their heads upward for a look at the majesty of the monument.

"Pushback," Zale said. "I'll take care of it."

"*Pushback?*" Roader said. "All you can say is 'pushback'? Christ Almighty, Victor, three federal buildings blown at the same instant. Eight dead. We are damn lucky it was in the middle of the night and it's only eight."

"Luck had nothing to do with it. She thinks she's teaching me a lesson, and Gray being Gray, she didn't want much collateral damage."

"A lesson?" Roader's face was reddening. "A fucking lesson? Victor, are you paying attention? Three federal office buildings bombed, and now the world thinks that April 19 is responsible."

Zale sighed. He put his hand over his eyes, shielding them from the murderous sun. "I know, Wade. But this is for my benefit. That line about 'the federal government and those who conduct business on its behalf.' She might as well have written my name on it. She thinks she's got the moral high ground or something."

"For God's sake, why?"

Zale slapped his hand down onto his knees. Landon, sitting beside him, jumped at the motion. "I sent a man to take her out. She's pissed about that."

Landon shook his head silently. Roader said, "She's pissed you tried to kill her? Imagine that. Maybe you should have taken a little more care in your hiring."

"We had some mutual professional acquaintances. She came highly recommended. She's gone crazy now, but she managed the project well in the beginning."

"But she's off the reservation now," Roader said.

"Totally," Zale said. "We're tying it off. All the people at the site have been given pink slips. They all think it's something corporate, and we'll put out a press release with the local media to that effect."

"You're hardly tying it off if your 'manager' is running around blowing up buildings," Roader said. "The country can't stand this, Victor. Last year we lost the Speaker of the House and the chief justice of the Supreme Court to violence, followed by President Harwell of a heart attack. We don't need this. President Mendoza's been rebuilding this nation, and this kind of thing pushes people to the breaking point."

"You talking politics at me now?" Zale said, half-turning on the bench. "Don't you get on the moral high horse, too. If you'd ever really served your country, if you'd done anything that required a little more effort than walking down the hall to get another bottle of mineral water, you might have a little more understanding about what it takes."

"What do you mean, 'if I'd ever really served my country'? What do you think I'm doing now?"

"Shit, Wade. You sit in a fancy office and you talk a lot about theories and poll numbers. You think that's the real world? You're not near as smart as you think you are. The fact is, this country doesn't run without someone like me. There's always someone like me who makes it possible for someone like you to do things. You've benefited from this project, so don't you talk to me about rebuilding this nation."

"It's getting messy, and I want to know what you're going to do about it."

"Gray has to die."

"Agreed," Roader said. "She was a great asset but now she's a liability. If she really wanted to, she could topple everything."

"She's connected everywhere," Landon said. "I don't know if killing her—"

"We've been over this, Terry," Zale said. "Because she is connected everywhere, she has to go. A freelance operator with a fucking conscience. That's a new one on me."

"Conscience?" Roader said. "Three federal buildings destroyed, eight dead, a threat of more. All that to send you a *message*. That's conscience?"

"She's a complicated individual," Landon said.

Zale laughed. "Well, I think we can all agree on that. But we'll find her and we'll get her."

"Then there's the matter of the RIO woman and her history consultant," Roader said.

"I had people on her starting in Wilmington the day after Dana Cable," Zale said. "I knew something was wrong when she started working with the locals. Who knew Cable was friends with someone in an agency like that?"

"And she's quite good," Roader said.

"Not *that* good," Zale said. "So she went to see this professor and they're working on it. We'll see that the trail stops there."

Roader took off his glasses and wiped his brow with a handkerchief. He was already sweating, long elliptical stains showing on his shirt. "You've said that before."

"Don't fuck around with me, Wade," Zale said.

Roader poked Zale's leg. "And don't you fuck around with me, Victor. I've been patient with you for months. You keep telling me the trail's going to stop, and it hasn't. If it doesn't, sooner or later someone is going to connect the dots. Whether it's your manager or Tolman or the history professor or none of the above. Do whatever it takes, but end it." He glanced at Landon. "You're tidying up the accounts?"

"In progress," Landon said, and he glanced at Zale. "At least my part of it is going smoothly."

Roader smiled, but there was no humor in it. "I believe your partner just took a serious dig at you, Victor."

Zale waved his hand. "Bullshit. People are more complicated than money."

"So they are," Roader said, standing up. "The car will take you to the airport. Have a nice flight back to the Berkshires. Beautiful up there this time of year, and not so damned hot." He looked thoughtful. "You may have forgotten, Victor, that I was a history professor once. My specialty was the colonial era, up to the American Revolution. I was pretty damn good at it. But that was a long, long time ago."

The Asian family passed them again. A tour group of twenty or more, all older people, went by going the other direction. Zale heard the droning voice of the guide, like listening to a bee buzzing in one ear.

"You have all the information you need on Tolman and the professor?"

"I'm assembling a dossier on the professor," Zale said.

"Don't," Roader said. "I have everything you need."

Zale looked surprised.

"I can play the game, too," Roader said. "But I play it in a different way." He dug in the pocket of his wrinkled khakis and pulled out a USB drive, handing it to Zale. "There's your dossier on Nick Allen Journey, and a more complete look at Margaret Isabell Tolman. They also contacted a colleague of Journey's, a Professor Graham Lashley, within the last few days." He started toward his bodyguards, then turned back after half a dozen steps. "End it, Victor. End it now."

Zale and Landon watched the rumpled, stoop-shouldered man walk away. An idea was blowing through Zale's brain, and for a moment Ann Gray and April 19 and the Silver Cross and the imminent protest/counterprotest in Chicago and President Robert Mendoza were all jumbled together. He began to sense an opportunity, perhaps a way to deal with more than one problem at a time. Victor Zale was nothing if not a problem solver. When Roader had disappeared, Zale pulled out his phone and began calling his people in the field. They had work to do, and they had to do it quickly.

A little over a mile northwest of the Washington Monument, Tolman stepped off the Metro at Farragut Square North and walked briskly to Connecticut and her office building. She'd been listening to her iPod all the way in from her apartment across the river in Alexandria, trying to stay centered, to keep her mind from straying into dark corners. Her taste was eclectic—jazz to singer-songwriters to bluegrass—but there was one notable absence in her music collection: no classical piano. Tolman had felt for many years that listening to other pianists' interpretations of works she might someday play interfered with her own reading of the piece.

So by the time she stepped onto the fourth floor, she was listening to a bluegrass band from the D.C. area, The Seldom Scene, tearing through a semi-gospel song called "Going Up on the Mountain." She was surprised to see a light on in suite 427 when she unlocked the door. "Hello?" she said, pulling out ear buds as The Seldom Scene started on its final chorus.

"Hello?" a voice came back.

Tolman turned left down the hall and found RIO's resident financial analyst, Kerry Voss, in her office. "Hey," Voss said, looking up and smoothing back her hair, which was reddish-brown and in a ponytail today. Tolman thought it had been black earlier in the week. Voss was wearing a Bob Marley T-shirt and denim shorts. "If I'd known the boss was going to be here this morning, I would have worn grown-up clothes."

Tolman smiled. "I still have a hard time getting my head around that whole 'boss' thing. You're probably more qualified than I am to do that, since you follow money for a living."

"Wouldn't have the job if you offered me a million a year," Voss said.

"Uh-huh. Kids must be with your ex this weekend."

"That they are, and I didn't even have a date last night. So here I am, finishing up a couple of cases. Hopping down the old money trail. You? You still distracted by the North Carolina thing?"

"You could say that." She waved. "I'll be in my office."

She went to the office, turned on the computer, and while it booted up, she went to the break room to start coffee. Voss wasn't a coffee drinker—"I get my caffeine from twelve-ounce cans," she liked to say—so Tolman knew there wouldn't be any ready.

She took a cup to her office and logged on to the Web. She checked a few news sites, and all the news was the same, with images of burning buildings filling the screen. She settled on ABC, which was streaming live video in a three-way split, with the anchors in the fourth corner of the window-type shot. "What's this?" Tolman said.

She turned up the volume, listening to the chatter about "overnight explosions in three federal office buildings." She froze when she saw footage she recognized, footage she'd watched again online yesterday, a clip of the GAO office in Rockville, and Barry Cable's body being removed from the building.

"April 19 is the same militant antigovernment group that claimed responsibility for the fatal shooting at a government office outside Washington last spring," said the reporter. "They have been silent since that incident, but they are apparently back, and in a big and frightening way."

Holy shit, Tolman thought.

Thoughts tumbled through her. Did that mean her hypothesis about April 19 existing only to murder Barry Cable was totally off base?

But why now? Why blow up federal buildings across the country now?

Tolman pushed herself away from the desk and ran down the hall to Kerry Voss's office. The door was closed and Voss was listening to something loud—crashing guitars, bass, drums, screaming vocals. Tolman didn't recognize it. She didn't bother knocking—Voss wouldn't hear her anyway.

Voss looked up and turned down the music. "What?" she said, seeing Tolman's face.

"April 19," Tolman said.

"Yeah, did you hear about those buildings? Good thing it was the middle of the night or a lot more people might have been hurt."

"April 19," Tolman said again, her mind racing.

"You're repeating yourself, Meg. What is it?"

"Can you find their money? They had to have money to orchestrate something like these bombings."

Voss folded her hands into her lap. "Here we go again. Is this a RIO case?"

"Not yet," Tolman said. "Then again, it may already be."

"What? You're not making sense."

"I know," Tolman said. "They may be connected to this investigation I'm already working on."

"Oh, not cool. What do you want to know?"

"Anything. Find their money. No one blows up three federal buildings at the same time without having money behind them. They're claiming responsibility all over the media. Maybe they're not phantoms after all. Maybe I was wrong . . . hell, I don't know."

"You're babbling," Voss pointed out.

"Yes," Tolman said. "I'm going to Norman, Oklahoma."

"What does that have to do with April 19?"

"I don't know yet. I have to go. Call me on my cell when you get something. This is top priority."

"Of course it is," Voss muttered as Tolman dashed down the hall.

"He sent me something," Jim Cable had written.

Time to find out what, Tolman thought.

CHAPTER
18

Sandra wasn't due at the house until nine o'clock to watch Andrew, so Journey held to Saturday morning tradition and took his son to a small donut shop on the square. After breakfast, they stepped out onto the bright sidewalk in front of the Donut Chef, and Journey looked across the square in time to see his ex-wife stepping out of the Carpenter Center branch of First Southwest Bank.

Andrew looked up and saw his mother, hooting as loudly as he could. He stamped his feet, waved his arms, and broke into a run toward her.

"Andrew!" Journey shouted.

It was no use—whenever Andrew saw his mother, he ran as fast as he could away from his father, oblivious to all else, including danger. He pounded down the steps by Maskil's Discount Store and into the street. "Andrew!" Journey screamed again.

Amelia turned when she heard his voice, her hand still on the bank door, her black and white banker power suit perfectly tailored, nails and hair and makeup just right, nothing out of place. She smiled at Andrew, but it quickly evaporated into the hard-edged look she had cultivated in her forties to go along with her professional and material success. She took a step forward, hands outstretched. "Andrew, no!" she shouted. "Not in the street! Go back!"

He reached the median, making happy vocalizations, flapping both hands wildly in the morning breeze. Journey looked both ways and scrambled into the street. "No, Andrew, no!" Journey shouted, and Amelia repeated the words.

Andrew bounded across the street. Amelia dashed down the steps and grabbed a handful of his shirt, pulling him onto the curb. Journey let out a breath, and seeing Andrew in his mother's arms with no cars on the square, jogged across the street.

"Don't ever do that," Amelia was saying. "You could get yourself killed. Don't ever do that, Andrew!" Her voice rose, and Andrew stepped back, his vocalizations turning angry.

"Lower your voice," Journey said.

"What?" Amelia said.

"You know what we talked about. The angry tone of voice."

"He doesn't get aggressive with me, Nick. He never has."

Journey absorbed the words like a slap. Andrew was calming himself, now dancing circles around his mother. Journey took a deep breath and let it out slowly, looking at Amelia. He was struck, as he always was when he saw them together, how much she and Andrew looked alike—the fair skin, the gray-green eyes, the beautiful hands with long, tapering fingers.

"What are you doing in town?" Journey finally asked.

"I'm making a swing through our branches in this area," Amelia said. "Just came down from Oklahoma City for a breakfast meeting with my management team here, then on to Durant, McAlester, and Poteau. Arkansas after that."

"On a Saturday? So much for bankers' hours."

"No such thing anymore. I was going to call you."

Journey smiled. "No, you weren't."

The hard lines of her face sharpened for an instant, then melted into a soft smile. "I can never fool you, can I? No, I wasn't. I don't have time. I'm on a pretty tight schedule and I didn't want to get Andrew excited." She glanced across the square. "Still doing the Donut Chef on Saturday mornings, huh?"

Journey shrugged. "It's routine."

"So it is." She looked at him. "What happened to your arm?"

"Nothing."

The silence drew out for half a minute. "That's the worst instance yet," Amelia finally said. "He could have really hurt you."

"Or himself." Journey waved toward the street.

"You know, a place opened not long ago in Oklahoma City. It's a specialty hospital. It's residential, especially for kids and teens on the autism spectrum. I called and talked to the clinical director and she seems to know what she's doing."

How would you know? Journey thought but didn't say. "When was this?"

"A couple of months ago, before he came for his two weeks with me."

"You were thinking you might put him in there for those two weeks, is that it? Without consulting me?"

Amelia raised both hands, then let them drop to her sides. "No, of course not. I wouldn't . . . I just wanted to ask. They do all the latest therapies, they're ABA certified. He could get some intense testing, maybe help us . . . help *you* . . . to learn some more things to do with him, to get through some of these behaviors."

"I'm not rich, Amelia."

"They take Medicaid, and since he's Medicaid qualified because of the disability, he could get in that way. And I could help pay for it, too. I'm doing all right."

Andrew had taken his mother's hand, holding her index and middle fingers with his entire hand. He rocked back and forth on his heels. Journey said nothing.

"Just give it some thought," Amelia said.

Journey hesitated, then nodded. "I will."

"It wouldn't be forever, you know," Amelia said. "But maybe they could get a handle on some of these things. A few months might do a lot of good. They've toilet-trained kids, some even older than Andrew. They've worked with aggression and kids who hurt themselves. They've had nonverbal kids who started talking. It couldn't hurt to look into it."

Journey reached out his hand toward Andrew, even though he knew what would happen.

Andrew hid behind his mother and stamped his foot.

Journey swallowed hard. "Andrew, it's time to let your mom go. I'm glad you saw her for a minute, but she has to go, and we need to get home."

Andrew screamed, and it almost sounded like he said "no."

"Come on, honey," Amelia said, and took his hand. She glanced at Journey. "Where are you parked?"

Journey pointed.

"You ever going to trade in that van?" she asked.

"Oh, I figure it has about another hundred thousand miles left in it," Journey said.

Amelia led Andrew across the square. She had to put him in the van, and it took another couple of minutes before he let go of her hand. She finally slammed the door and began walking away. Andrew hooted after her.

Journey rolled down his window. "Hey," he called.

Amelia turned.

"What's the name of the place?"

"It's called Grace. Grace of Oklahoma. They have a website."

Journey nodded to her, then started the car and pulled away from the curb.

Sandra arrived at the house at nine o'clock sharp, carrying a plastic bag filled with puzzles. "I found a bunch of them at a garage sale," she said, "and thought we might try to do them together this morning." She breezed into the living room, kissing Journey on the cheek as she went by. Andrew gave her a wary look. "Some of them have fifty pieces or more. You think that's too advanced for him?"

Journey looked at Andrew, then at Sandra, thinking of how different she was from Amelia. After a moment Sandra said, "Hello?"

"Sorry," Journey said. "Anything that engages him is good. I bet he'll like them."

"We'll give them a try, then," Sandra said, and dropped her bag. "Morning, Andrew."

Andrew looked away and made a clicking sound with his tongue.

"You seem distracted," Sandra said.

"I am," Journey said, then leaned over and kissed her on the mouth.

*   *   *

Fifteen minutes later Journey was in his spot in the fourth-floor carrel of the library, armed with laptop and legal pad. He hoped the French-speaking librarian was working today, and she was.

"I need to find journals or collections of letters from chaplains who would have been attached to French military units in Mexico during the French occupation in the 1860s," he said.

The librarian started laughing. "Could you be a little more specific, Dr. Journey?"

"What?"

The librarian, who looked young enough to be a grad student, put a hand on his arm. "I'm kidding. That's way more specific than you need to be. In fact, I don't know that I have anything indexed that way. This is a little outside your usual field, isn't it? I mean, aren't you the Civil War guy?"

"Trust me, it all comes together in the end," Journey said. "Or at least I hope it does."

The librarian shrugged. "This kind of stuff is usually Dr. Lashley's business."

"He and I may wind up working on it together."

"Oh sure, you made that pretty clear in here last night."

"You heard that?"

"Oh yes. About time someone told him off, too. He's an asshole. Pardon my French." She smiled. "That's a joke, too."

She brought him several books, a few ragged journals, and pointed him to a number of online sources as well. Journey read multiple accounts of the French occupation of Mexico, including the Battle of Puebla on May 5, 1862—a Mexican victory against the occupying French, leading to the modern Mexican celebration of Cinco de Mayo. He read a journal by Maximilian's personal confessor. Lots of piety, a bit of corruption, politics, sex—all good, but nothing about expeditions across the Rio Grande.

Journey opened the poorly written Leveque book again, pestering the librarian to translate the chapters before and after the one he'd already highlighted. There was nothing.

A greater treasure than may be believed," Leveque had written.

And yet no one else wrote anything about this great treasure? Journey wondered.

"There has to be something," he said, going back to the librarian's desk after he'd been at it over an hour.

"If you're specifically looking for writings by priests, you might try theology instead of history," the librarian said. "I mean, a lot of theological writings turn up in history journals and texts, but the opposite is true, too: lots of history in the theological journals. I know a good one, and it's really interesting. We carry it because Dr. Stern in Humanities has contributed to it a few times. It's called *Cross Currents*. But I know it has an online index."

"Is it French?" Journey asked.

"Scottish, actually, published in Glasgow. But it has contributors from all over the world. It's small but pretty interesting."

Journey found the website for *Cross Currents: A Multidisciplinary Journal of Theological Studies* and worked his way to the index. It had been published in Glasgow since 1983, and the name was no lie: history, politics, sociology, psychology, literature, even the "harder" sciences, all viewed through a theological lens.

He entered "Napoleon III" and the index showed thirty-six entries.

He cross-indexed "Napoleon III" and "Mexico." Four hits. The first three were dry as dust, with no relevance. The fourth article was published six years ago, and its author was Reverend Claude Michel. It was an examination of the life and work of Reverend Henri Fournier, who had served as priest of St. Pierre's Church in Montluçon in central France from 1872 to 1901. A journal belonging to Fournier had recently been discovered and Michel—the current priest at St. Pierre's—believed it offered a "breathtaking" glimpse into the life of the nineteenth-century clergy.

Fournier's journal began when he volunteered to serve Emperor Napoleon III's army in Mexico as a chaplain in 1862. Journey read the translated words:

We face many hardships. The country is dry and the heat is oppressive. The peasants here are not happy to see our soldiers, but the gentry are quite welcoming. I have served the Lord's Supper to many here, and was even asked to baptize an infant in one village where there is no church. I was happy to oblige. I serve Christ first, the Emperor second, and finally, my comrades. Captain Prideux says we will soon under-

take a new mission, with only a small force. Several men I do not know are joining us for this mission—some of them are not soldiers. Two are Mexican natives. They do not speak French, but Prideux speaks fluent Spanish, and I know a smattering of words. Prideux will not tell me what the mission is, or why we have taken on these new men, but he expects that we will be away for many months.

The entry was dated November 1, 1862.

Journey read on. A company of fifteen men, including the priest, left Sonora on December 3. They spent time in several villages along the way. Fournier met many Mexicans who wanted to make confessions to him, as they rarely saw priests along the frontier.

On Christmas Day, the French contingent camped alongside the Rio Grande. Then:

December 26, 1862

Today we will cross the great river. We are leaving Mexico to enter Texas. Texas! By Christ, I did not know that we would be crossing into the land where war rages. The Americans fight each other, and Texas is part of the faction that has withdrawn from the Union. Why are we to enter Texas?

February 22, 1863

I have not set pen to paper these many weeks. The wind here will be our destruction. God shows no mercy to His servants in this country. Every few days we camp and small parties of men go in different directions. The horses are dry, the nights cold and long, the days filled with wind and dust. We have encountered small parties of Indians. Captain Prideux has shot two of them.

April 2, 1863

We make our way north through this empty country. There are a few small settlements scattered about, and when I ask the inhabitants about the war, they say, "What war? This is Texas, not Virginia."

April 9, 1863

We have lost a man, a foot soldier, a rifleman. His name was Marc-Andre Bernard, and he was out with one of the scouting parties today, where he fell down a ravine, breaking his neck. He is from Bayonne, and I must write to his family and tell them their beloved son lies in the desert of Texas. I do not know why we have come to this place and Prideux will not say.

April 10, 1863

Prideux says I must not tell Bernard's family that he died in Texas. No one in France is to know we are in Texas. I am to say he died in Sonora. I do not know if I can tell them this lie. Prideux is angry with me. He threatens to leave me for the Indians and the wolves if I do not do as he says.

May 23, 1863

This country is rugged, more so than Mexico. Still, we press on, searching, searching! This is madness! I have prayed to know God's mission in this wilderness. The men occasionally act excited, as if they have discovered something of great importance, but I am privy to nothing.

May 31, 1863

One of the men, who had gone with a scouting party to the east today, returned and gave something to Prideux. I could not see it, as they were on the other side of the wagon and horses and there were men between us. They were all excited, more so than usual. I ventured to ask Prideux the source of this excitement and he said, "Tend to your rosary, priest, and leave the rest to me. Tomorrow we start for Mexico."

Later that night, I encountered two of the men from the party and asked them what had happened. I bribed them with whiskey from the last settlement we passed. "You should be grateful, Father," said the one. "We have seen the Silver Cross." Then he laughed as if he had made a joke.

Journey was sweating. A contingent of French troops was in Texas for several months in 1862–63, and there found something called the Silver Cross.

"Texas," Journey whispered.

June 1, 1863

We turned back today, as Prideux had said. We are returning to Mexico. At dinner all the men were drunk on whiskey and a bottle of wine Prideux had brought from Sonora. In their drunkenness, they fell asleep around the wagon. I made my way stealthily to Prideux's horse, a fine gray with a calm temperament. I spoke softly to the animal and gave him a cube of sugar from the cook's supply. I opened Prideux's saddlebag, as this is where I saw the man give Prideux the mysterious item. But there was nothing there, only maps and other papers. I looked at them quickly, but it was dark and the fire was dying. There was nothing. The Silver Cross?

What is this Silver Cross? Is it a crucifix of our Lord's Passion? If so, it should rightly be in my possession. I searched all of Prideux's things, until I heard men stirring and ceased my efforts lest I be found out.

But there is nothing. For what have we come?

Michel's narrative spent a few paragraphs in conjecture about what the Silver Cross could be, while praising Fournier's rare glimpse inside a French military unit in the western hemisphere. Michel then skipped to Fournier's time in Veracruz and Mexico City, his return trip to France, and his time in Paris before settling as priest of St. Pierre's in Montluçon.

"Texas," Journey said.

But if French soldiers had already found the Silver Cross and removed it from Texas, why would Napoleon need to make a bargain with Jefferson Davis?

Questions inside of questions, Journey thought.

He looked at his watch. Three hours had passed. He called Sandra quickly.

"Any luck?" she said.

"Yes," Journey said. "I found some things, but they raise more questions. Look, I'm sorry about the time—"

"It's okay," Sandra said. "We've had a great time with the puzzles and going for a walk by the lake."

"I'll be home soon."

As he hung up with Sandra, his phone vibrated. Meg Tolman.

"Do you know the city of Norman?" Tolman asked without preamble.

"What? Norman, Oklahoma?"

"Yes, Norman, Oklahoma! What other Norman would I be asking you about?"

"I know it a little. I used to know someone who taught at OU. Why?"

"We're going there."

"We?"

"I'm about to get on a plane for Oklahoma City. I'll be getting in around four o'clock. Pick me up, then we're going to Norman."

"Why?"

"To visit Jim Cable's ex-wife, and hopefully to get inside his house. Anything happening on your end?"

"Oh, yes," Journey said. "But Meg . . . it's Saturday."

"I know what day it is, Nick. What's your point?"

"Andrew. During the week he's in day camp."

"So?"

"I would have to bring him along, and I—" Journey walked out of the library and into the sun. He stopped, looking out at the college common, thinking of the bullet hole in Tolman's bag.

"Oh, hell," Tolman said. "Now I see where you're going. Someone took a shot at me." She waited a moment. "You know, it would be much more convenient for me at times if you weren't so damn conscientious."

Journey started toward the parking lot. "But you understand."

"Yeah, I understand. And you couldn't ask—"

"Sandra's already watched Andrew this morning while I was doing this research for you. I don't want to ask too much of her."

"And his mother?"

"His mother's unavailable," Journey said, thinking of Amelia and the tour of all "her" banks.

"Look, Nick . . . I need you on this. I like to bounce ideas off you, even the nonhistorical parts. Don't you do anything for self-protection?"

"In Carpenter Center? No, but I do have a baseball bat."

"Put it in your van. I'll have my SIG, and this time it's not getting out of my reach. As federal law enforcement, I even get to carry it onto the plane. All I have to do is identify myself to the air marshals."

Journey reached the van and leaned against it, feeling the hot metal against his back. "I don't know."

"I don't want anything to happen to Andrew either. And I'm a pretty good shot when I have to be. I need you, Nick."

"All right, we'll pick you up. I'll keep Andrew nearby while we're talking to the ex-wife."

"Don't forget the bat."

"I won't."

"Something's happening. Both Jim and Dana thought so. They were right."

Journey thought of the young priest Fournier in the wilderness of Texas. "Yes, they were," he said.

CHAPTER
19

Shortly after three o'clock, Journey steered the old minivan off Interstate 44 and exited on Airport Road in Oklahoma City. Even after living in Oklahoma for more than a decade, Journey was still amused that the state's major airport was named after a man who had died in a plane crash. To be sure, Will Rogers was a favorite son, but the irony of Will Rogers World Airport still made Journey smile. Once he had parked and was in the arrivals terminal, he checked the flight monitors and found the baggage carousel for Tolman's flight while Andrew whistled his three-note melody.

Tolman came down the escalator ten minutes later. "Didn't think I'd see you here again so soon," Journey said.

"Glad you're driving," Tolman said. She waved at Andrew. "Hey, big guy."

Andrew didn't look at her, fixated on the baggage carousel as it began to move. He took a step toward it, flapping both hands. The whistling stopped and he began to make high-pitched sounds. A few people turned to look.

"Come on, Andrew," Journey said in a soft voice. "Time to go to the car."

* * *

"So what about Jim Cable?" Journey asked in the van. "What did you find out about his suicide?"

"I read the police reports. It seems straightforward. No sign of forced entry to the house, no fingerprints of anyone but Jim and his son. He had a pergola over his back porch, he looped a rope over the beams, stood on a chair, kicked the chair out from under him. When he didn't show up to class for two straight days, one of his colleagues went looking for him. The gate was unlocked, and that's where he found him. The Norman police talked to the ex-wife. With the divorce and his brother's murder coming so close together, they had a couple of pretty good indicators of depression. Colleagues and students said he had been quieter than usual the last few weeks. On the surface, it's pretty clear. You can't fault the local cops."

"What do you mean, 'on the surface'? Do you think it wasn't really suicide?"

"He knew something was happening," Tolman said. "In fact, he used those exact words to Dana: 'something is happening.' Maybe he was caught in the middle."

Journey accelerated onto I-44, retracing the route he had taken a few minutes ago. "The middle child, the second to die."

"Yeah." Tolman sighed. "So tell me what you found."

Journey explained Father Fournier's mission across Texas with the French troops, and the soldier's revelation of the Silver Cross.

"But there was no cross," Tolman said when he finished. "He didn't find it."

"Apparently not. But it tells us the French were in Texas during the Civil War, looking for something."

"Which the priest says they found . . . but didn't find."

"Exactly," Journey said.

"And this helps us . . . how?"

"It's the first corroboration of the fact that there was such a thing as the Silver Cross, and that Napoleon wanted it badly enough to send soldiers secretly into another country, a country engaged in a war of its own at the time. That was risky."

"All this to get something to symbolize that he was right in invading Mexico?"

"Don't minimize the symbolism. It was a time when that sort of thing was huge. The Mexico invasion was politically shaky for Napoleon. He needed all the help he could get, divine or otherwise."

"Symbolism doesn't mean anything," Tolman said. "Symbolism doesn't tell me who lured Dana to North Carolina and onto that seawall, and why this damned Silver Cross is such a big deal to people here and now." She sighed. "And I had to be the one to tell Melissa Cable that Dana was dead. Called her before I got on the plane. Not fun."

Journey worked his way back to I-35 South, leaving behind Oklahoma City proper and coming into suburbia. The city of Norman, clinging to the southern edge of the metro, had always been a college town, home to the state's largest university. But in recent decades it had grown into a suburb as well, a progressive and interesting community with a distinct personality.

Melissa Cable and her son Alex lived in a middle-class neighborhood on the north side of Norman. The boy was at a friend's house, but they spent ten minutes with Melissa and obtained the name of the realtor with whom Dana had listed her brother's house. Melissa Cable didn't think her ex-husband had seemed especially depressed in the weeks before his death.

"But," she said, "he wasn't a big talker, and certainly not about feelings. He'd talk about work or Sooners football, but that's about it. I just couldn't believe he would do this. He and I may not have been a very good couple when we were married, but I know he loved Alex, even if he never said it."

Five minutes later, Tolman and Journey had an appointment with the realtor. Jim Cable had lived in a 1930s arts-and-crafts-style home on Boyd Street, east of the University of Oklahoma, with an abundance of dark wood and a circle driveway. A real estate sign was staked into the ground at the curb. The realtor was a tall and tanned blond woman in her fifties whose name was something like Gigi or Mimi. She chattered away about proximity to campus, the home's character, and "lots of extras" until Tolman stopped her with a business card.

"I'm not here to buy," she said. "I'm here to investigate."

The woman's face fell. "So you know what happened here, then."

"Yes. You met with Dana Cable to put the house on the market?"

"She was here over Fourth of July weekend and asked me to list it. She was supposed to schedule an estate sale to take care of the furniture and such, but I haven't heard from her. I've called and e-mailed her, but can't seem to reach her."

"She's dead," Tolman said.

"Excuse me?"

"Someone killed her, and I'm investigating," Tolman said. "Let us in, please."

The realtor let them in to the house, then retreated to her BMW, where she began making phone calls. Jim Cable's house had the expected musty smell after weeks of being uninhabited, and it seemed incomplete: vacant spots on walls, empty spaces in several of the rooms.

"He didn't do too much after his wife and son moved out," Journey observed.

"Yeah," Tolman said, thinking of her father's house in D.C. Sixteen years after her mother's death, it still had the same feeling, as if her mother had just left and her father was waiting for her to return.

There were no books to speak of in the house, but many engineering journals. No music, no art. It was very utilitarian and clean and organized. Alex Cable's room showed a little more life, with posters of Oklahoma Sooners football players on the walls and books by Mike Lupica on the dresser, alongside a handsome carved chess set. But the bed was neatly made, the closet empty. It looked like Jim Cable was waiting for the day his son came home.

They crossed the wood floors, Andrew thumping his feet on the hollow planks, liking the sound it made. They stepped onto the back porch, a comfortable spot with a pergola covered in vines. A straight-backed wooden chair—not a lawn chair, as it looked like it had come from the dining room—lay pitched forward on the patio. Tolman looked up—a chalk mark "X" was on one beam.

Her eyes trailed down to the chair. She remembered something from the police report on Cable's suicide. One of the officers on the scene had questioned the chair's position.

Tolman stood under the beam with the mark. The chair was upturned in front of her. "This isn't right," she said.

Andrew had wandered into the bright sunshine of the backyard and was dipping his fingers into the marble birdbath. Journey, keeping an eye on his son, returned to the shade of the patio. "What do you mean?"

"Look at the X." She pointed. "If that's the spot on the beam where he tied the rope, and he was facing the back of the house, how could he kick the chair out from under himself and have it wind up facing that way?"

Journey looked. "I'm not following you."

"You have a rope around your neck. You've used a chair to climb up, and you're going to kick it out from under you to hang yourself. How would you do that? Easiest way, with this kind of chair, is to kick backward against the back of the chair. It falls backward, you dangle, you're dead. Or you even move side to side, swing your foot out, and kick the chair that way. But then the chair falls off to one side."

Journey looked at the fallen chair, then up at the beam. "You're sure he was facing the house and not the yard?"

"It was in the police report. One of the officers noted that he was facing the back door."

Journey squatted down and ran a hand over the woven chair back. "But if you were hanging right there, you'd have to get your feet somehow *behind* the chair back to be able to kick it forward so it landed like this. The police didn't catch this?"

"They caught it, but they didn't follow up on it." Tolman spread her hands apart. "Why would they? You had no forced entry, nothing amiss, and a guy who had gone through a tough divorce and the murder of his brother, all in the space of a couple of months. To be honest, I wouldn't have followed up on it either. I would have done exactly what the Norman police did—made a note of the chair for the sake of thoroughness, and let it go. If I didn't know what I do now—and that's not much—it wouldn't say anything to me either."

Journey stood up. "There's no way he could get his legs around to kick this chair forward. My God, Meg."

"Yeah. But you know something? This reminds me of Dana's death. It's sloppy. Whoever killed Dana wanted it to appear like an accident, like she was drunk and slipped and fell. But she was pointed the wrong way. Same thing here. Our killer wanted this to appear as a suicide, an obvious suicide. But the killer didn't quite get the details right."

"This changes everything, Meg."

"Yes. No. I don't know." Tolman glanced toward the yard, where Andrew had progressed from dipping his fingers in the birdbath to splashing both his hands in it. "He's going to get soaked."

Journey followed her look. "I keep spare clothes in the van. What are you thinking?"

"Barry sent Jim something, and I think both of them, and Dana, were killed because of it."

Journey turned abruptly and started for the back door.

"Where are you going?" Tolman asked.

"I'm going to search the house."

"Good idea. I'll start with Jim's computer."

Jim Cable's computer was in his study, off the home's front entry. It felt more complete to Tolman than any other room in the house. Of course, it was *his* room. It wasn't built around the life he shared with Melissa and Alex. It was no "man cave," but was still undeniably masculine, with its neatly sorted engineering journals, several working sets of gears and other gadgets Tolman didn't recognize, and a few bits of Oklahoma Sooners sports memorabilia.

She booted up the computer, but found it was password protected. She expected no less—Jim Cable was an engineer, someone who lived in the technical world. But he was also very organized, and such an organized mind would no doubt have a list of passwords tucked away somewhere for reference.

It took her half an hour, but she found it between the pages of the program for an Oklahoma-Nebraska football game from 2000, one of many such items on Jim's bookshelf.

"Sweet Jesus," Tolman muttered, looking at the neat computer printing on the page. Jim Cable had more than fifty passwords. The man must have come up with a new password for every single computer function he did—from online banking to utility payments to online magazine subscriptions. And he didn't note what password went with what function. Each function was assigned a number, but she found no key to the numbers.

Damn anal-retentive engineers, Tolman thought, then smiled a little. Jim Cable and his sister could not have been more different.

Gigi-or-Mimi stuck her head in the door, said she had another showing, and left Tolman the key with instructions on how to manage the lockbox. Journey returned from his search, reporting nothing unusual. Lots of empty space, no unopened boxes or packages.

Andrew was beginning to vocalize loudly. Journey told Tolman he was taking the boy for a walk, maybe to get a cold drink. They'd passed a Sonic drive-in on Porter Avenue. Tolman said something about a Diet Coke, but she was feeling the pull of the hunt, the immersion into a technological place that would yield information to help her put it all together. She took the list of passwords to Cable's padded leather office chair and sat down. She went down the list—none of them were the obvious, such as his birthday, wife's name, son's name, employer, Social Security number. They were random alphanumeric collections—Tolman wondered if he'd had a password generator create this, so that no hacker could get into his computer.

Starting at the top was too easy. If Jim Cable was this security conscious, he wouldn't make it that simple. Still, she gave in to the obvious and entered the first password at the desktop prompt.

"Incorrect password."

Thank you for the challenge, Jim, she thought, and started down the list.

The thirty-eighth password on the list let her log on to the system. She went straight to his Gmail account. She already had the username from the e-mail Jim had sent to Dana. She caught a break when the third password she tried opened the e-mail account. Gmail was organized into conversations with different people. She clicked Dana's name and read the same e-mails she'd read on Dana's laptop.

Her pulse quickened when she clicked Barry's name. Twenty e-mails were in the folder. She saw instantly that only one had a file attachment.

Yes, she thought.

Then, just as quickly, her heartbeat slowed down. She stopped breathing.

"Holy shit," she said.

Journey and Andrew returned to the house with drinks. Andrew was rocking on the balls of his feet and hooting. Tolman jerked at the sound.

"What?" Journey said.

Tolman ignored him, clicking on the message. There was no subject line. The text of the e-mail was blank, leaving only the file attachment. Its title was a series of numbers, and its file extension indicated that it was a spreadsheet.

The e-mail had been sent on April 19, at 9:03 A.M. eastern time.

According to the police reports, the members of the April 19 extremist group had entered the GAO office in Rockville at 9:02 A.M. The time was symbolic—it was the same time as the original April 19 bombing in Oklahoma City in 1995. The shooting was over within two minutes.

Barry Cable had sent this e-mail to his brother as the killers entered his building and began firing.

April 19, 9:03 A.M.

"This was the last thing he did," she said, her voice raw. "Before they killed him, he e-mailed this file to Jim."

She turned around and met Journey's eyes. Andrew was still bouncing behind him, sipping from his Sonic drink. Journey's eyes widened. Tolman's thoughts raced: April 19 had killed Barry Cable, seconds after he sent this e-mail to his younger brother. But April 19 didn't exist before that killing, and the group had been silent ever since—until last night and three burning federal buildings in different parts of the country.

Tolman turned slowly to the computer and clicked the mouse to open the file.

CHAPTER

20

The Michigan State Scholastic Chess Championship was held at the University of Michigan in Ann Arbor, and Ann Gray drove with Rick and Joseph from their home in Fremont. They had spent Friday night in a hotel near the campus, and Gray had read the text from Barrientos in the middle of the night.

"What is it?" her husband had asked sleepily, in bed beside her.

"Nothing," she said. "Go back to sleep."

Joseph was up before dawn, his excitement palpable at participating in the state chess tournament again this year. Rooms in the Michigan Union were set up for students from across the state, long rows of tables with dozens of chessboards. Gray always felt a rush of pride when she saw her son sitting down, shaking hands with his opponent, and when the official said, "Begin," bending to the board in total concentration.

Joseph won his first game, then his second. At noon, Gray and her husband were watching the third game from the roped-off spectators' area when she heard her phone beep in her purse.

She dug it out and read the text from Barrientos: "I'm outside in the east parking lot."

"Be there soon," she typed, then put her phone away.

Rick was staring at her. She put on an exasperated look. "Bad news?" he whispered.

She nodded.

"Do you have to go?"

Gray frowned and nodded again.

Rick sighed. Gray's frown deepened. She knew how he felt, and why. But she had to be very careful now. The project was being shut down without her, and The Associates wanted to kill her. She'd set April 19 in motion to send a message to Zale and company, to begin the process of bringing The Associates down. But when it was over, she might have to move, to ensure the family's safety. Perhaps Canada would be next. She loved Montreal, and all three of them spoke fluent French. She smiled a bit at the irony of that.

Joseph's third game had lasted over an hour, and he lost. But he was an even-tempered kid, and he showed no emotion over the loss.

"I have to go," she said in the lobby after the game. "An emergency in Belgium. I was afraid of this."

"Mom!" Joseph said.

Gray sent a stern look his way. He knew better than to take that tone with her.

"Sorry," he said, head down.

"I'll be back when I can. After this project is finished, I should have a lot of free time."

"Let's hope so," Rick said.

She glared at her husband, then softened the look. Of course he didn't understand. To him, she was an international attorney who would rather trot the globe than be at home with her family. He had no idea the sacrifices she made every day to have a life with the two of them, to even still be alive. He could never understand.

She kissed her husband's cheek, squeezed her son's arm, gathered up her purse, and left the building.

Barrientos was waiting in a car outside and around the corner. "Did you pack a bag for me?" she asked as she slid into his car.

"In the trunk."

"Good. My husband will take my things home from the hotel here."

Barrientos nodded. "So what's happening on the campus? Why here?"

Gray smiled. "Never mind about that. It's from the other part of my life. Is the second wave ready?"

"Waiting for your word."

"Good."

April 19 wasn't finished yet. And she had other work to do as well. The noose must be tightened around The Associates, and Tolman and Journey must have time to do what she needed them to do.

"Where are you going?" Barrientos asked.

"First to Washington."

"Really? Is that safe?"

Gray looked amused. "Do not worry about me, Mark."

"What are you doing in D.C.?"

"Visiting the French embassy."

"What?"

"The French are about to become very angry with the U.S. government."

"Jesus Christ, Ann."

"Don't be sacrilegious, Mark. It shows poor manners."

"I mean, are you sure—"

"Yes," Gray said, and didn't elaborate.

"So you mean—"

"I mean, to use an interesting American expression, that all bets are off. I've finally seen Victor for what he is, and he isn't going to be allowed to hurt any more families. His power is going to be broken, absolutely and thoroughly."

Barrientos stared at her for a long, silent moment.

"I know what I am doing, Mark," Gray said.

"I guess I really don't understand you. What about after D.C.?"

"Then," Gray said, "I'm going to Texas."

Tolman sipped from the Diet Coke Journey handed her and looked at the box on the screen:

"Enter key to open file."

It made sense. Barry Cable had sent it from his government e-mail account, but he had sent it while men with automatic weapons were in the building, shooting his coworker, destroying the office, coming his way. Panicked, under duress, he'd sent the file to his brother.

But he hadn't written anything. There was no time.

No time to send Jim a key that would open the file.

After the shock of his brother's murder had time to wear off—along with his divorce at the same time—Jim Cable began to wonder about his brother's death. In June he e-mailed his sister and voiced his concern that Barry's death wasn't as random as it seemed.

Five days later, he was found hanging on the back porch of this house.

"Maybe he finally started asking questions," Tolman said.

"What?" Journey said.

Tolman looked around. She'd almost forgotten he was there. "Jim," she said. "He survived all the crap from his brother's killing and his divorce and maybe he asked some questions in June about what happened to Barry. He told Dana he was going to check into it. And maybe when he started asking questions, they killed him."

"Who is 'they'? April 19 came in with guns blazing in a big public statement. Jim was killed at his house, and whoever did it tried to make it look like suicide."

"Different killers?" Tolman said. "It still doesn't add up, and it still doesn't explain why no one had ever heard of April 19 before they shot up the GAO. Then they quietly kill Jim on his porch, and weeks after that they tell Dana to go to Wilmington and kill her there?"

"Lots of holes in that story," Journey said.

"No shit, Professor." Andrew had sat down on the wooden floor, cross-legged, alternately sipping and slurping his drink. He giggled, then laughed out loud.

Tolman looked down at him. *What do you think, Andrew?* she wondered.

He stopped laughing and looked up at her.

She was startled. His gray-green eyes made contact with hers for a long second, then looked away. But he began to whistle, and it was the same pattern as when she'd stood with him in Journey's living room. The second pattern, the one with the lower note.

He glanced at her again, and this time held the eye contact longer, almost three seconds.

He associated that pattern of notes with her. Somehow, in Andrew's mind, those notes were what he knew about her.

Patterns.

She whistled back at Andrew.

He smiled and whistled the same pattern again.

"What's with you two?" Journey said. "Are you whistling buddies now, or what?"

Patterns.

Jim Cable was right. Barry's murder wasn't a random terrorist nutcase. There was more to April 19 than violent antigovernment ideology. Maybe that wasn't what the group was about at all. Maybe that was a front, a cover for something deeper. What if they killed Barry Cable for some other reason—shooting up the government office and wounding Barry's coworker to make it *look* like they were terrorist nut-cases? What if they blew up those buildings last night as part of something else?

April 19 was part of a larger whole. If she stopped thinking of them as political extremists and started thinking of them as an instrument of some other agenda, some other plan, some other *pattern,* there would be answers.

Some other plan that involved Napoleon III's Silver Cross, and whatever Barry Cable was working on at the GAO when he was killed . . . and the woman in the cemetery at Cassville, coolly handing her a 150-year-old letter and then vanishing down a country road.

Andrew whistled again, but he was playing with the straw of his drink, looking at the floor.

Tolman whistled the notes, and Andrew smiled without looking up.

Tolman glanced at Journey. "I'm going to forward this file to my own e-mail. Could I stay with you another day or two? I think Andrew inspires me to think in different ways, to look at things in ways that aren't obvious."

Journey smiled with genuine pride. "Amazing how he reaches people, isn't it?"

Andrew looked up. "Yes, you," his father said, looking down at him.

"Yes, it is," Tolman said.

Journey pointed at the computer. "How does this fit with what I found out about the Silver Cross?"

"Don't know yet. But it's there."

"You're sure?"

Tolman looked at Andrew again. "I'm sure."

"You realize that everyone who's touched this file, whatever it is, has been killed," Journey said.

Tolman patted her purse. "The SIG is right here. You really should get yourself a gun."

"I'd shoot off my foot, probably. And with Andrew in the house, I think it might be more danger than protection. But the bat is under the seat of the van, and maybe I'll start keeping it by my bed at night."

Tolman returned to the computer. She forwarded the message, in the knowledge that it had been sent by a dead man to a dead man. As they left the house and dropped the key in the realtors' lockbox, Andrew took his father's hand. With his other hand, he reached out and held Tolman's elbow, and the boy walked between them that way, all the way to the car.

CHAPTER

22

The last of the light was gone by the time Journey steered the van toward the Madill city limits. "We'll be in Carpenter Center in ten minutes," he said, then glanced in his rearview mirror. A pair of headlights appeared behind him. He had slowed as he approached Madill, expecting the other car to pass. But the driver stayed put behind him, the lights creeping closer.

"Come on, driver, pass or back off," Journey said, glancing in the mirror again.

"What's going on?" Tolman said, sitting up in her seat.

"Some guy riding my tail. Big times on a Saturday night."

With his acute hearing, Journey heard the roar of the powerful engine accelerating behind him. The vehicle behind him was large, some kind of dark-colored SUV. It was closing fast.

"Hey!" Journey said.

Tolman turned and looked. "Oh, shit," she said.

The SUV slammed into the minivan's back bumper. The steering wheel pulled to the right. Journey shouted without words. Tolman began digging in her purse, wrapping her hands around her SIG.

The van's tires touched the gravel shoulder of the road as Journey stepped hard on the brake. He felt the right front tire blow out as the big SUV followed him and tapped the van's bumper again. Journey locked his hands to the wheel. Andrew hooted.

Tolman shouted, "Goddammit!" and the minivan careened off the road. Journey saw yellow in his field of vision, and he knew they were heading straight for the abandoned brick building that had once housed KMAD, the town's only radio station. The van dipped into a narrow depression, what the locals called a "bar ditch."

"Andrew!" Journey shouted, then he was fighting the steering column. He spun the wheel to the left; the van fishtailed and slammed sideways into the building, the passenger side flush against the radio station's long-broken front window. Glass shattered on that side of the van, bits of safety glass raining down on Tolman. In the backseat, Andrew was on the driver's side, directly behind his father. The force of the crash pulled at him, but the seat belt snapped him back.

Journey's head banged against the steering wheel. His vision went black for a few seconds, then he could see in his headlights the faint outlines of the letters "KMAD" and the numbers "1550" on the front of the building. He put his head down on the wheel. Blood trickled from under his hairline.

Then, footsteps. He turned in time to see the man racing down from the SUV. He held a gun in his hand.

Journey's vision blurred. "Can you—," he said to Tolman.

She was fumbling with the latch on the seat belt. "It's stuck, and I can't get out this side!"

Journey's vision cleared, then blurred again. The van was spinning. Blood ran into his eye. He slapped at the seat belt latch with the palm of his hand, pressing it three times before letting go.

Air bag? he wondered, then he remembered: the van was old enough to not have mandatory air bags.

He freed himself and reached under the seat. He pulled out the Louisville Slugger as he heard the driver's side door behind him slide open.

"No!" he shouted, turning.

The man grabbed Andrew, and in one swift, well-trained motion, released the latch on his seat belt and dragged the boy out of the van.

"Let him go!" Journey shouted. "I don't know who you are, but you let him go now!"

The man said nothing, wrapping one arm around Andrew's neck and pulling him backward. With the other hand he jammed the muzzle of his gun against Andrew's temple. Andrew hooted once but was otherwise silent—maybe it was a game to him.

Journey tumbled out of the van, scraping his knees on the concrete sidewalk that ran along the front of the building. He heard Tolman behind him. "I'll cover you," she said in a hoarse whisper.

But all Journey could see was Andrew, the man's muscular arm around his neck, gun to his head. Andrew said nothing. His hands flapped, patting at the air around him, then slapping the legs of his jeans.

Journey rolled, gripping the bat, and came up in a crouch.

"I'll kill him," the man said, his voice low and calm. "He wasn't part of my assignment, but I *will* kill him if you don't drop the bat."

Tolman crawled out of the van, the SIG snapping upward.

"And you drop the weapon," the man said. He hadn't moved a muscle. "This boy dies right now if you don't drop it. Butt first, and throw it out to your right, toward the parking lot. Do it now."

Tolman tossed the SIG into the darkness.

"Let him go," Journey said. He took a step forward, the bat tight in his left hand. "He has severe autism. He's nonverbal. He doesn't understand what's happening."

"You don't get it," the man said. "See, I have a job to do."

"I bet you do," Tolman said. "Who sent you? The woman in the cemetery? Tall woman, midforties, refined voice?"

"I don't know what you're talking about," the man said. He pulled back the hammer on his weapon. It hadn't moved from the side of Andrew's head.

Journey hadn't prayed in thirty years, but he thought, *Dear God, Dear God,* over and over again, and then he didn't know what else to think. He thought of the cross Sandra Kelly always wore. *Give me strength,* he thought, and opened his eyes.

He stamped his foot and shouted "Andrew!" in a sharp voice.

"Keep your fucking voice down," the man said. "And you better drop that fucking bat."

He's cursing now, Journey thought. *He's starting to feel rattled. Good.*

"Andrew!" Journey said, his voice rising to a shout.

Andrew stamped his foot.

"Hey!" the man shouted.

"Nick, your tone of voice," Tolman whispered. "But he'll—"

"Yes," Journey said, and made his voice as angry as he could. "Andrew, look at me!"

A light went on in the building next door, behind them.

"Drop the bat," the man said.

Andrew emitted a low, throaty voice and spat toward his father.

"What the fuck—," the man said.

Andrew reached up, grabbed the hand holding his neck, and raked his fingernails down the man's arm.

The man jumped and the hand holding Andrew moved. He looked down, his grip on the gun loosened for a split second. Andrew spat again.

As soon as the assassin cut his eyes downward to Andrew, Journey moved. He saw Andrew spitting, reaching up to scratch the man again, and the gun, an inch or two from where it had been. He would only have an instant.

Journey sprang forward, circling toward the side away from Andrew. The assassin saw the movement.

"Don't—," he said, and his gun hand came up again.

Journey swung the bat, crashing it into the assassin's kneecap. He heard the bone crunch.

The man grunted. His knee buckled, but he didn't fall. But his grip on Andrew loosened further.

Andrew stamped both feet, raked the man's arm with his nails again, and spun away from him. Behind him, Tolman broke into a run, grabbed Andrew around the waist—even though he was nine inches taller than she—and wrestled him to the ground. She covered his body with her own.

Journey raised the bat and aimed it at the crook of the assassin's arm. Wood connected with bone and the gun flipped out of the man's hand. Journey swung again, breaking the elbow, then went for the knee again. The man grunted and his legs went out from under him.

"What's going on out there?" a woman's voice shouted, from the building to the north of the old radio station.

"Call the police!" Tolman shouted.

Journey rammed his knee into the man's chest and poked the barrel of the bat against his eye. "So help me God," Journey said, his voice shaking, "give me one good reason not to beat your brains in. You sorry son of a bitch. He's a child!"

"Fuck you," the man whispered. "They'll send someone else, you know. You're dead, both of you. When they want someone dead, they're dead."

"You shouldn't have touched my son," Journey said, and he realized tears were streaming down his face, mingling with the blood from the cut on his forehead. He swung the bat and broke the man's other kneecap.

"Nick!" Tolman screamed.

"You don't know me very well," Journey said.

"Nick!" Tolman screamed again.

Andrew shrieked. Journey heard sirens.

"Don't kill him, Nick!" Tolman said, rolling off Andrew and helping the boy to his feet. "He can talk!"

"I don't know anything," the man said. "They don't tell us anything. You're nothing to me. You're an assignment."

Two Marshall County sheriff's units arrived, an ambulance close behind. One of the deputies was Scott Parsons, whose younger brother had died last year coming to Journey's aid. "Professor Journey?" he drawled.

"He tried to kill us," Journey said. "He had a gun to Andrew's head."

"Where's your boy?" Parsons asked.

"Over here," Tolman said. "He's safe."

"Is that Meg Tolman?" Parsons said. "Well, this is a fine little reunion, isn't it?"

Andrew shrieked again. Journey stood and watched as the paramedics tended to the assassin. "He tried to kill us," Journey said again.

"All right, Professor," Parsons said. "You stay over there. We're going to sort this out."

More deputies arrived on the scene. Journey dropped the bat and ran to Andrew. He lowered his voice and threw his arms around his son. Andrew spat on his father's arm, but then the aggression seemed to drain out of him. "It's okay," Journey said. "You're okay."

"Damn," Tolman said. "You surprise me more all the time. You've got balls of solid rock."

"He shouldn't have touched Andrew," Journey said.

CHAPTER
23

Journey and Tolman and the woman next door gave statements to Deputy Parsons. The assassin, whose New York driver's license identified him as Matthew Jackson, was transported to the Madill hospital, then transferred to the trauma center at Medical Center of Southeastern Oklahoma in Durant. Journey called Sandra, and she met them at the hospital in Madill, staying with Andrew while Journey and Tolman were treated for cuts and lacerations.

In the front lobby of Integris Marshall County Medical Center, standing beside the darkened gift shop while Andrew high-stepped and vocalized, Tolman held up one hand and said, "I need to make a call."

With small bandages on her arm and one on her cheek, she walked out the automatic doors and into the hot August night. Andrew clung to his father's arm. Sandra watched Tolman go.

"You like to show a girl a good time," Sandra said. "And I thought you were only picking her up at the airport."

"So did I," Journey said.

Sandra took his hand and they walked through the doors, Andrew following. Tolman was coming toward them. "I pulled a little RIO muscle and have ordered our friend Mr. Jackson to be taken into federal custody. Two deputy U.S. marshals are on their way from Oklahoma City. They'll be with him round the clock in the hospital, then when he's well enough to travel, he'll go into a federal lockup."

"You can do that?" Sandra said.

"It appears I can." Tolman smiled. "This is actually the first time I've ever done anything like that. Being deputy director has its advantages after all." The smile faded. "Nick, I also called Darrell Sharp. Remember him?"

"He's hard to forget," Journey said.

"Who's this?" Sandra asked.

"A friend of mine," Tolman said. "We went to the Academy together. Toughest man I know. He was a deputy U.S. marshal and walked into a bloodbath on his very first assignment a few years ago. Eight people died, and he was the only one left standing. Now he lives by himself in the middle of nowhere in Arkansas."

"Why did you call him?" Journey asked.

"I talked him into coming here and providing some protection for you and Andrew."

Journey was silent.

"Come on, Nick," Tolman said. "Accepting some help from a professional doesn't mean you can't take care of Andrew. It means some extra muscle until this thing is over. That's all."

Journey said nothing.

"Nick," Tolman said, not bothering to hide her exasperation. "Dammit all to hell. You were right. Something happened, and I'm the one who talked you into coming and bringing Andrew. Do you get that, Nick? I convinced you to bring your child into a situation where all of us could have been killed."

"But—"

"No, not *but*!" Tolman shouted. "As long as we are in this, you are going to have security for you and Andrew. That is not negotiable. Darrell may be on disability retirement, but he will be well armed, and he is well trained, and once he gets here, I don't want the two of you out of his sight. I don't know where all this is going to take us, and I also know how you feel about other people watching Andrew. The solution is to make goddamn sure that both of you are protected."

"Meg—"

"*Not* negotiable. If you want to look at it as being for *my* peace of mind, that's fine. But he's coming, and he's your bodyguard."

"Just for the record, that last one wasn't a protest," Journey said. "You're right. We might not see them coming the next time. But I thought Darrell never left his house."

"He will for me," Tolman said.

Sandra looked at her.

"It's complicated," Tolman said. "Darrell said he'd leave within the hour. His place in Arkansas is about four and a half hours from here. He'll be here early in the morning." She glanced at Sandra again. "He has PTSD and severe depression. Give him plenty of space and don't expect him to say much, but he'll have our backs."

Journey's van had been towed, and Sandra drove them to Carpenter Center in her VW Beetle, with Tolman and Andrew wedged into the backseat. At home, Journey gave Andrew a shower and put the boy immediately to bed. Journey thought his son was asleep before he closed the bedroom door. He set Tolman up in the guest room and walked Sandra to the door.

"Another woman sleeping in your house," Sandra said. "Do I get to be jealous?"

Journey looked hard at her. "Meg? No, she's—"

"I'm kidding," Sandra said. "Don't be so serious, Nick. I'm not a possessive person. And besides, I'm not sure what we have to be possessive of at this point."

She reads me so well, Journey thought. *Better than Amelia ever did. Better than anyone, better than . . .*

Meg Tolman.

Journey still had a dull ache in his head from where he'd hit the steering wheel. For an instant the two women were jumbled in his mind. Then his thoughts cleared and he focused on the tall woman with the red hair and the green eyes that always seemed slightly amused. He looked at the little silver cross around her neck.

Journey pulled her to him and kissed her hard on the mouth.

When he let her go, she was gasping. "My God," she whispered. She traced her hand along his cheek, his jawline, his neck.

"Thank you," he said.

"For what?"

"Just . . . thank you."

"Okay. That's good enough." She turned around and walked quickly to the VW. In a moment she was gone.

Journey turned toward the house. Tolman was standing in the middle of the living room. She winked at him. "Good for you," she said, then walked down the hall toward the guest bedroom.

Of course, Journey couldn't sleep, thinking of the words of "Matthew Jackson": *They'll send someone else, you know.*

He kept the bat within reach and settled in at the computer in the living room, even though it was 1:30 in the morning. He scrolled through a few e-mails, responded to a few students, a few colleagues. Anything to occupy his mind.

Then he thought about the morning—had that only been a few hours ago, downtown on the square, when he'd spotted Amelia coming out of the bank? He remembered what she'd said, and the name of the place.

Grace of Oklahoma.

He typed the words into Google and waited. When the search results settled onto the screen, all Journey saw was Andrew, in the faint headlights by the side of the highway, a gun pressed to his head.

I don't know the right thing to do. I'm bluffing . . . I have everyone fooled into thinking I'm this great, caring father of a child with a disability . . . but I don't have a clue.

The thoughts weren't new. He had some variation of the same thought every day of Andrew's life. And yet, every day he and Andrew survived.

Would a facility like Grace really be best for him? At least for a while? Would it give Andrew—and me—tools to help face the rest of his adolescence, as he grows toward adulthood?

Or, Journey wondered, *does it mean I'm not the parent I think I am, or should be?*

I don't know.

He clicked one of the links, and Journey began to read about Grace of Oklahoma.

* * *

He left the computer on and fell into the recliner beside it, then jerked awake to a tapping sound. He pressed the button on the luminescent dial of his watch: 5:36 A.M., and someone was at the front door.

He wrapped both his hands around the handle of the bat, but thought, *Do assassins knock?*

Journey peered through the three glass rectangles cut into the top of his front door and saw the brooding form of Darrell Sharp on his porch, the porch light glinting off his shaven head. Tolman, barefoot but otherwise still dressed, came around the corner, her SIG in her hand.

"Sharp," Journey said, and opened the door.

"Darrell," he said. He started to put out his hand, then remembered that the big man didn't shake hands.

Sharp glanced at him and Journey stepped aside.

"Hey," Tolman said.

"Hey," Sharp said in a Deep South accent, dropping his backpack and small overnight bag beside the door. "Came as quick as I could."

"You made good time."

Sharp shrugged. Journey could see his eyes wandering over the room, checking corners. "Thanks for coming," Journey said.

Sharp nodded.

"You can put your things in the guest bedroom," Tolman said. She glanced at Journey as she spoke. "What did you bring?"

"Brought all I need," Sharp drawled, his mustache twitching a bit.

Tolman smiled. "I believe you."

For the first time in at least five years, Andrew slept well past eight o'clock. Tolman made coffee for Sharp and they sat at the dining room table while she briefed him on the situation. Journey was helping Andrew get dressed when he heard the door. No subtle tapping this time. It was a loud and insistent pounding.

Three uniformed officers stood on the front porch. Two were Carpenter Center policemen, and the other was Deputy Scott Parsons.

"Aren't you off shift yet?" Journey asked Parsons.

"Just went off," the deputy said. "You have a minute, Dr. Journey?"

"Come in," Journey said.

Andrew came into the room, whistling. He stopped short when he saw all the unfamiliar people. He made a vaguely interrogative sound, then turned and went back into his room.

Sharp stood up. Tolman laid a hand over his forearm.

The older of the two Carpenter Center cops was named Poteet. The younger was Natale. Journey knew his family—the young cop's father and uncle ran the Italian restaurant where he and Sandra had had dinner two nights ago. His eyes took in the room.

Journey followed him. "Officer, this is Meg Tolman, from Washington. I work with her on consulting projects from time to time. This is her friend Darrell Sharp. He's here to help us out a bit."

Poteet looked from the others to Journey. "A few questions, sir?" he asked.

"This is about last night?" Journey said. "We were outside of Madill, not in Carpenter Center. Wouldn't it be the Sheriff's Department's jurisdiction?"

"It's about last night, but not what you think," Parsons said.

"What?"

"Dr. Journey, you know Dr. Lashley. He's a history professor, too. Professor Graham Lashley."

"Of course I know him. I saw him on Friday."

"Yes, sir," Poteet said. "That's why we're here. Dr. Lashley was shot and killed in his home last night."

CHAPTER

24

W hat?" Journey said.

"Oh, shit," Tolman said.

Journey looked at all three officers. Natale, the young one, stood behind his partner, arms folded. Parsons leaned against the wall, eyes locked on Journey.

"Sometime last night, best guess between ten P.M. and two A.M., someone broke into Dr. Lashley's house," Poteet said. "It's about three blocks from here. He was shot in the head. If this were a movie, they'd call it 'execution style.' Know what I mean?"

Journey looked up at Scott Parsons. The deputy shrugged.

"We've heard that you've had a couple of run-ins with Dr. Lashley in the last few days," Poteet said.

"You can't be serious," Journey said.

"How about it, Professor?" Poteet said. "You had an argument with him over at Uncle Charley's, and then people in the campus library heard you two arguing again on Friday night. Threatened to kick his ass, did you?"

"This is bullshit," Tolman said.

Journey held up a hand. "No, Meg, I'll handle this. I was with Meg from about four o'clock on yesterday. We were in Norman. As we were coming into Madill on the way here, *we* were attacked." He looked at Tolman. "They sent someone after Lashley, too. Somehow they found out we talked to him."

"Scott here has shown me his report," Poteet said coolly. "I see what happened to you over at Madill. What time did you get home?"

"About one o'clock," Journey said. "You can't seriously think that I—"

"It's a murder investigation, Professor, and you had two very public disagreements with Dr. Lashley. What was that about? Some big historical find, is that right?"

Tolman handed the officers her ID. "Officer, we're working on a case, and in the course of that case, we've been attacked. I can guarantee you, the people who came after us also went after Dr. Lashley."

Poteet looked Tolman up and down, examined her ID, and glanced at Journey again. "Banged you up a little last night, did they?"

"A bit."

"You'll want to stay close, Dr. Journey," the officer said. "You don't happen to own a gun, do you?"

"I've never fired a gun in my life," Journey said. "I don't even *like* guns."

"Uh-huh." Poteet looked at Tolman's card. "Research and Investigations Office. Deputy director. Well, that's good to know, I suppose."

Tolman started to say something, but Journey cut her off. "My whereabouts are accounted for. Deputy Parsons can vouch for that."

"Oh, we read Scotty's report this morning. Took a baseball bat to the guy who attacked your son, did you?"

Journey stiffened.

"I don't have any kids," Natale said, "but I have a little niece. Someone grabbed her and put a gun to her head, I'd break a few bones, too."

Journey said nothing.

"Officer Poteet, are you finished here?" Tolman said.

"Research and Investigations Office," Poteet said, looking at the card again. "Interesting. I've never heard of it."

"Now you have," Tolman said.

"We'll be in touch," Poteet said.

Journey looked at Parsons, and the three officers left. From the porch, Parsons called, "There's a package on your porch, Dr. Journey. I almost tripped on it."

Tolman pulled out her phone.

"What are you doing?" Journey asked.

"Getting protection called in for Melissa and Alex Cable. If they know we talked to Lashley, if they tracked us last night, then the odds are they know we were in Norman yesterday. I'm not going to be responsible for the death of another Cable."

Journey opened the screen door, watching the three officers go to their cars. He looked down and saw the box to the left of the door. It had been sent from a mailing service in Big Rapids, Michigan, shipped UPS overnight on Friday. It must have come when he was in Norman yesterday, and he hadn't noticed it on the darkened porch when they all finally returned to the house a few hours ago.

Michigan? he thought.

There was no telling. He received textbooks for review all the time, both at home and the office. He took the package into the living room. Andrew was sitting on the couch with a puzzle, humming. Tolman was still on the phone. Sharp hovered behind her. Journey noticed for the first time that Sharp was actually wearing a gun in a holster on his hip.

I'm a suspect in Graham Lashley's murder, he thought. *The man may have been unpleasant to work with . . . but he was killed because he talked to me.*

Journey's head began to throb. He started to open the box, slitting the tape with a box knife from his desk drawer.

"Don't know if I'd do that," Sharp said.

Journey stopped cutting. "What?"

With his long arms, Sharp reached between Journey and the table and picked up the box.

"What are you doing?" Journey said.

Sharp said nothing, carrying the box out of the house and into the front yard. Tolman had been on the phone, and she followed Sharp. Journey looked at Andrew, and his son hooted.

"I don't know," Journey said. "Let's go see." He took Andrew's hand and they walked to the door.

Tolman had just reached Sharp and the box. He'd placed it on the ground in the center of the open space in the front yard. "Meg, you go back," Sharp said in a very soft voice.

"Darrell, I can—," Tolman started.

Sharp shook his head.

Tolman opened her mouth to say something else, but Sharp shook his head again, looking directly at Tolman. She raised both hands, palms out, and backed onto the porch.

"What's all this?" Journey asked.

"Nick, someone tried to kill us last night, and that package is addressed to you. Who knows what could be in it?"

Journey rubbed the back of his neck. Andrew whistled. "I never thought—"

"Yeah, Darrell's smarter than the two of us combined," Tolman said.

"It's probably just a book. I get them all the time."

"Probably. You want to gamble on that?" She looked pointedly at Andrew.

Journey followed the look. He squeezed his son's hand and Andrew squeezed back. "But what about Darrell? If it's something—"

"You don't argue with him about things like this. He knows what he's doing."

Journey said nothing, watching Sharp touch all sides of the box, his big hands moving delicately, almost tenderly. He hefted it, seemed to be weighing it.

"Looks like it's pretty light," Tolman said. "That's a good sign."

Sharp put the box carefully on the ground again, then began to open it, running his hands along the slits Journey had already made.

Journey found he was holding his breath. He let it out slowly when Sharp pulled out some bubble wrap with one piece of paper taped to the outside, and another sheet inside the wrap.

"Paper," Sharp said. "All clear." He brought the box and its contents back to the porch.

"Thanks, Darrell," Tolman said.

Sharp shrugged and moved past them into the house. Journey watched him go, then looked at the note taped to the top of the bubble wrap. In beautiful, flowing, feminine cursive was written:

*Dr. Journey, please call as soon as you have examined this
package's contents.*

A phone number followed, area code 773. Journey took the package back in the house and slid the bubble wrap out onto the kitchen table. Very carefully, he undid the tape, laid the wrap open, and looked at the paper inside.

It was a map.

"What—," Journey said, and the sentence died in his throat.

"Nick?" Tolman said.

The map was of the western part of Texas. Journey recognized the distinctive shape, from El Paso all the way up to the Panhandle. The paper was very old, and it had been well preserved. There were no modern landmarks, but rivers and mountains had been carefully drawn.

Journey's eyes went to the area near the top, the modern-day Texas Panhandle. Roughly southeast of where Amarillo would be today, something had been drawn over the original printed map.

A cross.

The bottom of the cross was squarely in the center of a river. The two arms reached out along tiny, jagged lines that Journey assumed were creeks, little tributaries of the river. The top of the cross extended farther along the larger river.

Written in black, in a heavy hand, as if by an old-fashioned quill pen, to the left of the top of the cross, were the words *La Croix d'Argent*.

Journey's French wasn't good, but he didn't need a translator for this.

"The Silver Cross."

CHAPTER
25

It had been several years since Gray last stayed in the Hay-Adams, Washington's famous hotel in Lafayette Square, across the street from the White House. She rarely allowed herself such opulent surroundings, preferring to remain carefully anonymous. But for this trip, she felt like treating herself. She was dealing with The Associates on several fronts, and the pugnacious and dangerous Mr. Zale would soon find himself a great deal more uncomfortable than he was now.

When the cell phone rang, she knew the call was from Nick Journey. She'd programmed a special ring for it, and this was the only call for which she would use this phone. "Hello, Dr. Journey," she said on answering it.

"Who is this?"

"You may call me Ann Gray for the purposes of this call. I trust you are well."

"Well? We were almost killed last night. Is that your doing?"

"Certainly not. Are you all right? Is Ms. Tolman with you?"

"We're all right, but—"

"And your son? He wasn't hurt?"

"Leave him out of it."

"I wasn't responsible for the attempt on your life last night, Dr.

Journey. You must trust me on that point. The people who came after you have no sense of morals at all. But your son—is he all right? I know about his condition."

"Do you? I guess that shouldn't surprise me. If you didn't do it, who did?"

"I suspect you will know that soon enough," Gray said. "Did you see the map?"

"I did. Why did you send this to me? Are you the same person who gave Meg that letter in Missouri?"

Gray smiled. "You're a scholar and your questions are legitimate. I've read some of your journal articles, by the way. You write well, and have a fine understanding of your subject."

"Don't patronize me, Ann Gray."

"I assure you, I would not be so rude. My feelings are sincere. But I do understand your frustration, and I am as frustrated as you are. The same people tried to kill me in the last few days as well."

"I don't understand this," Journey said. "Who are you?"

"A manager. A problem solver. Someone who likes an interesting challenge here and there. What do you think of the map?"

Journey was quiet for a moment. "The Silver Cross isn't some artifact that Napoleon III wanted as a symbol of his invasion of Mexico. It's a place in Texas, a place Father Fournier saw and wrote about in 1863."

"Indeed."

"What is out there? There's not much in that part of Texas."

"Indeed," Gray said again. "You have all you need to find everything you need to find. Can you put Meg Tolman on the phone, please?"

Words were exchanged, then a female voice: "Meg Tolman. Who's this?"

"As I told Dr. Journey, I believe that you have everything you need. I can't protect you, though—my resources are spread rather thin at the moment. But I understand you are quite capable, Ms. Tolman."

"What kind of bullshit is this?"

"Capable, but rather foul-mouthed. That notwithstanding, I'm sorry we didn't have more of a chance to chat in Cassville."

"Who shot at me?"

"Don't concern yourself with that. But do be on the lookout. I am doing all I can to bring the Silver Cross to light."

"What does it mean?"

"You have everything you need."

"Why don't you tell me?"

"I don't exist, Ms. Tolman. This will eventually all be public, out in the light for the world to see. But someone else will have to do that. I can facilitate others, but cannot stand in the light myself."

"Dammit, you're not making any sense."

"I am rather annoyed with some people who do business on behalf of the U.S. government."

"Yeah, well—"

"Please, Ms. Tolman, I don't want to see more bloodshed in Oklahoma."

"You killed Dana Cable. You lured her to North Carolina and killed her."

"No, I did not kill her." Gray sat down on the bed. "In fact, I was trying to correct an error. I tried to protect her, and I made another error. I'm trying to correct those mistakes now."

"And Jim Cable—you were sloppy there, too."

"I tried to stop his death as well. But as I've said, I must stay out of sight. Others will make the revelations. You will be the one to do it, I suspect, if you stay alive."

"Goddammit!"

"You should know that April 19 will free its brothers," Gray said. "The leader will not be silenced."

"But you're not—"

Gray pressed end, then turned off the phone and removed the battery. She would toss it in a dumpster when she left the hotel.

The Associates would pay. They were already paying . . . for the deaths of two of the three Cables, for the attempt on her life on the *S.S. Badger* . . . for the attempt last night on Nick Journey and Andrew Journey and Meg Tolman.

She thought of her own son, at the chess tournament in Ann Arbor. She called Rick, who told her that Joseph had won four of five games yesterday. He was in his first Sunday game now.

After she hung up the phone with her husband, she called Barrientos. "The second wave is tonight," she said. "Make sure the personnel and the equipment are ready."

She clicked off before Barrientos could reply. Gray found she was perspiring.

Control! she thought. She had never lost control in twenty-five years of living in this shadow world, of managing diverse operations for governments and corporations and individuals around the world.

Control.

She focused on her breathing and soon she was better. She left her room, walked out of the hotel, and hailed a taxi.

"To the French embassy," she told the driver.

France's embassy in the United States was not on the famed Embassy Row, but rather on Washington's Reservoir Road, north of the Georgetown University campus. It was not particularly impressive from the outside, a simple black and white office building set back from the road, with a guardhouse and automated traffic control arm blocking the entrance to the parking lot.

Gray directed the cab driver to the guardhouse, and the uniformed guard issued a visitor permit. The arm went up and the taxi entered sovereign French territory.

On the phone, Gray had been able to convince a deputy attaché for Commercial and Economic Affairs to meet her on Sunday morning, that she had something important to pass on to the French diplomatic mission. Robert Caron, the young deputy attaché, met Gray in the main lobby of the embassy.

"Anne Arceneaux," she said, using the name she'd given him on the phone and shaking his hand. "It's a lovely morning. Perhaps we could walk about your grounds," she added in perfect French.

"It is lovely," Caron said. "But the heat will be deadly in two hours or so."

Gray steered him outside and they walked among the landscaped grounds. "I have information of great importance for the French people," she said.

Caron acted as if he had heard it all before. "How may the embassy be of service?"

Gray handed an envelope to him. He shook out the photocopied papers and gave them a cursory glance, then looked at Gray.

"Should this not go to a historian or cultural expert?"

"One of these papers—the letter—sets out a rather significant historic statement. But the map . . ." Gray shook her head, as if in disbelief of it all. "The map concerns things more modern. And it was stolen from French soil."

Caron stopped walking.

"*Oui,*" Gray said. "From a church, no less. St. Pierre's in Montluçon, where it rested for many years."

"Stolen, you say?" Caron said. "From France? By whom?"

Gray gestured in a sweeping motion.

"Americans?" Caron said. He looked at the map again. "This is Texas, if I am not mistaken. Why was it in Montluçon?"

"I do not know all," Gray said. "I am only a messenger."

"How did you come to have these copies? Where are the originals?"

"You will want to take care to have the documents authenticated."

Caron watched her, rubbing the week's worth of blond stubble that covered his chin.

"You do not need to accept my word," Gray said. "You will do your due diligence and you will discover the importance of these two documents. The French people have been cheated, are still being cheated."

"You bring me photocopies and claim they are stolen from a church in France," the young diplomat said. "I do not know you. Nor do I know your interest. Why does an old map of Texas so interest you?"

"It does not interest me. But it interests the Americans. And it should interest France, especially in these difficult times. Goodbye, *monsieur.*"

Gray watched the man as she returned to the waiting taxi. He was young and sharp, and like so many men in their twenties, he was looking for some sort of break, some way to make a name for himself. She suspected he would be on the phone very soon. By the end of the day the letter and the map would be exactly where she wanted them.

As the cab left the embassy complex, the driver asked, "Back to your hotel?"

"No," Gray said. "Take me to the Capitol."

* * *

Ninety minutes later, Gray emerged from the Rayburn House Office Building. Instead of Ann Gray, she had been Diane Corbin, and affected a mild Southern accent.

Representative Delmas Mercer of Louisiana had been chosen carefully. He was a centrist, a true moderate, not an ideologue. But he was also a fierce Southern regionalist in Congress. Plus, his undergraduate degree was in history. Gray had done her homework.

She had laid out her proposal for Mercer, and at first he pointed the way to the door. But then he listened, and she grew more persuasive. When she placed the briefcase with three hundred thousand dollars in cash on his desk, he looked at her, nodded without saying a word, and put the case under his desk.

Gray knew why Mercer was a centrist. His vote was for sale—whichever lobbyist funneled the most cash his direction won his vote. Sometimes on the left, sometimes the right, with just enough of what remained of his real convictions thrown in to be convincing to the voters every two years. Mercer was a Southern partisan, educated in history, and as corrupt as they came.

He was perfect for her purposes.

And he would soon make more of a name for himself than he ever had as a back-bench House member in his previous eight terms. Delmas Mercer was about to be a household name, and The Associates would soon be no more. The United States was about to erupt—once again—into division and chaos. And, sadly, blood. But she had planned it well, and the bloodshed would be minimal. That is what separated Ann Gray from the likes of Victor Zale.

I wish it had not come to this, she thought, then asked the cab driver to take her back to the Hay-Adams. They would pass the White House on the way. Gray thought it quite appropriate.

As soon as the phone went dead in her hand, Tolman raced into the spare bedroom and grabbed her laptop. "Give me that paper with the phone number on it."

In fifteen minutes, she knew that the phone was a prepaid cell, purchased in suburban Chicago. "A throwaway. Chances are she's already disposed of it. What did she say her name was?"

"Ann Gray," Journey said. "What are you doing?"

"I'm doing a RACER search for Ann Gray," Tolman said. "With a name like that, it's going to pop up a million or so hits, and I suppose that's her point, using a name like that. I'll have to narrow the search. She told you that she's basically a freelance operator. Someone's heard of her, even if they've only heard the cover name. I'll do some cross-references." She worked the keyboard and thumb bar and set RACER to work, then looked up at Journey. She pointed at the map. "So tell me about that. Napoleon III wanted . . . what? A spot in the middle of nowhere in Texas?"

Journey ran a hand along the map's parchment. "Again, religious symbolism or geographic reality? It's impossible to tell—"

"Without seeing it for ourselves," Tolman finished. "I get it. Can you pinpoint a location from that?"

"There are a lot of little rivers and creeks in West Texas. But using GIS, we should be able to get a fix on a modern location."

"GIS," Tolman said. "Geographic Information System. Why, Dr. Journey, I thought I was the technology person here."

Andrew giggled from the couch. He seemed completely unfazed by last night's ordeal. *A blessing of sorts,* Journey thought. "Don't get too excited," Journey said. "The geography department uses it. I can call—" He reached for the phone, then put his hand down.

"What?" Tolman said.

"Lashley." Journey met Tolman's blue eyes. "Someone murdered Graham Lashley in cold blood, and why? Because we talked to him about this."

"I know, you don't want to put another professor in danger. I get it, Nick. But whatever all this is, it starts with the Silver Cross. The woman on the phone was talking in circles, but she said we had everything we needed." Tolman thumped her fingers on the table. Andrew looked up at her, then thumped his own fingers. "She said she didn't want to see any more bloodshed in Oklahoma. But she also said she didn't kill Jim or Dana. Said she'd made mistakes, tried to prevent their deaths."

"But not Barry," Journey said.

Tolman stared at him. "That's right. But April 19 killed Barry. That's never been in dispute."

"The dispute is what April 19 really means."

Tolman nodded. "Nick, I'm not going to put anyone else in danger." She glanced at Andrew. "There's been enough of that already."

Journey looked at her for a long moment, then touched the map. "I'm going to find where the Silver Cross is located. By lunch if possible."

"I like the way you think, Professor."

Andrew thumped his feet on the wood floor. Tolman thumped hers in response, then returned to her computer.

Kerry Voss had tried every door, both front and back, to trace the financing of April 19, and when she woke up Sunday morning, she still knew nothing. As an organization, April 19 simply had no money trail. Clearly, the organization existed. It had carried out the shooting at the GAO, and its four operatives were in prison. She'd read something about them a few days ago, before the latest round of bombings, about how they were being moved to a different facility.

Now they were taking credit for the bombings. They *had* to have money behind them.

Voss sat at her breakfast bar, still stained with purple crayon from where her youngest son had tried to scribble his name a few days ago. The house was quiet—her three kids were with her ex-husband for the weekend. *Too quiet.* She flipped on the TV, then turned it off just as quickly. Images of Albuquerque, Kansas City, and Cleveland filled every channel, with the occasional story about "Left vs. Right in Middle America," hordes of protesters and counterprotesters arriving in Chicago. There was nothing new, so the pundits had taken over, and as usual, the pundits knew nothing and used a lot of words to say so. Some of them drew parallels between the April 19 bombings and the dueling protests that were unfolding in Chicago. Voss opened her first Diet Coke of the day and ate a banana.

April 19. She thought about what she *knew* of the group. Not speculation, not supposition, but what was actually known.

Antigovernment ideology. A fanatical reverence for the Oklahoma City bombers. A willingness to use extreme violence.

And there were four men, now in prison.

Four men.

No others had been identified. No one came forward to claim leadership of the group after these four were convicted and sentenced. The e-mails two nights ago to media outlets after the federal buildings were bombed came from anonymous servers. There were no names.

Except four.

Almost spilling her Diet Coke, Voss ran into her bedroom and dressed quickly. She jammed a baseball cap on her head, not even brushing her hair. She didn't put on makeup or her contacts—just put on her glasses and ran. She almost went out without a bra, but thought better of that one. She had to get to the office.

Sunday morning traffic was light, and she was in the RIO office in less than twenty minutes. She turned up Rush's *Moving Pictures* album as loud as she dared and logged on to her computer.

Maybe April 19 was so loosely organized that they had no bank accounts—or maybe as part of their ideology they didn't believe in banks—but here were four men who had carried out the shootings in Rockville. At least one of them must have had a job at some point. If she couldn't find the organization, she would at least find its four most famous members.

She pulled up the names: Jeremy Rayburn, thirty-one, Spokane, Washington, an unemployed sheet metal worker; Logan Hampton, thirty-three, unemployed medical technologist from Mobile, Alabama; David Phipps, twenty-five, self-employed auto mechanic from Vermilion, South Dakota; and Douglas Clay, thirty-eight, unemployed print shop worker from Staunton, Virginia.

She started with the bank records of David Phipps, the only one to have a recent verifiable income. Nothing extraordinary—the guy barely scraped by. She accessed his tax returns from the last three years. He never made more than twenty thousand dollars in a year.

Hampton and Clay had no unusual bank activity. Clay had received unemployment benefits. Voss wondered how he squared that with his antigovernment message.

When she found the bank records for self-appointed April 19 spokesman Jeremy Rayburn, she saw nothing unusual in the account at his hometown bank. But she found something else with his Social Security number: an account at a large regional bank based in Seattle.

Voss leaned forward. When looking at lines of numbers on computer screens, she often found herself actually touching the screen, tracing the lines. She adjusted her glasses and ran her finger across the screen.

Rush's "Tom Sawyer" was throbbing in her ears as she looked at Rayburn's Seattle account. It had been opened on April 12, one week before Rockville. It showed an opening deposit of fifty dollars.

Two days later, on April 14, Rayburn received an electronic funds transfer of two hundred fifty thousand dollars.

A quarter of a million dollars for a sheet metal worker without a job.

There had been no further activity on the account.

Voss's heart pounded. She began moving her mouse.

Where did you come from, quarter million? she thought.

She isolated the transaction number with the Seattle bank, then started the backward trace. She worried that she'd run in to an off-shore account. She wouldn't be able to track it if that were the case—that exceeded RIO's legal mandate. Of course, she had a hacker on retainer who could find such things if needed. Unofficially.

The trace stopped at a number. Voss breathed a sigh of relief. A domestic account, at least. But that was where the trail went cold. A series of firewalls stopped her from going further, and she was left with only the number. The account was probably in a private bank somewhere. She would need more paperwork completed—not to mention an order by a federal court—to do anything else in official channels.

She didn't know who owned the account, but she could get a sense of what else the account was doing. She asked the computer to do a search for other transactions originating with the numbered account. She'd traced the payment to Jeremy Rayburn backward from the recipient. Now she was going the other direction, starting from the originating account to see where its funds were sent.

The search went to five minutes, then ten. Voss took off the baseball cap and smoothed her hair. The screen flickered, then the results settled onto it.

The bank account that had paid Jeremy Rayburn had transferred funds into accounts at various banks around the country. All were in the names of anonymous-sounding business entities—Midwest Enterprises, Affiliated Distribution Systems, Western Data. All but one.

Another numbered account. Voss clicked the number.

Nothing happened.

She traced her finger along the screen again. The first set of numbers was familiar. She'd seen it many times. Voss worked with accounts having the same prefix on a daily basis. But the number was incomplete. The last seven-digit sequence was grayed out.

Voss reached over and turned off the music in midchord. Rush fell silent.

She reached for the phone and called Meg Tolman. "Meg? It's Kerry. Did I wake you?"

"Trust me, Kerry, you didn't wake me," Tolman said. "What's up?"

"The April 19 money," Voss said, still staring at her monitor.

"What about it?"

"There is none."

"What?"

Voss explained, then detailed how she'd traced Rayburn's deposit backward.

"But you can't find out who owns the account," Tolman said.

"Not yet, but I—"

She blinked at the screen. Her cursor had moved, ever so slightly.

Voss's right hand, the one nearest the mouse, was holding the phone. Her left hand was on the other side of her keyboard. She couldn't have bumped the mouse by accident.

"Kerry?" Tolman said.

Voss blinked. The cursor was still.

Overactive imagination, Voss thought.

"This account," she said, "the one that's being fed by the account that paid Rayburn—"

She cradled the phone against her shoulder and put her hand on the mouse. The cursor jumped before she could move it.

"Dear God," she said.

"What's the matter, Kerry?"

"Someone's in our system, Meg. My cursor—someone knows I'm looking at this, and is tracking me live right now."

"Shit," Tolman said. "Get out of there, Kerry. Leave the building. Don't go home."

"But the kids," Voss said, rolling her chair away from the desk. "They're coming back from their dad's at six o'clock. I—"

"Kerry, listen to me. Leave . . . the . . . building. Go to my dad's. You remember the address? He'll be able to help you. Just get out of there. You're on a RIO line, right? Hang it up and call me from your cell when you're out of the building."

Voss had an image of her cell phone, on the breakfast bar in her house, right beside the Diet Coke can she had almost spilled. "My cell . . . I left it at home. I had this idea, and I ran out of the house—"

"Okay, Kerry, okay," Tolman said. "Get out. I'll call my dad."

"I'm going . . . ."

"The account," Tolman said. "What is it?"

"It's us," Voss said.

"What the hell do you mean, it's us?"

"It's a federal government account. I recognize the number sequence."

"Oh Jesus, Kerry," Tolman said. "What department? Can you tell what department? Where does it go?"

"The last numbers are grayed out. But I've seen that before. That means it's a black account, off the books, off budget." Voss jumped, as she heard the front door to the RIO suite rattling. Thank God she'd locked herself in when she came into the office. "Meg, the door. The door to our—"

"Go, go, go! Go down the corridor by the break room, and out that emergency exit. It opens onto the back stairs."

Voss threw the phone in the cradle and ran.

The door thumped once, twice. She bit her lip and sprinted for the corridor. The lights were off and she caromed off the wall twice before finding the exit sign. Voss crashed through the door and into a tiny alcove with concrete flooring, hearing the RIO door splintering open somewhere behind her.

She pushed open the second door and onto the stairs, moving quickly, silently, thankful for all the times she'd tortured herself at the gym. Four floors below, she emerged from the stairwell behind the building's main elevator bank. She heard footsteps, both above her and from the other side of the elevator in the lobby.

Voss spun away from the elevators and out a glass door, into the bright sunshine. The back door of the building opened onto an alley, with the expected dumpsters. She turned right and ran for the parking lot. At the edge of the building, she stopped, scanning the lot. It was almost empty—there was a small SUV that she thought belonged to a lawyer who officed on the second floor, a couple of old pickup trucks that always seemed to be there, and her red Nissan Altima. Otherwise, the lot was Sunday-morning empty.

Voss ran. *But the kids . . .*

She would have to call her ex from Ray Tolman's house. He would understand. He had to. The kids would be okay to stay with him until—until *what?*

She made it to the Altima and reached into her pocket, then dropped her keys on the pavement.

The footsteps came from nowhere, everywhere, the other side of her car, behind her . . .

Then hands were grabbing her, the hands of a strong, muscular man.

"Easy," he said. "Don't fight. That just pisses me off."

"No!" Voss screamed, and the big man clapped a hand over her mouth.

"All the smart people are either asleep or off praying somewhere," said the man. "You should have stayed in bed."

A car pulled alongside, a black SUV, larger than the one that belonged to the second-floor lawyer. Voss struggled, but the man was at least a foot taller than she. He tossed her into the back of the SUV as if she were a sack of flour, then put his weight on top of her. Her head rested against the car door.

A door slammed. "Go!" the man said, and the engine accelerated.

Voss started to struggle, to crane her neck and see out the SUV's window.

"No, no," said the man on top of her.

Voss kept moving.

Then the man's fist crashed into the side of her head. "I don't get off on hitting women," he said, "but I've got a job to do, and you better be still and be quiet."

Voss felt nauseous. "Who hired you?" she managed to say.

The fist rained down again, this time in her eye. The pain bloomed bright and hot and hard.

"Where are you taking me?"

This time, the blow was on her cheek.

"Don't be stupid," the man said. "You won't be so pretty with your face all rearranged."

The kids, Voss thought. *The kids are coming back tonight.*

Voss fell silent, resting her head against the seat, no longer trying to see outside. The man loosened his grip, but she was still pinned. "Better," he said.

She blinked. Even that simple action hurt. The eye was beginning to swell already. But Voss's mind wouldn't stop racing. The anonymous account had paid terrorist Jeremy Rayburn. It had also paid large sums of money to a federal government account. A "black" account. Money that didn't really exist. But Voss knew that money had to sit somewhere, and while it was sitting there, she could track it. Unless it was tens and twenties stuffed under someone's bed—and clearly it wasn't—she could track anything.

No, I can't. I'm in this SUV with a swollen eye, probably a broken cheekbone, and my face hurts like hell. I can't do anything. I don't even know if I'll be alive in another hour.

The kids, she thought, jumbled up with *seven more numbers . . .*

The two thoughts ran together. A plan began to form in Voss's mind.

"S hit!" Tolman shouted. *"Shit, shit, shit!"*

She arched her arm as if she were going to throw her phone across the dining room table. Andrew stopped whistling in midnote and glared at her. She pushed her chair away and turned her back to him. He spat in her direction.

"Andrew," Journey said, keeping his voice down. He glanced at Tolman. "Remember . . ."

"Sorry," she muttered, walking in long strides across the living room, throwing open the front door, and stepping onto the porch. Sharp followed.

"Shit," she said again when he joined her.

"What?" Sharp said.

"Kerry. They tapped into RIO's network somehow. They saw what she was doing—"

"Who?"

"Kerry Voss, my financial analyst." Tolman paced the length of the long porch. "She said the money went out of an account to the April 19 leader, but also into a government account. An off-the-books account. A nonexistent account."

Sharp said nothing. The screen door opened and Journey and

Andrew came out. Journey pointed and his son sat in a lawn chair with soccer balls emblazoned across it. Tolman looked at him. "If these people, whoever they are, can get into RIO's network, they can do a hell of a lot of damage."

"Not to mention three buildings blown up at the same time," Journey said.

"I'm thinking we need to go to West Texas," Tolman said, meeting his eyes.

"You're getting ahead of yourself. There's a lot of space in the Texas Panhandle, and in most of it, there's nothing there. We have to get a clear picture of where it is. Otherwise we're wasting our time."

"Can you access GIS from the college?"

"The Geography Department. But I don't have keys—"

"They'll let you in," Tolman said. "Make arrangements for Andrew. We have to get out of here. I wonder if Kerry made it to Dad's yet." She pulled out her phone. "Dad?" she said when her father answered. "I'm sending a friend to your house."

"What? What's going on?" Ray Tolman said.

"No time, Dad. You remember Kerry Voss? She came over to dinner a few times."

"I remember. The short one with the Big Bird tattoo and all the kids. What's wrong?"

"She's in trouble and needs a safe place. I'll explain later."

"I'll be ready," Ray Tolman said, and clicked off.

Her dad was a pro. He didn't ask questions when there was no time for questions.

"We should get our things and go," Tolman said. "First the college, then we plan the next step."

"What's in Texas?" Sharp asked.

"The Silver Cross," Journey said. "And that links the past with the present."

"We hope," Tolman said.

"We hope," Journey echoed.

Half an hour later, as they were piling bags into Sharp's Jeep, Ray Tolman called. "She's not here, Meg," he said.

Tolman closed her eyes and leaned against the Jeep. "My office building," she said. "There was someone there. Take your weapon. And backup. Can you call your friend Pat Moore from the Bureau? Does he have a line into Hostage Rescue at Quantico?"

"I'll call him," her father said. "Pat can get whatever we need. Your friend's a federal employee with ties to DOJ, so it'll be a priority. And I'm guessing that I'll be feeding the cat for a few more days."

"You better not let Rocky starve. Sit with him awhile when you're there."

"Like I've said before, that cat hates me."

"No, he doesn't. He just—well, maybe he does. He's a one-person cat."

Ray Tolman's voice turned serious again. "Heading out the door now. I'll find your friend."

Twenty minutes later, Ray Tolman was on the phone again as the Jeep pulled into the SCC gates. "Found her car. Keys were on the ground beside it. She's gone, Meg."

"Shit," Tolman whispered. "Kerry's not an investigator. She's a financial analyst." She pounded the seat in frustration. "Jesus, she has three little kids."

"What do you need me to do?"

"I—" Meg Tolman stopped. She pounded the seat again.

I don't know what to do.

It was, as an adult, as an investigator, an unusual place for her to be. She always had options. She always had ideas about where to go, and that's where she went. But now she felt nothing, only a windy emptiness.

Her father always used to say, in any situation: *Just be ready.*

"Just be ready," she finally told him. "I don't know what else to say."

Ray Tolman was silent for a long time. "Let me know. I'll be here."

"I know," his daughter said, and clicked off the call.

Journey directed Sharp to drive around the common to Cullen Hall. Ten minutes later, a South Central security officer let them in to the Geography Department's computer lab on the fourth floor of Cullen. The room was covered with high-tech color maps on the walls. A dozen computers sat at workstations.

"I can log in using my ID," Journey said. "Come on, Andrew."

He'd brought puzzles and a ball for Andrew, and he parked him in a corner.

Surprising them, Sharp said, "I'll sit with him. Does he like to play ball?"

"Sometimes," Journey said. "Roll it back and forth to him. He enjoys that for a while."

Tolman settled into an empty desk and took out her laptop. "My Ann Gray search was still too broad—thousands of responses." She tapped the computer. Across the room, Andrew laughed—a happy and genuine laugh. She and Journey both looked. Sharp was tossing the ball to him, not simply rolling it on the floor. Sometimes Andrew caught it, sometimes he simply raised his hands and the plush ball bounced off his chest. But he was clearly enjoying himself. Sharp was smiling as well. Tolman hadn't seen Darrell Sharp smile since their Academy days.

Journey and Tolman looked at each other. "You never know," Journey said.

Tolman returned to her computer and Ann Gray. "I'll query our database again. Someone like an Ann Gray has to show up somewhere. The government has to know about her. *Someone* has seen her, knows what she is." She began tapping keys again.

Journey scanned the map of West Texas into the computer he was using. He brought it up on the screen, thinking about the times he'd used this system, usually with geography faculty nearby in case he became stuck. The resolution on the old map wasn't great, and he tried to sharpen it, setting up the process of georeferencing: first he had to select control points on the old map, places that were known. Then he would overlay a modern, digital map of the same area onto the historic map, matching up the control points.

The surveyor or cartographer who drew this map—Journey guessed it was one of Father Fournier's "new men" or one of the Mexicans, who would have been more familiar with the region—had done a good job outlining Texas. The shape was distinctive, from the straight line at the top of the Panhandle, to El Paso clinging to the tip at the extreme western edge. These were natural control points. Moving the mouse, Journey clicked at the northwest and northeast edges of the Panhandle, where it hung beneath No Man's Land—now the Panhandle of Oklahoma. Red dots appeared on the screen where he had placed the markers. Then he scrolled down and placed another point at El Paso—another known quantity on the old map. In between were hundreds of miles of rough country, largely the realm of the Comanche and Kiowa at the time of the Civil War. And of course, the hand-drawn cross—Le Croix d'Argent—in one of the region's rivers.

With his control points in place, Journey went searching in the college's GIS database for a current map of Texas. He had it in less than five minutes and was ready to layer the modern map onto the one from 1863. Journey didn't pretend to understand the mathematic algorithms involved in the process. His geography colleague had tried to explain it to him, but Journey had no interest in algorithms, only results and context. He remembered that the geographer had told him that the computer would "warp" the original map, a process sometimes called "rubber sheeting," because the program stretched and shrank the image, much akin to a thin sheet of rubber being pulled to fit a certain form.

Journey clicked "OK" and watched the two images begin to merge, the French map from 1863 and the modern digital one.

"Amazing," Journey said.

"What?" Tolman looked up from her laptop, frowning.

"Technology. You live in a fascinating world, Meg. I don't live there, but it's interesting to visit now and again. They didn't even have this technology when I was in grad school."

Tolman smiled, her forehead smoothing away the frown lines. "What do you have?"

"Give me a couple of minutes, and with any luck, I'll have a much closer fix on the Silver Cross. How are you coming along?"

"Hell, there are so many things going on I can't keep up. Kerry and Ann Gray and Lashley and our pal Jackson from last night, and April 19 and all the Cables. It's like playing Liszt with no score."

"I take it that's difficult?"

"You have no idea."

The GIS had completed its function. The modern map, with its highways and landmarks and cities, settled onto the old brown parchment with the heavy quill-pen writing.

"Amazing," Journey said again.

He checked the control points, then found the cross that had been drawn in 1863.

The Silver Cross, as mapped by the French, was in present-day Hall County, Texas. The river was a small tributary of the Red, which to the east would form the northern boundary of Texas with Oklahoma. The river crossed Texas Highway 70, a few miles north of the town of Turkey.

Journey had driven through West Texas a few times, and it was a land of stark beauty. In some areas the land was table-flat; in others there were craggy stone formations and canyons. Trees were few, and the ones that grew in that landscape tended to clump together and bend to the north, constantly buffeted by relentless southerly winds. But the thing Journey remembered about West Texas was the sheer hugeness of it. It was what outsiders thought of when they referred to the mythical American West, both of yesterday and today.

"Found it," he said, and Tolman came and stood at his shoulder. "Hall County, Texas, north of Turkey."

"There's a town called Turkey, Texas?"

"The home of Bob Wills. You're a musician. Surely you've heard of Bob Wills." Journey smiled.

"Western swing, 'San Antonio Rose.' Yes, I've heard of it. This is where it is?"

"Pretty close," Journey said. "This isn't one hundred percent accurate."

"Name something that is."

"Point taken."

"Can you get someone to look after Andrew? This time someone has to take care of him."

"I—"

"Start calling, Nick. We need to go to Texas. We're going to see what old Napoleon was so desperate to find."

"Maybe," Journey said.

Tolman pointed. "Call. I want Andrew to be safe."

Tolman's phone rang and she crossed to it. "Meg Tolman," she said.

"Ms. Tolman, it's Mark Raines in Oklahoma City."

Raines was the chief deputy of the U.S. Marshals Service office.

She'd spoken to him last night and again this morning. "What's up, Chief? You get people onto the Cables?"

"Yes," Raines said. "Melissa Cable and her son are secured."

"And my guy in the hospital in"—she looked at Journey—"what's the town again?"

"Durant," Journey mouthed.

"Durant," Tolman said into the phone.

"That's the problem, Ms. Tolman."

"What?"

"He's not there," Raines said.

Tolman was silent, then said, "And where did he go? He has two broken kneecaps and a broken arm."

"He was transferred before my men arrived there this morning."

"Transferred? Who transferred him? He's in my custody."

"Not anymore. The U.S. attorney received an order from D.C. to have him taken somewhere else."

"Where, goddammit? I need to question him."

"I don't know."

"You're not telling me you *lost* my fucking prisoner?"

"Your prisoner was transferred. The paperwork was all in order."

"Who authorized the paperwork?"

"I don't know. It came from D.C. I'm sorry, Ms. Tolman."

"Wait a minute! Chief, you wait a goddamned—"

The line went dead.

Tolman slammed a fist on the desk, rattling her laptop. Andrew and Sharp looked up from their game. She kicked at the chair, sending it rolling halfway across the room, crashing into another desk.

Sharp stood up. Journey said, "What, Meg?"

"Someone's fucking with me," Tolman said. "There's someone inside somewhere, tied up in all this shit. Not again . . . not *fucking* again!"

Sharp took a step. Andrew laughed hysterically, then shrieked, then whistled.

"My prisoner's been moved," Tolman said, "and someone hacked RIO's network, and Kerry is God knows where. There has to be someone inside. Somewhere."

"What do you mean, inside?" Journey said.

"Inside the federal government. This makes me angry, Nick. I'm not going through this again."

No one spoke.

"Dammit to hell," she said, the anger seeming to fade. She sagged into a chair.

"Meg?" Journey said, sliding into the chair beside her.

Tolman said nothing. She pulled a hand through her hair, then slowly looked up at Journey. "You want to hear something crazy? Total batshit crazy?"

"Tell me."

"This is going to sound like civics class, or . . . I don't know, a campaign commercial or something. But, Nick, I believe in the government. I could make a lot more money in a private tech security company. But after I flamed out as a full-time musician, I did this instead. My father did it—still does—my grandfather did it. They spent their lives protecting our government. And now, I do, too, in my own weird way." She blinked. Journey saw that her eyes were moist. "And then this kind of thing happens . . . again and again. I'm no flag waver, Nick, I'm really not, but . . ." Her voice trailed away.

"But you take the job seriously."

"Yeah, I guess I do."

"Meg," Journey said, and his voice was quiet but firm. "Let's move on this. Now."

Tolman stood up. "Yes," she said. "Let's move."

CHAPTER
28

Since they arrived at the house—a generically furnished but fairly spacious ranch-style somewhere in the suburbs—the two men had not treated Voss badly. They gave her ice to put on her eye and one of them—not the one who'd hit her—actually apologized that they'd been so rough. They made her sandwiches and brought her bottles of water.

But she was kept in an interior room with no window and no closet. It held a small futon and nothing else. When she had to use the bathroom, one of them went with her and stood outside the door. The bathroom had no windows either. She suspected this was a classic "safe house," and Voss wondered who had the capability to tuck her away in such a location. She didn't like the places those thoughts led her.

I need those seven numbers, she thought.

The plan had formed over several hours, and she'd been over it and over it in her mind. Every word had to be precise. There was no room for mistakes. Her life—and God knows what else, since all this was somehow wrapped up with those April 19 wackos—might depend on it.

She banged on the door and shouted, "Hey, you guys! Hey!"

"What?" said the driver—the apologetic one.

"I need to use the phone."

"You must be kidding."

"I need to call my ex-husband. The kids are supposed to come back from their dad's at six o'clock. If he drops them off and I'm not home, he's going to be suspicious. Look, I don't know where we are here—I can't tell anyone. I'll make up a story about a sick relative. Then no one will worry. But I need to let him know and make sure the kids are all right." Voss put a little break into her voice. Most men—even vicious ones—couldn't stand it when a woman cried. A man would do almost anything to get a woman not to cry. "Please," she added.

Voss heard Apologetic's voice. "She wants to call her kids. See if it's all right."

The tough one was on the phone, then, but Voss couldn't pick up the words. Then: "Go. But put the phone on speaker. One wrong word and we're out."

Voss didn't ask what "out" meant in this case. The door opened a crack and Apologetic came in. Tough hovered in the doorway. "Sit on the futon," Apologetic said. "If you say something wrong, I'll break the phone and your fingers, not necessarily in that order, and I'm fixing the phone to block the caller ID."

"Of course," Voss said. "I'm not stupid." *Get it right!*

He handed her the phone, enabling the speaker function. She punched in the number, one committed to memory years ago, in another job, another life.

"Yo," said a man's voice.

"It's me," she said. "How are the girls?"

Please, she thought. It had been so many years, she hoped he hadn't forgotten. . . .

The line was silent for ten long seconds. "Kerry? Uh, girls are fine. What's up?"

"Something came up," Voss said. "Can you keep them for . . . well, for a little while longer?"

"I guess so. Yeah, I guess I can do that. What's the problem?"

"You remember my great-uncle Ray, don't you? The really, really tall man with the bad hairpiece. You met him a couple of times, years ago. He's sick again, and you know, he doesn't have a wife or kids or anyone else, and I'm going to the hospital to see him."

"Yeah, yeah, I remember. Is he going to be all right?"

"I'm sure he'll be fine, but I just can't get home right now." Voss looked up—Apologetic was staring at her intently. *Every word*, she thought. "But I also need a favor. Could you go by my place and take the dogs out? Will you do that? You know where I leave the emergency key."

The line was silent. Voss's heart pounded. *Come on, come on, I know you remember. . . .*

Then, a deep sigh. "I guess so."

"Thanks," Voss said. "I really appreciate it. Tell the girls I called, okay? And tell them not to worry. I'm sure Uncle Ray will be fine. They just have to do some tests."

"Okay. How long will you be?"

"I don't know. Just kiss the girls for me and take the dogs out."

"Yeah, I will."

The phone clicked. Voss handed it to Apologetic. He immediately turned it off, then threw it on the floor and brought his shoe down on top of it, shattering the instrument.

"Don't worry, we have others," Apologetic said. "At least we didn't have to break your fingers. Your ex sounds like a loser, but I guess the two of you get along okay."

"We get along fine," Voss said. "We still try to help each other out when we can."

"'Course you do." He crossed the room and closed and locked the door. Voss exhaled and leaned back on the futon. She hoped she had pulled it off. Apologetic, at least, seemed to have no clue that the man she'd spoken to was not her ex-husband.

Duke sat in his Springfield apartment, surrounded by his professional wrestling posters and multiple computers, and looked at his screen. Despite the blocked caller ID—as if that would make a difference to a real hacker—he already knew the phone was a prepaid cell, purchased in the District, and he'd triangulated the signal to isolate it in Fairfax County. He'd have to work harder to pinpoint the exact location.

A few years ago, when Voss had worked for a different, much more clandestine government agency and recruited Duke as a freelance hacker, they'd worked out the code phrases in case something happened to her. If she mentioned "girls," that was a sign that she was in trouble and others might be listening in on the call, to just play along. Voss had one girl and two boys, so the plural was the giveaway. "Take the dogs out" meant he was supposed to find what she had been working on and that would point the way to what had happened to her.

Duke knew he could do that easily. There wasn't a computer system or code around he couldn't break. He was on contract to half a dozen federal agencies, and truth be told, he made a good living at it. He had most of it in mutual funds and lived in a modest apartment, away from noise and bustle. He had no car, never left his apartment, and the only things he spent money on were food and computer equipment.

Duke knew the stereotype of the hacker: an overweight guy with thick glasses, living in his mother's basement. But he was six-foot-six and thin as a post with perfect eyesight. He paid someone to come to the apartment and give him a haircut twice a month. He always attended to his hygiene. He dressed in khakis and a button-down shirt every day. He had a fairly healthy relationship with his parents and brother. He'd once played college basketball for Butler University. But he couldn't go out. There were . . . *things* . . . out there that he couldn't handle.

He'd been given medication for his anxiety, but he hated the way it made him feel. His head was full of mush when he was on the meds, and he couldn't be as sharp as he needed to be when a job came his way. So he stayed off the pills and inside his apartment.

Duke would have done anything for Kerry Voss . . . except leave his apartment. And now she was in trouble.

He thought about what else she'd said, knowing there was more to the message. He picked up the business about the tall man. He'd never met Meg Tolman face to face, of course, but he'd talked to her on the phone. Kerry had "introduced" them, asking Tolman to put him on permanent retainer as a contract employee of RIO. That was last fall, after Duke had traced some sizable bank accounts.

Now, someone had Kerry.

And she needed *him*.

He had to find what she'd been working on and get the information to Meg Tolman. He used his back-door password and logged in to RIO's network. He wandered around until he found Voss's computer. It was easy—whatever she'd been doing was still on the screen. He did a screen capture, looking at the bank accounts, seeing the grayed-out numbers. Duke knew about this—he'd hacked these kinds of things hundreds of times. The encryption was good.

But he was better.

He settled in to work. He would not move from this chair—well, he might get up to take a piss—until he had what Kerry Voss wanted him to know, and he passed it on to Meg Tolman. Tolman would know what to do next. That was her job.

CHAPTER
29

The airplane was a ten-seat Cessna Caravan that Tolman "borrowed" from the Marshals Service, along with a pilot. It had been fairly easy—the national air fleet operations center of the Justice Prisoner and Alien Transportation System, or JPATS, was headquartered in Oklahoma City, near the FAA and the Federal Transfer Center. Sitting in the copilot's seat, Tolman turned and looked at Journey, Andrew, Sharp . . . and Sandra Kelly, sitting next to Journey and holding his hand.

Journey had first called his ex-wife, but Amelia Boettcher was still on the road, somewhere in eastern Oklahoma visiting more bank branches and would be unavailable for another week. "Unavailable" was the word she'd used when she told Journey she couldn't take Andrew. Tolman, of course, had only heard one end of the conversation, and she knew it would have been easy to stereotype Amelia as a cold-hearted bitch whose special needs child didn't fit in to her high-flying executive lifestyle. Tolman also knew the reality was much more complex than that. She still didn't like Amelia much—not that it mattered—but she sensed there was much more of an undercurrent in the relationship between Nick Journey and his ex-wife than she understood.

Tolman could tell Journey was torn. He wouldn't willingly put Andrew in danger again, but he didn't trust others with his son's care. And whether out of historical curiosity, work ethic—he *was* being paid as a RIO consultant—or a sense of personal duty to Tolman, she knew he wouldn't walk away from the investigation, either. So Tolman suggested Sandra, and they worked out a compromise: Sandra would accompany them, then they would get a motel room, where Sandra would stay with Andrew while Journey went with Tolman and Sharp. To complete the picture, Tolman talked to the sheriff in Hall County, Texas, explained that a federal team was coming to his county, and requested round-the-clock security for Sandra and Andrew. She also lined up a vehicle through the sheriff's office.

The plane taxied in to the municipal airport in the town of Memphis, Texas, seat of Hall County and about forty miles northeast of their destination. As soon as she stepped off the plane, she sensed the flatness of the land, the dry air, and the incredible, stifling heat. Sheriff Walt Nichols was waiting for them on the runway.

"Welcome to Hall County," he said.

Tolman shook hands with the sheriff, noting his brown cowboy boots and the badge clipped to his belt.

"Hello, Sheriff," she said, and introduced the others. "Thanks for helping us out."

"Well, we don't get too many visitors from the Research and Investigations Office out here," Nichols said. "Y'all are on hush-hush business, is that right?"

"Pretty much," Tolman said. "At least for now."

"And you'll put in a good word for our department? We've applied for some federal grants for new equipment, and haven't heard anything."

"You know what, Sheriff?" Tolman said. "I don't know how much I could influence such a thing, but I'll certainly check into it. You've been very helpful."

"We always like to maintain a good relationship with our federal partners," Nichols said.

Tolman didn't think the man was bullshitting her. It was interesting how different cops could be from each other. With some of them, you had to threaten them with obstruction to get anywhere. With others you promised to look into their grant applications. "I appreciate it," she said. "You have a car for us, and someone to stay with Dr. Kelly and Andrew?"

"We've booked rooms for you over at the motel, and there's a pool. The young man there might like it."

Andrew was holding on to his father's hand. He'd been silent and wide-eyed for much of the short flight, and he seemed subdued.

"Thanks," Tolman said.

"Deputy Hills will take them on into town and watch over them," Nichols said. "I'm lending you an Explorer we use as a mobile command post. Most of the time it's for when we have tornadoes or fires and such. You know where you're headed?"

"We have a map," Tolman said, and thought it was the understatement of the century.

Sharp drove. His Glock 21 rode on his hip and his Smith & Wesson M&P340 was on the dashboard. He'd brought his FN Special Police Rifle as well, and it was between the driver's and passenger seats. Tolman's SIG was in her purse. The people who'd attacked them near Madill had long arms. They had the money and personnel and resources to track them. They could be waiting up ahead along the winding Texas roads, around any one of these bends.

They headed southwest out of Memphis into the country on Texas 256. It was all tall-grass prairie, sage and mesquite, giving way to short, craggy buttes and small mesas. Cattle grazed inside low barbed-wire fences. Tolman began to feel uneasy with the open emptiness of the landscape and the huge sky. The road bent sharply south and joined Texas 70. No one spoke. Tolman looked at the digital temperature readout on the Explorer's dash. It was ninety-nine degrees.

They crossed the Red River, which was true to its name, wide and muddy, like most rivers in this part of the country. "It shouldn't be much farther," Journey said from the backseat. "The way the map reads, this little tributary of the Red is a few miles south."

The road curved and bent. Craggy caprock formations rose on both sides. Sharp steered around a curve facing a long, low bridge over a bone-dry riverbed. "Look," Journey said. "This has to be it. Slow down, Darrell."

Tolman stared out the window. In the middle of the dry bed of the river to their right, extending as far as she could see on the other side of the bridge, was a fence.

"A fence in the middle of a riverbed?" she said. "That's not a common thing out here, is it?"

"No," Journey said.

It was no ordinary barbed-wire cattle fence, either. At least ten feet tall, it was topped with rolls of razor wire. It looked like it belonged in a prison.

Sharp slowed the Explorer to a crawl. On the north side of the riverbed, where the hard-baked ground began to slope upward from the banks, the fence turned at a sharp right angle and ran as far as the eye could see into the western distance.

They crossed the bridge. A white-tailed deer ran along the road to their left, then disappeared under the bridge. Tolman blinked.

Several yards beyond the bridge, a gravel road turned off the highway to the right. Sharp turned onto the road and drove until the vehicle was nose-to-nose with the fence's gate. An empty guardhouse sat inside the fence. The gate was sealed with a heavy-duty padlock and a length of chain.

All three of them climbed out of the Explorer, moving slowly. Sharp scooped up his rifle, scanning the banks of the dry river and glancing toward the highway behind them. Clearly, he didn't like having their backs to the road. "I'll go watch the highway," he said.

Tolman and Journey trotted to the fence. A white metal sign to the left of the gate read:

PANHANDLE MINING COMPANY, INC.
Hall County Production Facility
Trespassers will be prosecuted.

In the bottom left corner of the sign was a graphic representation of a cross.

CHAPTER
30

Journey's eyes zeroed in on the graphic. "The Silver Cross," he whispered. Perspiration ran into his eye and he wiped it away.

"It's a mine," Tolman said. "By God, Nick, it's a silver mine."

She lifted her phone, clicked the camera button, and snapped a photo of the sign, then took more pictures of the fence, the bridge, and the riverbed. Journey said nothing.

Tolman peered through the wire of the fence at the empty guardhouse. "You think they're closed on Sundays?"

Journey was still silent. He walked along the line of the fence to where it began to slope down toward the river. The gravel road snaked over a rise, and Journey couldn't see past it. The open country went on and on past this dry river.

"This has to be the base of the cross," he finally said. "The arms will be up that way, to the west. But they'll be dry, too. I'm willing to bet that when Father Fournier first saw this place, it was a real river. But other than that . . ." His voice trailed away as he walked along the fence line toward Tolman and the gate.

"So it's a mine," Tolman said.

"Napoleon sent his armies out prospecting for more silver. The mines in Sonora were rich, but he wanted—*needed*—even more. The silver situation was a crisis, like Lashley said, and while his forces were in the neighborhood, Napoleon was going to make sure they scoured the countryside for more deposits of silver. They must have found them here." Journey listened to the wind and the ticking of the Explorer's engine as it cooled. "In Fournier's journal, he talked about the different men being attached to the unit before it left Sonora, and a couple of 'native Mexicans.' They knew the country, and the other men—"

"Engineers," Tolman said. "Geologists. What do you bet he had teams like this all over Mexico and the Southwest?"

"Including this little piece of the Confederacy," Journey said. "I just thought of something. . . . In the letter that Rose was carrying to Jefferson Davis, it didn't just say Napoleon wanted the Silver Cross. He said he wanted 'legal possession' of it. I should have seen that before, but I was too busy thinking it was an artifact, a crucifix or something made of silver. But 'legal possession' sounds more like land. He wanted Davis to give the title to this land over to the French."

"And that would help him solve his silver problem. Would Davis have done that? Wouldn't that be a big scandal, handing over American soil to a foreign country?"

"Yes to both. But I think Davis would have promised Napoleon *anything* if it meant French money and troops, and I think the governor of Texas would have gone right along with it. At that time, this part of Texas was Comanche country. That would turn Texas's 'Indian problem' into a French problem. I suspect that if Rose had lived and delivered that letter, this would have been French territory in record time."

"Must have been a hell of a discovery," Tolman said.

"'A treasure greater than may be believed.' That's what one French writer said about it."

Tolman looked toward the gate. "How does it get from your French priest to Rose to Panhandle Mining Company?"

"The question," Journey said, "is whether Panhandle Mining has been here awhile, or if they found out about it recently, say, since Barry Cable was killed."

"But where's the connection?" Tolman said. "Okay, so Napoleon wanted this land to mine the silver. Obviously he didn't get it, since Rose died. *Someone* eventually saw the letter and the map."

"Or, Panhandle Mining discovered it on its own and is a legitimate business with no connection to any of this."

"You think so?" Tolman asked. Her shirt was sticking to her, after only a few minutes in the sun.

"I don't know. There's still no clear connection to April 19 or the Cables or—"

An engine sounded and they turned. Sharp, near the road, gripped his rifle a little more tightly. A dusty blue Chevy pickup truck slowed beside the highway and a single man emerged, smoking a cigarette. "Y'all need some help?" he called in a deep Texas drawl.

Sharp looked over his shoulder. Tolman walked toward the road and the heavyset, balding man. Sharp scanned the horizon.

"Has this operation been here a long time?" she said.

"About four years," the man said, scuffing a dusty work boot against some stray gravel. "Guess it played out, though, but they seemed to have a pretty good run." He looked at the Hall County logo on the door of the Explorer. "I don't think I know you."

Tolman followed the look. "Sheriff Nichols was kind enough to lend us the truck."

"Uh-huh. Who did you say you were?"

"We're with the Research and Investigations Office in Washington, following up on an investigation here."

"Well, now," the man said, but his expression had gone stony.

"What do you mean, it played out?" Journey asked.

"Closed," the man said. "They gave pink slips a few days ago. Way I hear it, everyone cleared out. Left all their equipment, left everything. Just up and walked away."

"Do you know anything about Panhandle Mining Company?"

The man spat on the road. "They're not from the Panhandle, I'll tell you that. I don't care what the name says. They built places, sort of like dorms, for the workers to live on the property. Didn't hire very many local people. They liked to brag about making four hundred jobs in Hall County, but hell, all the jobs went to people they brought in."

"About four years, you say," Tolman said, glancing at Journey.

"Yeah. They roared away in there, all day, every day—twenty-four seven, I guess is how people like to say it—and must've mined it all out in four years. But I hear they were a big producer in the silver market.

Real big. Strange outfit." He looked at Sharp, who stood silent and brooding. The man didn't seem to be alarmed by the rifle in his hand. He ground out his cigarette on the road under his boot. "What kind of investigation are you doing?"

"Just some follow-up work," Tolman said.

"Follow-up work. You don't want to tell some dumb redneck, is that what you mean?"

"Pretty much," Tolman said. "Except for the 'dumb redneck' part. I hadn't thought of that until you mentioned it."

The man surprised them by laughing. "You're not going to find out anything about Panhandle Mining. I'm on the board of the chamber of commerce in Turkey, and we tried to get friendly with them ever since they came in. They paid their membership dues, cosponsored our Bob Wills festival every year . . . they did the right things, but no one really *knew* them. You get what I mean?"

Tolman took a few more steps toward the man, leaning on the Explorer. "Who owned this land before they came in?"

"Oh, this was all Jack Hebden's spread. He ran cattle on it for about fifty years, and his dad before that, and his granddad before that. But Jack's kids all left here. They didn't want the place. All three of them moved down to Dallas, and Jack was getting up in his seventies and he was tired of cows, so it didn't take a lot of convincing for him to sell."

"You don't happen to know how we could reach Mr. Hebden, do you?"

"You'll have to see the Pearly Gates for that. He died less than a year after he moved out of here. Heart attack, just like that."

"That's sad," Journey said. "So it had been in one family for a long time."

"Oh, yeah," the man said. "That's pretty common around here. We had a lot of the big ranches in this part of Texas. The JA Ranch, one of the really famous ones, isn't too far away. Started by Charles Goodnight himself, and J. A. Adair. And before that, of course, most of this was what they call public domain."

"Public domain," Tolman said, and looked at Journey.

"Yeah," said the man, wiping his forehead. "It was owned by the government."

They were quiet. Sharp shuffled his feet.

"Nice rifle," the man said. "A little much to take down deer, but nice. Good range?"

Sharp shrugged.

"If I were to call up Walt Nichols, would he know who you were?" the man said.

"Of course," Tolman said. "I told you—"

"Yeah, that he lent you the truck. I heard you. Walt's pretty protective of his equipment, though."

"Do you know him?"

The man smiled. "My brother-in-law."

"Go ahead," Tolman said. "You go ahead and confirm who we are. And thanks for the information."

"Information? I'm having a little chat by the side of the road, that's all."

The man returned to his truck and slammed the door. He lit another cigarette and blew smoke out the window. "I hope you find whatever it is you're looking for," he said. "And if you find that lady, tell her our tax base is sure going to miss the income."

"Lady?" Tolman said. "What lady?"

"The boss of Panhandle Mining. At least she was the one who came around for a week once a month to supervise things. She was in charge of the business here. Never saw a woman in charge of something like this before." He looked at Tolman. "No offense."

"None taken. What was her name?"

"Diane Corbin. She was from back east somewhere. Pretty tall. I'm six feet and she could look me in the eye. Kind of brown hair, forty-something. Nice looking, I guess, but not a head turner. Like after you talked to her, then you couldn't really remember what she looked like five minutes later. You know what I mean?"

"Yes, I do," Tolman said.

"So our friend 'Ann Gray' gets around," Tolman said, in the Explorer on the road to Memphis. "She buys a phone in Chicago, mails the map from Michigan, she supervises the mine in Texas. But why give me the letter? Why send you the map? On the phone, she said she didn't exist.

She couldn't be in the light or something like that. And she said we had everything we needed." She pounded the car door. "Every time I answer a question, I think of ten more. How is it possible that no one else found this deposit of silver for nearly one hundred and fifty years?"

"Maybe no one looked," Sharp said.

"What?"

"He's right," Journey said. "Remember what our friend back there said? Look around—this is cattle country. Ranching is the business out here. You don't even see that many oil wells in this area. Texas was never much of a silver-producing state. No one was looking for silver out here. It was good country to graze cattle, and that's what people did . . . still do."

"But that much silver—"

"Yes, that much silver. But there really aren't many sudden 'Eureka!' moments in the real world. Oil gushers don't come shooting up out of the ground when you're out hunting, and you don't see silver nuggets shining in a river while you're fishing. Napoleon, on the other hand, was looking hard. He had a terrible economy, a foreign war disrupting his supplies, and a shaky foreign policy adventure that he was trying to prop up. He was a desperate man, and he believed Mexico and the American West had what he needed. Since then, people haven't been desperate for silver. Yes, it's a good mineral resource, and there's money to be made, but do people frantically search for it? I don't think so."

Tolman allowed herself a small smile. "I need to come sit in on one of your classes sometime, Nick. When you get wound up about something historical, you are a different person."

Sharp's mustache twitched and he almost smiled.

Tolman caught the motion. "Don't you think so, Darrell?"

"Maybe," Sharp said.

"I need my computer," Tolman said. "All I can say is, that motel better be air-conditioned."

The Travelodge in Memphis was on U.S. 287, the town's main thoroughfare. They found Sandra and Andrew in the pool, Andrew merrily bobbing up and down, ducking his head underwater, coming up with a mouthful of pool water and blowing it out. Sandra, in a one-piece swimsuit with a UCLA T-shirt pulled over it, was trying in vain to stop him from drinking the water. A uniformed sheriff's deputy sat nearby in the shade of a pool umbrella. Tolman noticed that the holster on his belt was unsnapped.

"All okay?" Journey said.

"We're fine," Sandra said. "This kid loves the water."

"I guess I should have warned you."

"It's okay. It was kind of nice for me to discover on my own."

Journey looked at her, then leaned down and squeezed her shoulder. "Thanks."

Sandra shrugged. "Good thing I'm not teaching this summer, either. What did you find?"

Journey filled her in, adding his thoughts on how the Silver Cross had been untapped until four years ago. "That's a sound conclusion," she said when he finished. "I don't know much about West Texas, but I do know that most of the silver in the U.S., at least these days, is in Nevada and Idaho."

Andrew splashed, drenching his father's shoes. He laughed.

"Get in and join him," Tolman said. "I'm going to my room and get busy on my computer. For the moment you have a little downtime. Enjoy it. We don't know what's coming next."

Journey glanced at Sandra. Tolman saw the subtle shift in his face, the hint of a smile. "I might," he said.

The room was standard small-town motel, but it was cool. Tolman turned up the air conditioner all the way, booted up her computer, and opened the curtains so she could see the others at the pool. Sharp put his rifle down on the queen-size bed, but didn't lay down his pistol. "How long, Meg?" he said.

"How long what?"

"How long you figure we'll be here?"

"I don't know. I want to get inside that mine, and I want to know who these people are. As long as I have this"—she tapped the computer—"I can work anywhere. I'm not too wild about these wide-open spaces, but for now this is as good a place as any."

Sharp looked uncomfortable. "I don't like it."

"I know, Darrell. We'll get you back to your place as soon as possible."

"I miss my house and my road and my hills."

"I know. And I miss my old deaf cat, too."

"I wish I could paint." He sat on the bed. "I wish you could play the piano. If you ever come to my place again, you can play."

Sharp's father had been a successful pianist and left Darrell a Steinway concert grand, which filled a room of his tiny house in Arkansas. He'd had it when he and Tolman were students at the Federal Law Enforcement Academy, and their bond had formed around that piano.

"I haven't played in a few days," Tolman said. "That would be nice. I promise to come see you when I can."

Sharp shrugged.

"And RIO will pay you for this job," Tolman said. "I know you're here for me, but we can pay you."

"Don't need any more money. I can help, but I don't need money." He looked out the window. "Hope no one tries to hurt that little boy."

"They better not," she said.

"He's different," Sharp said. "He doesn't talk."

"He has autism and yes, he's nonverbal."

Sharp waited, then said, "I guess I'm verbal, but I don't really talk either."

Tolman reached out and put her hand over Sharp's much larger one. Sharp looked down at their hands.

"So maybe you and Andrew understand each other," Tolman said.

"Maybe," Sharp said. "I don't think very many people understand him."

Tolman nodded. "But not many people understand you, either." Sharp dropped his eyes and Tolman added, "Sorry. You know what I mean, Darrell. *I* understand you." She squeezed his hand, looking up at him. "We're not going to let anything happen to each other, right? Just like old times."

"Yeah," he said. "And the little boy, too."

Tolman turned back to her computer screen and started a preliminary search for Panhandle Mining Company. The local address was a post office box in Turkey. The company was a Delaware corporation, created just over five years ago and privately held by another corporation. And so it went. She wanted to see the bank accounts, but didn't know how—that was Kerry Voss's job.

Tolman flinched at the thought of her friend. She still didn't know what had happened to Voss. She could be anywhere. She could be dead. Given the propensities these people had already shown for violence, Tolman had to accept it as a real possibility.

Please, not Kerry, she thought. *Too many good people have died already.*

Two hours later, the others were still at the pool. "I hope you used sunscreen," Tolman said as she walked up to them.

"Always," Journey said. He'd been swimming laps, pausing to play hand games with Andrew—touch each finger, fold it in, then do a fist bump when they were all folded. Andrew held his hand out to his father again and again. "Find anything?"

"Yeah," Tolman said. Sharp was right behind her, gun on his hip. Deputy Hills, still under the umbrella, looked him up and down but said nothing. Tolman kicked off her tennis shoes and socks, rolled up the legs of her pants, and dangled her feet in the water.

"Come on in," Sandra said.

"Not much of a swimmer," Tolman said. "I like water in bottles, mostly." She looked at Journey. "I believe what your guy said about a treasure greater than is to believed, or whatever it was."

Journey stopped in mid hand game. Andrew frowned but didn't vocalize. "What?" Journey said.

"They have taken one hell of a lot of silver out of the ground here in the last four years," Tolman said.

"Yes?"

"Last year this mine produced forty-two million ounces of silver."

Sandra took off her sunglasses and looked at Tolman. "How does that compare to other producers?"

"All the other silver producers in the United States *combined* produced thirty-eight million ounces."

"More than the entire national output," Journey said, color draining from his face.

"Anyone know the price of silver?" Sandra said.

"Lots of things affect it," Tolman said, splashing her feet a bit. The water felt good on her ankles. "Inflation, debt ceilings, the currency markets, and of course, Economics 101 . . ."

"Supply and demand," Journey said. "I'm willing to bet that with this mine more than doubling the available supply, the price has gone down in the last few years."

"It has. But you know how supply and demand goes. In the last few years before this mine opened, production had been declining, and so the price on the COMEX division of the New York Mercantile Exchange had gone up steadily. That's where the industry says that silver has 'strong fundamentals.'" She smiled. "In English, of course, that means it costs more per ounce. At the time the mine here started producing, the price was around thirty-five dollars an ounce. Now it's dropped to about twenty dollars."

"But still—," Journey said.

"Right. Forty million ounces, at twenty dollars, is eight hundred million dollars."

Sandra drew in a breath. Journey said, "My God, Meg."

"Multiply that by four years," Tolman said, "and it's three point two billion dollars. That's billion with a B. Someone's getting rich."

Journey swam to the edge of the pool, where Sandra and Tolman sat. "The question is, who? Where does all that money go? Is this the account that transferred funds to the April 19 guy and—"

Tolman cleared her throat, cutting her eyes toward the silent deputy under the pool umbrella.

"I need Kerry's expertise," Tolman said, "and I don't have it. All those bank account numbers are gibberish to me."

"You still haven't heard from her," Sandra said. A statement, not a question.

"No, and I checked with my dad three more times. He's on high alert, and he and his FBI buddy searched the area around the building. There's nothing." Tolman dipped her hand in the water and rubbed it over her face, letting droplets run down her chin. "If something happens to Kerry . . . I just keep thinking about her three little kids. I had them all over to dinner at my dad's house a couple of times. We played Boggle and Yahtzee. Kerry's ten-year-old daughter beat my dad at

Boggle every time." Tolman ran her hand over her face again. "I have to find Kerry. How was RIO's network compromised? Who was in it? Why, Ann Gray, of course, or Diane Corbin, or whatever the hell her name is."

"But we still don't know that," Journey said. "We don't know what Gray is."

"No, and my RACER search still has too many hits. The name's too damn common. In a case like this RACER is almost too good a search engine. I've referenced it with 'manager' and with 'freelance' and with 'freelance operator' and with 'silver.' Thousands of hits. On the other end of it, I've referenced it with the names of all the Cables and April 19. Nothing there."

"Assassin," Sandra said, then lowered her head. "God, I can't believe I'm thinking this way."

"What?" Tolman said.

"You've entered all these mundane titles to cross-reference her name," Sandra said. "That's what she called herself when you talked to her, right? Manager, operator, all that? But what if she's behind all these killings? Wouldn't someone like that show up in your government databases? Cross-reference her name with the word 'assassin' or 'murder.'"

"Yes," Tolman said. She drew her feet out of the water, pushed herself up, and took off for her room at a dead run.

Duke spent his time alone and liked it that way, but he couldn't stand silence. Usually he ran the TV, his iPod, streamed videos, even ran the dishwasher and clothes dryer for noise. Occasionally he had several of them going at once.

As Sunday afternoon clicked into evening, the TV was on full blast. Some incarnation of "Law and Order" was on, as it usually was. He'd seen most of them by now and could recite the dialogue almost as well as Jerry Orbach and Sam Waterston, but he watched them anyway. It was better than silence.

The seven grayed-out numbers had vexed him, and he had hacked into several federal government agencies already, browsing through their financials to see if the numbers matched. He'd barely moved from his chair since Kerry Voss called. He hoped she was okay. He hoped he could help her.

But the numbers stayed hidden from him. He'd tried the obvious choices for security-conscious departments, like Defense, Justice, and Homeland Security, then started on Energy, Commerce, Treasury, and on down the line. He was careful to shield himself when he was in the different departments' networks, and he didn't stay inside and poke around for fun as he did sometimes. Kerry was depending on him, and the longer he was in, the greater the chances he would be seen. Voss knew how to do some of this, but mainly she was on the up-and-up, and didn't go hacking. That's why she kept him around.

None of the numbers matched, and Duke's eyes were getting tired. He opened a Diet Mountain Dew and thought about what he'd already done. He'd tried all the cabinet-level agencies. He'd tried the FBI, the CIA . . . he didn't try NSA. *No one* could hack the NSA and he didn't even try. He'd spent hours, and Kerry was . . . God only knew where she was.

Duke glanced at the TV. Now President Mendoza was on the screen, a replay of a speech he'd given earlier in the day about those buildings that had been blown up. *People are crazy,* Duke thought. Thank God he stayed in his apartment where it was safe.

Duke patted his pants legs. He knew what Voss wanted him to do: find those account numbers and call Meg Tolman when he figured it out. It sounded so simple.

Mendoza was talking about "justice being served" and "hunting down the cowards" and words like that. It was what politicians always said when these things happened. But Duke liked Mendoza. Liked him a lot better than the last one, Harwell, who had died last year. Duke had read all about Mendoza after he became president—he'd been raised in Charlotte, North Carolina, where he worked in his grandparents' restaurant from the time he was twelve years old. He'd had real jobs, not like Harwell—or most politicians, for that matter. Plus, the president wasn't afraid to wear glasses. A lot of them thought it ruined their looks, but Mendoza was honest about the fact that he was blind as a bat.

The president kept talking, and Duke kept patting his legs. Then he thought, *Oh, what the hell? Better cover the bases.*

The White House's network was better protected than most, but not as well as NSA's. It took nearly an hour, but he found his way in. The financials were a little trickier, because the White House budget came from different "pots" of money, but he could see the list of accounts. Nothing there. Then he tried clicking on a subdirectory and found it empty.

Duke frowned.

He returned to the root directory and checked the code, made sure the path was right. The path had been changed, and it went deeper into several layers of the network. Now his natural curiosity was up. He wanted to see what was there, what had once rested in the empty subdirectory.

Four layers deeper, he saw the complete number, and the seven digits were clear. It was a match.

"Well, fuck me," Duke whispered.

The account Kerry Voss had been searching for belonged to the White House. A black, off-the-books account, buried deep.

And there had been a shitload of money in it.

Until yesterday.

All the money had been transferred out of the account, and it was now closed. He couldn't see where the money had gone. It was just . . . *gone*.

The clock on the computer said it was 10:21 P.M. He'd been at this all day. He glanced over at the TV. The anchors were talking in urgent tones. A BREAKING NEWS banner scrolled across the top of the screen.

There were images of buildings in flames, all with the word "LIVE" in one corner of the picture. Duke grabbed the remote and turned up the volume even further.

". . . have struck again," said the male anchor. "The militant antigovernment group April 19 is claiming credit for a string of bombings in six American cities tonight. Within the last few minutes, facilities housing federal offices in Portland, Oregon, Buffalo, New York, Chico, California, St. Petersburg, Florida, Nashua, New Hampshire, and Duluth, Minnesota, have exploded."

The graphic identified the young anchor as Megan Nguyen. "But these are not all federal buildings. Security at most federal office buildings across the country has been ramped up since Friday night's bombings in Cleveland, Kansas City, and Albuquerque. These are all smaller facilities, usually satellite offices with only a few employees. Offices range from the Social Security Administration to the Department of Agriculture to military recruitment centers. The blasts happened at exactly ten P.M. eastern daylight time, and it's going to be a while before we know an injury or death toll."

"That's right, Megan," said the male anchor, a bland, middle-aged white guy. "April 19, in an e-mail to CNN tonight, has claimed credit.

And once again they use the phrase, 'We are April 19. Maybe now the U.S. government and those who conduct business on its behalf will get the message.' That's the exact wording from Friday night's e-mail as well."

"We're starting to get some casualty reports," the woman said, touching her ear.

Duke watched as the screen changed from one city to the next. "In St. Petersburg, the offices were next door to a popular local sports bar, and as of right now, at least twenty-seven are reported dead there. We're told that the bar is ordinarily empty on Sunday nights, but a large private party was going on at the time of the explosion. Fortunately, the late hour on a weekend night means there were not a lot of people in most of the other blast areas. We're hearing of one dead in Portland, three in Duluth, and three in Nashua. Is April 19 finished with their reign of terror? Derek, that remains to be seen."

"Wow," Duke said, and he was glad, again, that he never left his apartment.

He wondered if President Mendoza would be making another speech, a live statement from the White House.

The White House.

The thought jarred him away from the bombings on the TV to the account he'd uncovered. He grabbed the phone and scrolled through his address book until he found Meg Tolman. Duke had only talked to her once, when Kerry arranged a conference call last fall. But Kerry liked her, and she was RIO's boss now, and Kerry had said to call her.

The White House, Duke thought, his thoughts racing wildly, bouncing like a ball in an old-fashioned pinball machine, as he looked at the images of the burning buildings on his TV.

The sun was finally going down across the Texas high plains as Tolman flipped the laptop open again and logged into RACER. Across the motel courtyard, Andrew and his father and Sandra Kelly were getting out of the pool. Andrew jumped up and down while his father dried him.

RACER took its time coming up, and Tolman could barely type fast enough to enter Ann Gray's name and the word "assassin."

Searching. Please wait.

The motel's wireless wasn't particularly fast, so this might take a few hours. But while Sandra's idea was a good one, Tolman was still bothered by various aspects of the whole dynamic. Ann Gray had insisted she didn't kill Dana or Jim Cable, but she was silent about Barry.

Next on the list was opening the file Barry had sent to his brother.

My damn list is getting longer, she thought.

She could have delegated some of these tasks to other people in the RIO office. They were capable, intelligent, dedicated people, and this was now an official RIO case.

But she couldn't.

She had to handle it, for Dana. And for Kerry Voss. Tolman squeezed her eyes closed, trying not to think about what might have happened to Voss.

The phone rang. The caller ID read, "Duke."

Voss's hacker.

"Yes?" she said as she reached for the phone. She didn't know if Duke was his first or last name, and she'd never seen him face to face. He was a strange guy, but Voss trusted him implicitly.

"Umm, is this Meg Tolman?"

"Hello, Duke."

"This is Duke— oh, okay. I guess you saw the caller ID. Umm, Kerry called me—"

"She called you? Was she okay? Where is she?"

Duke sounded rattled. "I don't know. I mean, yes, she called me, but I don't know where she is. There's this code we worked out a long time ago, for when she was in trouble."

"Where is she, Duke? Please tell me you know where she is." Tolman kept her voice tightly controlled.

"I . . . I don't know. She just called . . . well, she was working on something—"

"I know what she was working on. She was trying to find an account for me."

"Okay, yeah. Well, I did a screen capture and then I found it. So, see, I had to go through these layers—"

"Duke."

"Yeah, I get you. Okay. Umm, well, the account is really deep, like an off-the-books thing. And you know where it is? The White House."

"Oh, shit," Tolman said. "Goddamn, motherfucking, *shit.*"

"Yeah," Duke said. "Um, Ms. Tolman? Or can I call you Meg?"

"What?"

"And the account is closed. It was closed yesterday morning. All the money's gone out of it. There was a lot of money there."

"Can you find it?"

"Well, yeah, but it'll take some time."

"Do it. Duke, how much money was in there?"

"It was, like, five hundred and eighty-three million dollars, plus change."

Sandra and the two Journeys had come up from the pool and entered the room next door. The night deputy stayed outside. Sharp sat unmoving, silent as stone, on the bed behind Tolman.

"That's a lot of money," Duke said.

"Yes." *The White House. The money tied the leader of April 19 to the White House. They'd both received funds from the same account. And now the money was gone from the White House.*

This is insane. This is black-helicopter stuff. There has to be another layer, another connection somewhere.

Ann Gray. Diane Corbin.

She tied it all together. She was the missing piece. She was the unknown.

Duke said something else.

"What?" Tolman said.

"I said, does this help Kerry?"

"God, I hope so. Find that money for me, Duke."

Tolman disconnected the call.

She hoped Kerry Voss was still alive, and able to be helped.

Ann Gray. The Cables. The file that Barry had sent . . .

Tolman dropped the phone. Journey appeared in the doorway, Andrew bouncing up and down behind him. She snatched the phone from the floor and hit the redial button.

"Yo," Duke said.

"Duke, it's me again, Meg Tolman. Don't trace the money yet. I have something more important for you to do."

"More important than the money?"

"A hundred times more important, and I need a serious hacker for this. I'm going to send you a zip file. It's encrypted with an AES. I need you to find the key and open it."

"Cool," Duke said. "I love cracking AES."

"Okay, I'm sending you the file now. This is totally confidential. Don't talk to anyone but me, Duke. Only me. If anyone else calls you and says they're from, say, the White House, don't believe them. You understand?"

"Yeah, I understand. I'll get this for you."

"I believe you."

"The White House. Man, I was sitting here watching the TV and all those buildings that were blown up and I wondered if the president was going to talk—"

"Didn't he make a speech earlier? I've been a little busy today."

"No, I mean the new buildings."

"What do you mean, 'new' buildings?"

"Oh, didn't you hear? Those wacky antigovernment guys blew up six more buildings in different cities tonight. It's really bad, worse than the ones on Friday."

"Oh, Jesus," Tolman said, grabbing the TV remote. "I have to go."

"What?" Journey said as the TV came on.

Tolman pointed. The TV was on ABC News, and the video was of buildings burning, firefighters, stretchers with bodies covered. A graphic in one corner of the screen showed the number of fatalities combined from the six locations: thirty-four confirmed so far.

"They did it again," Journey said, and his voice was very quiet.

Tolman couldn't speak. She turned up the volume when she heard the anchors say something about Oklahoma City. She went to the edge of the bed and leaned forward.

". . . the members of April 19," said the anchor. "Of course, the first time the world heard of this group was last spring, when four of its members murdered one employee and wounded another at the Government Accountability Office in Rockville, Maryland. Those four are in the process of being moved from the federal prison in Hazelton, West Virginia, to a high-security facility in Atwater, California. Currently housed at the Federal Transfer Center in Oklahoma City, Oklahoma, they are scheduled to be transported to California tomorrow. It seems quite ironic that the members of a group calling itself April 19 are being housed in the very same city where the original April 19 bombing took place. Security will be high for the transport at noon tomorrow."

"I don't want to see more bloodshed in Oklahoma," Ann Gray had said on the phone.

"You should know that April 19 will free its brothers."

At the time, on the phone early this morning, it had been so much double-talk.

"Bloodshed in Oklahoma" . . . *"April 19 will free its brothers."*

The members of April 19 were in Oklahoma City right now, awaiting transfer to California. April 19 had just blown up another set of buildings.

Tolman turned to Sharp. "Go get the pilot. He's two rooms down. We have to get to Oklahoma City. She's going to try to break out the other members of April 19 tomorrow."

"What are you talking about?" Journey said.

"We have to get there. They need to double the security detail for the prisoner transfer. Something's going to happen. Gray's going to—"

"Gray runs the Silver Cross mine, but blows up buildings in her spare time?" Sandra said.

"You said she was an assassin," Tolman said. "You were right."

"Meg," Sharp said.

Tolman was packing her laptop and stuffing clothes into her travel bag. She didn't speak.

"Meg!" Sharp said. It was the first time Journey had heard the man raise his voice.

Tolman jumped. "What? For God's sake, what, Darrell?"

"Can we do anything tonight? Really?"

"What?"

"They're not going to transfer them in the middle of the night," Sharp said. The words came slowly, as if he weren't accustomed to stringing that many of them together. "Won't go until noon, the TV said. What could we do?"

"I don't fucking know, Darrell, but"—she stabbed a hand at the TV screen—"look at that! Look at what's happening!"

"Meg," Sharp said, and inclined his head toward Andrew. "I think the little boy's tired. Been through a lot today."

"He has," Journey said, his voice low. "This is a lot of stimulation for him."

Tolman slumped her shoulders. They were right. She couldn't do anything overnight. She would call and mobilize a larger security detail, see if she could arrange a few minutes with the prisoners before they were put on the plane for California. Gray was trying to tell her something. Why else would she have said "April 19 will free its brothers"? Why tell her in advance? She wanted them to see something, to know something.

They blew up the buildings, and the prisoners were being transported tomorrow. . . .

Tolman felt herself bending into the exhaustion, the mental overload, the emotional strain. She was bending, much like those trees bent in the face of the brutal Texas wind.

"You're right," she said. "We need some rest. We'll leave at first light."

CHAPTER

32

Tolman slept beside Sharp, her SIG and his Glock on their respective sides of the bed. Their relationship hadn't been sexual since a handful of times in their Academy days, but it seemed perfectly natural that they would sleep in the same bed. Tolman slept lightly, and Sharp muttered in his sleep, indistinct sounds of pain. At one point Tolman awoke with her arm thrown over him, her hand on the edge of the scar tissue that ran the length of his stomach, a grim reminder of the slaughter that had ended his law enforcement career before the age of thirty.

She woke up for good at 3:45, put her bare feet on the floor, sat in the motel armchair, and opened her laptop. Her RACER search for "Ann Gray" and "assassin" had finished.

There were three hits.

Tolman rubbed her eyes to be sure of what she was seeing.

All of the documents were highly classified, and all were found in the network of the CIA.

"Jesus," she whispered.

Sharp came awake and sat up, reaching instantly for his pistol. "It's okay, Darrell," Tolman said. "I just woke up." She turned around and looked at him, saw the scar across his belly. "I'm sorry I woke you. Go back to sleep."

He grunted but didn't lie down, and Tolman knew he wouldn't go back to sleep. "The CIA," she said. "Gray has CIA files." Tolman couldn't open the files—RIO was strictly a domestic agency, and CIA was, at least in theory, only authorized for international operations, so her clearance didn't get her into the classified material.

But on each of the files was the name of a control officer: B. Denison. She wrote down the name and the phone number beside it, then picked up the phone. It was a little before 5:00 A.M. in the D.C. area—if B. Denison wasn't up yet, it was high time he was. The number given was at Langley, but Tolman was willing to bet that most operations officers at the Agency had their phones roll over to a cell after a certain number of rings.

On the sixth ring, a deep male voice said, "Denison."

"This is Meg Tolman from RIO," she said. "Do you know an Ann Gray?"

Silence.

"I know I woke you up," Tolman said. "So I'll say it again—"

"Don't say it again," Denison said.

"Do you know her?"

"How did you happen to come by that name?"

"I've seen her. I've talked to her. Tall, middle-aged, brown hair, nondescript. I'm in your database. She has three files. Three operations. She's a contract assassin. Don't bullshit me. I'm really tired of bullshit."

"We should meet," Denison said.

Tolman laughed. "Nice to see I have your attention, Mr. Denison. But I'm in a motel in Memphis, Texas, right now."

"Last I checked, Memphis was in Tennessee, not Texas."

"Not this one. In a couple of hours I'll be flying out to Oklahoma City, Oklahoma. So you see, I'm nowhere near D.C. right now."

"Oklahoma City," Denison said. "I can get there. I'm getting dressed now."

"You'll fly all the way to Oklahoma because I dropped this name?"

"Yes."

Tolman waited, but Denison said nothing else.

"You Agency guys don't talk much," she finally said.

"Name a place in Oklahoma City. Where can we meet?"

"I have a meeting at the Federal Transfer Center. It's at the airport. I should be there by eight o'clock."

"I can't get there that soon. Make it ten o'clock."

"Deal. Is Ann Gray a dirty little Agency secret?"

Denison's tone didn't change. "Ms. Tolman, there are days when I wish RIO had never been created."

Tolman laughed. "I feel the same way sometimes, Mr. Denison. See you at ten o'clock."

Seventy-seven miles from the Travelodge in Memphis, Texas, Ann Gray stepped off the plane at Rick Husband Amarillo International Airport from her early flight. She'd flown from Washington to Chicago last night, slept in a hotel, picked up Barrientos, and flew on to Amarillo, changing planes in Dallas.

As soon as they landed, Barrientos had his phone to his ear. He spoke in quiet tones. "Final death toll at thirty-eight. They don't think they're going to find any more. What do you think Zale is doing right now?"

"Wondering how I got the best of him," Gray said, but she didn't smile. She would rather not have been put in this position. But Zale had forced her to take drastic actions. With any luck, Victor Zale and The Associates would be ruined soon. She looked at her watch. Delmas Mercer's news conference had probably happened while she was in transit. She wanted to get to a television and see how the gentleman from Louisiana looked on camera beside the French ambassador. That thought almost did make her smile, as she imagined twisting the knife a bit more in the back of Victor Zale.

There were televisions in the Amarillo terminal, and they stopped to watch. NBC's screaming graphic read: AMERICA UNDER SIEGE. Another TV was tuned to CBS: ANTIGOVERNMENT VIOLENCE . . . FRENCH DIPLOMATIC CRISIS . . . CONFEDERATE SOVEREIGNTY RESOLUTION. A little further on, Fox News: TIME OF CRISIS: SILVER, THE CIVIL WAR, THE SOUTH . . . AND TERROR AS DEATH TOLL MOUNTS FROM FEDERAL BOMBINGS.

Gray stopped to watch the last one, as it was running video of Representative Delmas Mercer and the press conference he'd held that morning with the French ambassador, a dour man named Daquin. Mercer waved his papers and pounded the podium. Daquin took over and spoke about violation of French sovereignty and relations chilling between the two countries if the United States Congress didn't act on Mercer's resolution immediately—a resolution Gray had written, and paid the congressman three hundred thousand dollars to introduce in the House and promote in front of the TV cameras.

"Is it what you wanted?" Barrientos asked quietly as they collected their bags.

"What I *want* is beside the point," Gray said. "None of this has anything to do with what I want. I have no agenda, I never have. You know that. I have no allegiance to political borders. I am a professional, and The Associates—and by extension, the United States—have disrespected my professional services." She glanced at her young associate. "And Mark, why do you think we set the explosions for late at night? If these had been done on a weekday, say, at noon, the death toll would probably exceed what New York saw on September 11. I didn't see Victor Zale for what he was until he started ordering the killings of people who were no threat to the project."

"But, Ann . . ." Barrientos seemed to be struggling for the words. "All this seems like . . . too much. You're going to have Congress screaming over Mercer's resolution. It's going to open up a lot of emotions. You always told me there's no room for emotions in this business. When you get emotional, you lose your effectiveness. You taught me that."

"I've sent a very important message. Zale is twisting in the wind now."

"It's a hell of an expensive message."

"Mark, that's enough. Your opinion is noted. Leave it alone."

"Kids were killed, Ann. Last night. There were kids."

Gray stopped in her tracks and grabbed Barrientos's arm. "The targets were supposed to be in areas where no children would be around at that time of night. What happened? How could that happen?"

"In Nashua, a guy who worked for the Department of Energy office had taken his kids, boy and a girl, seven and nine, to a baseball game. On the way home he stopped by his office for a few minutes. The kids went in with him. They—"

Gray raised her hand and silenced him. "No more. They shouldn't have been there."

"Ann, I think you should—"

"I don't want to know what you think. No more, I said."

They walked toward the National car rental counter. "So why are we here? What's the point of being here? They shut it down. All the real employees at the mine were let go, the accounts are all closed. It's done."

"I ran this from the beginning, Mark. From *before* the beginning. I hired the engineers, the managers. I made Panhandle Mining a part of its community. They can't shut it down without me."

"They did, Ann. It is finished."

"Not quite," Gray said.

Wade Roader had not slept, and as his driver took him toward the Washington Monument, he thought of the horrific pictures from Oregon to Florida to New Hampshire. He had excused himself several times during the night, and he went to his office's personal bathroom and vomited until he could barely stand. But he could not leave and he could not sleep. All through the long night, he stayed close to his boss, President Robert Mendoza, who thought his chief of staff was simply upset—as all Americans were—at what was unfolding on their television screens.

If only the president knew, Roader thought.

But Mendoza could never know that Roader wasn't just sick because of what had happened in six American cities, but because Roader had indirectly caused it. All of it.

It was out of control. Zale and Landon and their "manager," the mysterious Ann Gray. The Associates.

And Meg Tolman and Kerry Voss. Roader almost became ill again when he thought of the two RIO employees. Meg Tolman had an infuriating habit of not going away, and Voss was just as tenacious. He'd been monitoring RIO's networks remotely, had been notified by secure e-mail when the financial analyst logged in and found the account reference numbers. She couldn't see all of it, thank God, but it added one more layer to the mess. He'd immediately dispatched men to get Voss. Zale's response would have been *kill, kill, kill.* But Roader only wanted her out of the way while the rest of the situation resolved itself. So he sent his own men—a personal crew, not associated with the White House—to take Voss. She was in a safe house in Fairfax County. Roughed up a bit, according to the troops, but alive.

"Don't touch her again," Roader warned them. "Extend her every courtesy."

Courtesy? Roader thought. *I kidnapped one of my own employees. Courtesy!*

And Tolman . . . he'd gone along with Zale's order to have RIO's deputy director killed. *Dear God, what have I become?*

More and more these days, he wished he were still teaching colonial history at Yale. But that had been a long, long time ago. Before he rode into politics with his old friend, James Harwell, who had been president until his death of a heart attack last September. But Roader had kept his job. Robert Mendoza was a thoughtful and capable man— though an unknown quantity. He even seemed honest, whatever that meant in American politics today.

More honest than I am, Roader thought.

He arrived at the Washington Monument and found Zale and Landon in the same place as the last meeting, two mornings ago. When Roader spoke, his voice was a rasp, raw from all the retching he had done. He'd told the president he was going home to sleep for a couple of hours, and would return in time for Mendoza to make his statement to the nation.

"If this is your idea of tying it off," Roader said, "I think we're in pretty piss-poor shape here."

"I had no idea she would—," Zale said.

Roader stopped him with a look. "I don't want to hear it. I want it to *go . . . away.* Permanently. The information I gave you on that USB drive was supposed to help you finish it."

"We got the other professor, Lashley," Zale said.

"Yes, as usual, you killed the person on the periphery, and the ones causing the problems are still out there. And I had to rescue your man 'Jackson' from the hospital in Oklahoma. But Meg Tolman will not quit until she has all of it. With what I had to do to get Jackson away from her, she's already going to be questioning how far up this goes. I may have been able to slow them down a bit—"

"What else did you do?"

"Never mind," Roader said, thinking of Kerry Voss and her computer. "But you will stop this. Now. The president will not stand—"

"Don't tell me about the president," Zale said. "Now you're getting on your moral high horse. That's what Gray did, and she's going to get her ass killed because of it."

"You think so? Looks like she and her funny little band of terrorists have been doing all the killing."

"She's doing that to get at me," Zale said, "doing this and claiming it's April 19. It's a dig."

"Goddammit, Victor, I don't care what it is! She's killing innocent Americans."

"Innocent," Zale snorted. "That's a laugh. When have any of us ever been innocent? When we're born, maybe, then we spend the rest of our lives getting corrupted. There is no such thing as innocent."

Landon was looking at his partner with something like horror. "Good God, Victor. Why did those people in Minnesota and Florida and all those places have to pay? They *were* innocent. All these people, all this blood . . ."

"I just do my job," Zale said. "Sometimes a few people die so that a society's way of life can be preserved. That's just the way it is."

"Maybe it's time for your job to be finished," Roader said.

"Sorry, Wade, that's not the way The Associates work. You know how it goes."

"You disgust me."

"Save your disgust and your righteous indignation. I'm you, Wade. I'm all of you. I do what you and all the other hand-wringers are afraid to do. Do I like it? Not especially. But I do it because I have to. Where would this country be without me and people like me? We'd be bankrupt, and we'd still be sending men in to die by the thousands all over the world, with no hope of winning, just like they sent me to Vietnam." He raised his right hand and held the stumps of his fingers in front of Roader's face. "I left three fingers in that miserable shithole of a country in '69. A lot of guys left a lot more there. A lot of guys never came back. I saw then, more than forty fucking years ago, that there was no chance. Vietnam was lost—it was always going to be lost. But I could see that it didn't happen again, and I found ways to make things work. Things that your poll numbers don't tell you. Things that most Americans don't want to think about."

Roader stood up, his face burning, his guts churning again. "I don't want to see you again. I *won't* see you again." The chief of staff turned and walked toward his waiting car.

"He's weak," Zale said. "He's a weak asshole, a poor excuse for a man and an American." He watched Roader go. "But I have an idea, and it'll take care of many of our problems. Many of this country's problems. And that's our job, isn't it?"

Landon turned to look at him.

"I'm going to beat Ann at her own game," Zale said. "She's conjured up April 19, but you and I both know it's not about ideology. Ann prides herself on no agenda, being a professional, all that shit. So the people she's hired will be the same. Hired hands. Mercenaries. And what do you do if you want a mercenary to turn against the one who hired him?"

"You offer him more money."

Zale smiled. "Exactly."

"To do what?"

"We're going to send April 19 to Chicago."

"*What?*"

"I've been thinking about these damn protests. They're eating up the country, breaking down the social order, undermining the civil authority. *Our* authority. They have to stop, and this is the opportunity to do it. I'm going to take care of a festering problem, throw April 19 back in Ann's face, and in the process, Mendoza will be so weakened that he'll be dead politically. He makes me nervous—I think he's too independent, and he should never have been anything but just another junior senator."

Landon's face went slack. "April 19 to Chicago . . . the protest and counterprotest. Victor, there will be thousands of people there. I don't understand this. You're going to send Ann Gray's April 19 people into the middle of that protest? But Ann doesn't have anything to do with the protests. What does that—"

"I'm going to wipe them out and restore order. That's what we do. We find ways to maintain order and control, things that people like Roader won't do. Ann is also going to find out she shouldn't be trying to send 'messages.' And I'm going to use her own people to do it and use the money she made for us from the mine. Maybe then she'll understand who's in control."

"Victor, you can't. All those protesters . . . they're going to be packed so tight, thousands of them—"

"I can't?" Zale looked down at the other man. "You're telling me what I can't do, Terry? Really?"

A silence fell between them, and Zale could feel the other man's fear.

"Don't get any ideas in your head," Zale said. "You tend to your accounting."

Landon shook his head. "You're wrong about one thing, Victor."

"And what is that?"

"I think you do like it. I think you like the manipulation and the behind-the-throne power. And I think you like the killing. In all these years, I've never seen it as clearly as I do now. You like it, don't you?" Landon stood up. "Don't bother answering that."

Landon turned and walked in a different direction from Roader, leaving Zale sitting alone in the shadow of the Washington Monument.

CHAPTER

33

The Cessna Caravan landed in Oklahoma City a little before eight o'clock in the morning and taxied to the extreme western edge of Will Rogers World Airport, to the JPATS hangar and the Federal Transfer Center. The FTC was a low-profile facility of the Justice Department's Bureau of Prisons, a holding center for federal prisoners and illegal aliens who were in the process of being moved elsewhere. The Oklahoma City location in the center of the nation was ideal—early each morning one MD-80 jet took off flying east, the other west, moving hundreds of prisoners in federal custody between locations.

The SOAP flights were another matter. Originally the acronym had stood for Service Owned Aircraft Program, but nowadays it was a generic term for smaller planes used to transport "special" prisoners—politicians or athletes or particularly notorious and violent prisoners, those convicted of terrorism-related charges. Like the members of April 19. They would fly to their new "home" in California on a smaller plane, similar to the Caravan. Tolman had asked to meet with the April 19 shooters as soon as possible, but the facility's warden told her she could only see them right before they boarded the

plane. He steadfastly refused, even in the face of Tolman's broad jurisdiction, to deviate from his protocols. Tolman respected him a little
for that.

The warden set them up in an unused office in the FTC and Tolman ordered breakfast, seeing that the others were fed. At a few minutes before ten, the warden came into the office and said, "There's a
man at the gate, a Bart Denison. He won't come inside the facility, and
says he's here to see you."

Tolman stood up. "Showtime, kids."

"Ms. Tolman," the warden said, "what the hell is going on? This
transfer better not be turned into a circus. It's bad enough with the
media around, since these nuts have blown up more buildings. We're
all a little on edge, and whatever you're doing isn't helping."

"I'll handle it," Tolman said, and the warden scowled after her.

They left the building, passed a guardhouse, and walked outside
the high walls surrounding the three-story brick building. The sun was
already high. Bart Denison was waiting for her just outside the walls.
"Meg Tolman," she said, and shook his hand. "Care to come inside
where it's cool? You're going to wilt if you stand outside in that suit for
very long."

"No, thank you," Denison said. "I'd prefer we not have this conversation inside a government building, Ms. Tolman."

Tolman looked amused. "Think I've put a bug in the Federal Transfer Center, do you?"

Denison didn't smile, his dark face remaining impassive.

Tolman cleared her throat and gestured at the others. "Dr. Nick
Journey, RIO consultant. His son Andrew, his friend Dr. Sandra Kelly.
Darrell Sharp, U.S. Marshals Service, retired."

Denison looked Sharp up and down. "You look a little young to be
retired."

Sharp said nothing, folding his arms.

"Ann Gray," Tolman said.

Denison pointed at the others. Andrew was hopping up and down,
holding Sandra's elbow and his father's hand. "Only you, Ms. Tolman.
Not your consultants and . . . friends."

Tolman pointed at Journey. "We were attacked on Saturday night.

That boy had a gun held to his head. His father has a right to know what's going on."

"No," Denison said. "He doesn't."

They stared each other down, Denison completely unmoving.

"We'll go," Journey said. "We'll wait in the building. Do what you have to do, Meg."

Tolman looked at Denison. "I'm going to tell them later. You know that, right?"

"I wouldn't advise it," Denison said.

"Don't advise me."

Denison shrugged. Journey and Andrew, Sandra, and Sharp turned toward the building. Sharp looked toward Tolman several times, and she inclined her head toward him—*It's okay.*

"Ann Gray," Tolman said. "She's a freelance assassin who has done three jobs for the Agency."

Denison took a few steps along the grass at the edge of the FTC property. To his right, on the other side of the FTC entrance, the street was blocked off. High fencing with razor wire stretched into the distance. It reminded Tolman of the mine site in Hall County. She looked at the CIA man. He was compact, trim, and fit, and despite her comment about him wearing a dark suit in the sun, he didn't seem to be perspiring at all.

"The Agency doesn't conduct assassinations," Denison said. "It's against the law."

"I don't have time to dance with you. Let's get to it. I found the connection to CIA by cross-referencing her name with the word 'assassin.' You know Ann Gray. You're listed as the control officer. You were her handler."

"I know her professionally."

"Professionally, she's an assassin."

"Not exactly," Denison said. "Ann Gray likes to call herself—"

"A manager, an operator. Yeah, I get it. But let's dispense with—"

"You talked to her?"

"Yes."

"Then you know that she's rather more interesting than the average operator. Ann Gray specializes in helping individuals or corporations or governments achieve certain objectives. She's schooled in international business and law, and of course has other talents as well. If, in the course of managing a project, a situation comes up that requires some wet work, then she does that, too."

"Wet work. Jesus, you guys are a riot. 'Wet work.' 'Black operations.' You like your euphemisms, don't you?"

"Where did you talk to Gray?"

"Sorry, Mr. Denison," Tolman said. "I'm asking the questions. Gray has worked for the Agency, right?"

Denison hesitated a bit. "We've used her as a contractor in the past."

"To do what?"

"I'm not getting into past contracts."

"Where does she come from?"

Denison shrugged. "We think she was born in South Africa, lived in Spain, Austria, the Netherlands, and the States. But no one can be sure. She covers herself too well."

"Is she working for you now?"

"No."

"Should I believe that?"

"It's the truth."

"Of course it is. Why did you fly all the way out here to meet me when I dropped her name?"

"Have you seen the news this morning?"

"No, what is it now? Aside from April 19?"

"No, not them," Denison said. "We received word late yesterday that France's ambassador to the U.S., and one idiot congressman, were going to hold a joint news conference this morning. They did."

Tolman stopped walking. "The French ambassador?"

"Yes. Congressman Delmas Mercer of Louisiana is introducing a resolution in the House to retroactively recognize the Confederate States of America as a sovereign nation during the four years of the Civil War, in order to give the French treaty rights. Ambassador Daquin is claiming that the French negotiated a deal with the Confederacy, and that if this woman, this spy, hadn't died, it would have been law. If the Confederacy is legitimized, they could possibly have legal recourse, as insane as it sounds."

"That can't be right," Tolman said. "No one will buy it."

The CIA man looked at her. "Have you been paying attention to the state of American politics? Have you seen the desperation of the French government's monetary crisis? Desperate and troubled people will buy almost anything, if it furthers their own agenda. Mercer is telling the world that we stole the map from France, and we must be true to our steadfast allies, and on and on."

"Holy shit," Tolman said. "Christ, Denison. How did this happen?"

"We think Gray told someone—whether it was Mercer or the French, we don't know—about the map."

"What the hell is she doing?" Tolman said. "And how did she get the map in the first place?"

She almost told Denison that Gray had sent the map to Journey, but thought better of it. She didn't trust Denison.

Hell, who can *I trust?* she wondered.

"To answer your first question, the Agency would like to know," Denison said. "To answer the second . . . Gray stole the map from the French. She stole it for the Agency."

CHAPTER
34

All this—," Tolman said.

"No," Denison said quickly. "Whatever you're involved in has nothing to do with the Agency."

"Maybe you'd better explain this to me, Mr. Denison. We're in the business of stealing maps from churches in other countries? *Friendly* countries, I might add."

"Don't be naïve, Ms. Tolman. When we find things in other countries that have a bearing on our national interest, we take them. Other countries do the same here. It's the perfect kind of job for a contractor like Gray. We'd used her on a couple of other jobs over the years—and no, I'm not going to discuss those operations with you. Six years ago, we found out through our regular assets in Europe that some old papers and maps had been found in this church in Montluçon, France, things that related to the French in North America in the 1860s. We have an interest in historical documents—our analysts can piece together past operations, get a picture of how certain regimes behaved, consider the possibility of future operations. We never know what we're going to get."

"But you steal artifacts on a regular basis."

"I'm not going to respond directly to that. We heard of this discovery, and when we learned that there was a map of Texas in the 1860s, the decision was made to try to obtain it."

"Why didn't you offer to buy it?"

"I'm not going to respond to that, either. We approached Ann Gray and she obtained the map for us and took it out of France."

"What did you do with it?"

"Nothing," Denison said.

"Nothing."

"Our analysts looked at it, people determined the actual site, and went to it. There was nothing there. It was determined that the map was of no further use to us, and the file was closed."

"Why didn't you just give the map back to the French?"

"And admit we took it in the first place? Be serious."

"So what did you do with it?"

"We sold it."

"You *what*?"

"It became surplus government property. We sold it. Not through the Agency, of course, but through the General Services Administration, the GSA. It was sold, along with hundreds of other items."

"Jesus," Tolman said. "You guys . . ."

"It was worthless to us. The letter that Congressman Mercer talked about . . . we didn't have it. We knew nothing about some proposed treaty between the French and the Confederates."

"You didn't know what the Silver Cross was?"

"Not until we heard last night about what Daquin and Mercer were going to do."

Tolman's mind was racing. "And now you want to find Gray because you're afraid the French are about to name the CIA as having stolen the map from their soil."

"It becomes a difficult situation to navigate."

"No shit. 'Difficult to navigate.' Tell me about April 19."

Denison pointed toward the walls of the FTC. "I suspect you know more about that than I do."

"Gray is April 19," Tolman said. "Somehow. She also ran the Silver Cross . . . Panhandle Mining . . . she ran the operation that mined all that silver. But she's also April 19."

"Ann Gray and April 19? I don't think so. Gray has no political agenda. She has no ideology. She only believes in herself. She only takes on jobs that are 'interesting' or 'challenging.' Early in her career, from what we can piece together, she did anything. The first traces of her are at the end of the Cold War, when Communism was falling apart in Eastern Europe. She was a courier, then reportedly assassinated a high-ranking member of the East German Stasi, days before the Wall fell. And no, that job was not for us. As her reputation grew, she became more selective. She's very, very good at what she does. One of the best in the world, actually, and that is precisely because she has no political agenda of any kind."

"But you've been out of touch with her for six years?"

"We paid her for the job in France, then she vanished. You see why I think it's interesting that you may have talked to her."

Tolman massaged the muscles in her neck, feeling the sun beating down on her. She wished she had water. "What do you know about Edwin Barry Cable?"

"Who?"

"April 19," Tolman said. "The GAO shooting last April."

"I know nothing about it. I know what everyone else who watches TV or uses the Internet knows."

"You talk in circles," Tolman said. "You know that, right?"

Denison shrugged. He took off his gold-framed glasses, cleaned them with a crisp white handkerchief, and put them on again. "Comes with the territory."

"Who bought the map?"

"You understand that the Agency had no part in the sale of the map. The GSA—"

"Who bought the fucking map?"

Denison was still and quiet. His gaze bore into Tolman, unblinking.

Tolman raised both hands, then let them drop, slapping against the legs of her dusty jeans. "Don't you Agency guys ever sweat?"

"No," Denison said.

Tolman almost smiled at his deadpan tone.

"Ann Gray has put us in a difficult position," Denison said. "No one else could have leaked the existence of the map—and your alleged letter from Napoleon III—to the French. The French government is just about bankrupt and their economy is on the edge of collapsing.

They see an opportunity for money here, and one idiot congressman decides to renew the debate over secession so the French can have 'treaty rights' with the Confederacy, retroactive to the Civil War. This is not a good place for our country—or the world—to be, is it, Ms. Tolman?"

"Well, we agree on that," Tolman said. "So the CIA paid Gray to steal that map from the French. But you knew nothing about Napoleon's letter? The letter and the map are worthless separately, but together—"

"You see, then. I wish the Agency had known about the letter. Together they are apparently quite valuable."

"What's still missing?" Tolman said, almost to herself. "Somehow, the map and the letter came together, and Gray wound up with both of them. How else do you explain Panhandle Mining and all that money going—"

"Going where?"

The sentence died, and Tolman looked at him, his face carefully impassive, the sun glinting off his glasses.

The CIA didn't know about the White House connection. They didn't know about four billion dollars in silver sales. All they knew was they had Ann Gray steal a map—a map they determined was worthless, until now.

And now . . . they *wanted* to know.

It never ended.

"That money went into someone's pocket," she finally said.

"That's not what you were going to say."

"You don't think so?"

"No."

"Well, tough shit, Mr. Denison. And Ann Gray *is* part of April 19. I don't know what the game is, or exactly what Barry Cable found, but she's part of it. They're going to try to break these guys out today. She said they were going to 'free their brothers.'"

"Ann Gray is not a terrorist," Denison said. "She's the ultimate professional. If she said something to you about April 19, it's because she wants you to think she's a part of it. Ann is all riddles and rhymes . . . she's a master of sending people in circles. It's how she's stayed alive doing what she does, for over twenty years."

They reached a side gate to the FTC, then turned around and worked their way along the strip of grass between the fence and the street. Denison's phone rang, and he reached into his suit jacket. He listened, then hung up and looked at Tolman again. "That was Langley. The French are recalling their ambassador."

"What does that mean?"

"It means that one of our strongest allies in the international community is about to break off diplomatic relations with the United States. And they're threatening legal action in international court to force us to pay restitution, with interest, on royalties for money earned from this place in Texas."

"They're breaking off relations? The French are breaking off relations with us?"

"They are going to close their embassy. They're already in a financial crisis that has the entire European Union teetering. This is not Greece or Ireland we're talking about. This is France, the eighth largest economy in the world. It's about to be a diplomatic problem, too—other EU countries may follow the French, just for the sake of a united Europe, standing against us. The French government of today is about as desperate as Napoleon III was one hundred and fifty years ago." Denison looked straight at Tolman, unflinching. "And while they may be playing a game of diplomatic chicken, so to speak, they may not even think they really 'deserve' those funds. But they are certainly going to make a great deal of noise about it. They are showing the world their moral outrage and indignation and they are going to do everything they can at this point to make the United States look bad on the world stage. Now . . . are you sure you have nothing else to tell me, Ms. Tolman?"

Tolman's head was spinning. What had started with Dana Cable's murder had become an international crisis.

"Are you sure you have nothing else to tell me, Mr. Denison?" Tolman said.

For the first time, Denison showed his exasperation. He blew out a breath. "America is in flames. I don't know what you think Ann Gray has to do with that, but be that as it may, it is a fact. And we're about to lose one of our longest-standing political allies in the world. At this stage of the game, the French will do anything to prop up their economy, and if they think there's an opportunity to squeeze money out of this situation, they will. So don't play games with me, Ms. Tolman."

"Games? Don't talk to me about fucking games, Denison. You guys stole that map from the French, then when you decided it wasn't worth your time, you chucked it aside. Well, apparently *someone* knew it was worth the time . . . and you are screwed. You set this mess—all of this!—into motion when you hired Ann Gray to steal that map. And you say *I'm* the one playing games."

Tolman turned and strode toward the main gate of the FTC.

"Ms. Tolman?" Denison called after her. His voice was soft, but carried well.

She turned.

"The GSA sold the map to a private collector, a wealthy elderly gentleman named Noah Brandon."

"Where? Where do I find this guy?"

"I have no records. The GSA informed the Agency as a courtesy—"

"Goddammit, Denison!"

Denison folded his hands together in front of him, as if he were about to pray. "As of six years ago, I understood that Mr. Brandon lived in Wilmington, North Carolina."

CHAPTER
35

Bart Denison watched Meg Tolman walk to the guardhouse, pass through the checkpoint, and disappear inside the Federal Transfer Center. A plane took off from a nearby runway, and he watched it lift into the clear Oklahoma sky.

Oklahoma, for God's sake, he thought.

Then Denison pulled out his phone and punched in a number. When a man answered, he said, "This is Bart Denison."

"Go ahead," growled the voice on the other end.

"Do you recall asking me some time ago if a short young blond woman who works on a certain river had ever asked about a certain mutual acquaintance of ours?"

"You heard from her?"

"Oklahoma City," Denison said. "The Federal Transfer Center at the airport."

"What the fuck's she doing there?"

"She is under the impression that our mutual acquaintance is somehow connected with some prisoners who are being housed here."

"You must be kidding."

"I don't kid."

"Well, hell. No, you don't. I still have assets in the area. Thanks for the call. I'll remember it."

"I'd rather you didn't, Mr. Zale," Denison said. "This was only a professional courtesy to a former employee of the Agency. We never talked."

"I know the tune," Victor Zale said.

"So you do. But, Mr. Zale, if I may ask . . . exactly what is going on?"

The line went dead, and Denison began to walk across the street toward his rental car. He slid into the seat, waited a moment, then placed another call.

When a woman answered, he said, "Run a full scan on a former Agency employee, Victor Zale. He's been retired for a few years and is supposedly in private business. He was in the Operations directorate. Had a reputation for doing things no one else would do, and on occasion he surfaces and asks the Agency for certain professional considerations. I want to know everything. I want access to his communications. No paper on this. It's strictly an internal matter, but I must know as soon as possible."

Denison ended the call and sat with his hands on the steering wheel. *What are you doing, Zale? What do you have to do with all this?*

And what can I do about it? he thought as he dropped the car into gear.

A TV was on in one corner of the vacant office, with CNN cutting back and forth between burning federal buildings, protesters descending on Grant Park in Chicago for tomorrow's competing rallies, and the scene right outside the FTC's window—the tarmac where the April 19 killers would soon be transferred. Tolman glanced at the screen once, then looked away, filling the others in on what she'd learned from Denison.

"Wilmington," Journey said. "Wilmington again." He was sitting at a desk with Andrew, working a puzzle from his backpack. Andrew was very vocal, and FTC officers had checked the office several times.

"Ever been there?" Tolman said.

"No, can't say that I have."

"You might be going soon."

"Meg," Journey said.

She looked up at him.

"Andrew needs to go home. This has been a lot for him to process. He needs familiar surroundings."

Andrew screamed, then shot up out of the chair, both hands waggling and flapping furiously.

"I know, son," Journey said, keeping his voice level. "We'll go home soon."

"But, Nick—," Tolman said, then broke off, thinking of all Journey had done for her on this case. Things he didn't have to do. She cut her eyes to Sandra, who sat quietly in the corner, reading a magazine and looking very tired. She'd dragged all of them through the mud in trying to find the truth of the Silver Cross . . . which was really about understanding the dying words of her friend.

"You're right," she said. "I'm sorry. When we're finished here, we'll figure out a way to get you home." She glanced at Sharp. "But I still want Darrell to stay with you until we know what's happening."

"Meg," Journey said, and Tolman looked up at the tone. "Don't misunderstand me. You're not getting rid of me."

"But you said—"

"I said *Andrew* needs to go home. It's a detour, but I'll be back. I can't walk away from this now. You should know me better than that."

Tolman shook her head. "I guess I don't. Just when I think I have you figured out, you surprise me."

"Then you should stop trying to figure me out. I'll see that Andrew is safely at home and cared for, then I'll go."

"Who's going to look after him?"

"Haven't gotten that far yet, but I'll think of something," Journey said. "You're always trying to get me to talk about myself, so here's something you might not have found in any of your databases: when I was pitching, I led my conference in complete games all four years of college. After I signed with the Tigers and was playing in the minor leagues, I led the league in complete games three of the four years, until I injured my arm."

"Complete games. In baseball, that means—"

"Just what it says. It means I like to finish what I start."

Tolman nodded, then glanced toward Sandra, who was looking at

Journey with a vague, tired smile on her face. She cut her eyes to Tolman, and the two women looked at each other for a moment. "Looks like he's made up his mind," Tolman finally said.

"Looks like it," Sandra said. Tolman thought she detected a note of something like pride in her voice.

Tolman moved to the desk and began working her phone and laptop. Journey sat down beside Sandra. She touched his hand. "These April 19 bombings," she said. "All those buildings, all those people . . ."

Journey looked at her.

"It's all mixed up with this, with the Silver Cross and Meg's friend and the Civil War. Those people . . . all those people died because of this."

It was a statement, not a question. "I think so," Journey said.

"Dear God, Nick. I mean—for a while there, it could be academic, a puzzle, a series of questions to answer. Even after you were attacked, I still didn't get it. But these people are blowing up buildings, all over the country . . . because of *this*. There's an international crisis with France . . . because of *this*."

"Yes," Journey said, then went silent. Across the room, Andrew laughed loudly.

"I don't know. . . ." Sandra let go of his hand, and folded her own back into her lap. "It isn't academic anymore. It's buildings on fire and people dying. God, Nick, it's real, and no one seems to be able to stop it. It was three buildings on Friday, six last night. How many next time? Twelve or twenty or fifty?"

"We're going to stop them."

"How? We still aren't even sure who they are. We're a couple of history professors, Nick."

"True. But you know that the answers to the present are often in history. And Sandra"—she looked into his eyes when he spoke her name—"no one else can do this. No one else knows as much of what is happening than the people in this room."

Sandra waited, then nodded. She closed her eyes. "I should have taught summer classes this year."

Journey smiled.

"I wish I didn't know about all this," Sandra said. "I should be working on my Eugene Debs paper. I shouldn't know anything about how the world works. I should be blissfully unaware and watching TV like everyone else. You know that, right?"

"I know."

"This is so much more than you first thought."

"Yes."

"You can't walk away. *We* can't walk away." Sandra pulled her hair away from her face. "Man, I could tell some stories to my cousin the former federal marshal. I thought she was the one in the family who dealt with the dangerous stuff."

There was a sharp knock on the door, and the warden entered, staring at Andrew, then looking at Tolman. "They're in iron and we're about to take them to the SOAP plane. If you want to talk to them, it's now or never."

"Thanks, Warden."

"I do this under protest, Ms. Tolman. But because you're federal, I guess I have to."

"Doing my job. I won't keep them long. Come on, Nick."

The warden pointed at Andrew. "The boy can't come. No minors in there. I won't bend that regulation, even for RIO."

Tolman looked at Andrew, then the warden. "That's a good regulation, Warden." She glanced at Sandra. "Can you—"

Sandra closed her magazine. "Of course I will."

"We won't be long," Tolman said. "Darrell, will you stay with Sandra and Andrew?"

Sharp nodded.

"Now," Tolman said, "let's go meet April 19."

The warden led them down a series of hallways, through metal detectors—Tolman had already checked her SIG when she entered the facility—and a series of heavy metal doors, until they found themselves in a long, narrow hallway. It was the last section before prisoners at the FTC were taken on to the jetway and put on board the airplanes.

As they approached the end of the hallway, they encountered more officers. The aviation enforcement officers, or AEOs, wore tan pants with U.S. Marshals shirts and caps. ASOs, aviation security officers, were contract employees, in blue shirts and uniform trousers. Tolman counted over a dozen in the hallway.

"You still think there's a threat of someone trying to break these guys out?" the warden asked Tolman.

"That's why I called and had you double the security. You have armed people on the tarmac?"

"Six men with shotguns," the warden said. "This is a hell of a lot more than we'd usually do for four prisoners, even SOAP prisoners like these."

"I have credible information that members of April 19 are going to try to break them out," Tolman said.

"Thought these assholes were busy blowing up buildings," said one of the ASOs as they passed.

"Yeah, that's why all the damn TV reporters are out there," said another. "If these guys had stayed quiet like they were before, this wouldn't be such a circus."

Tolman started to snap out a reply, then the sentence faded away.

"If she said something to you about April 19," Denison had said, *"it's because she wants you to think she's a part of it. Ann is all riddles and rhymes . . . she's a master of sending people in circles."*

Tolman stopped in her tracks, so abruptly that Journey bumped into her.

"Meg?" he said.

"She wants you to think she's a part of it."

"Riddles and rhymes . . . sending people in circles . . ."

She wasn't part of April 19. Ann Gray *was* April 19.

Except April 19 wasn't what it claimed to be.

"Son of a bitch," Tolman whispered.

"What?" Journey said.

"Nothing's going to happen here," Tolman said. Her words sounded thick as she said them, as if she'd been shaken awake from a strange dream.

"What?" Journey said again.

Tolman looked at him, blue eyes boring into his brown ones. "No one's going to try to break these guys out of here. April 19 freeing their 'brothers'? It's a con, a fake. Gray sent us here. She wants us to see something."

"What are you talking about?" the warden said.

"What's she telling us?" Journey said, ignoring the warden. "The

CIA, the map, the French . . . what? The collector in Wilmington? These guys, the terrorists?"

"They're not terrorists," Tolman said.

"Are you out of your mind?" the warden said.

"Murderers, yes," Tolman said. "Terrorists, no."

They reached the holding room off the long hallway and the warden opened the door. Surrounded by officers, the four men were dressed identically in tan shirts and elastic-waistband pants, similar to hospital scrubs. They all wore slip-on tennis shoes, and all were shackled at their feet, chains looped around their midsections. Their hands were cuffed in front of them, at waist level.

Tolman recognized them from the famous picture of them being arrested outside the GAO building. The one in front was Jeremy Rayburn. This was no crew-cut Timothy McVeigh with ramrod military posture and cold eyes. Rayburn slouched, had a bit of a belly, and long, stringy hair. He was looking straight at her.

As she walked up to him, she remembered Ann Gray on the phone, when talking about April 19 freeing its brothers: *The leader will not be silenced.*

"The leader."

She wants me to talk to him, Tolman thought.

"April 19 isn't real, is it?" Tolman said to Rayburn.

Rayburn laughed in his throat. "Here we are," he said. "Don't we look real?"

"Ann Gray hired you to kill Barry Cable, to take out the GAO building and make it look like an antigovernment terrorist group," Tolman said.

One of the others shuffled his feet and cleared his throat.

"No, lady," Rayburn said. "I hate the fucking federal government. It's got too much power, takes away our freedom."

"But there was no such thing as April 19 before you hit the GAO. Yet somehow you received a quarter of a million dollars a week before the hit."

"I played the lottery." Rayburn smiled brokenly.

"You pled guilty," Tolman said. "Why?"

"'Cause we did it. We hate the fucking government and we're not afraid to say so. We're martyrs for the cause."

"Ms. Tolman," the warden said, "I need to take these prisoners out to the plane."

"She cut you loose, didn't she?" Tolman said. "Gray hired you, paid you, probably told you that you'd be making a statement, told you what to say. Guaranteed that she'd hide you, that you'd get away with it. What do you owe her? She set you up—she probably called the FBI herself and sent them to arrest you before you'd even finished the hit." Tolman tilted her head up, staring into the eyes of Jeremy Rayburn.

"Hey, shit," said one of the other three.

"I'm in charge," Rayburn said, and stared down at Tolman. "Everyone knows I'm the leader of April 19. Everyone in the fucking world knows Jeremy Rayburn's name. I hate the fucking government, you know?"

"She cut you loose, and hung you out to dry. You don't owe her shit, Jeremy. You're going to spend the rest of your life in prison, and she's making money."

"But everyone knows who I am, and no one knows who she is. So what does it matter?"

"No one's coming for you. No one's going to break you out. She made up April 19 to suit her own purposes. Those buildings that were blown up, those people who were killed? That's not because of hatred of the government. That's her, that's Gray, making some kind of a point, isn't it?"

Rayburn smirked at her.

"*Isn't it?*" Tolman shouted.

"Meg," Journey said.

One of the ASOs said, "We need to—"

Tolman took another step toward Rayburn. "What are we supposed to see here? What does she want us to know?"

"Don't get too close," said the ASO, stepping between them.

"Get out of my way!" Tolman shouted, and the ASO looked at the warden.

"Ms. Tolman, I'm putting a stop to this," the warden said, behind her.

"Tell me!" Tolman shouted in Rayburn's face.

"Tick-tock," Rayburn said. "Time is a-fleeting."

"What? What does that mean?"

"We all need a little extra time, don't we?"

"What did she tell you? She visited you, didn't she? Recently, since all this started."

"They haven't had any visitors while they've been at the FTC," the warden said.

"Check the logs from the last place they were housed," Tolman said.

"But—"

"Find them, Warden. Please . . . it could be critical."

The warden scurried from the room and Tolman said, "Extra time for what?"

"To do everything that needs to be done," Rayburn said. His eyes had sharpened, and Tolman thought he'd dropped the façade of the slow-witted antigovernment militant. "But now I have nothing but time, see? You, maybe not so much."

"Where is she?"

"Back off," the ASO warned again.

"Where is Gray?"

Rayburn dropped his voice to a whisper and leaned down toward Tolman.

"Hey," said the ASO. "You don't want to be doing that."

"Sixty-eight GTO," Rayburn whispered, then straightened up. "Can we get going?" he said in full voice.

"But—"

"Jeremy Rayburn," Rayburn said again. "I hate the fucking federal government, and everyone in the world knows it. Washington, D.C., steals our money and our liberty and they promise we'll be safe. Well, we're not safe. I fought back, and now everyone knows I fought back. Everyone in the world knows that Jeremy Rayburn stood up to their goddamn lies."

Then the guards led the four men out of the room and down the long hall. Tolman watched them enter the jetway and cross to the small plane. She held her breath, looking at the men with shotguns. The four murderers boarded the plane. The AEOs and ASOs followed. The lead AEO carried a Tazer stun gun on his hip. Within ten minutes, the plane was pulling away from the building.

"Time to do everything that needs to be done."

Tolman felt like screaming. Her brain was on overload. The CIA, Ann Gray, Barry Cable . . .

"Sending people in circles."

Who needed time to do everything that needed to be done?

Gray? Rayburn? Tolman herself? What did Rayburn mean by that?

"Sixty-eight GTO."

Tolman knew it should mean something to her, in context. But she couldn't reach it. She didn't know what it meant, what Gray—via Rayburn—was saying to her.

The warden was at her elbow. "I talked to the assistant warden at Hazelton," he said. "Rayburn had one visitor the day before he left there. Supposedly it was one of his lawyers. The name on the log was Kristin Leneski."

Tolman was staring in the direction the plane had gone. "Don't tell me: tall, middle-aged, brown hair, average looking, right?"

"That's right," the warden said.

"Meg, what does it mean?" Journey said.

She looked up at him. She'd almost forgotten he was there, this good man, this historian, this father. . . .

"I'm sorry," she said.

"For what?"

"Dragging everyone else down into the mud. This started out personal, and now it's turned into an international incident. But it's going to end personal. That much I know."

She started moving in long strides down the hallway toward the office where Sandra, Andrew, and Sharp waited. Tolman asked Sharp to bring his Jeep around to the main entrance, then she stepped out into the sun and began making phone calls. She was on the phone with her assistant at RIO when the phone beeped with another call coming in. The caller ID said: "Duke."

She disconnected from the office and picked up Duke's call. "I hope it's good news, Duke."

"Uh, yeah . . . well, kind of."

"What does 'kind of' mean?"

"I broke through and found the encryption key for the file. See, I was trying a brute force attack, using two machines to—"

"Duke."

"Yeah, well, you don't want to know how I did it. You just want results, right?"

"You are right. Now tell me."

"So I found the key. I found it in a file Barry Cable e-mailed to himself, all sixty-four characters. But there's a problem. It has a sub-password."

She heard Andrew screaming. One of the FTC officers walked past and stared. She thought she heard Journey singing to Andrew in an off-key baritone. "A subpassword," she said.

"Yeah, it's like a shorter—"

"I know what it means, Duke. Can you dig around some more?"

"Already did. He didn't keep a record of any five-character pass-words that I could see."

"That's just grand," Tolman said, and started to say something else. Then the sound seemed to die all around her, as if someone had pressed a mute button. She saw Andrew dancing around, saw his mouth moving, heard nothing. Sharp was pulling up in his Jeep, but she heard no engine sounds. She saw a plane rising off the runway, but heard nothing.

A five-character password.

She thought of Jeremy Rayburn and his bad breath, stringy hair falling around his face.

"Sixty-eight GTO."

And then she remembered: Barry Cable was into classic muscle cars. At the time of his murder, he'd been restoring a 1968 Pontiac GTO.

But how could Rayburn have known? How could Ann Gray have known?

She shook it off. *Answer the questions later, Meg.*

"Duke," she said slowly, "type in the numbers six and eight, followed by the letters G, T, and O. All uppercase."

"What's that?"

"Enter it."

She heard Duke typing. She held her breath, still in a cocoon of silence.

"That's it," Duke said. "We're in."

Oh, Barry, Tolman thought. "Open the file," she said.

CHAPTER
36

The Berkshire Mountains shimmered in the midday sun as Terrence Landon sat in his office in the well-kept colonial on the outskirts of Hillsdale and watched his TV in horror. He felt physically ill, watching the coverage of an actual fistfight on the House floor between Delmas Mercer and a Pennsylvania congressman named Sherman, who had come to blows over Mercer's resolution to retroactively recognize the Confederacy and give "treaty rights" to France. The video of Mercer's press conference with Ambassador Daquin also played again and again. Mercer waved his map, proclaiming that he would be releasing copies of it to the media later in the day.

All the coverage was interspersed with shots of the burning office buildings where nearly forty had died on Sunday night. The e-mail from "April 19" was splashed across every screen.

"... the U.S. government and those who do business on its behalf..."

But still, no one had made the connection between all of this mayhem shaking the country and The Associates. No one mentioned secret accounts flowing into the White House. The president appeared on TV, typically calm, saying he was dispatching Secretary of State Sean

Boss to Paris for talks with the French foreign minister to smooth out the unfolding diplomatic crisis.

All this, Landon thought, *because Zale was too zealous in pursuing The Associates' agenda.*

The irony was that The Associates had accomplished many of their goals with the latest project. The Silver Cross had been profitable beyond their wildest imaginations. Even after paying their legitimate employees at the mine and meeting all expenses, they made huge profits. Zale and Landon took their "fees," and the rest, per The Associates' mandate, quietly went into the off-book accounts managed by the White House. But it was all infinitely more complicated than funneling money into politics, and The Associates had existed long, long before he and Victor Zale were even born.

And now he wanted out.

The Silver Cross project was over, and he thought that Wade Roader was right. The Associates should quietly fade away. Close *all* the accounts, not only the one Barry Cable had found in the spring, which had started unraveling the whole thing. Then, Landon would get as far away from Zale as he could.

Landon closed his office door, picked up his desk phone, and input the number.

"Yes?" Ann Gray said.

"Hello, Ann."

Gray was silent.

"I'm not Victor," Landon said. "Please don't lump us together simply because we've run The Associates together."

"What do you want, Terrence?"

"Victor is crazy, Ann. He will do anything to see you dead. All those buildings . . . you shouldn't have done that."

"The Associates acted unprofessionally," Gray said. Landon thought he heard wind blowing on her end of the call. "That renders any contract between us null and void. When you act in bad faith, I take action to see that it won't happen again."

"You could destroy this country," Landon said. "Doesn't that mean anything to you?"

"No, national boundaries mean nothing to me. It's interesting that you think so little of your country that you believe a few bombs and an international scandal would actually destroy it. Isn't the United States bigger than that?"

"Ann . . ." Landon was struggling. "Have you seen what's been going on? I don't know how much you paid that congressman from Louisiana, but is it worth it? Is it really worth it? Victor and I get the point. We understand. Don't do anything else. Just leave, Ann. Walk away."

"You think Victor gets the point? You said he was crazy."

"He *is* crazy. But we understand. We disrespected you and we did some things that were unnecessary. It won't happen again."

"No, it certainly won't, will it?" Gray said.

"Where are you now?"

"I'm surprised at you, Terrence. You don't know? You haven't figured it out?"

"No, I . . . no. What do you mean?"

"Why, I'm at the Silver Cross, Terrence. Right where I should be."

"Oh God, Ann, there's nothing there for you to do now."

"Indeed," Gray said. "It has a bit of the ghost town atmosphere to it."

"Why are you there? If Victor finds out you're there . . . Ann, I'm trying to save your life. Victor's gone off the deep end. He's . . . oh, God help me, he's reaching your people, the people you used for the bombings. He's going after those protesters in Chicago and April 19 is going to be blamed for that, too. See what you've started?"

There was a long silence on the line. "You cannot possibly be serious."

Landon nodded. "There are thousands of people there. He was going on about restoring civil order and beating you at your own game at the same time."

"April 19 is mine," Gray said. "The people are mine."

"Yes, and you're paying them money to do a job."

Another long pause. "He's going to offer them more money?" Gray's voice rose. "There will be thousands of people at that protest, and they have nothing to do with the Silver Cross. I was very careful in planning the April 19 bombings—"

"Not careful enough! Where does this stop, Ann? God in heaven, where does it stop?"

The phone clicked in his ear.

Landon looked up and saw Zale standing in the doorway, pointing his Les Baer 1911 Boss .45 with its ivory handle at him.

Landon jumped. "Victor—"

"You think I'm crazy? Trying to save that bitch's life, are you?"

Landon started to get up. He saw Zale's wild eyes and the fear began to grip him, cold and hard.

"Sit down!" Zale said. "Have you seen what she's done to this country?"

"I know," Landon said. "But in the end, Victor, maybe it's not what she's done. Maybe it's what we've done."

"You weak-minded bastard. You're a traitor," Zale said, and squeezed the trigger three times.

Zale bundled Landon's body into a closet, locked up the colonial, and drove to the airport at Great Barrington. He fueled the Cirrus, consulted his aviation charts, and did a quick preflight inspection.

He took off and set a course that would take him southwest.

Gray stood in the sweltering West Texas heat, Barrientos beside her as she tried ten different phone numbers. "I can't reach them," Gray said. "I can't reach any of them. The April 19 people in the field . . . I can't . . ." She shook her head, the words leaving her.

"Ann, I don't—"

"How could he get to them? How could he turn them? Money? For money, Mark?"

Barrientos nudged a stray piece of gravel with his shoe. "This has always been about money. Money, power . . . it's all the same. It was never about anything else."

"They betrayed me," Gray said. "Because he offered them a few more dollars. I hired them, I trained most of them myself, some of them nearly twenty years ago. Now they're gone, just like that. And he's going to use them to kill those protesters—college students and single mothers and laborers, and some of them will have their own children with them. It's a protest movement, it's freedom of speech. You prize your First Amendment so highly, and yet—"

"I don't see the point in all this," Barrientos said. "In being here."

Gray withdrew a pair of needle-nosed wire cutters from the back of the rented van and took them to the gate of the mine.

"What are you going to do?" Barrientos asked.

"I'm tending to business, as I've done from the start."

"Dammit, Ann! If Zale knows you're here, he's going to send people after you."

"He'll do what he must," Gray said. She gazed up the road past the guardhouse. "But if I know Victor, now he'll come himself."

"And that's what you want, isn't it? That's what you've wanted all along."

"Now I have more reason than ever." Gray began to work the chain cutters on the gate.

"What about all those people in Florida and Oregon and everywhere else? Those two little kids in New Hampshire? They were all a way to get to Zale so you could make him come after you? You're talking about the protesters, but what about the people we killed? You've made this personal, Ann. You taught me that it's *never* personal!"

Gray threw the chain cutters on the ground and turned so quickly that Barrientos took a step back. "*He* made it personal!" she shouted. "When he left Alex Cable without a father, he made it personal."

"What?"

"Jim Cable's son! He's just an eleven-year-old boy who likes to play chess. He . . . he could have been *my* son. And now he has to live the rest of his life thinking his father killed himself. And Dana Cable was a musician and a teacher. Neither of them could touch us—and now that boy has no father. I tried to stop it and didn't . . . and now, Alex Cable *has no father!*"

Barrientos stood there looking at her. He'd never heard her raise her voice or lose control before. "I think you're losing your perspective."

Gray picked up the cutters and bent to the chain again. Droplets of sweat were running down her back. "Thank you for your good work, Mark, and for not betraying me like the rest of them."

"What the hell is the matter with you? You're going to get yourself killed out here, and then those people in Chicago will still die and *your* son won't have a mother. Have you thought of that? You should leave the country—that's what I'm going to do. You have enough money to live, and you can't stop this from happening. Just get your husband and your son and go! The Associates have resources—people just like us. You think you can stop anything Zale wants to do?"

Gray shook her head. "I don't leave things unfinished. Where will you go?"

"I don't know. Brazil, maybe. I like Brazil."

"Wait."

"What do you mean, wait?"

"There may yet be a way."

"What are you talking about? A way to do what?"

"Mark, he didn't get to you. Zale never called you?"

"Good God, Ann." Barrientos kicked more gravel. A dust cloud rose around him. "I'm here. No, he didn't call me. And I wouldn't—"

Gray held up one hand. "I need you to do one more thing for me, Mark. Then you can go to Brazil or wherever you want."

"What?"

"I want you to go to Chicago."

Barrientos backed up against the grill of the van. Their eyes met. Nearly a minute passed. "Jesus, Ann. It won't work. I'm only one guy, and the protests are tomorrow. No one else is with us, not anymore."

"We'll see about that."

"You're not making sense. What about you? How are you going to get out of here?"

"Don't worry about me, Mark. Let Victor come after me now. I'll be ready."

W hat's in the file?" Tolman asked, her hands trembling a little. She was in the front passenger seat of the Jeep, Sharp
driving. Journey, Andrew, and Sandra were wedged into the back.
Andrew was being very loud, and Tolman had to put a finger in one ear
to hear Duke on the phone.

"It's a spreadsheet," Duke said. "It's money. Oh, man . . . look,
here's the account that we found in the White House with all that
money in it. Hoo boy, look at this . . . it has all the transfers into the
account, and all the source accounts. These things . . . wait a minute,
I'm scrolling down now. The deposits go back about four years. Man,
that's a shitload of money."

Tolman's heart was racing. She looked over her shoulder at Journey.
"Barry found it. Barry found all the money. That was GAO's job, government accountability. Somehow he came across those accounts, and
he tracked them to the source." She spoke into the phone again. "Duke,
tell me about the source accounts. Did he name them?"

"Hell, yeah," Duke said. "They all started with an account belonging to Panhandle Mining at a bank in Memphis, Texas. Then they
go to a bunch of other accounts, mostly in New York. There are a few

more layers, then they feed the White House account number. There are dates of fund transfers . . . it's really detailed. This guy was good."

Tolman closed her eyes. *A bean counter,* Dana had laughingly called her brother. *A minor bureaucrat.*

Tolman could see it: Barry Cable, GAO auditor, had come across some irregularities with White House accounts and began to investigate. He found enormous sums of money, money that no one acknowledged, money earmarked for the highest levels of power. Money that came from a silver mine in West Texas. He began to build a case, documenting everything he found, placing it in an encrypted file.

And eventually, someone realized he was onto the scheme. Someone figured out that Barry Cable could bring it all down, exposing their dirty money.

So Ann Gray recruited four losers who hated the U.S. government, coached them, trained them, *used* them to kill Barry Cable—making it look like an antigovernment terrorist attack.

But Barry, in the last seconds of his life, e-mailed the file to someone he knew he could trust: his brother.

"I tried to stop his death as well," Gray had said on the phone.

"No, I did not kill her," she'd said of Dana.

Then who did?

"So what did they do with the money?" she said aloud.

"Don't know," Duke said in her ear.

Hundreds of millions of dollars. That kind of cash could buy a lot of influence. That kind of cash could effectively buy the White House. Tolman shivered.

"Duke," Tolman said slowly, "this file has names and dates and amounts. Don't say anything to anyone. You get how serious this is?"

"No shit," Duke said. "Yeah, I do."

"Forward the file to me with the encryption key. Also make a copy. Make two copies. Store them in different places. Things may get very, very bad."

"Things are pretty damn bad already," Duke said.

But then the paradox reared up at Tolman. Someone leaked the existence of the mine to the French, and April 19—the group created for the sole purpose of eliminating Barry Cable and protecting the existence of the scheme—was claiming credit for blowing up buildings.

Why was Ann Gray giving them the tools to expose her own secret operation?

"You have everything you need," she'd said on the phone.

"They may get worse," Tolman said, and hung up the phone.

Zale's three men in Oklahoma City traveled under the names of Fillmore, Pierce, and Buchanan. Fillmore was alone in a silver Ford F-150 pickup truck at the corner of Southwest Seventy-fourth Street and Regina Avenue at the western edge of the airport. After moving into position, he'd pulled to the shoulder and pretended to study a map. Pierce and Buchanan were in a Chevy Suburban north of the intersection, at a turnout of the entrance to the FAA's Mike Monroney Aeronautical Center, where many of the nation's air traffic controllers came for training.

Their orders were clear and succinct. They did not know why, but as part of The Associates' operational task force, they were to take out Margaret Isabell Tolman and Nick Allen Journey and anyone who was with them. Zale had been clear on that point. He'd also been clear that their colleague Jackson had been put in the hospital Saturday night because of this same group of people.

Fillmore saw the dusty Jeep Cherokee come to the light at the corner, across the street from his position. The right turn signal went on. Fillmore smiled. They were correct. Journey and Tolman—who, according to his visual of the Jeep, had at least three other people in the car with them—would leave the airport complex and head north toward the highway. Their intelligence was good.

Fillmore spoke into his secure cell and said, "Subjects are turning north. Visual ID confirmed of the Jeep. Five inside. I'll fall in behind. Wait for my mark. Let's get clear of the immediate airport vicinity first."

"Affirmative," Buchanan said.

The Jeep turned north. Fillmore pulled into the flow of traffic and followed.

Sharp drove, with Journey directing him from the backseat. They were going to drop him and Sandra and Andrew in Carpenter Center, where Journey would make arrangements for Andrew. He didn't know what the arrangements were yet, but Tolman was impressed that he was going to find someone to stay with his son. *Complete games, indeed,* she thought.

A few yards before the main entrance to the FAA center, a black SUV pulled in front of the Jeep. Sharp slowed, checking the traffic, his eyes always in motion. The M&P340 was on the dash, his rifle between the seats.

The street curved and crossed another thoroughfare, becoming MacArthur Boulevard as it wound north. As the Jeep cleared the cross street, Sharp said, "Company."

Tolman was doing something on her laptop, and she snapped her head up. "What?"

"Front and back," Sharp said. "Don't like the way they're driving."

The SUV in front had slowed to a crawl. The truck was less than half a car length behind them. Sharp checked over his shoulder and moved into the left lane to pass the SUV. It matched his speed.

"Uh-huh," Sharp said. He pulled the M&P340 down from the dash and put it in his lap. A traffic light was coming at Southwest Forty-fourth. Ahead to the left was a large oilfield supply company, with a huge fenced yard containing pipes and other equipment.

Journey squeezed Andrew's hand. Sandra's hand touched his shoulder. He turned, looked into her huge green eyes, and shrugged. Tolman looked back at both of them. She wished Journey still had his baseball bat.

Pierce was driving the SUV, and he sped up when the Jeep's driver, a big guy with a shaven head, pulled out to pass. Pierce glanced into the Jeep and spoke into his radio. "Positive ID on the subjects. There's a kid in the backseat."

Fillmore waited before replying. "Orders say everyone."

"Even the kid?"

"Orders are for everyone."

Pierce clicked off the radio. "Ah, hell," he said to himself.

Ten seconds went by. The three vehicles were approaching the light at Forty-fourth. For the moment, the street was clear on all sides.

"Now," Fillmore said.

Buchanan's pistol was in his hand. Pierce's was at his side. Behind them, Fillmore had a rifle. Pierce slammed on the brakes.

Sharp acted on reflex, sensing something was about to happen. He twisted the steering wheel to the left and floored the accelerator. A split second later he saw the SUV's brake lights. "Hang on," he said, barely above a whisper.

The Jeep shot across three lanes of traffic and jumped the curb, angling toward the oilfield business. The SUV sped up and spun to the left, trying to cut off the Jeep. The driver laid a trail of rubber across MacArthur, jumped the light, and spun around to face the Jeep.

Journey looked behind. The truck was stopped, the driver's door open. He saw the driver raising the rifle.

"Get down!" Journey shouted, instinctively grabbing both Andrew's and Sandra's heads.

The back glass of the Jeep shattered and the bullet thudded into the floorboard, no more than a foot behind the backseat. Tolman whipped around, her SIG in her hand. "Stay down," she said. "Darrell—"

Journey heard another shot from the other direction. Sharp spun the wheel and braked hard.

"Gotta get out," he muttered, grabbing both rifle and pistol. He kicked open the driver's door and immediately went into a crouch, using the Jeep as a shield. Its grill was inches from the fence. Tolman lowered her head, staying in the Jeep.

Andrew let out a mighty scream and tumbled out of his seat. Journey realized the boy had released the catch on his seat belt. It was something Andrew had learned to do only recently, and Journey had had to reattach Andrew's belt many times, as he would undo it while the car was in motion. Andrew had seemed proud of his new skill.

In an instinctive motion, Andrew opened his car door. To his mind, Journey thought, that was what you did when a car stopped. He raced out.

"No!" Journey screamed, fumbling at his own belt. But Sandra was quicker, and without hesitation she took off after Andrew.

Andrew ran ten steps toward the street, then froze. He looked over his shoulder toward his father, a smile on his face. Journey undid his belt, but Sandra was ahead of him.

It didn't happen in slow motion. It was almost the exact opposite, Journey thought, as he saw Sandra running, both arms outstretched, mouthing Andrew's name. He saw the gunman from the truck running toward them, stopping, taking aim.

Sharp's voice: "Hey!"

Then, a shot from the other direction. Then another, though it sounded different, as if it had been fired from another gun, louder than the first. He heard a body falling, but his eyes were fixed on Andrew and Sandra.

Sandra reached Andrew, stepped in front of him, and grabbed one of his arms, moving him away from the gunman. The gunman from the truck fired, and Journey shouted wordlessly as he saw the shot explode into Sandra Kelly's chest.

CHAPTER
38

Journey was three long steps behind, and he felt his legs go out from under him. He crawled the rest of the way, pulling Andrew down and tripping over Sandra's legs. The blood was everywhere—Sandra had been wearing one of her tie-dyed T-shirts, and now it was soaked in red, above her right breast.

"No, no, no!" he shouted, and looked up in time to see Darrell Sharp charging around the edge of the Jeep with a look of pure and unadulterated rage in his eyes. Journey had never seen such an expression on the face of another human being—and in fact, it seemed almost inhuman to him. Sharp had his M&P340 in one hand and the FN rifle in the other. The gunman in the street was aiming again, cool, confident.

Journey couldn't tell which gun Sharp fired, but the top of the gunman's head exploded. The rifle slid out of his hands as if it had been greased, but he didn't fall, wobbling on his legs. Sharp fired again, and the rest of the man's head was gone as he toppled to the side. Sharp fired again and then again, and all of the assassin's clothes were soaked in blood. When the man fell, Sharp whipped around.

"Okay?" he said.

Journey couldn't speak, staring at the carnage of the assassin in front of him. Underneath him, Andrew whimpered, a strange sound, not one of his typical vocalizations. Not fear, exactly, but a lack of understanding, an uncertainty, as if Andrew knew something bad had happened here, but he didn't know what.

Journey raised his head a couple of inches. He couldn't see Tolman, but he saw one body in the street beside the SUV. Then he saw her unmistakable blond hair rise up from beside the Jeep's right front tire. Her SIG was still in her hand. The Jeep's headlight was shattered.

"There's still one!" she shouted.

Journey heard sirens, not distant, but almost on top of them. He saw movement from inside the fence, people at the periphery of his vision, workers from the oilfield company. Voices reached him, indistinct but urgent. Two Oklahoma City police units screamed into the intersection of Forty-fourth and MacArthur, one from the north, one from the east. Other traffic was to the side, none moving.

Officers spilled out of the police cars.

"I'm a federal officer!" Tolman screamed. "We're under attack!" She pointed with her SIG at the SUV.

Pierce shuddered. He'd thought Fillmore was going to get the kid, and he secretly hoped for something to happen . . . anything. Fillmore was a hard son of a bitch, didn't seem to care about the kid. Pierce had breathed a sigh of relief when he shot the tall red-haired woman instead. She threw herself right in front of the kid. Pierce wondered if she was the boy's mother.

But now . . . now the cops were here. The big bald guy, the one who'd destroyed Fillmore a moment later, had taken down Buchanan.

Now it was only Pierce, and cops were fanning out into the street.

Our goddamn intelligence wasn't so good after all, he thought as he crouched behind the open door of the SUV. *We were told that maybe Tolman would have a pistol, Journey a baseball bat. But the bald guy had some serious weaponry and clearly knew how to use it . . . who the hell is he?*

If he went back like this, Victor Zale would kill him. Would probably pull out the Les Baer 1911 he was so proud of, the one with the ivory grip, and shoot him, right in the middle of The Associates' office.

Hell of a choice.

Pierce checked his weapon, stood up, and came out shooting.

He heard all the things he expected to hear: *Drop it! Drop the weapon!*

He fired in all directions, getting off one decent shot that took down a cop who was moving in beside the traffic light pole. The guy went down quick, and Pierce thought it was a kill. But then he heard shots from all directions and felt the pain in his ribs. He staggered, but was determined to get off more shots.

He aimed at Tolman, but now he was wounded and wobbling and she was running straight at him.

Good God, she's tiny, he thought, and felt disgusted. He was going to let himself get killed by a woman who was barely five feet tall. He swung his gun arm around.

"Don't do it!" Tolman shouted at him.

Pierce snorted.

"Who do you work for?" Tolman said.

Pierce squeezed another shot, but his balance was bad and the shot went way high.

"Do you work for Ann Gray?" Tolman said. She was fifteen steps away, now twelve, ten . . .

Pierce looked at her.

"Noah Brandon?" Tolman said. "The CIA? *Who?*"

It's all over, he thought. The pain in his side was blinding, and he was about to go down. His legs wouldn't work. He fired at Tolman and she fired at him.

"The Associates," he said, and he felt the weight in his chest. Then Pierce went down.

The noise was everywhere now . . . cars coming and going, voices, screams, sobs. But the ringing in Journey's ears from the gunfire had stopped. Sharp knelt next to him, and at first he recoiled, remembering the rage on the big man's face a few seconds ago, the way he'd kept shooting the other man. But Sharp's eyes were normal now, guarded, cautious, wary. He looked human again.

Sharp pulled off his T-shirt and wrapped it around Sandra's wound, looping it under her arm to stop the blood flow. Journey glanced at Sharp, noticing the scar tissue on his stomach.

"She's alive," Sharp said, and that was all.

Sandra was breathing, but it was labored. "Sandra," Journey said, then said it over and over again. Andrew was sitting on the ground beside him, rocking silently back and forth. The boy looked at his father with real concern, then reached toward Sandra's head and touched her hair.

"Okay," Sandra managed to whisper. "Andrew okay?"

She turned her head, and a little sound of pain, a sharp stab of a sound, escaped her. She saw Andrew, but couldn't feel him touching her hair.

"He's fine," Journey said. "You—"

"Shhh," Sandra said. "Later." Journey could see she was struggling not to pass out. He moved a couple of steps away, giving the paramedics room to work. Her blood was all over him. He reached out for Andrew, who let himself be held. Journey couldn't tell what anyone was saying—they were all talking at the same time.

He looked at Sharp, who had gently put his weapons on the grass and showed his hands to the officers. Sharp looked his way. "He was going to shoot your little boy," the big man said. "He shouldn't have done that."

"The Associates," Tolman said. "What the hell does that mean?"

One of the local cops was screaming at her. "Gun on the ground in front of you!"

Tolman complied and said, "I'm a federal officer. Meg Tolman, deputy director, Research and Investigations Office, Washington. My ID is in my purse, in the Jeep, on the passenger side."

One of the other cops ran for the Jeep. Tolman looked around. Sandra Kelly was being loaded into an ambulance. "Dammit," she whispered. Kelly was the ultimate innocent civilian, and Tolman had convinced Journey to have her come along to watch Andrew.

And she had saved Andrew's life.

Tolman only hoped she didn't pay with her own.

The cop returned, looking at Tolman's ID and saying, "We'll have to sort this out. What happened?"

Tolman found herself in a familiar position—with the world almost literally blowing up around her and a local law enforcement officer trying to do his job by innocently asking her for a statement.

"It's complicated," she said.

The cop didn't seem fazed. "I'm sure it is. We have an officer down, a civilian down, and these three men dead."

Tolman looked at the cop's nametag. "Officer Owens, I think you'd better get me connected to your superior. Where will they take Dr. Kelly?" She pointed at the ambulance.

The cop followed her look. "OU Trauma Center, most likely."

"I need to go with them."

"We have to sort out—"

Tolman held up one hand. "I know. How's your man?"

"Not as bad as we thought at first. He took a round in the shoulder, but should be all right."

"Good. Now let's find your captain and start sorting, but I want you to understand that I need to go to the hospital with Dr. Kelly. Can you have a unit take Dr. Journey—that's the man in the khakis over there—and his son with them? He'll want to be with her."

"We'll talk to the captain. What's wrong with the boy?"

Tolman felt a shard of anger, and she thought she knew how Journey must feel at times. "He doesn't seem to be hurt, now does he?"

"That's not what I meant."

"I know what you meant. There's nothing 'wrong' with him. But he does have autism."

"Does he understand all this?"

Tolman hesitated, then answered honestly. "I don't know."

"Okay, let's go, then."

Tolman talked to several officers, steadily increasing in rank from sergeant to captain to deputy chief. She told them she was in the middle of an ongoing investigation into conspiracy to commit acts of terror and implied that it involved the recent spate of bombings. Tolman was pleasantly surprised by the Oklahoma City Police Department. All the officers she talked to were intelligent, articulate, and professional, and only one showed any sort of jurisdictional jealousy, which she quickly tamped down.

Andrew was stomping around the waiting area in the ER of the trauma center. Journey had bought cheese and crackers and a Coke from a vending machine and was handing them to his son. Tolman separated herself from the cops and walked over to him.

"You okay?" she said.

Journey looked down at her.

"That's a stupid-ass question, isn't it?" Tolman said. "What are they saying about Sandra?"

"Nothing yet. They may have to get her into surgery. She lost a lot of blood." He rubbed the back of his neck. "She jumped out in front of him without stopping to think. It's exactly what I was going to do, but I was—"

"Stop right there, Nick," Tolman said. "Don't go blaming yourself because she got there faster than you did."

"I know, I know. Who were they? Were they Gray's?"

"That last one said something before he took his shot at me. He said 'The Associates.'"

"'The Associates'? That could be anything."

"My thoughts exactly." Tolman scuffed a foot on the floor. "It's another piece in one gigantic fucking jigsaw puzzle. You know how much I hate jigsaw puzzles?"

Journey smiled. "Andrew loves them. He's all about puzzles lately."

"Well, he can have my share. We know what Barry found. We know where the money from the mine went. We don't know about the buildings being blown up, or why Gray seems to have wanted us to find all this. It's like she's trying to hang herself." She ran her hands through her hair. "This changes things, Nick. No one will blame you for staying here with Sandra."

Journey said nothing. His mind strayed, thinking about the residential program at Grace of Oklahoma. Could they teach Andrew to understand danger, to control his impulses? Could they reach him in ways he—and the educators in Carpenter Center—could not?

A nurse, a middle-aged Native American woman, came into the waiting area. "Mr. Journey? Is there a Mr. Journey here?"

"Here," Journey said, running to her. "Is Sandra all right? May I see her?"

"They're prepping her to go up to surgery now," the nurse said.

"How bad is it?"

"Bad enough to go straight to surgery. Are you family?"

"No, I'm . . . I guess I'm a friend. But I've called her parents in Illinois and her brother in Missouri. They're on their way."

"Everyone's talking about her," the nurse said, and smiled a little. "Said she took a bullet for a little boy."

"My son," Journey said, and his voice broke.

He felt Tolman's hand on his back. "Is there any way Nick can go be with her?" she asked.

"On her way in to surgery. Nothing you can do for a while."

Journey reached out and grabbed Andrew's hand and pulled the boy to him.

"This the boy?" the nurse said.

"Yes. His name is Andrew."

Andrew rocked on the balls of his feet and whistled.

The nurse nodded with a seen-it-all kind of look. "You must be a pretty good friend."

"What do you mean?"

"Before we put her under, she insisted on giving this to you. She said you'd know what it meant."

The nurse dug in the pocket of her scrubs and handed Journey the silver cross necklace, the one Sandra always wore.

"There was some blood on it," the nurse said, "but we washed off most of it. It was really important to her that you get this."

"Thank you," Journey said. "I know what it means."

"What?"

Journey thought of Sandra, back in the office at the FTC. *You can't walk away. We can't walk away.*

Journey looked at Tolman and folded the silver cross into his palm. "It means I'm going to Wilmington."

"Yes," Tolman said, then she said it again.

She moved away from Journey a few steps and pulled out her phone. She pulled up its call log and punched in the number she'd called a few hours ago.

"Denison?" she said when the man picked up. "I want some answers."

"Ms. Tolman," Bart Denison said. "I didn't expect to hear from you again."

"I have a woman—a civilian, for Christ's sake, a fucking history teacher—with a bullet in her chest, and I don't know if she's going to live. Stop screwing around with me. The Associates. Ever heard the name?"

Denison waited.

"Now," Tolman said. "Today. Come on, Denison."

"I have heard the name, within the last few minutes."

"What?"

"I made some calls after we met earlier. Because, Ms. Tolman, I don't know what's going on. I do not like not knowing what's going on."

"Come on, The Associates."

"A business consulting firm headquartered in upstate New York. It's operated by a former Agency employee. My people are still digging. This is off the books, you understand. The Agency—"

"Goddammit, I know. The Agency can't operate domestically. Enough with the disclaimers. What do you know about The Associates?"

Denison's tone was measured. "They make and move around a great deal of money from many different enterprises. But there's something else happening. Today. Right now. We picked up some whispers about a move against the protesters in Chicago. A move by April 19."

Tolman nearly dropped the phone. "What does that have to do with April 19? Neither of those groups has—"

"I can't pick up the specifics."

"Can't pick up or won't tell me?"

Denison was silent.

"Denison, we're on the same fucking side!"

"Are we, Ms. Tolman?"

"Yes! Jesus, yes! I don't want any more people to die, or buildings blown up. That protest—if April 19 is somehow moving on that tomorrow, thousands of people could die. But why would they? Your former Agency employee—why?"

"I don't know." Denison sounded frustrated for the first time. "I honestly do not know. It's troubling."

"It's Gray. She's April 19, like I told you before."

"No. Impossible. It's too imprecise, too volatile. Ann Gray sending in bombers against an unarmed crowd? She doesn't work that way."

"But The Associates. They do?"

"Apparently."

"*Apparently*. Keep your people digging . . . we have to know."

"I don't take orders from you," Denison said.

"This is all connected," Tolman said. "You're not stupid. You know it's connected. Put your resources on it. You want to resolve the mess with France, you want to keep more people from dying. You want to save your own ass. Whatever you want, find out what The Associates are doing. Jesus God, if they attack those protests . . ."

"And you, Ms. Tolman? What are you going to do?"

Tolman looked across the room at Journey, at Andrew bouncing up and down. Journey's face was guarded.

The game had changed. The stakes had changed. "I'm going to find Ann Gray," she said.

CHAPTER

39

Duke knew he'd done what he was supposed to do, what Voss wanted him to do. He'd found the money, tracked it all the way to the White House. *The White House!* It was the kind of job a hacker lived to do, and he'd cracked it.

But still he worried about Voss. Someone had her, and he *had* to do something more. She needed him, and he was the only one who could help her.

When Duke began doing consulting jobs for the government a few years ago—basically, when Kerry Voss had recruited him—he'd started routinely tracking all incoming calls. He had the software to pull up name and address on landlines, and the same GPS tracker that law enforcement used for cell calls. He wanted to know where people were when they called him, and the information was sometimes useful when he was working on a project.

He'd seen that the phone Voss was calling from was in Fairfax County, but he hadn't tracked it further at the time. He'd been too intent on doing what Voss told him, on finishing her work. But now, it was in his power to find her, and he wasn't going to let her down.

He'd done a screen capture of the GPS coordinates, and he pulled it up again on his number-one desktop. In five minutes he had the address in McLean.

Yes! he thought, pumping his fist in the air. Then his excitement faded. *What the hell do I do with it now?*

What if they were moving Voss from place to place? What if the kidnapers weren't in the same place as when she'd called?

It's a starting place.

Duke went to the kitchen and poured himself another Diet Mountain Dew—no ice, he couldn't stand ice—and wandered around the apartment. He thought about President Mendoza. Duke wondered how much of that money that he'd found had gone into Mendoza's pocket. The thought disappointed and depressed him. He'd really liked Mendoza, but in the end, he supposed all politicians were alike. He didn't like thinking that way.

He considered Voss's phone call, all the coded references. "Take the dogs out" meant for him to find what she was working on. "The tall man": Meg Tolman.

He turned the conversation over in his mind, and a slow realization came over him.

That's not all. There was something else.

Uncle Ray.

The first time he'd talked to Meg Tolman on the phone, when Voss had "introduced" them via conference call several months ago, she'd mentioned that her father was Secret Service. Her father, Ray Tolman.

Duke shot up out of the chair. Meg Tolman's father worked for the Secret Service. He would know things, he would know how to *do* things. He could rescue Kerry Voss.

Duke's fingers flew over his keyboard and in less than two minutes he had Ray Tolman's direct phone number. He punched it in before he could lose his nerve.

"Ray Tolman," answered a gruff voice.

"Um, hi," Duke said. "Mr. Tolman? Hello, my name is Duke. I kind of work with your daughter. Well, I work *for* her, is what I mean to say."

"Yeah? What's going on? Have you heard from her?"

"Well, yes. I talked to her, and . . . but, I'm not calling about her.

You see, I have a friend who also works for RIO. Her name is Kerry Voss—"

"Is she all right?" Ray Tolman said. "Meg called me, said people were after her. I was supposed to meet her, but she was gone. Do you know where she is?"

Duke smiled. He knew he'd done the right thing. "Yes, sir, I do," he said.

Voss's cheek and eye still hurt from where Tough had hit her, but Apologetic had given her ice to put on it to keep the swelling down. She didn't think the bone was broken, or the pain would have been much worse. Voss had been in more difficult positions than this in her lifetime, and with much harder people than these two.

Since the phone call, they had essentially left her alone except for meal and bathroom breaks. They were well armed, and she knew that physically she didn't stand a chance against the two of them. They were both big men, and both looked like they could snap her in two if they tried.

So Voss lay on the cot and thought about the kids. Her ex-husband would be annoyed, and maybe even worried. They actually had a good relationship—better than when they were married—and worked hard at the joint custody, helping each other when they could. But Voss missed the kids. No doubt her daughter would be trying to act grown-up and concerned, but the boys, who were six and four, wouldn't understand, and her ex would do his best to be low-key.

The room had no window, so when she heard several cars go down the street outside, she couldn't see what was happening. But Voss had "mom hearing," and suddenly the traffic sounds had increased several times over. Then she heard cars stopping and people moving. She stood up from the cot.

Out in the hallway, she heard Tough say, "What the fuck—"

More sounds, more movement. Then the door opened and Apologetic came in, gun drawn. "Let's go!" he shouted.

"What's happening?" Voss said.

"Now!"

He took two more steps toward her, then Voss heard crashing and many more footsteps in the hallway.

"Let's go!" Apologetic screamed. "Move, move . . ."

Then the room filled with men in full riot gear, with FBI HRT across their jackets. "On the floor!" one of them shouted at Apologetic. He dropped his gun as if it had burned him and fell to the floor.

An older man in suit pants and tie, but with an FBI windbreaker over it, stepped into the room. "Kerry Voss?" he said.

Voss nodded, watching Apologetic on the floor.

"Special Agent Pat Moore, FBI," the balding man said. He spoke into a wrist radio. "She's secure, Ray."

Voss smiled and closed her eyes in relief. "I'd like to call my kids."

"In a minute," Moore said.

The Hostage Rescue Team members had already cuffed Apologetic and were leading him away. "Do you have the other guy?" Voss asked.

"In the living room," Moore said. "Are you all right?"

They turned into the hallway. "A little banged up, but okay overall," Voss said, touching her cheek.

"Assholes," said another voice, and Voss looked up to see Ray Tolman.

Voss smiled—Duke had figured it out. *Uncle Ray.* She made a mental note to send him a case of Diet Mountain Dew.

"Glad you brought some friends," Voss said.

"Thought we'd make it a party," Ray Tolman said. "You okay, Kerry?"

"I'll be fine. Duke called you?"

"He did. Interesting kid, but he was concerned about you."

"I owe him . . . and you. Have you heard from Meg?"

"Not since yesterday. You can call her if you want."

"The kids first," Voss said. "Then Meg . . . but on a secure phone."

In the sparsely furnished living room, Tough was on the floor, hands cuffed behind his back. "I have something I need to do before we go," Voss said, and sidled up beside him. She poked at him with her foot.

"Leave me the fuck alone," Tough said.

"Don't whine," Voss said. "Get up."

"You heard the woman," Ray Tolman said.

Tough struggled to his feet, while multiple HRT members followed him, weapons at the ready. He glared down at Voss.

"Who hired you?" Voss asked him.

"Fuck off," Tough said.

"I see," Voss said, then she stood on her toes and punched him on the side of the face. "Мудак," she said.

"What's that mean?" Tolman asked.

"It's a Russian word my grandfather taught me," Voss said. "It applies to this scum."

Voss hit the man again, on the other side of his face, then turned toward the door. "Okay, I'm ready," she said.

"I think I like your style, Kerry," Ray Tolman said.

No more JPATS planes were available, and after frustrating conversations with several local officials in Oklahoma City, Tolman gave up and went to a charter service, where she booked two small planes.

"Bill it to the U.S. government," she'd said to the owner.

"That the same government that's falling apart left and right?" the man had asked, earning a glare from Tolman.

"You find out how that map—and the letter, too, if that's possible—made its way from point A to point Z," Tolman said to Journey while the planes were being fueled. "Brandon is the place to start. I want to know *everything*. How did it go working out something for Andrew?"

"The Gardners are good people, and they've agreed to look after him. Dale is a Carpenter Center police officer—he helped us out of a problem a few days ago downtown. His wife Sharon works at the college in financial aid. They have a daughter with cerebral palsy, and Dale volunteers at the therapeutic riding program where Andrew goes every week."

"They're your friends, then?" Tolman touched his arm. "You're okay about leaving him with them?"

"As for me being okay about it . . . best not to think too hard on that one. I'm trying to be better about that. I wouldn't necessarily say the Gardners are friends. More like good acquaintances."

"You don't have many friends, do you, Nick?"

Journey stared down at her. "My life— no, never mind. I'm not going there, not now. I do wish you'd stop doing that."

"Doing what?"

"Asking me blunt personal questions."

"Sorry. Well, no, I'm not sorry. The way to find out information is to ask questions, blunt and personal included."

"The Gardners agreed to stay with Andrew. They'll even go to my house, so that he can sleep in his own bed."

"He's a cop," Tolman said, "so he'll have access to weapons. Andrew will be protected. You're sure he doesn't still think you're a suspect in Lashley's death?"

"He said that no one seriously believes I killed Graham Lashley, and my whereabouts are accounted for at the time of the murder. But the town's in an uproar over it. It's a small town—this sort of thing doesn't happen in Carpenter Center very often."

"Okay, then. I'm going to request another deputy marshal to go to Wilmington with you, and I'm going to take Darrell with me to the mine. I think he'd be . . . let's say, nervous . . . without me nearby. And frankly, I may need him."

"I still don't like it. I'm worried about you."

"Worried about *me*?" Tolman punched him on the shoulder. "I can take care of myself, and I'll have Darrell."

They both looked at Sharp and Andrew. "He's taken quite a liking to Andrew," Journey said. "The way he went after that man who shot Sandra . . ."

"Yeah," Tolman said. "Best not to dwell on it. I'm glad he's on our side."

The charter owner returned to the office and announced that both planes were almost ready: one to go to Carpenter Center to drop Andrew with the Gardners, then to fly on to Wilmington, North Carolina, the other headed west for the Texas Panhandle.

They gathered their things. Sharp said an awkward goodbye to Andrew, then came and stood beside Tolman.

"Darrell," Journey said, "I want to thank you—"

"Don't," Sharp said. "Don't thank me for killing a guy."

"I didn't mean that," Journey said. "You—"

"Don't," Sharp said, and Journey went silent.

Tolman's phone rang. She walked a few steps away, talked for a few minutes, then said, "Thanks, Dad," and rejoined the group. "Kerry's safe. Duke figured out where she was and called Dad, who happens to have good connections with the Bureau. Two of the RIO guys are going to stay with Kerry while we sort this out. I need to meet this Duke in person sometime."

They all stood in silence. Andrew rocked on the balls of his feet, then let out a stream of high-pitched laughter, his eyes fixed somewhere over Sharp's shoulder. He held his father's elbow and pulled gently.

"Okay, we're going, Andrew," Journey said. He looked at Tolman again. "Sandra's family should be here by tonight. I feel strange about leaving her." He pulled the silver cross necklace out of his pocket and ran his hands over it.

"Quite a woman," Tolman said. "I think she gets it."

"'Gets it'?"

"Gets *you*. You should hold on to her. She's crazy about you."

"I'm not so sure about that."

"She took a bullet to save your son's life," Tolman said, her tone turning hard. "I would think that would tell you something."

"No, I—," Journey began, then let the sentence fade. "Getting shot could change a person's mind. She may never want to see me again."

Tolman pointed at the necklace. "You don't believe that."

"I don't know what I believe. But you're right—she's quite a woman. And she understands what's going on here, how critical this is."

"Get going," Tolman said. "We have things to do." She watched Journey and Andrew leave, then looked at Sharp. "Come on, Darrell. Let's go open up the Silver Cross."

CHAPTER

40

T he restaurant was called The Oceanic, and it was in Wrightsville Beach, North Carolina, across the Intracoastal Waterway
from Wilmington—and not far from Fort Fisher.

Wrightsville Beach was a tourist town through and through, filled
with condos advertising beach access, and bumper-to-bumper summer
traffic, with college-age kids and families with young children vying
for supremacy. In the rented Chevy, Journey twisted through narrow
streets onto Lumina Avenue, with the bodyguard Tolman had arranged for him, a silent deputy U.S. marshal named McCaffree, in the
passenger seat. The Oceanic advertised itself as the "only restaurant on
the ocean in Wrightsville Beach," and it was a three-story building
meant to resemble a plantation house.

Journey mentioned Brandon's name at the door, and he was whisked
through a noisy downstairs dining room, up to an open-air covered pier
running outward from the building over the beach. The view was breathtaking.

Brandon sat at a corner table, away from others, a glass of iced tea
in front of him. "Mr. Brandon?" Journey said.

"Dr. Journey," the man said, and his voice was a resonant baritone.
"Sit, please. You've come a long way. I trust you had a pleasant flight.

Would you like some good Southern-style sweet tea, or something stronger?"

"Tea is fine," Journey said. "I've been doing a lot of traveling the last few days, and I think if I have anything alcoholic, I may fall asleep."

"Of course," Brandon said, shifting a cane from one knee to the other. "I've taken the liberty of ordering a plate of hush puppies. And you must try the Carolina crab cakes. Have you been to the Carolina coast before?"

"I don't believe so. I lived in Florida as a teenager, but I've never seen the ocean from this perspective."

"Welcome, then. We are, as you know, rich in history." Brandon sipped his tea, taking care to be very careful when he put the glass down on the table. He spread his hands apart. "So you've come all the way from South Central College of Oklahoma to ask me about the map."

"You bought it six years ago."

"I did. And you want to know if I realized what I had at the time." Journey smiled.

"Of course," Brandon said. "I am what you might call a 'freelance historian,' Dr. Journey. I keep an eye out for auctions and estate sales, and frankly, the government has been a fine supplier to my collection. They auction off all kinds of documents, artifacts, things they think they don't need but believe some fool—like yours truly—is crazy enough to buy." The old man glanced toward the ocean and adjusted his thick glasses. Even though the sun was low, the beach was still crowded. "The map has caused quite a stir today."

"So it is the same map that Congressman Mercer has," Journey said.

"Oh yes, Dr. Journey. I once owned the Silver Cross map."

"How did you come by it?"

"As I've said, it was a government auction. And I look for things, Dr. Journey. I most assuredly do look for things. But when I saw the description of this map—one item in a long, long list of thousands up for auction—I knew I had to have it."

"Did you know its history? If so, how?" Journey leaned forward and plucked a hush puppy off the plate. He realized he was very hungry.

"Let me tell you a story," Brandon said. "It's a story about a young

British sailor who became caught up in America's most horrible war. His name was Charles Roberts, and as a teenager he served on board a ship called the *Condor*."

Journey stopped with another hush puppy halfway to his mouth.

Brandon smiled. "So you know the story of the *Condor*."

"She ran aground just down the coast."

"Good, good," Brandon said. "No doubt you know the name of Rose O'Neale Greenhow."

"I do."

"Young Roberts was one of the crewmen assigned to row Mrs. Greenhow to shore the night the *Condor* ran aground near Fort Fisher. He was closest to Mrs. Greenhow and she gave him something. A letter."

"And the map?" Journey said.

"No. That comes later. She gave him a letter, from Napoleon III to President Jefferson Davis, promising an alliance between France and the Confederacy in exchange for something called the Silver Cross. Can you imagine what it might have meant, if Mrs. Greenhow hadn't drowned? The Confederacy might have won the war. The world as we know it might be a very different place, Dr. Journey. Very different indeed." Brandon waved his hand. "But we're not dealing with 'what if.' Mrs. Greenhow drowned, and young Roberts kept the letter, the letter she told him to protect with his life. So he did, for the rest of his life, for more than fifty years."

"He never read it?"

"Remember, in that day and age, it wasn't uncommon for the working classes—including sailors, *especially* sailors, if you will—to be illiterate. All he knew was that this captivating woman, who had drowned in front of him, told him to protect it with his life. More than fifty years later, Roberts was old and sick and was tended by a young man from his village, a tailor and schoolteacher. The young man's named was John Brandon."

Journey leaned forward and Brandon smiled again, the seams in his aged face knitting together.

"My great-uncle. John Brandon read the letter Roberts gave him and knew it was of vital importance. He sent it to his older brother, William Brandon, who had immigrated to Boston around the turn of the twentieth century. Will Brandon was my grandfather. He was a clerk for a Boston lawyer. When he received the letter, he contacted the War Department in Washington. Surely they would be interested in such an artifact." Brandon thumped his cane on the wooden floor. A strong sea breeze came up and stirred the air.

"What year was this?"

"Very good, Professor. It was in 1917."

"World War I," he said. "I'm betting they told your grandfather they didn't have time to fool around with a paper that was fifty years old and meant nothing to anyone."

"Rather shortsighted, weren't they?" Brandon said, and chuckled. "But understandable, given the times. So Will kept the letter. He researched Rose Greenhow, and in 1918 he packed up and moved his family and everything he owned to Wilmington."

"He moved here because of the letter?"

"Yes, he most certainly did. Because, you see, he believed the Silver Cross was a thing, not a place."

"I made the same mistake," Journey said.

"Of course, of course." The old man's blue eyes gleamed. "We'll come back to that. But he settled here, made his fortune here, and he kept the letter."

"He never tried to find the 'further documentation' that Napoleon mentioned in the letter?"

Brandon raised both index fingers and shook them at Journey. "Yes, yes. He spent his life—and quite a lot of money—trying to find them. He died in 1949, and never found them. My father was never interested in history. He lived for the moment, and for whatever would make him the most money in the moment. History meant *nothing* to him. I was my grandfather's true spiritual heir, and I swore I would find whatever was out there to be found. But, and this is very important, I was not interested in so-called treasures or in making money from history. History is who we are as a people. The collection of historical data is its own reward. Understanding is its own reward. Do you see what I mean?"

"Yes, I do," Journey said. "You kept the letter, but never tried to find what was out there."

"I simply wanted it to be complete, to find Napoleon's other documents, so the collection would be complete, to deepen my own under-standing. And money? Bah . . . I had more than enough money. A rarity in this society, yes? Of course." Brandon seemed to falter a bit. He took another sip of tea. "The heat gets to me at times. My apologies."

"Should we go inside?"

"No, no, I love to sit out here. You must try the crab cakes, sir. I highly recommend them." He nodded to a waiter standing patiently behind Journey. "Two orders of crab cakes."

The waiter scurried away and Journey said, "So the letter stayed with your family."

"Yes," Brandon said. "Until six years ago."

Journey's heart raced. "What happened?"

Brandon pursed his lips and looked toward the Atlantic. "I follow what is happening around the world. When you have money and a bit of influence, you can look into places others might not look. I do not mean this to be boastful. Six years ago, I heard that a journal by a French priest had been discovered in a church in Montluçon in central France."

"Father Fournier," Journey said.

"Yes, yes. You most certainly have done your due diligence, Dr. Jour-ney. Along with the discovery of this journal was a map that purported to show exactly where Fournier and the soldiers had gone. The Silver Cross mentioned in Napoleon's letter, and in Fournier's journal . . . there was a detailed map. I had to have it. I sent a man to France, but—"

"It had been stolen before he got there," Journey finished.

"Less than two days before my man arrived, Father Michel re-ported the map stolen in the night. The journal was hidden in a sepa-rate place, but he had left the map on his desk. He'd been looking at it before vespers, and the poor man simply forgot to put it away. Father Michel is not a young man, and he was beside himself. I'd been prepared to pay whatever price he asked. But it was gone." Brandon slammed a hand on the table. A bit of tea spilled. "And now, I hear Congressman Mercer and Ambassador Daquin saying that agents of our government stole it."

Brandon looked toward the sea again, and Journey thought he'd lost himself in the story of his family's relationship with the Silver Cross.

When he looked at Journey again, his eyes were bright. "I thought my chance to complete the collection was gone. You may have noticed that I am not a young man either."

"You don't look a day over eighty."

"Hah! I'm only five years short of one hundred, but we will see. Imagine my surprise when, less than a year after the map disappeared from Montluçon, I saw a map listed for auction on the GSA's website . . . a map that sounded very similar. Yes, I use the Internet, Dr. Journey—don't look so surprised. When I saw the image, I knew that was it and I bought it. I couldn't believe my luck, to get a second chance. . . ."

Somewhere on the pier, a child screamed and for one wild instant Journey thought, *Andrew?* But Andrew was safe with the Gardners in Carpenter Center. "Let's return to the map. How did it get to St. Pierre's Church? According to Michel's article, Fournier never saw the map, or if he did, he didn't understand the significance of it."

"Excellent question," Brandon said. "When I spoke to Father Michel, he said that Father Fournier's account of the expedition into Texas stopped after they returned to Mexico. Fournier kept other journals, of course, but nothing more was written about this subject. Of course, the French were thrown out of Mexico in another couple of years, and Fournier went home to France. He served churches in Paris for a few years before settling at St. Pierre's in Montluçon. He hid the journal of his time in Mexico and Texas behind some stones in the rectory—stones that stayed in place until a renovation of the church was begun."

"Six years ago."

"Yes. But during the twenty-nine years Father Fournier served St. Pierre's, he couldn't forget what he had seen and heard in Texas. Of course, by 1901, Napoleon III was long dead and France was a very different place. But, an old man by then—though not as old as I am now—Fournier went to Paris, to the national archives. He described the map, he showed them his journal, which proved he'd actually been with the French soldiers on the expedition, and they released it to him."

"They gave it to him?"

"A different age, Dr. Journey, a different age. He'd proven he was there when the map was created, and for the service he had shown to France, he was rewarded with this one little map, a map that no one deemed significant."

"But—" Journey was struggling, trying to put himself into the time period. "How did the map get from Fournier's military unit to France?"

"Ah," Brandon said. "The archivist in Paris told the old priest that the captain of the soldiers—Prideux, I believe his name was—gave the map to his commander in Sonora. It was then given to an aide to Maximilian, the puppet that Napoleon had put on the throne of Mexico. The aide took it to France and gave it to the emperor. Of course, that's when he came up with the idea of supporting the Confederacy in exchange for this land. He knew Davis would go for the idea, as Davis was desperate by that point of the war. What was some worthless scrubland in Texas, when the French were dangling military and economic support? Davis sent Rose Greenhow to Paris, and Napoleon sent the letter with her. Once Davis agreed to the deal, he'd send the map."

"The 'further documentation' mentioned in the letter."

"Exactly. But then the *Condor* ran aground, Rose drowned . . . and the Confederacy lost the war. By the next spring it was over."

Journey tapped his index finger three times on the table. "And Napoleon was out of luck. He'd made the offer to the South when they were losing the war and desperate for assistance from Europe. But after the Union won, there was no need of French help."

"Napoleon was, as we say, between a rock and a hard place. It always helps to be friends with the winners, and he couldn't very well reveal that he'd offered to help the losers. There was nothing he could do. He was—as some of the kids of today put it—screwed."

Journey laughed out loud. "So here he was, with knowledge of this huge deposit of silver, and now he couldn't do anything about it without making the U.S. angry that he'd offered to help the Confederates. And he couldn't offer to purchase the land either. Then he would have had to explain that he'd had French soldiers illegally roaming around Texas. So he had no recourse, and he put it away in the archives."

Brandon smiled. "So you see. It must have been quite difficult for the most powerful ruler in Europe to know of these incredible riches, yet be unable to do anything about it."

"But," Journey said, "you sold the map and the letter. After all that, you sold them."

Brandon's face darkened. The sun had sunk low on the horizon, and the crowd on the beach had thinned somewhat. The noise level on the pier was down a notch.

"I only had them for a few months," the old man said.

"What happened?"

"The Associates," Brandon said, and lowered his head.

"Who are they?" Journey said.

"Two men, one quiet, reserved. One loud-voiced, insistent, threatening. They said they wanted to know about the Silver Cross map. I thought they were treasure hunters, and I've dealt with more than a few of those in my day. Then they said—well, the loudmouth said—that they were businessmen, always on the lookout for opportunity. I made the mistake of showing them the map, and the letter." Brandon bowed his head again. "God forgive me. But someone had shown an interest. No one had shown an interest in my collection in so long. I've buried two wives and both my children, Dr. Journey. My only son died in Vietnam in 1969, and my only daughter died of breast cancer in 1981. Her son, my only grandchild, lives in California and has no use for me. I haven't seen him in fifteen years. And here before me were two men with a strong interest in my world, my life. My own history, my family's history . . ."

Journey thought of Tolman, how she'd said, *"You don't have many friends, do you, Nick?"*

Is this me? he thought. *Am I this man in another fifty years or so? Lost in history, talking about the Civil War to anyone who looks in my direction?*

He swallowed, reached out, and covered the old man's hand with his own. "I'm sorry," he said, and he meant it.

"Yes, pathetic," Brandon said. "I could be seduced by a degree of interest. They became very excited about the map and the letter. I asked them how they knew I had both the letter and the map at all. They implied they were 'well connected.' I suspect they meant government connections. And as you are certainly aware, Dr. Journey, there is no such thing as privacy in this day and age. Anyone can read anyone else's mail, look at their bank records, listen in on their phone calls . . . it seems our society is willing to trade some liberties for a degree of security, though of course we aren't secure, either." Brandon thumped his cane. "You must forgive my editorializing. These men weren't historians, but they wondered what the map and letter meant. I was somewhat familiar with Napoleon III's 'silver problem' and his adventure in Mexico, and I casually mentioned that to them. Treasure hunters, businessmen . . . it's all about treasure, though, isn't it? In one way or another, that's always what it is about."

Journey nodded, for in the end, Brandon was right, based on what he had seen.

"They wanted to buy the letter and the map. I said they weren't for sale. The loud one threatened me, first with tax investigations. I laughed at him. I am absolutely scrupulous about my business affairs, Dr. Journey. I have no dark corners in my financial life. Taxes are the price we pay for freedom and I never complain about taxes. Some people have called me a 'liberal' for such a stance, and that word is heresy in these parts. But be that as it may, it did not scare me. He began to make veiled threats about actual bodily harm, and I confess that the man frightened me."

Journey thought about what he knew. "I think you were right to be afraid of him."

"Yes. So I gave in, and I sold them for two hundred thousand dollars. He walked off this very pier with them in his hands. I couldn't help thinking of Charles Roberts, and that night on the *Condor*, a few miles south of here, and how Rose Greenhow went to her death thinking she was serving the Confederacy and that there was a still a chance for the South to win the war. And I thought of John Brandon and Will Brandon spending his life trying to understand all this. And I watched that vile man walk out of here with those papers, and I heard nothing more until I saw Congressman Mercer on television. If he gets his way, we'll fight the war again, and again, there will be divisions. There will be no winner in this debate, and it's all because I sold those papers for a few coins."

"I don't think you had a choice," Journey said. "These people are vicious. Did they say anything about what they did? The Associates? What are they all about?"

Brandon reached into the pocket of his shirt and took out a white card that had been repeatedly bent. "This won't tell you much, but you are welcome to it. You are a legitimate scholar, Dr. Journey . . . after your call, I looked up your credentials on the Internet. You may keep that."

Journey looked at the card in the fading light. The black printing simply read: THE ASSOCIATES, INTERNATIONAL BUSINESS CONSUL-TANTS, followed by a phone number and two names: Victor F. Zale, J. Terrence Landon.

"Did they mention a woman named Ann Gray?" Journey asked.

"What a common sort of name," Brandon said. "No, they mentioned no one else. The quiet one, Mr. Landon, said maybe ten words the entire time they were here. Zale did all the talking. A rude, disagreeable man. He is missing three fingers on his right hand, and he kept putting it on the table between us, almost as if he were daring me to stare at it. So do these men have some connection to Mr. Mercer? And who is this Ann Gray?"

"I'm not sure. We don't understand who she is. These men, The Associates . . . did they have any connection to the government? To the White House?"

Brandon looked startled. "I've told you they implied a government connection. But they certainly never came out and said such a thing. Surely the White House was not responsible for the theft."

"No, the CIA did that, and that is—at least we think—where this Ann Gray enters the picture. But we're exploring—"

"The White House," Brandon said softly. "You know, our president is a North Carolinian. Though of course he was vice president at the time all this happened. I am acquainted with him. I met with him when he first ran for attorney general of this state, and was an honorary chair of his first campaign for the Senate. He's an honest man, Dr. Journey. I realize the popular view is that no politician is honest, but Robert Mendoza is a fine man, and I've contributed to his campaign to win the job in his own right this November. You cannot think he has some knowledge of all of this."

"Mr. Brandon," Journey said, "I don't know. I truly don't know. But there are some troubling things happening in this country."

"That is true, sir. I was born the same year that Charles Roberts died, the year John Brandon sent that letter to his brother in the

United States. I've lived through two world wars, a Depression, a Cold War, the invention of technology that could not even be imagined when I was born. I've lived through scandals and terror and uncertainty and fear. And what's happening right now—buildings being destroyed and people being killed, civil unrest that hasn't been seen since the Vietnam and civil rights era, a petition to in essence revisit the issues that led to the War Between the States in the first place—it does frighten me." Brandon closed his eyes. "And all because a lonely old man was hoodwinked by a couple of 'businessmen.' I am very sorry, Dr. Journey. I am truly sorry for what I have done to my country."

To Journey's horror, the old man began to weep, quiet tears streaking his weathered face. Journey put his hand over Brandon's again, but didn't speak.

They sat that way for a few minutes, then the waiter arrived with their crab cakes. Journey pulled his hand away and Brandon wiped his face with a napkin. "I must have forgotten my handkerchief," Brandon said. "A gentleman carries a handkerchief, my father always said. None of this silly business with paper tissues." The waiter departed. The sun was down. "What is your part in all this? Where do you come into the picture?"

"I'm not even sure how to answer that, Mr. Brandon. I'm a historian, and I'm helping . . . a friend, who is trying to figure all this out."

"Will you do justice, Dr. Journey? With all that has happened, will you see justice done?"

"I don't know."

"An honest answer. I appreciate your candor. Bear in mind that justice does not mean revenge."

Journey felt in his pocket and closed his fingers around the silver cross. "Yes."

"Do you have the letter and the map now, Dr. Journey?" the old man asked.

"My friend has them."

"I have one more thing to tell you, and something to give you," Brandon said. "It will complete the set. There is one more piece to this story, and it is written nowhere. No record of it exists. There are only a few words that point to its existence, but I have it. It has stayed with my family for almost my entire lifetime, and I'm going to give it to you."

"What are you talking about?"

Brandon folded his aged hand over Journey's, a reversal from a few moments earlier. "Come, sir," he said. "You must try the crab cakes."

CHAPTER
41

Five minutes before takeoff, Tolman's pilot told her that a cell of summer thunderstorms had broken out over the Texas Panhandle, and he refused to fly into them. Tolman paced the charter service office for hours, waiting for the pilot to check the weather, which he did hourly. Sharp sat without speaking, even dozing at times.

Tolman made phone calls, talked to Erin at RIO four times, catching up what administrative business she could over the phone. She talked with her father, with Voss, even called Duke to thank him for what he'd done for Voss and for RIO.

Late in the afternoon, her phone beeped once—a text message coming in. Tolman checked the screen and didn't recognize the number. She opened the message.

"Would you care to meet me at the Silver Cross? You may find further enlightenment here."

The text was signed: "A.G."

"She's there," Tolman said.

Sharp looked up but said nothing.

"She's there right now," Tolman said. "Gray is at the mine right now."

"Might be a trick," Sharp said.

"I don't think Gray is the one playing all the tricks."

"What about those guys this morning?"

"She isn't The Associates," Tolman said, pacing again. "Since this whole thing started, Gray has been hanging around in the shadows, and every now and then gives us a nudge in the direction of finding things. I don't think she's the danger. She has the answers, but she isn't the danger to us."

Sharp shrugged.

"That's not to say that we aren't still in danger, because we are. But I don't think it's from her."

The pilot came in and said, "Storm cells still strong. Forecast says they'll still be over the Panhandle for another four hours or so."

Tolman slammed a hand on the table. "Dammit!" She flipped open her laptop and pulled up Google Maps, asking for directions from Oklahoma City to Memphis, Texas.

"About four and a half hours to drive it," she said, then looked up at the pilot. "And you're telling me you're not clear to fly for at least four hours?"

"I won't fly into a storm cell," the pilot said. "No responsible pilot will."

Tolman closed the laptop and shoved it into the bag. "If we drive it, we could be there before the planes are clear to fly. What do you think, Darrell?"

Sharp arched his eyebrows at her.

"Your Jeep's still running after this morning, right?"

"Might be a trap."

"I don't think so. I think I'm starting to understand Ann Gray a little. If there's a trap, she's not the one who set it."

"That message might not even be from her."

"Possible," Tolman said. "But we were going anyway. Like I told Nick, maybe we don't find all the answers there. But everything points back to the Silver Cross."

Sharp shrugged and stood up. "Better be ready, then."

Tolman wrote a reply to the A.G. text: "I am all about enlightenment."

She sent it. There was no further reply. She hadn't really expected one.

* * *

Journey's head was still reeling as he left The Oceanic, his bodyguard trailing five steps behind. "Are you all right, sir?" Deputy McCaffree asked.

"Fine," Journey said, but he wasn't fine. His heart was racing and his blood pressure was probably off the charts. He couldn't even remember the last time he'd taken his medication. Days ago, at least.

They reached the rental car and Journey slid behind the wheel. He very carefully took the package Noah Brandon had given him and slid it under the driver's seat.

"What's the package?" the guard asked.

The Silver Cross, Journey thought, then said, "It's nothing."

"Where are we going now?"

"Texas," Journey said. "We have to get to West Texas."

CHAPTER
42

The storms had passed on to the east, but the sky remained gray. It was a few degrees cooler than Tolman remembered, but she didn't expect it to last. Sharp pulled the Jeep off Highway 70 on the gravel path toward the mine. The gate was standing open, the chain and padlock lying in pieces beside it. "Well, that's one less thing to worry about," Tolman said, and Sharp pulled slowly forward.

The gravel road wound into the backcountry, with small mesas to the left, the dry bed of the river to the right. Nearly a mile from the highway, they bent around a sharp curve. Several buildings came into view. All were institutional looking, single stories. A sign in front of one identified it as PANHANDLE MINING COMPANY OFFICES. The others, set back across the gravel road, were long and low. Tolman remembered that the company had built dormitories for its workers.

They drove on, Sharp keeping a wary eye all around as he drove. His guns were within easy reach. Tolman's SIG was in her hand.

The road rose, and at the top of the rise, they spotted the open pit of the mine below. It was kidney-shaped, with an outcropping of rock jutting into its curve. Tolman had no sense of distance, but it was deep, and the land had been blasted away in tiers, with shelflike protrusions on each tier. It looked almost like a natural amphitheater on one side. The other side was sheer rock on its face. The floor of the pit looked oddly smooth. Tolman had expected it to be craggy, jagged—but then, she'd never been around a working mine before.

Nothing working here anymore, she thought as Sharp steered the Jeep onto the road that ran around the top edge of the pit. The road dipped as another shelflike wall rose to their left. The road then split, one fork going down into the pit, the other rising. Tolman pointed to the higher road.

They climbed again, and Tolman noticed that to the left, another thirty yards or so beyond the road, vegetation began again, the tall grass of the prairie. On the other side, toward the mine, the land had been scrubbed clean, stripped of its outer covering. The Jeep rounded another curve and they found the way blocked by a massive dump truck. The tires alone were nearly ten feet tall.

"Jesus," Tolman said. "Guess we're not getting around that thing."

"Big truck," Sharp said, then backed the Jeep into a clearing and turned it around.

"Let's go down to the office. You see any signs of anyone?"

"Nope. Could be hidden, though."

He drove around the pit and down to the office building. They got out of the Jeep, Tolman with her SIG still in her hand. Sharp was wearing double holsters, the M&P340 on his hip, the Glock on his shoulder. He held his rifle in his hand.

The sun was fully up, but it still wasn't hot yet. When Tolman's shoes touched the ground, it felt mushy. The storms had loosened the hard-baked Texas earth. She pointed to Sharp, and the two of them approached the office building from different sides. A screen door was in place, but the building's frame door was wide open.

"Creepy," Tolman said. "I don't like all this quiet."

Sharp's mustache twitched a bit as he moved toward the door.

"Wait," Victor Zale said to his men, watching through binoculars from the top of the ridge behind the office building. He was near the mine's crushing facility, where the ore was brought after extraction from the pit. Trucks dumped the ore and non-ore rock, called "overburden," into the crusher, and the rock slid down a long chute to another truck. One of the two-hundred-ton trucks sat immobile under the chute.

"They're going inside," Zale said. "We're going to get them all at once. What a cute idea, Ann, to have Tolman come out here. Now the history teacher and I'll have all the loose ends tied up."

He motioned the team into position, coordinating by radio. He didn't know who the big bald man was, but he had Ann Gray—with a bonus of Meg Tolman—right where he wanted her.

Once the men were placed, Zale drew his Les Baer 1911 in his left hand. With his missing fingers, he'd had to learn to shoot left-handed a long time ago. He was a pretty damn good left-handed shot. Zale started to pick his way down the ridge.

The office was like any office, with a paneled reception area, some plaques on the walls from chambers of commerce and such, commending Panhandle Mining for being a good corporate citizen. Computers, filing cabinets, printers . . . all the ordinary ingredients of any business operation. Cubicles, a few offices with doors. Tolman heard nothing.

With her SIG, she pointed down a hallway and they moved silently into it. All the doors were closed, except the one at the end of the hall. She motioned at Sharp to hang back a couple of steps, then Tolman stepped into the office, leading with her pistol.

"Good of you to come," Ann Gray said. "I'm so pleased you received my message."

She was sitting behind the desk. A placard on the edge read DIANE CORBIN – CEO. The desk was otherwise empty. A table to the side held a computer, printer, and fax machine.

"I was already coming anyway," Tolman said. "Keep your hands where I can see them."

"I have no business arrangement concerning you, Ms. Tolman," Gray said. "You have nothing to fear from me."

"And I don't believe a thing you say."

"Of course not. I'm so sorry we didn't have time to talk more in Cassville."

"You shot at me," Tolman said. "You gave me the letter, then you shot at me. It finally occurred to me that it had to be you. More of this little game of illusions that you play."

Gray smiled and crossed her legs at the knee. She was wearing tan slacks and a white blouse, and looked perfectly at ease behind the desk. "The Associates wanted you dead, but that was unnecessary. Still, at that moment, there was a possibility of salvaging the project. But The Associates were watching me, and I had to at least give the appearance of doing their bidding."

Sharp entered the room, rifle at the ready.

"You're right to have backup," Gray said. "They're here somewhere."

"The Associates?"

"Of course."

"Who are they? *What* are they? What the fuck are The Associates? And what is April 19? For real, not the cover story."

Gray placed one hand on the desk. "Please, Ms. Tolman—may I call you Margaret, or Meg?—there's no need to be crude. By the way, I'd love to hear you perform sometime. I understand you are fond of Rachmaninov. I'm more of a classicist, personally. Mozart is a favorite of mine, but I do enjoy some of the early romantics, Schubert and Mendelssohn. Early Beethoven, of course."

"Get up," Tolman said. "We're not having tea and discussing composers. We're getting out of here. You're responsible for a lot of deaths, and you diverted money from this mine into a secret White House slush fund. The CIA hired you as a 'contract agent' to steal that French map, and somehow you found the letter, put it together, and found this place. You, and whatever these fucking 'Associates' are, made this little enterprise into a secret moneymaker. And when Barry Cable found it, you killed him and made it look like antigovernment extremists. I know it all."

"I assume you've talked to Bart Denison," Gray said. "Lovely man. He has four children, did you know that? I'd done a few other freelance jobs for your CIA, and this was quite an easy one. The church wasn't secured, and the map was in plain view on the priest's desk. I never knew it would lead to the most interesting project of my career. But let's not talk about me. And trust me, Meg, you don't know it all."

Sharp had been standing in the doorway, shuffling his feet. "I'll go outside and watch the perimeter," he said, and moved silently down the hall.

Tolman looked over her shoulder, then back at Gray, the SIG never wavering. "You said on the phone you didn't kill Jim or Dana, but you said nothing about Barry."

"Correct. Barry Cable's discovery of the accounts was a legitimate threat to the project. He was in a position to do something about it. So yes, the decision was made to eliminate him, but it could not be done in such a way as to point to his work. I created April 19 and did a nationwide search for a few men who would fit the profile. They already had antigovernment sentiments. All I had to do was fire them up, arm them, and point the way. You might be surprised by how easy it was."

"Then you made sure they were captured. Nice and neat—nutty antigovernment guys shot up the GAO office, case closed. It was lucky that five of the six other people who worked in the office were at a workshop in D.C. that day."

"Luck had nothing to do with it. I made sure the others would be away that day."

"And how did you accomplish that?"

"A fairly minor detail. It was unfortunate, though, that another member of the team stopped by the office before going to the workshop. I am thankful that Rayburn and company didn't get too carried away. The woman was only shot in the arm. I saw to it that her hospital bills were paid. It was the least I could do."

"But you still had Rayburn and the others shoot up the building, destroy all the computers, shout their antigovernment slogans when the media showed up."

"It was necessary to continue the illusion," Gray said. "This had to be an act of terror, not the murder of a specific individual." Gray spread her hands apart. "And I have no doubts that young Mr. Rayburn would have gone on to commit some rather serious acts on his own, if left to his devices. Now he is in prison for the rest of his life."

Tolman shook her head in disbelief. "Barry sent the file to his brother," Tolman said, "and that screwed it all up for you."

"Apparently so," Gray said. "In the last seconds of his life, no less. I did not believe Jim Cable was a threat, even after he started asking questions. He sent an e-mail to his sister with his thoughts that what happened to Barry wasn't what it appeared to be, and that he was going to check into it. Still, he really couldn't harm the project. He was an engineering professor. But The Associates disagreed. I refused to kill an innocent like Jim Cable, so they went around me. They wanted it to look like a suicide." Gray's eyes clouded. "I was outraged. I had read the dossier they compiled on Dr. Cable. There were a few lines about his family, and it mentioned his son—" The sentence died away.

"What? What about his son?"

"His son played chess."

"Excuse me?"

"His son was a chess player. A champion, apparently."

"What difference does that make?"

Gray hesitated, and for a quick moment Tolman thought she was somewhere else, that her thoughts had strayed to a different place. Then the sheen of the cool professional assassin was back.

"None," Gray said. "No difference at all. Be that as it may, Jim Cable was not a threat."

Tolman felt rage rising in her throat, at how this woman could sit at this desk and talk so dispassionately about the destruction of an entire family. "Dana," she said.

"A few weeks ago, she went to Oklahoma to close up her brother's home. When I heard, I decided to meet her. I didn't know if she'd seen anything, but it was time. The Associates had gone too far in murdering Jim. I had to protect Dana—she deserved to know what happened to her brothers. Then I would shut the project down and move on."

"You lured her to Wilmington. You were going to give *her* the letter and the map."

"Yes, though I don't think 'lured' is quite the right word. I thought it appropriate that we meet there, where it all started, with Rose Greenhow's death. I met her at the Fort Fisher Museum, told her I knew the truth about her brothers' deaths, and would explain it all to her. I told her that we would talk about Rose Greenhow and the Silver Cross. It was late. We made plans to meet the next day."

"But something else happened."

"I made a tactical error. I wasn't paying close enough attention. My son . . . no, never mind. I wanted to get home. I wasn't watching. The

Associates had people there, in Wilmington. I don't know the particulars, but my guess is that they called her that night, said they were working with me, and that the meeting had been moved up. They intercepted her somewhere, poured alcohol into her, took her out on the seawall, and bashed her head against the rocks. Again, sloppy. The Associates employ people with the wrong backgrounds for nuanced work."

"Nuanced work?" Tolman shook with anger. "Who are you fucking people? Nuanced work—you killed Dana Cable because of who her brothers were! She couldn't do anything to you. She was a cellist, for God's sake!"

"I understand your feelings, Meg. I did not kill Dana Cable, and I made it clear to The Associates that what they had done was wrong. The unnecessary violence jeopardized the project."

"The project? But you jeopardized the project yourself by giving me the letter, sending Nick the map. You built all this up, killed Barry Cable to protect it, and then . . . what?"

"I'm a professional, Meg. When The Associates killed Dana, I decided then that enough was enough. Then when The Associates shut all this down without me, and even sent a man to kill *me*, something had to be done. But as I told you on the phone, I couldn't expose them myself. It had to come from others. I've taken lives, but only when necessary. I have no thirst for blood."

"What about April 19? What about the buildings blown up this week, all those people? Don't preach to me about not having a thirst for blood. What was that about?"

A shadow crossed Gray's face. "That was a message. That was a lesson that needed to be taught. I tried to ensure minimal loss of life in the bombings. I couldn't control every factor, but many more could have been killed in those buildings."

"What about Chicago? Another lesson? I know you're sending people in there against those protesters today. You have to pull the plug on it. Denison's digging, he has the whole CIA on this. He's probably coordinating with the FBI. We'll find your connection to The Associates."

The shadow deepened. "No, you don't understand. April 19 is . . . no longer mine."

"No longer yours . . . what the hell does that mean?"

Gray bowed her head. "I'm no longer in control of it. I'm not involved in Chicago. The Associates somehow reached my people, offered them more money, turned them against me. Please, you must understand that I would never move against a mass protest. I do not operate in that way. I can't stop it. I no longer have the resources. But you can."

"How? For God's sake, how?"

"It's already in motion," said a man's voice. "There's no stopping it." Both women turned.

"Your people are good, Ann," Victor Zale said as he walked into the office. "They worked all night. Amazing what a little money—a little silver, if you will—can do. The bombs are placed. The rallies start in a couple of hours. All those dead protesters. All those self-righteous people disrupting the life of this country, shouting to be heard, yelling at each other, yelling at the media. They are a distraction, and you're about to kill them. You, Ann . . . the assassin with a conscience."

"Stop it," Gray whispered, steadying herself against the desk.

"You're not in control now, are you?" Zale said. "But you never were, Ann. You never were."

Sharp thought he saw movement on the ridge, a tiny sliver of motion, a patch of grass disturbed. He was worried about shooters on the high ground, aiming down toward the office building, and he gradually worked his way higher, cutting a wide swath around the building and the edge of the pit, coming around from behind.

He moved silently, always focusing on his breathing. When he saw the man in the grass with an assault rifle trained on the building below, he sighed inwardly. He put his rifle on the ground and drew the Glock.

"Hey," he whispered.

The man jumped, then swung his weapon around. Sharp put a round between his eyes with the Glock, then he dove to the ground, grabbing his rifle from the grass as other shots erupted from higher on the ridge. He rolled down the hill, scanning the horizon above to see where the other shooters were.

At least two of them, he thought, one at two o'clock, the other at about ten o'clock. Sharp wriggled on his belly toward the lip of the mine pit. He peered over the side. The drop onto the first shelf was only a few feet. He swung his legs over it and dropped into the pit.

"Your man went looking for my men," Zale said, looking at Tolman. "Gave me a nice opening. That's good. I don't have time to screw around. Drop the pistol, Tolman."

"Who are you?" Tolman said.

"He's one of The Associates," Gray said.

"The only one left," Zale said. "Had to eliminate Terry. The little bastard, trying to help you. Treason is a capital offense, Ann."

"Treason?" Gray said. "Treason against whom?"

"The gun, Tolman. On the floor and kick it to me."

Tolman looked at the pistol with the ivory grip. Zale was only five feet from her. She had no chance. She complied, and Zale kicked the gun into the hallway. "What are The Associates?" she said.

"Nope, not doing that," Zale said. "You think I'm going to make a big speech? Sort of a 'you have the right to know before you die' kind of thing? Sorry, I don't do speeches." He gestured with the gun. "Out from behind the desk, Ann. You went off the reservation. Not good."

"You broke our arrangement," Gray said. She hadn't moved. "Killing Jim and Dana Cable was completely unnecessary. And when you sent that man after me . . . I couldn't allow it."

"Wait a minute," Tolman said. "Wait one goddamned minute!" She glared at Gray. "You worked for him, running this 'project,' and when it went bad, you started blowing up buildings to send him a message? And that led to him hijacking your people to crush the protesters? Couldn't 'allow' it? Sending a message? Do you know how many people are dead?"

Gray shuffled her feet behind the desk. "But his behavior was unacceptable." Her voice strained. "You see, I had to show him—and more importantly, any potential future clients—that such behavior would not be tolerated. It was time to expose the operation—minus my own role in it. This was a way to bring The Associates' world crashing down, while protecting myself. April 19, Representative Mercer, the

French . . . all designed to thoroughly destroy The Associates' power, to expose them for what they have been doing. April 19 is a domestic crisis. Pairing Mercer with the French created an international crisis. It raised the stakes, and it brought everything to light. The Associates' power is broken." She pointed at Zale. "He is out of control. You have to call off Chicago, Victor. Alex Cable shouldn't have had to pay, and those people in Chicago shouldn't pay, either."

"High and mighty, aren't you?" Zale said. "But we're not broken. I do what has to be done. Now stand up."

"No," Gray said. One of her hands snaked out of sight.

"You crazy bitch," Zale muttered.

Gunfire sounded on the ridge behind the building. Zale jumped, turning toward the door. Tolman saw her chance and took it, rushing him on his blind side. He was a big man, and she had no thought to disable him . . . only disarm him. She needed both Gray and Zale alive. She launched a flying kick at his arm as he swung it back to aim at Gray. He took his shot, but it went awry, shattering the window behind the desk. If Tolman hadn't moved when she did, the shot would have taken Gray in the chest.

Thank God, Tolman thought. She saw Gray's eyes go wide, in realization that Tolman had just saved her life. Gray moved from behind the desk, her motions smooth, fluid, silent.

Zale's gun arm arched toward Tolman, swinging like a crane with a wrecking ball. Tolman dodged but was too slow, as Zale slammed the pistol into the side of Tolman's head. Tolman went down, her vision going black just as she heard another gunshot and the sound of a body falling to the floor.

Journey steered the Hall County Sheriff's Department's Explorer onto the gravel path that led into the mine. He was exhausted from the late-night flight, the intensity of feelings, a few hours of bad sleep in another anonymous motel. But he'd called the Gardners, and Andrew was all right. Sharon had put the phone to Andrew's ear and Journey had talked to him. Andrew hooted a couple of times, but otherwise attended to his father's voice. It comforted Journey.

Journey's mind was still careening with the knowledge of what

Noah Brandon had told him. With his foot, he nudged the package under the seat. Napoleon's letter to Jefferson Davis wasn't the only thing Rose Greenhow took with her into the lifeboat after the *Condor* ran aground.

Sharp landed on his feet, bent his knees to balance himself, then straightened. He edged sideways several steps along the shelf, sloping upward until his head was almost level with the top of the lip. He propped the FN Special on the lip and watched for movement. He'd counted three shots after he shot the man in the grass, then the guns had fallen silent after he went into the pit.

He watched; he listened. He was sure one of the shots had come from above and behind him. He heard some movement, but couldn't tell from which direction. Gunshots did that to him. The ringing in his ears stunned his hearing, confused his senses for a time. He blinked—he would have to be alert. Any sound, any movement . . .

He strained, listening for gravel being displaced. But his ears were still ringing. Sharp shook his head violently, and then he wasn't in dusty West Texas, but in muggy Key West, Florida, with a bunch of drug dealers opening fire on his partner and him. Then he could almost feel the knife as one of the dealers lunged at him and drew the blade across his stomach.

Sharp flinched, trying to quiet the sounds in his head. *I'm not in Florida, I'm in Texas, and I'm helping Meg. . . .*

Meg.

Meg Tolman had been the only person to visit him in the hospital when he checked himself into the mental health unit. No one else had known what to say to him. They all cast their eyes down and mumbled about how Sharp hadn't been able to handle the pressure, and wasn't it a shame . . . his very first assignment . . .

Sharp squeezed his eyes closed. *I'm helping Meg.*

The sounds and colors crashed together in his head. The rifle slipped from his fingers, clattered against the floor of the shelf, and flipped end over end down to the bottom of the pit.

Sharp went crazy . . . Sharp couldn't stop crying . . . Sharp couldn't hack it . . .

And he heard piano music, Meg Tolman playing something by Rachmaninov. She loved all those little preludes, and Sharp's dad had once played them, too. What was the famous one? It was in the key of C-sharp minor, wasn't it? And Meg had played it for him once, a long time ago.

Sharp was standing, arms at his sides, listening to the music, when he heard another sound—loud, sudden, something that didn't belong with Rachmaninov. He opened his eyes. He heard running footsteps, two sets of them from different directions. One set was almost on top of him. He started edging down the shelf, toward the pit.

The Rachmaninov faded away as the man came over the edge of the lip and landed three feet from him. Sharp had a good five inches on the man, and he lifted his boot and kicked the man, knocking his legs out from under him. But the man was good, and he popped up again immediately. He stumbled a little, but he had a nasty-looking pistol, similar to Sharp's Glock, and was raising it.

The Glock.

Sharp had the advantage of size and balance, and the other man was still off balance. He brought his Glock up in a smooth, practiced motion and placed a round in the man's Adam's apple. Then Sharp kicked him again and the man tumbled off the shelf, falling downward into the pit.

Then the other steps were upon him, and before he could turn around, he felt pain explode in his back, somewhere below his right shoulder blade. He fell, and then, just like the man he'd shot, Sharp began to roll off the shelf and toward the bottom of the mine.

Zale turned toward the office's back door, which led out toward the ridge and the crushing facility. He'd heard three different sets of gunfire.

He took one look at Gray on the floor, another at Tolman, then stepped halfway out the back door, the 1911 still ready. "What's going on?" he shouted. The only thing his men were supposed to shoot at was Ann Gray or Meg Tolman. They were covering him. *What the hell are they doing?*

"What are you doing?" he yelled.

He heard more shots, a shout, the scrabbling sound of bodies falling.

Idiots! Incompetent asshole idiots. Like Landon. Like Roader. Like Ann Gray. Like President Robert Mendoza.

Zale took another step.

Gray had been shot once before, seventeen years ago in Prague. She'd been sent to assassinate the finance minister of the Czech Republic by a cabal of former Communist party leaders who still thought Communism would survive in the former Soviet satellite states. She'd thought they were fools—Communism was bound to fail, even from its inception—but it had been a challenging job, and they paid well. That bullet, fired by one of the minister's bodyguards, had lodged between two ribs, and the wound had pained her for years afterward.

Zale's second wild shot—he was still off balance from Tolman having rushed the big man—had taken her in the soft tissue of her upper left arm. Blood soaked her sleeve. The pain was intense, but she'd felt much worse.

With her right arm, she began to pull herself along the floor. Across the room, Tolman was stirring.

Gray had to reach her bag, had to reach the desk. "Meg," she whispered. "Meg, if you're conscious, move toward the hallway. He's easily distracted, but he'll be back. *Move now!*"

She watched. Tolman started to crawl along the tile floor toward the hallway.

She is a tough one, Gray thought, upping her respect for Meg Tolman yet again. Inching along, dragging her left arm, grinding her teeth against the pain, Gray reached the edge of the desk.

"You have to get out of this building," Gray whispered.

"You—," Tolman said.

Gray reached her bag and dug into it. She withdrew a black three-ring binder and slid it across the floor. "Take it," she said.

"What?" Tolman mouthed.

"It's a history of The Associates. It has everything you need. Do with it—or don't do with it—as you will. The choice is yours. But look at the first page first. It has what you need today, *right now.*"

"What?"

"I told you I no longer had the resources to stop April 19 from wiping out the protesters in Chicago. But you do. You do, and now you have the information to stop it."

"You can still stop it."

Gray shook her head. "Do you think I'm going to call Bart Denison? And if I did, do you think he would believe me? No, I don't exist, Meg. You will have to do it."

"You are out of your—"

"Get out of this building," Gray said. "Go around the front, turn right toward the pit, and go up the ridge to the crushing facility. Get to the high ground."

"But I'm not—"

"I'll deal with The Associates," Gray said. "After today, they are no more. And I won't be taking any further actions. My points have been made. You have my word."

"Dammit!"

"Go," Gray said, then added, "I'm sorry for your friend. I left her alone that night and Victor's men killed her. It was a lapse in judgment, but it hasn't gone unpunished."

Tolman took the book and scrabbled to her feet. The wound on her head was nasty looking and she would have a headache, but Gray knew from experience that it looked worse than it was. "Go now," she said to Tolman. "Give my regrets to Dr. Journey. I had hoped I would be able to meet him today."

She and Tolman locked eyes. Tolman took the binder under her arm, staggering a little against the door, then she turned and ran down the hallway. Gray reached for her bag again.

Zale was dizzy with the rage that coursed through him. After all he'd done, coming from nowhere in north Georgia to serve his country in Vietnam, in Panama, in Grenada, in Iraq . . . the army, the Agency, The Associates . . . and everyone around him was incompetent. Unworthy of someone like Victor Zale, who had dedicated his life to something greater than himself, to ensuring that America did what it was supposed to do, regardless of the whims of idiot politicians and mindless generals and inept business "leaders."

He turned to the doorway to finish Tolman and Gray. These women would not get the best of Victor Zale. When he turned around, Ann Gray filled the doorway, and she was pointing a CZ 75 at his chest.

"You won't do it, Ann," Zale sneered, and took another step toward her.

"I am not that predictable," Gray said, lowered the gun, and shot him in the left knee, then the right.

Zale went down, the 1911 still in his hand. He fired one shot, but it went wild. He looked up at Gray, with her bloody sleeve. "I should have hired a man for this fucking job," he spat.

Gray smiled, walking to him, her arm throbbing. She kicked the 1911 away from him and into the mud.

"Get it over with, then," Zale said. He looked toward the ridge. A few more steps and she'd be in the open and one of the snipers could take her down. "Come on and do it! Or are you too moral and ethical and *professional* to kill me, Ann?"

She stopped, still smiling. "Oh yes, I'm going to kill you, Victor. You shouldn't have gone around me with Jim and Dana Cable, and you shouldn't have tried to kill Journey and Tolman, certainly not with Journey's son around. That was inexcusable. And trying to turn April 19—my own creation—against me to wipe out the ultimate innocents. You have no sense of ethics."

"But what I do will save my country. No matter what you think, even if you kill me right here, right now, Chicago goes on. The people die, the goddamn idiot protests stop, April 19 is blamed, then Mendoza is blamed for not doing enough to stop it. The Associates will go on, with or without me. You can't do anything about it, Ann."

"Don't you think so?"

"Do it! Get it over with!"

"On *my* terms, Victor. On *my* terms."

Zale looked up at her. Gray was still smiling, and for the first time, Zale began to feel afraid.

The Explorer came around the sharp curve and into the clearing in front of the office as Tolman ran out the front door. She sprinted around the edge of the building and headed up the slope behind it, carrying something under her arm.

"Meg," Journey breathed, and laid on the horn.

Tolman turned but didn't break stride. Her look was blank.

She doesn't know it's me, Journey thought. *I'm supposed to be safe and sound in another time zone. . . .*

He hit the button to lower the Explorer's window. "Meg!" he shouted and he pulled off the gravel of the parking lot to follow her up the slope. She zigged and zagged, still running.

Journey saw movement on the ridge, a man, a rifle. He heard the shot and saw Tolman hesitate, doing something of a slide-step, then she fell.

"No!" Journey roared, twisting the steering wheel.

He closed to within a few feet of where Tolman lay, then braked hard. He tumbled out of the driver's seat and grabbed Tolman's arms, looking for the wound.

"I don't think you're hit," he said.

"Just fell, goddammit," Tolman muttered.

Journey grinned and McCaffree helped him get her into the Explorer's backseat as more shots rippled down the ridge. One of the Explorer's windows shattered. Three seconds later Deputy Marshal McCaffree was buried under a hail of safety glass with a bullet in the side of his head.

"Oh, shit," Journey said softly.

"Up," Tolman said. "Up, up, up! By the crusher." She pointed. Journey spun the wheel to the left and floored the accelerator, with McCaffree's blood coating the other seat.

"What are you doing here?" Tolman said. "You're supposed to be in North Carolina interviewing an old man."

"I did," Journey said. "I came back."

"No shit," Tolman said.

"Are you okay?"

"I'm not shot, if that's what you mean. But I was knocked in the head."

"Again?" Journey said, thinking of last year.

"Don't be a smart-ass, Nick."

"Where's Darrell?"

"Jesus, I don't know," Tolman breathed. "He was outside. He went to do a perimeter patrol. . . ."

More gunfire sounded from above them. One shot thudded into the side of the Explorer. Twenty more yards to the crushing facility with the giant truck sitting under its empty chute. Journey steered around a wide puddle of mud and glanced down into the pit below.

"There are people down there," he said.

Sharp had snagged an arm on one of the lower shelves of the pit, but he couldn't hold it because of the pain in his back. It slowed his fall, and he slid more than fell the rest of the way to the pit floor. He'd already lost his Glock, and he'd felt the M&P340 slide out of the unsnapped holster on the way down. He didn't see where it went.

He came to rest on his butt and stayed that way, in a sitting position. He tried to stand up, but the pain knocked him down again. But strangely, as one minute passed, then another, he felt the pain begin to dull.

It had been this way in Key West. The intense moment of impact, whether by gun or knife, was unlike any pain he had ever known, but after a while, it began to ebb. Shock? Adrenaline? Blood loss? He didn't know, but he knew to take advantage of the precious time he had before the pain seeped in again to destroy him.

I won't let this destroy me, he thought.

He had paintings to do. He wanted to go home to his Arkansas hills. He wanted to have Meg come over and play his piano.

Sharp squinted.

I'm helping Meg.

He steadied himself against the lowest shelf and slowly got to his feet. The bottom of the pit was smooth, almost as if it had been polished, with puddles of water standing at the edges from last night's rain. He saw a few little green and pink flags staked into the ground. He glanced to the left and saw the body of the second man he'd shot, unmoving.

He looked to the right and saw the other man, the one who'd shot him, coming closer. He looked surprised that Sharp was standing.

"Think you're a tough bastard, do you?" the man said.

"No," Sharp said.

The man stopped, as if the word surprised him. Sharp scanned the pit, then his eyes found what he was looking for: his FN Special, near the body of the other man. Ten, maybe twelve feet away, toward the center of the pit.

Now or never.

Sharp slide-stepped to the right and the man shot him again. He was a moving target, so the bullet went a little lower than the assassin wanted, but he felt it go into his belly, right at the edge of his knife scar.

He fell toward his rifle, arms outstretched. His arms were long, but he couldn't quite reach it. . . .

Sharp heard the man moving.

"Okay, tough guy," the killer said.

A footstep, two, three. Lying on his side, the pain in his stomach worse than that he'd felt in his back, he inched forward. His fingers stretched. He could almost get it. . . .

He thought of how Meg's hands looked on the piano keys when

she played, the way she always found the right notes, the way they never missed, the way they could reach. . . .

He laid his hands on the stock of the rifle, swung it around, sighted, and fired. He stopped the man in his tracks, red blooming on his torso. Before he could fall, Sharp shot him again, putting a second round almost on top of the first. The man fell, twitched a few times, then didn't move again.

Move! Sharp thought. *Move or die.* . . .

Still on his side, he began to crawl toward the road that led out of the pit. He left a wide trail of his own blood behind him.

"Oh God, that's Darrell," Tolman said. "Can you get to him?"

"Don't know," Journey said, and spun the wheel the other direction. Now instead of going up, the Explorer started down toward the pit road.

"They shot him," Tolman said. "Oh God, they shot Darrell. He's—we have to get him, Nick! If something happens to him—"

"I know," Journey said, steering onto the narrow pit road. He was thinking of Sandra.

Without stepping from the shadow of the office building, Gray put the CZ 75—a weapon exactly like the one she'd thrown into Lake Michigan after killing Zale's man on the *S.S. Badger*—into the waistband of her slacks and grabbed one of Zale's arms with her own good arm.

"What—," Zale said.

"I don't think you should talk," Gray said. "This is going to be rather labor intensive."

"—are you doing?"

"We're going inside. If your man shoots now, all he'll hit is you."

"Goddammit, Ann—"

"Shhh," Gray said. She pulled him a few inches, then stopped. It was slow going with only one good arm, and she was feeling a little light-headed. She pulled again, getting Zale onto the concrete stoop at the back door of her office.

* * *

Zale's closest man to the office was named Harrison, and he came out of cover in time to see the tall woman—their primary target—pulling his boss by one arm. Harrison squinted. Blood on the woman's shirt, blood on both of Zale's legs.

"This operation is screwed," Harrison muttered.

He sighted down his rifle, but the woman had disappeared around the edge of the building, and all he could see of Zale were the boss's bloodied legs.

Very slowly, Harrison put down his rifle and left it on the ground.

Screwed, he thought again. Then: *I'm not dying for Zale. The mine is shut down, the project is over, and Zale was shot through both legs.*

No way.

Harrison began to trot away from the office, toward the front gate of the mine. After a few steps, he broke into a run.

Journey made the turn at the foot of the pit road and braked. He and Tolman tumbled out as shots rained down on either side of them. Using the Explorer as a shield, they crept to Sharp. Tolman cradled his head. "Oh God, Darrell," she said. "I'm so sorry. . . ."

Journey was examining the wounds. "He's been shot twice." He tried to keep the worry out of his voice.

"Meg," Sharp said, "will you come over and play the piano?"

"Oh Jesus, Darrell," Tolman said. "Yes, I will. I'll play anything you want. Come on, let's get you in the car. We have to get out of this pit."

Together they helped the big man struggle to his feet. He moaned and breathed loudly but said nothing. They moved him into the backseat and Tolman cradled him. "He's losing blood," she said.

"Right," Journey said, and drove the Explorer up the road.

At the top, he cut the wheel hard toward the crushing facility. As he began his turn by the giant dump truck, the Explorer went out of his control and skidded to the side.

"What happened?" he said.

"Tires," Tolman said. "They probably shot one or two of the tires. Get out!"

They pulled Sharp out, and he half-walked and was half-dragged around the edge of the chute that fed the truck, eerily silent now.

"Okay, lay him down," Journey said. He worked Sharp's shirt off and ripped it, using it to apply pressure to the wounds.

Sharp moaned again and said, "My rifle?"

"We didn't get it," Tolman said, shaking her head.

"Expensive rifle," Sharp said.

"Later, Darrell."

Journey looked at her and mouthed, *Do you have your gun?*

Tolman mouthed, *No,* and inclined her head down toward the office.

Journey grimaced, then said, "Wait." He crawled to the Explorer, held his breath and averted his eyes from Deputy McCaffree, then pulled the man's pistol from the floorboard. He handed it to Tolman.

Shots pinged into the chute above them. Gravel flew. "Back there," Journey whispered. They dragged Sharp farther from the edge of the chute, under the awning of the crusher. Journey crouched and looked under the wheels of the dump truck.

He could see the man's legs, coming over the rise. Only two legs, one man.

"Wait," Journey said. He edged along the side of the truck and reached the front, where a steel ladder led up into the cab.

He swung onto the ladder. He was breathing hard and he felt shaky and weak. But he was gambling that in the apparently hasty withdrawal from the mine, The Associates' people—or were they Gray's people? he wondered—hadn't tended to all the small details.

He swung into the open cab and found the keys dangling from the ignition. He peered through the window. He could see the man now—young, reddish hair, in fatigue pants, a dark T-shirt, and holding a rifle.

Journey stabbed at the key and the huge engine roared. The instrument panel wasn't much like anything Journey had ever seen, but he pulled at a lever that looked like a gearshift—he hoped it was a gearshift. The truck jumped forward.

The assassin jerked his head up, raised the rifle, and fired. The bullets pinged harmlessly into the huge grill of the truck. He lifted the weapon higher.

Journey inched the truck forward, feeling his way around the controls.

The man on the road stopped, seeing what was about to happen. "Drop it!" Journey screamed at the top of his lungs. "Put the rifle down!"

The assassin skidded, then began to backpedal. The truck rolled toward him, gaining speed.

Come on, drop it, Journey thought, and he remembered Noah Brandon's words about justice and revenge. *Drop it, please. . . .*

He pushed the truck forward. The assassin opened his mouth in a wordless scream, then flung the rifle away from him, down the ridge toward the office. He raised his hands. Journey pulled hard on the brake and the giant vehicle ground to a stop. He heard the sounds of running feet, and then Tolman was pointing McCaffree's SIG at the man and binding his hands with a rope.

Journey laid his head against the wheel. "Where's Gray?" he called down to Tolman.

"Down there!" Tolman shouted.

When Zale was fully inside the office, Gray closed the door, stepped around the bleeding man, and busied herself behind her desk. "What are you doing?" Zale asked again.

"You said you were shutting it down," Gray said. "It's being shut down."

Zale heard a clatter behind the desk, as if something bulky were being lifted. Gray was breathing heavily, one arm hanging limp at her side. She straightened from the waist, and in her good hand, she was holding a small rectangular silver box, about the size of a TV remote.

Zale's eyes widened. He tried to sit up. "No," he whispered. "Ann, you can't—"

"Tying it off. Snipping loose ends. Shutting it down. Wasn't that the plan, Victor? Except I'm not the loose end. You are."

She pressed a button on the box.

Zale reached toward her, and he was looking straight into her eyes. Then, in an instant, she was gone.

How could she be there, and then not be there? Zale thought, then his mind wandered. *Was she ever really here? Does Ann Gray even exist?*

Then he heard the explosions begin, felt the ground rumble. The last thing he thought before the tons of steel and wood and concrete collapsed on top of him was to wonder how Ann Gray could completely vanish, right before his eyes.

44

Journey and Tolman had tied the assassin's legs with a length of chain they found in the crusher and bundled him into the cargo compartment of the Explorer. They were helping Sharp into the backseat when the office building exploded.

Then a series of other explosions rocked the ground, boiling up from the pit of the mine. The shelves collapsed into themselves, and plumes of dust, followed by black smoke, drifted into the sky. Shrapnel rained down. Journey felt the blast, and a stray piece of concrete hit him on the side of the face.

"That's why she wanted me out of the building," Tolman said. "She blew herself and Zale up with the building, with the mine." She remembered Jeremy Rayburn, with his greasy hair, standing in the FTC yesterday morning: *"Tick-tock. Time to do what needs to be done."*

She needed time to set the explosives, then she texted me when she was ready . . . and she waited.

Tolman flipped open the book Gray had given her.

"A history of The Associates," Gray had said.

"Look at the first page first."

It was a grainy paper that looked as if it had been copied from a brochure and hastily faxed.

"What—," Tolman said, then the sentence died in her throat.

At the top was the legend, GRANT PARK MAP.

Tolman's heart thundered. In the center of the map was a grassy open area—the park's public outdoor spaces. On the northwest side of the open area, in masculine block printing, was the letter "L." Diagonally across the area to the southeast, the letter "R."

The places where the protesters and counterprotesters would face each other.

Tolman scanned the page. On two structures—the Art Institute of Chicago on Wabash Avenue, and the open-air Petrillo Music Shell, which sat to the southeast along Columbus Drive—the same hand had written, "A19" and circled the notation repeatedly.

"My God," Tolman whispered.

"What?" Journey said.

"That's where the bombs are. Jesus Christ. . . ." She fumbled out her phone—*But who the hell do I call?*

Instinctively, she opened the call log.

Yes.

Denison answered on the first ring.

"Chicago," she said. "I know where the bombs are."

"What?"

"Gray. I got it from Gray."

"But she is not—"

"No, she's not, but somehow she got the information."

I can't stop it, Gray had said. *But you can.*

"We can still stop it. Call FBI—get the Chicago Field Office, then get Hostage Rescue from Quantico in the air now. Get explosives people. The bombs are in the Art Institute of Chicago and the Petrillo Music Shell. Do you have that? They're on different sides of the park."

"The Art Institute and the music shell. Is Gray with you?"

Tolman glanced down toward the burning office building. "Not anymore. We can still stop this from happening, Denison."

"I'll call the Bureau now. What about The Associates?"

Tolman sagged against the ground, tapping the book in her hand. "I don't think you need to be concerned about them anymore, but I do think I met your former employee today. Nasty man." She rolled over and sat up. "I'm trusting you on this, Denison. This isn't a turf battle.

We can sort it out after the bombs are defused and all those people are no longer in any danger."

"Ms. Tolman, you told me not long ago that we were on the same side. I may believe you, after all."

Tolman almost smiled. "I'm sure we'll talk again."

"Count on it."

"Let's get out of here," Tolman said, ending the call.

She and Journey could feel the heat from the fire, but it was fairly contained, thanks to the moist ground from last night's rain. The mine pit had caved in completely. The office was a smoking pile of rubble.

Journey drove the Explorer down the road, cutting a path through the smoke. At the office parking lot, they switched to Sharp's Cherokee, leaving Deputy McCaffree's body in the Explorer. They would send someone for it later. Journey took the package Noah Brandon had given him and put it under the seat of the Cherokee. He turned left toward the gate and drove out to the highway. When he turned onto Texas 70, he took one look back and saw the smoke rising from the Silver Cross.

Gray hurried through the tunnel, working to stay ahead of the smoke. She'd had the tunnel system built under the office when construction had begun five years ago. She knew the time would come when she— or someone—would need to escape quickly. It was three hundred yards long, passing under the dry bed of the river and emerging from the base of one of the small buttes on the other side. She could smell the smoke, and she knew it would fill the passageway soon. She'd opened the tunnel door beneath her desk after she pulled Zale into the office, and in the split second after she pressed the button, she had stepped down onto the ladder and dropped into the tunnel.

Nearly half an hour later, bloody and gritty, she emerged from the base of the butte and climbed into the tan Mazda Tribute she'd parked there long ago and driven periodically, to ensure that it would be operable and ready when she needed it. She opened her first aid kit and took three Tylenol, then wrapped a bandage around her bloody arm. Gray started the Tribute and turned toward the highway.

In a few miles, she called the house in Fremont. Her son answered the phone.

"I'm coming home," she said.

"Yeah, but for how long?" Joseph said.

"For a long time, son," Gray said. She felt a little woozy, but she smiled. "I quit my job. It wasn't worth it anymore. See you soon."

In the Jeep, Tolman ran a hand through her hair. She felt dusty, smoky, battered. "Jesus, my head hurts." She glanced at Sharp, sprawled across the backseat. "But I don't have anything to complain about. How you doing, Darrell?"

"Okay," Sharp said, but he was pale and his voice was a whisper.

"What's the nearest real city?" she asked.

"Amarillo," Journey said. "But it's a good hour and a half drive from here, and we don't know where the hospitals are. Call Sheriff Nichols in Memphis and get him to arrange for a Medevac helicopter. We'll take him to Memphis and the helicopter can meet us there. If we move fast, they can get him to a trauma center in half the time it would take us to drive it."

"Then let's move fast."

"Already there," Journey said, as the Jeep's speedometer topped ninety.

The helicopter was waiting by the time they reached Memphis, and the pilot told them Sharp would be taken to Northwest Texas Hospital in Amarillo, the region's only trauma center. As soon as the chopper left the ground, Nichols led the way with siren blaring and escorted the Jeep all the way to Amarillo.

Sharp was already in surgery by the time Journey and Tolman arrived. Journey thought of how much time he'd spent in hospitals lately—*too much*. He sat with Tolman and held her hand, watching as the tough-talking façade of the investigator fell away.

"He better be all right," Tolman said. "After all this . . ."

"He's tough," Journey said. "I think being shot probably just annoyed him."

That brought a tight smile, then Tolman started to cry in huge sobs that shook her tiny frame. Journey pulled her to him and put his arms around her and let her sob into his dusty shirt. He said nothing, but kept his arms steady around her. She didn't pull away.

"I never cry," she finally muttered.

"Yeah, you said that the last time I saw you cry."

Tolman laughed and wiped tears from her face. "I want him to be okay. He needs to be okay."

"Yes," Journey said, and Tolman finally pulled away.

Two hours later, a nurse in bloody scrubs entered the waiting area. She spoke in short, clinical terms about gunshots and surgery and recovery rooms, then said, "I think Mr. Sharp may be the toughest man I've ever seen."

Tolman nodded. "Can we see him?"

"He'll be up in recovery in about fifteen minutes."

They sat down again and Journey said, "Brandon gave me something."

"Yeah?" Tolman said.

"The letter wasn't the only thing Rose Greenhow had with her that night."

Tolman waited. "What the hell is that supposed to mean?"

He handed her the package Noah Brandon had given him, which was actually a piece of very soft cloth. She began to unwrap it gently. When she saw what was inside, she drew in a breath.

It was a silver cross, about twelve inches tall, with rubies embedded in the base and at the top, and sparkling emeralds along the arms.

"It's—," Tolman said, and the sentence faded.

"A real silver cross," Journey said.

"Rose had this? But I don't . . . the Silver Cross was there. It was the place where they found the silver. All of this . . . it was all because of the mine. How can this—"

"Remember at the beginning of all this, when Lashley said that there were stories of an artifact, something that would show the world that God had blessed Napoleon's invasion of Mexico?"

"I remember."

"Symbolism was so important at that time," Journey said. "Even though Napoleon knew what he meant by the Silver Cross, he needed a public relations victory, a symbol of what he had done. He had this made as a gift for Jefferson Davis."

"Wait a minute," Tolman said. "The letter. In the letter, Napoleon said something about sending a 'token of our friendship.'"

"Right. Some token, yes? Not only a gesture of good faith from one ruler to another, but also a symbol."

"But wait . . . how did Brandon get it?"

Journey told her the story of Charles Roberts and John and Will Brandon, and Noah Brandon's desire to complete his collection.

"But I still don't understand, Nick," Tolman said when he'd finished. "So Rose gave the cross to Roberts, too?"

"No. Maybe she had it in another pouch, maybe she didn't want to give it up. I don't know. But it went down with her. Still, it wasn't with her things when her body washed ashore."

"So Brandon's grandfather thought the Silver Cross was real—"

"Just as we did."

"Just as we did," Tolman said. "And he went looking for it."

"He dived on the wreck of the *Condor*. Noah told me his grandfather dived on the wreck for two years before he found the cross. Once he found it, Will Brandon thought it was so stunning that he couldn't share it. He wanted to keep it, not sell it, not donate it, simply . . . *possess* it. 'A treasure greater than may be believed.' He was right. There was a real, tangible silver cross."

"My God, my God, Nick. It's amazing." She hefted the cross in her hand, ran her fingers along the jewels.

"Turn it over."

Tolman turned it over and squinted at an inscription on the back, along the main bar of the cross. She looked up slowly. "What is this? What are these numbers? They look like . . . degrees and minutes. This looks like latitude and longitude, Nick."

"That's right. They're coordinates."

"To the place that became the mine?"

"No."

"What do you mean, no? What else could it be?"

"I double-checked. When I used the GIS and found the mine, those were not the coordinates. If my calculations are right, this points to a location about sixty miles south of there."

"*What?*"

"Look beside the numbers."

Tolman held the cross close to her face. "What's this word?"

"*L'or*," Journey said. "It's French for 'gold.'"

"Gold?"

"Napoleon's men weren't looking for gold. Napoleon had plenty of gold. He was short of silver to pay India for cotton, remember? But if his men, in their exploration, found a deposit of gold, they'd be crazy not to document it. No one ignored gold in those days."

"So there's a gold mine there now? More of Panhandle Mining, more funneling illicit funds—"

"No, no," Journey said. "I already checked. There's no mine. If there's gold there, it's been untouched since the 1860s."

Tolman looked out the window toward the hospital parking lot. "And if it's as rich a strike as the Silver Cross was—" She slowly turned to face Journey. "Napoleon was giving a little gift to Davis. 'A token of our friendship.' Let me have the silver, and you can keep the gold . . . if you can find it. Napoleon III was a lot of things, but stupid wasn't one of them. And it's lying there, untapped, in the middle of West Nowhere, Texas."

"Just like the Silver Cross was," Journey said.

"Good God, Nick. This means—"

"I don't know what it means." He pointed at the cross. "But I know what that is, and I know why Rose Greenhow died. She literally protected that letter and this cross with her last breath, and then Charles Roberts did the same for the letter—without even understanding what it was. How many people in the world today would do that? Not many. Noah Brandon, I think. I never saw a more selfless person . . . he has no interest whatsoever in fame or notoriety. He values history for its own sake, for the depth of understanding it gives. That's rare."

"The silver cross that leads to gold," Tolman said.

"Yes. What did you get from Gray?"

"Not sure yet." She thought of the black binder. "A book. Some history, I think."

They both smiled a bit at that.

Five days later, Tolman waited in the White House Rose Garden, clutching the black binder. Before entering the White House for her appointment with Wade Roader, she'd called to check on Sharp. From Amarillo, he'd been flown to a hospital in Little Rock, near his home in Gravelly, Arkansas. He was still in ICU, and the doctors wouldn't tell her his prognosis.

"He never complains, though," one of the nurses told her. "He never wants pain meds." That had made Tolman smile, and she knew he would be all right.

When Roader approached her, with bodyguards at a discreet distance, his face was clouded. He waved at the guards to stay back.

"Good to see you," Roader said. "So sorry I haven't been able to meet with you for a while. A little busy, as you might imagine. How are things at RIO?"

Tolman ignored the chief of staff's question. "How are things with the French?" she asked.

Roader grimaced. "The secretary of state is still in Paris. We're trying to figure out what's happened. That idiot Mercer released the map to the media, and they swarmed all over the place, as you know. An explosion, still burning when they arrived, the place littered with bodies . . . we don't understand it. And that's all at the same time as the rally in Chicago, and the revelation that there were bombs in two of the surrounding buildings. It could have been total devastation, with that many people packed so tightly together. I may want RIO to do some follow-up work."

"Don't worry, I'm familiar with it."

Roader turned to face her. "Excuse me?"

"I passed on the locations of the bombs to a recent acquaintance of mine at CIA, who mobilized the FBI and local authorities to take care of the situation."

"You—," Roader said. "I don't understand."

"Sure you do," Tolman said, and dropped the black binder on Roader's lap.

"What is this?"

"The book is a history of The Associates. The fax page is the evidence of where April 19 had set the explosives at Grant Park. The best I can tell, it came from an associate of Ann Gray's who remained loyal to her after all her other field people defected to The Associates for more money. I'm just guessing here, because Gray is gone, but I would say that this associate, whose initials 'M.B.' are at the top of the fax page, was able to infiltrate the group that had turned against Gray, and he convinced them he'd turned, too."

"Ann Gray? The Associates?"

"Oh, and the letter clipped to the first page is my resignation from RIO."

"What?"

Tolman felt her color rising. "Don't play dumb with your plausible deniability and all that. The Associates. You knew all about it. Ultimately, it was you who ordered Nick Journey and me killed."

Roader's hand gripped the arm of the bench. "I think you'd better explain yourself, young woman. Where do you—"

"Nope, not playing anymore. Tired of the blood and all the lies and pure, unadulterated bullshit."

"The Associates?" Roader said, looking wildly around, as if he expected someone to come to his aid. "I don't know what you're—"

"And I thought you used to be a historian. Allow me to"—she paused, thinking of Ann Gray—"enlighten you. It started in the

McKinley administration, right after the Spanish-American War. A group of New York businessmen approached one of the president's unofficial advisors and suggested a private fund for the White House, a fund that would never appear on any budget. Sort of a discretionary fund, to be used for policy initiatives or for the president to buy booze, whatever struck his fancy.

"But McKinley's advisor said he'd have no part of it, so the original Associates told him he had no choice but to accept it. This is what was so ingenious. The Associates set themselves up as a legitimate business in a little town in upstate New York, and then arranged the fund for the White House anyway. If the White House complained or tried to give it back, The Associates would simply tell the world about the secret slush fund. The president was never to know, only his underlings. But if the underlings didn't cooperate with what The Associates wanted, they'd threaten to make it public. They'd ruin the president— even though the president didn't know about it. Sheer brilliance. They could steer him in one direction or another, whatever their agenda was—through whatever staffer or cabinet secretary or advisor actually knew about the funds. Years went by, and different Associates came and went, always looking for business opportunities, more money that would increase their hold over the White House. Sometimes it was the president's legal advisors in charge of the funds, sometimes a chief of staff, as you know. Only twice was it a cabinet member, under Coolidge and LBJ."

"You're crazy," Roader said.

"Maybe so, but it's all right there, along with the money Barry Cable found. Poor Barry—he did his job and you killed him for it. We don't know how Barry found the accounts, but he started to investigate, and when he did you had a keystroke tracker placed on his computer. That's how Gray knew his subpassword, 'sixty-eight GTO.' That's how she could tell Rayburn, and he could tell me. Once she decided to expose the scheme and bring The Associates down, when she was ready for me to find it, I could find it." Tolman propped an elbow on the arm of the bench, feeling weary. "After a cut to The Associates, and paying the expenses of running the mine, the White House still received over five hundred million dollars. That could buy a lot of votes, influence a lot of policy. But subtly, right? Your friend President Harwell had a difficult time making decisions. You probably helped him a lot with that, helped him with the 'vision thing.'"

"You are out of line," Roader said, but his voice had no strength in it.

"It's all right there, Mr. Roader, in black and white. Victor Zale and Terrence Landon were the leaders of The Associates for thirteen years, and they had some great schemes, but the Silver Cross was the biggest, a perfect opportunity to take advantage of something that no one knew existed, and make a shitload of money. But Zale was unstable, thought that he and he alone knew what was best for the United States. After Gray blew up the buildings, using April 19, he decided to turn it back on her, use her own people, and in the process wipe out the protesters—for some reason he hated both sides—and cripple the Mendoza administration." Tolman shook her head. "Tell me, how much of President Harwell's and Mendoza's agendas have been influenced by Associates money?"

Roader looked around. His guards were gone. Instead, striding through the garden toward him, was President Robert Mendoza, in a white open-collared shirt and dark pants, his glasses reflecting the sun, gray streaks in his dark hair.

"Meg," he said.

Tolman stood. "Mr. President."

Mendoza raised one hand, and a group of Secret Service agents surrounded Roader. Ray Tolman led the group. His daughter winked at him.

Roader was led away. Tolman thought she heard him crying.

When they were alone, Mendoza said, "Meg, I don't know what I can say to you."

"Nothing, sir. I'm leaving RIO."

"Don't, Meg. We need you."

"No, you don't, and I don't want to be a part of this anymore."

Mendoza sat down on the bench, as if they were two old friends chatting, and he motioned for her to sit next to him. "I knew nothing about it."

Tolman sighed. "I know that, sir. None of the presidents did, according to the book. That's not the issue. But sir, this went on for over a century. Were our elected leaders really in charge, or were the men who ran The Associates?"

"Who can say, Meg? Frankly, it's horrifying. But we don't know. Some Associates may have been content in knowing they had the leverage without ever using it. And yes, some may have actively influenced policy, for better or worse. But *we don't know.*" Mendoza spread his hands apart. "See, I was never supposed to be president. I was never even supposed to be vice president. I was one of those 'surprise' VP picks at the convention. I barely knew Harwell. Then when he died so suddenly last year, I didn't have time to assemble a staff, so I've kept most of his people. If I'm given the opportunity to serve a term of my own, I'll have my own people. But The Associates are history now, after holding these illegal funds over the heads of presidential advisors for more than a century."

"But, sir . . ."

"Say it, Meg."

"I'm tired of the lies. You're going to sweep this under the rug, and Roader will 'resign' for personal reasons, and no one will know what really happened. For the good of the country and all that, and I can't stomach it."

"No," Mendoza said.

Tolman looked at him.

"I've scheduled a news conference for tonight. It's all going to take place in the light. I'm tired of lies and bullshit, too, Meg." He smiled, leaning against the bench. "Are presidents allowed to swear? I hope so. I'm going to tell all of it, except for a couple of small things. I'm going to work out an agreement with the French—*without* giving in to Delmas Mercer's foolishness. I'm a Southerner, Meg, but I've no desire to fight that war again. I'm going to discuss Grant Park, and how we almost had a truly horrific act of terror there. Did you hear that the leaders of two main opposing groups actually sat down—right there in Grant Park—and talked to each other, after they found out about the bombs that were intended to wipe out all of them? Two leaders at extreme opposite ends of the spectrum sat down and *talked.*"

"You . . . you're going to come clean with all of it?"

"Every bit of it. And as for the gold, sixty miles south of the Silver

Cross? The current owners of the land keep all their mineral rights. The land belongs to them. But we'll add a provision to the French treaty and give them a percentage of any profits that might come from mining the land—*if* the owners choose to develop it. They already have geologists there now, so I think it's a safe bet we're about to see an extraordinary discovery—maybe as extraordinary as the Silver Cross. But France is an important ally for us in the world, and I'm not going to see this permanently damage our relationship. If the French economy collapses, the whole world is in a lot of trouble."

Tolman rocked back against the arm of the bench. "You're going to get killed politically."

"Probably," the president said. "I have the delegates locked up from the primaries, and the convention is in three weeks, but it's possible I may get a last-minute opponent for the nomination at the convention. The leaders of the party will start trying to make backroom deals and recruit someone to oppose me as soon as this becomes public. I'll be damaged goods. If, by some miracle, I do still get the nomination, the other party's going to be ready to carve me into little pieces."

Tolman said nothing, wide-eyed.

"Adlai Stevenson said, 'I would rather be right than president.' And he was never elected, was he? But he held to his principles. I am president, and I still want to do what is right. I don't think the two have to be mutually exclusive. Do you?"

"They shouldn't be."

"But most people don't believe that anymore, do they? Some days I do, some I don't. But I'm not going to make this go away and talk about it being 'for the good of the country.' This country is a lot stronger than that, we're better than that, and we can withstand more than most politicians think we can."

Tolman said nothing, staring at the president.

"Can't believe I'm saying this, can you?" Mendoza said, and laughed. "It's crazy, all right. A president telling the truth, even if it makes his own administration look bad." He shifted around on the bench, crossing one ankle on the other knee. "Look, Meg, I asked you to take over RIO last year because I thought you could make a difference, could clean it up and do things right. I still believe that. Especially after all this . . . after the Silver Cross."

"You're really going to release all of it?"

"I'm going to tell people the truth, and maybe they'll kick me out on my ass for it. But that's what I'm going to do. If I'm not reelected, I'll go home to Charlotte and practice law and spend time with my kids. My daughter is expecting my first grandchild in December. But if the American people see fit to give me a chance, they won't be disappointed. Will you stay with RIO?"

Tolman's mind tumbled and churned, and she thought of Barry and Jim and Dana Cable, lying side by side in the little cemetery in the Ozarks. And she thought of Sandra Kelly and Andrew and Nick Journey, and she thought of her father, spending his lifetime protecting presidents, serving a government that could sometimes be inept and corrupt, and at other times be a towering light for the rest of the world.

"I'm tired," she said.

"Take a month off," the president said. "Play piano all you want. Then come back and help us. The Wade Roaders and Victor Zales of the world aren't the whole story. There are also the Noah Brandons and the Nick Journeys and—"

"Don't say it," Tolman said. "I'll take that month."

"And then?"

She flipped open the book Ann Gray had given her in Texas, pulled out the letter she'd printed before coming to the White House, and tore it in two.

"I'll stay out of your way and let you work," Mendoza said with a smile. "We can make you director if you like."

"No, I think I'd rather stay as a deputy director, if it's all the same to you. Erin's better at the administrative part of it than I am. I'd rather work on individual cases."

"Whatever you like."

"Sir?" Tolman said. "Thanks."

"For what?"

"For taking this risk."

"On you or on the country?"

"Both, I think."

Mendoza smiled. "Oh, one more thing, Meg. Those little things I won't release? Your name and Nick Journey's. I want you to keep your privacy. I'm not going to turn you into heroes. We overuse that word these days anyway."

Tolman felt a weight drop away from her shoulders. "That's the best offer I've heard in a long time," she said, and watched as the president of the United States turned and left the Rose Garden.

A little less than twenty-four hours later, she stood on the seawall below Fort Fisher, at the spot where Dana Cable's blood had stained the rocks. She looked at the Cape Fear River to her right, and the Atlantic Ocean to her left.

Rose Greenhow had died near here. Dana Cable died here. Noah Brandon's grandfather had dived until he found the "real" silver cross here. Tolman went still, considering all that had happened, considering what she'd agreed to do, to stay with RIO, despite the betrayals, the deaths, the lies.

She tuned out the ocean, and she thought she could catch a little snippet of Beethoven's Cello Sonata no. 2, as played by her friend, long hair flying as she bowed her instrument in the second movement.

"We figured it out, Dana," she said, and wiped her eyes. "The rose and the silver cross. We figured it out."

There was no answer but the wind and the water. She lowered her head for a moment, then looked toward shore. Inspector Larry Poe was waiting there, and she waved to him. He waved back, and then Tolman started the long walk toward land.

CHAPTER

46

Journey and Andrew sat in Sandra's hospital room at the OU Medical Center in Oklahoma City, Andrew working puzzles two at a time, while Journey read *The Journal of the Civil War* and an occasional newspaper. He'd tried to avoid the mass media after President Mendoza's news conference. He'd seen enough uproar for a while.

But he couldn't help seeing one headline on *The Oklahoman's* education page: NORTH CAROLINA INDUSTRIALIST LEAVES COLLECTION TO OKLAHOMA COLLEGE.

Ten days after they'd met at The Oceanic, Noah Brandon died in his sleep of a brain hemorrhage. After his death, an attorney contacted the president of South Central College and said that Brandon had changed his will—the day after he met with Nick Journey—and had bequeathed his extensive collection of historic papers and artifacts to SCC. The collection was said to be worth several million dollars. Journey had to smile when thinking of the courtly old man.

He looked over at Sandra and the smile faded. The bullet had missed major organs, and while she had to have some arteries rerouted, Sandra had been miraculously lucky. She would survive, and with extensive rehab, she would only miss a month or so of the fall semester. Her parents had stayed for a week, her brother a little longer, and they'd worked through their initial anger at Journey. It would take a long time for them to fully trust him, and he didn't blame them. He and Sandra hadn't talked much about the shooting itself. He didn't know if he had the words within him.

She woke up and looked over at him. She smiled, and his heart nearly broke.

"Hey," she said.

"Hey yourself," he said.

"Andrew?"

"Loving those puzzles you got for him. He's getting really fast at them."

She went quiet for a long time. He sensed something big coming.

"Nick," she said.

He took her hand. She moved around on the bed, trying not to jostle her IV line.

"This is . . . hard," she said.

"Yes."

"I . . . I did what I did because . . . well, I guess I don't know. I didn't think about it. I saw Andrew running, and I knew he didn't understand that these were bad men, and I couldn't . . . it wasn't a heroic act or anything. It was just . . . what I did." She squeezed his hand. "I don't have the right words."

"Funny, I was just thinking the same thing."

"I'm scared, Nick. Is this what your life is like? What about the next job you do for RIO? What happens then?"

"I don't know. I can quit the RIO thing."

"No, you can't, and that's part of what is so amazing about you. You always try to do the right thing, even when it's difficult. Whether it's RIO or Andrew or helping a student, and even if it means trying to balance one or more of those things against each other."

"But I can't always figure out what the right thing is," he said.

"Yes, you can, but you're not going to believe me anyway, so I'm not going to die on that hill."

"Thanks, I think."

"I'm scared, Nick. Because I . . . I don't know how to say this and I'm confused and torn up."

Journey steeled himself and said, "You don't have to say it. If you don't want to see me again, I get it. Believe me, I get it. I understand. You could have died out there."

She slapped his hand. "No, dummy, you don't get it. Why do you think I gave you the cross? I wanted you to know it was okay to go, to do what needed to be done. I'm a big girl, and I could survive here without you beside me, if you needed to go and do the right thing, to finish what you started."

"I don't understand what you're saying."

Sandra closed her eyes. "Nick, I'm thirty-one years old and I've never said this to anyone in my life before today, and I'm saying it lying here recovering from a gunshot wound that could have killed me. But, Nick . . . I think I'm falling in love with you."

Andrew had been strangely quiet, and Journey heard him tap his feet on the floor. "I don't know what—"

"You don't have to say anything," Sandra said, and a single tear streaked down her cheek. "Not yet."

Journey brushed the tear away, pulled her beautiful red hair away from her face, touched her cheek.

"I think I'm going to sleep some more now," Sandra said, but then she smiled a little.

She closed her eyes, and he looked at her gorgeous young face. The feelings were so strong that he couldn't even name them, couldn't identify them, much less understand them.

He blinked several times, still holding her hand. He held it for a long time, then gently folded it over her stomach as she slept. He went over to Andrew and helped him with a puzzle, then they moved out of the room.

They stepped into the hallway and almost ran into Amelia.

Andrew whooped and jumped up and down.

Amelia was in one of her banker power suits, all black and white and sharp edges. "Hi, honey," she said to Andrew, then looked at her ex-husband. "How are you, Nick?"

"Not too bad."

Amelia gestured toward the door. "Is she all right?"

"She will be," Journey said.

"That's good. She sounds like a nice woman, Nick."

Journey nodded but said nothing.

"Can we walk a bit?"

They walked to a waiting area near the nurses' station. Andrew whistled, and Journey thought of Meg Tolman, how she'd whistled with the boy in the living room of his house. He'd talked to Tolman a couple of hours ago, when she called to check on Sandra. RIO was going to cover all of Sandra's medical expenses. That word, Tolman told him, came directly from the president of the United States.

"So you're sticking with it?" Journey had asked her. *"You're not going to quit after all?"*

"I think Mendoza might be a real statesman. No one uses that word anymore, but I think he might be one."

"Did you see his speech?"

"I did, and he was good as his word. He kept us out of it."

A pause, then Tolman said, *"I'm not going to quit. How about you?"*

"Probably not," Journey had said. *"I'll stay if you will, as long as I don't have to move to Washington."*

"That's a deal, Professor."

"Nick, are you listening to me?" Amelia said.

"Sorry," he said.

"I said, how does Andrew seem to you? I mean, after all he's been through."

Journey hesitated. "A little edgy. A couple of instances of aggression. When he was in the middle of things, he was fine. Afterward, some challenges."

"Challenges. Nick, he was almost killed twice."

Journey stiffened.

"Look," Amelia said, "I'm not going to try for full custody. I can't do that, and we both know why. I just . . . can't. But dammit, Nick, you're the great dad and all that, but twice he's been in serious danger, because of things you're doing."

"I couldn't control—"

"Don't misunderstand me. I'm sure you haven't told me all of it, and you don't have to. But maybe it's time to think a little differently. You still feel like you have to do everything yourself, and that's not good . . . for you, or for Andrew."

"I had him stay with the Gardners," Journey said. "They took good care of him for three days. Sharon Gardner was great with him."

"I'm sure she was. But"—she pointed at the healing scratches on his arm—"you can't deny what's happening. His adolescence is going to be hard, damn hard. We have options to help. Maybe you could learn something that would help him, and maybe—"

"I went to the website," Journey said.

"What?"

"Grace of Oklahoma. I checked out their website."

"And?"

Journey faltered a bit, with so many things skating around in his mind: *"Are you going to stick with it?" "I think I'm falling in love with you, Nick." "That's not good . . . for you, or for Andrew. . . ."*

"It's hard to think about," he said.

"I know. I never said it was easy for me, either."

Journey was quiet for a long time, looking out the window. He saw Andrew at the edge of his vision, thumping his fingers on the arm of the chair.

"You okay?" Amelia asked.

"Yeah," Journey said, and stood up. "It's near here, isn't it? It's not far."

"About three or four miles."

"We could go visit, while Andrew and I are here in the city. Just to see what it's like."

They started for the elevator. Andrew clung to his mother's arm, always keeping her between his father and himself, stamping his feet and humming and whistling. But as they rode down in the elevator, every few seconds he turned and made eye contact with his father. It was fleeting, as it always was, but it seemed to Journey as if Andrew were asking him a question.

"I don't know, son," he said, "but we'll see."

Amelia looked at him strangely, then the elevator doors opened and they walked into the hospital lobby, through the doors, and out into the hot Oklahoma sun. Andrew was quiet the entire way.

AUTHOR'S NOTE

Don't go looking for the Silver Cross in West Texas, because you won't find it. While Hall County and the surrounding locales are certainly real, the mine is not. Nor is there any factual evidence that Napoleon III's agents discovered silver (or gold) in Texas or sent a letter proposing to assist the Confederacy via Rose Greenhow. Likewise, there is no evidence to support the existence of such an entity as The Associates. Once again, the town of Carpenter Center, Oklahoma, is fictional, but all other settings are real, though somewhat altered at times for storytelling purposes.

So much for the fiction.

Now the facts: Rose O'Neale Greenhow died in the time, place, and manner described in *Silver Cross*. The circumstances of her death are as accurate as I can make them at a remove of nearly 150 years. Much of the detail of her mission to England and France, along with her death, is taken from Ann Blackman's magnificent biography *Wild Rose*.

Historical data on Napoleon III's occupation of Mexico is readily available from many sources, but Shirley J. Black's *Napoleon III and Mexican Silver* served as an excellent resource on Napoleon's dire need for silver during the period of the American Civil War.

Other resources I consulted while writing this book include: *Lifeline of the Confederacy* by Stephen R. Wise, a fascinating examination of the Union naval blockade and the role of the blockade runners. Special thanks to Ray Flowers of the Fort Fisher Historic Site for suggesting this book. Another invaluable and intriguing bit of reading was *Spies and Spymasters of the Civil War* by Donald E. Markle.

Not all individuals with autism exhibit aggressive behaviors. However, it is a fact of life for many families who live with the disorder, especially during adolescence and young adulthood. At times the aggression may be directed at others, or it may take the form of self-injury. Either way, it is one component of a highly complex and confusing developmental condition. There is also a stereotype of the individual with profound autism as being unable to connect with others, forever lost within himself or herself. This is not an accurate picture, either, as many people with the disorder are quite affectionate and loving. The condition is still poorly understood, but progress is being made. Such organizations as The Autism Society (www.autism-society.org) are working daily for deeper understanding and support of families living with autism. The portrayal of Andrew Journey, and his multilayered relationship with his father, is based in part on my own experience as the parent of a son with profound autism.

The impetus for writing this book was twofold. While doing research on spies and espionage in the Civil War, I came across the story of Rose Greenhow. More specifically, the accounts of her death intrigued me. Why did she insist on a lifeboat to go ashore in rough seas, only three hundred yards from Fort Fisher? Why didn't she wait out the night, as the *Condor's* captain suggested? What could possibly have made this coolly self-assured woman so frightened that she felt she must leave the grounded ship? The answer died with her on the North Carolina coast—we will never know what she was thinking that night, but the story haunted me, and it gave me the idea that became *Silver Cross*.

The other half of this book's origin is more contemporary and personal. Around twenty years ago, I attended a graveside service for a great-uncle. The service was at a small cemetery in rural Oklahoma on a hot summer day, and when it was over, I took a walk among the grave markers. Under a tree in the newest section of the cemetery was a trio of markers: two men and a woman, all with the same surname, all having died on different dates within the past two years, aged in their late twenties or early thirties. What happened to this family? I wondered. Who were they? Why did they all die so young, and so close together?

To this day, I have no idea what happened to the three young people buried beside each other in that small-town cemetery. But the image stayed with me for all these years, until I discovered a way to explore it fictionally in this book, via the three Cable siblings.